THE WOLF AND

THE RAVEN

Book 2 in *The Forest Lord* series

By Steven A. McKay

D1534239

1

For my son, Riley, and my daughter Lianna, with all of my love.

Acknowledgements

There are too many people I owe a debt of gratitude to, like all the lovely folk on social media who have shared my stuff, all the people who left nice reviews for *Wolfs Head* on Amazon and elsewhere, and those who helped me promote that book with interviews and blogs etc.

I'd also like to thank my beta-readers Bill Moore, Emma-Jayne Saanen, Pat Goodspeed, Neal Aplin, Luke Burns-McGruther, Paul Bennett, Robin Carter and Niall Hamilton, with special gratitude to Chris Verwijmeren for technical advice on the archery side of things.

To Gordon Doherty, author of the Legionary series of novels, for all his help and advice, particularly when I was working on *Wolf's Head* and Glyn Iliffe, author of The Adventures of Odysseus series for providing a glowing strapline for that first book – you guys rock.

To the people at Amazon, particularly the KDP team (you know who you are!), for making it possible to successfully publish my work when it had proved otherwise impossible and for continuing to support me on my self-publishing journey: thank you so much!

Thanks to my wife, Yvonne, my children Freya, Riley and Lianna and my mum, Bernadette, who all support and inspire me every day in different ways.

And finally – thank you to YOU, the readers who bought *Wolf's Head* and now *The Wolf and The Raven*. Your support means everything, believe me.

Apologies if I've forgotten anyone – let me know and I'll list you in the next book!

CHAPTER ONE

England, 16th March 1322

"Loose!" Robin roared, hoping the soldiers he commanded would be able to hear him over the deafening sounds of the battle.

His men, fifteen in total, released their arrows, along with dozens of other longbow men in Thomas Plantaganet, the Earl of Lancaster's, army.

The missiles formed an ominous dark mass in the sky before hammering down, into the forces of King Edward II, led by Sir Andrew Harclay, 1st Earl of Carlisle. The king's men desperately tried to shelter behind their shields, but many of them were killed or horribly injured. Their commanders screamed at those still standing to hold firm, as the rebel forces advanced upon them.

Robin shuddered at the screams of dying men, the thunder of horse's hooves and the looks of terror on the faces of the men being driven on by the mounted nobles behind them. He had never seen anything as horrifying as a full scale battle before, and the hellish atmosphere shocked him.

He forced himself to concentrate, fitting another arrow to his bow and bellowing again. "Keep firing; we have to allow the Earl's men a chance to reach the ford or we're finished here!"

It was true. The Earl of Lancaster's forces were badly outnumbered by the king's men. Sir Andrew had also managed to reach the river before the rebels which had allowed him to take full advantage of the surrounding terrain.

Positioning his knights and men-at-arms on the opposite end of the bridge, almost in a spear-wall, Harclay knew the Earl would have to try and break through as more of the king's forces were travelling to attack his rear.

It was becoming more and more obvious to Robin the battle was going badly. Lancaster was trying to lead his men, many of them wearing his livery of argent and azure, to a ford further upriver while his lieutenants, the Earl of Hereford, Humphrey de Bohun, and Roger de Clifford of Skipton, tried to storm the bridge. The king's longbow men were taking a terrible toll on Lancaster's men as they tried to reach the ford though, while Hereford had been killed by a pikeman hiding underneath the bridge. When Clifford was also wounded, the assault on the bridge threatened to grind to a complete standstill.

Robin and his men had been living as outlaws in the forests of Barnsdale a few months earlier, when the Earl of Lancaster had promised them all pardons if they joined his rebellion. It had been a simple choice for the outlaws. They could either continue to live like animals in the freezing winter, hunted by the foresters and sheriff's soldiers, or join a rebellion against the king whose unjust laws had driven them into the greenwood in the first place.

The weeks leading up to this point had been hectic for the outlaws, as the earl sent word summoning them to join his army besieging the royal stronghold of Tickhill Castle. From there the army had moved on to Burton-on Trent, setting fire to the town when they found out the king was coming after them, before heading for Dunstanburgh on the coast. They'd only managed a few miles before Harclay's men had caught up with them here at Boroughbridge.

For most of Robin's men this wasn't the first time they'd been a part of such a large, organized force; many of them had stood against the Scots or, like Will Scarlet, served as mercenaries, fighting in battles all across the world. In the past, though, they had joined up because they were either summoned to do so by their local lord, or were being well paid to fight for an employer.

Here, Robin and his friends felt like they were fighting for a cause that directly impacted on their own personal lives. Although none of them knew much about the wider political picture in England, they knew they wanted their freedom and the Earl of Lancaster promised that. It was widely known that the earl stood up for the lower classes living in his manors, while King Edward II spent more time playing around in boats or at sports than he did taking care of his people.

It was a simplistic view of the situation – black and white with no shades of grey in-between, although Robin had been outraged when the earl had set fire to Burton, and rumours of a treaty with the Scots had spread amongst the army, enraging many of them.

They were here now though, the rumours were nothing more than hearsay and no-one would convince Robin they weren't fighting for a just cause. They weren't just struggling to survive here, as they had been doing as outlaws for months or even years in some cases. They were trying to do some good, for themselves, yes, but also for their fellow countrymen.

As Robin had said to them all in a short, but rousing speech just before battle commenced: "We have a chance to actually *change* things here, lads. A chance to bring justice and some form of equality to the country. A chance to show the king we're not going to take his shit any more!"

The men had cheered their young leader's words and gone into the fight with pride and determination burning in their eyes,.

Robin grimaced as he let fly another arrow, knowing it would find its lethal mark in the closely packed line of soldiers on the other side of the river. A moment later he had pulled another from the ground at his feet and nocked it to his bowstring, the rock-hard shoulder muscles rolling as he drew back the great warbow and took aim again.

The earl had seemed confident in the success of the rebellion when Robin had agreed to join him, but it

3

was going badly wrong. The king's men were happy to stand safely behind their spears as the rebels tried to force their way across the river, and, with such an advantage in numbers and terrain, Lancaster's forces would soon be crushed.

The air was heavy with the harsh sounds of blade on blade, screams of wounded men and horses and ragged, desperate war-cries.

"What do we do, now, Robin?" the giant known as Little John shouted at his friend, his great voice carrying effortlessly even through the din of battle.

Robin was torn. It was against his nature to run from a fight. But the battle was lost – he could see that. Once Harclay's forces had killed enough of the rebels the king's man would surely lead his vastly superior force over the bridge to destroy the rest of them. It would mean certain death for Robin, and the men who had placed their trust in him to lead them.

His heart swelled with pride as he glanced along the line at his friends, still firing grimly into the enemy lines. Allan-a-Dale, Friar Tuck, Will Scaflock, his childhood friend Much...They were more than just outlaws; they were Robin's friends: blood brothers.

A great cry of victory went up from far to his left, and Little John, his great height giving him a better view of the battle, cursed. "The assault on the bridge has broken! It won't be long before the earl's men take it, and the bastards'll swarm over the bridge and circle us! We're done, Robin!"

The young leader looked around, trying to find their commander, the earl, but there was no sign of him. "Keep firing, John!" Robin bellowed. "We're not finished yet!"

He knew they *were* done – he just hated the idea of running from the battle, possibly taking a sword in the back as they were charged down by the enemy cavalry. Even if they did make it to the trees a short distance away, what then? Back to a life hiding in the forest, not only an outlaw, but a rebel too. He tried to shoot faster, desperation fuelling his enormous arms, but fatigue was beginning to set in and the enemy numbers seemed to be as overwhelming as they had been when the battle started.

Once Harclay's men came across the bridge Robin's outlaws would have to draw their swords and, with trembling, aching, spent limbs, fight a foe enraged by the arrows that had been killing and maiming them and their comrades.

Robin could see his men were beginning to realise the same thing, as they began to glance nervously in his direction. He shouted in rage and continued to release arrow after arrow, each one sailing up almost majestically, before tearing down, viciously, into a target. Yet still the enemy stood, a vast host of men, as immovable as a castle wall.

Suddenly another cry rose from dozens of throats, this time to their left, where the earl's men had given up their attempt to reach the ford, and, as their allies began to run for it, Robin knew the battle was as good as finished. An image of his wife, Matilda, smiling, her belly swollen with the child growing inside her, flashed into his mind and tears of frustration blurred his vision.

He would not die here.

"Retreat!" he cried. "Head for the trees! Head for the fucking trees!"

Only those closest to him heard, as his tired voice cracked with the strain.

Little John filled his great lungs and repeated the command. The outlaws looked along the line to make sure they had understood the order, then, seeing Robin, sword drawn, gesturing towards the copse of beech trees behind them, began to run.

Many of the earl's men on either side of the fleeing outlaws shouted in dismay, telling them to hold their positions, but the outlaws ignored the cries.

Robin waited until his men were all moving towards the forest before he began to follow. He felt a terrible sense of guilt to be leaving the earl's men behind to face their fate, but he knew the battle was lost. He could see other groups of soldiers on all sides streaming back towards the forest in desperation now and knew he had ordered his friends to retreat at exactly the right time.

Another great cheer went up from the bridge as the king's men realised they were close to smashing their enemy and began to run across the bridge in pursuit, and Robin forced himself to move faster, his whole body aching, lungs burning.

From the corner of his eye he saw a mounted nobleman screaming in rage, trying to order the men to hold the line. It was Thomas, the Earl of Lancaster. He had his sword drawn and was hacking at his own retreating men in fury, desperately trying to stop the rout.

Robin was horrified at the sight of the earl attacking his own men, but the sound of pounding feet behind him told him King Edward's army were coming fast and he grimly pushed on towards the trees, knowing he would be cut down should he falter or stumble.

Ahead in the trees, he could see Little John and Much waving to him, willing him onwards, and mixed emotions struggled within him: anger at them, for not getting as far into the safety of the forest as possible, but also gratitude that they hadn't simply left him behind.

As he raced towards his friends in desperation, he could feel the ground tremble beneath him and he knew enemy cavalry were close behind. He couldn't risk a look back to see how close they were, for fear of stumbling, but he expected any second to feel a sword hammer into his spine.

He was more frightened than he had ever been in his life, and again, Matilda, and an image of a little boy, came into his mind as, sobbing, he bared his teeth and tried one last time to make his legs move faster.

The metallic taste of blood filled his mouth and he knew he must have bitten his tongue as the pounding of hooves came closer and an enemy knight charged through the grass behind him. He imagined the pursuer laughing in grim satisfaction at the unresisting target fleeing desperately towards the trees.

Much and John looked on in frustrated disbelief as Robin suddenly came to a halt and turned, sword held before him.

"Come on then, you bastard!" he shouted, spreading his legs and moving into a defensive stance.

The enemy horseman thundered towards him, almost fifteen hundred pounds of muscle and steel. In comparison Robin was closer to two hundred pounds and only lightly armoured. The gambeson he wore was the same beaten-up one his old captain, Adam Bell, had given him almost a year ago. He never wore a helmet or carried a shield, needing both hands free to shoot his enormous longbow.

Even if he somehow managed to land a blow on the knight, the sheer weight of attacking horse and man would destroy Robin's body.

He lost his sense of fear as the knight bore down on him, and time seemed to slow to a crawl. The horse's eyes bulged, its great nostrils flaring, as its rider swept his longsword back, perfectly timed for the killing blow, and Robin felt a feral growl escape from his throat, enraged at the oncoming doom, but determined to meet it head on.

From behind Robin an arrow tore through the air, somehow finding its way through the thin visor on the horseman's helmet, lodging in his brain and catapulting him backwards to land, arms and legs flailing, on the hard ground behind.

The charging horse, with no one to control it, veered to one side, away from the grateful outlaw, who stood rooted to the spot, thinking inanely of King Harold and how an arrow to the eye had killed him nearly three hundred years earlier, changing England forever.

Hands grabbed his arm and he came back to the present, as Little John dragged him into the trees, towards Much, who held his longbow, ready to cut down any other pursuers. Robin grinned towards his childhood friend in gratitude, and Much laughed in relief.

"We'll talk about how lucky that shot was later," John grunted. "Once we're safely away from here. Come on, let's move!"

CHAPTER TWO

"Now what?" Will Scaflock demanded. "We're back where we started!"

When Robin's men had run from the battle, although they were scattered, they had slowly made their way back, in ones and twos, to meet up again in Barnsdale, at a prearranged spot well-hidden from the main roads.

The king's men had chased and harried all the fleeing rebels but many of them, including all of Robin's gang, who were experienced woodsmen, had managed to escape into the forest, and safety. For now.

Matt Groves slammed his open palm against a tree in frustration. "We're not back where we started at all, Scarlet!" he shouted at Will. "Before this we were outlaws, hunted by foresters and, now and again, the sheriff's men. Now we're rebels – the king's own soldiers will be after us!" He pointed an accusing finger at Robin. "This is all your fault, Hood! You told us to join the rebellion, and we followed you! Now what? We're fucked!"

Robin sat on a frost-covered fallen tree and shook his head wearily. He was tired of Matt Groves and his complaining. The rest of the group shared a strong bond of friendship and mutual respect, but Groves had slowly become something of an outsider in their small band. The sheriff had offered to sell Robin's wife, Matilda, a pardon a few months earlier, but Matt had refused to part with any money. Every one of the other outlaws had been happy to help the girl and, thankfully, she had won her freedom eventually, but the incident still angered Robin.

"I never told anyone to join the rebellion," Robin retorted. "I decided to throw my lot in with the

Earl of Lancaster and Sir Richard-at-Lee. The rest of you were free to do what you wanted."

"We all wanted to fight," Much nodded, agreeing with his big friend. "Not just for pardons, but to bring some sort of justice to the country. This was our one chance to make a difference – to help the common folk. To help our friends and families in places like Wakefield and Hathersage."

There were grunts of agreement at that, but Matt snorted, looking around at the rest of the men in disgust. "The common folk? You mean like the people at Burton where Lancaster burnt the place down about their ears?" He turned to glare at Robin again, barely drawing breath as he continued. "You're supposed to be our leader, Hood. We all trusted you to steer us right. You said it was a good idea – 'we'll all win pardons,' you said. Well, where's my fucking pardon then? And what about that king's man, Sir Guy of Gisbourne? That bastard has a hard-on for you and we're all going to suffer for it now!" As he ranted, his voice had grown steadily louder and he had moved slowly closer to Robin, so, his last, shouted words, were spat right in the young man's face.

Although Robin felt humiliated and angry, he also understood Matt's frustration. No, he hadn't told the men to join the Earl of Lancaster's rebellion but he had suggested it was a good idea. Robin was still a very young man, only eighteen, and his lack of experience often made him question his leadership skills. Deep down, he wondered if maybe Matt Groves was right, and it *was* all his fault.

Groves misread Robin's silence and downcast eyes, assuming his young leader was ignoring him. "Are you listening to me, you arrogant young prick?" he demanded, his hand shooting forward to grasp Robin round the neck.

Without realising what he was doing, Robin reacted instinctively. His left wrist flicked up and round, knocking Matt's hand past his shoulder, as his right fist shot out, slamming straight into Matt's nose with a crunch of bone and cartilage.

Groves fell back onto the frosty wet grass, his eyes wide in shock, but before he could react, Little John and Will pinned him to the ground.

"Just stay where you are, Matt," John grunted, as the fallen man struggled to rise, his face a mask of fury, blood trickling from his nostrils. The rest of the outlaws stood watching the confrontation in silence, wondering where it would lead.

Robin thought quickly. Although Matt Groves was not well liked amongst the outlaws, thanks to his sour nature and constant complaining, he *was* respected. All of the men had been in fights with Matt at their side, and many of them had been saved from the point of a forester's sword by his actions.

The young leader couldn't just tell Groves to leave their group; he had to deal with this situation properly, while retaining his authority in front of the men.

"Let him up," Robin muttered to Will and John, who warily let go of Matt's arms, the three of them climbing slowly to their feet, Groves wiping his upper lip and grimacing in disgust at the blood smeared on the back of his hand.

Robin looked around at the men, addressing them as one. "I'm going to head back to our last camp-site, and carry on as before. We have no other choice. Aye, it'll be hard – even harder than before the rebellion. But there's nothing else to do – so...I'm not ordering anyone to follow me. You're all big boys; you can make up your own minds. Barnsdale's a big place, with lots of trees to hide in, especially now as spring's on its way. I'm sure you can all find somewhere to try and keep out of the king's way. Anyone that wants to, though, is welcome to come with me." He looked into the eyes of the men, his face earnest. "I hope you all do."

Matt Groves hawked and spat a gob of blood onto the forest floor.

"You can do what you like," Robin glared at him. "For what it's worth, I'd be more than happy if you'd just fuck off. Go your own way, so we don't have to listen to your complaining all the time. But it's your choice: go where you will." He moved forward to stand in front of Groves and lowered his voice to a menacing growl, just loud enough for everyone else to hear. "If you ever try and lay a hand on me again though, old man, I'll rip your face off and nail it to a tree."

Matt held eye contact with the younger man for a moment then turned away with a sneer.

Robin collected his few belongings and moved off in the direction of Notton, not far from Wakefield, where the outlaws had spent the previous winter. It was as good a place as any to set up camp, he thought. He didn't look back as he made his way through the forest, but he muttered a quiet prayer to Mary Magdalene that his friends would all follow him.

Much caught up with him, clapping a big hand on his leader's back, sympathetically. "You all right?"

Robin shrugged. "Not really. Will's right – we're fucked. Back worse off than we were before Christmas. And not just us: the whole country." He shook his head angrily, the disappointment of being on the losing side in the rebellion threatening to overwhelm him. His hopes and dreams had gone up in smoke as he had shouted at his men to retreat from the battle of Boroughbridge. He had desperately wanted the pardon the Earl of Lancaster had promised him. His wife Matilda was carrying their unborn child and he wanted so much to be a part of the little one's life; a real father. A real husband.

That would be nigh on impossible living as a wolf's head in the forest. His rage boiled impotently inside him, and he almost hoped Matt Groves would attack him again so he could take his frustration out on the bastard.

He felt suddenly ashamed as he looked over at Much, a young man who had lost his home and his entire family and been left with nothing. At least Robin still had his parents and his wife in Wakefield, even if he couldn't be with them as often as he'd like. He put an arm around Much's shoulder and threw his old friend a grin. "We'll be all right – we just need to find some other way to earn a pardon now."

There was a sarcastic laugh from behind him at that, and he turned to see Will Scarlet following, his green eyes twinkling. Little John and Friar Tuck were a little way behind and, as he looked back along the trail Robin's heart soared as he realised his men had all decided to follow him.

He might not have his family beside him, but this gang of outlaws was a brotherhood. He grinned at them all and walked on with his head high.

Matt Groves traipsed along at the rear, shoving branches and foliage out of the way angrily, his face twisted in a scowl. It would be suicide to head into the forest on his own just now though, with the king's men still hunting the rebels, so he followed Robin and the others bitterly.

His nose ached, and the blood drying around his mouth cracked uncomfortably as it dried in the chilly morning breeze. Hood had beaten him today – humiliated him in front of these men he had known for years. But Matt Groves was a man that knew how to hold a grudge – he would find a way to pay the young arsehole back eventually.

He just had to be patient, and watch for his chance.

* * *

"Shut up, you scum!" Henricus Chapman, steward to the Sheriff of Nottingham and Yorkshire, roared at the people gathered in the great hall of the castle. "The king is at the gate! Make yourselves presentable, and keep your mouths shut!"

The sheriff, Sir Henry de Faucumberg, shook his head at his steward's harsh words, but his own nervousness at the impending royal visit stopped him from reprimanding the over-zealous official.

As a result of the failed rebellion many men from the surrounding villages who had thrown their lot in with the defeated Earl of Lancaster had either been killed or chased into the forests as outlaws. Now, their families – wives, children, brothers, parents – came to the sheriff pleading for mercy. Who would work the land if so many men were declared outlaws and hunted down? Who would support their children? More importantly to the sheriff and his noble peers, who would pay their rents?

De Faucumberg was prepared to grudgingly allow the hundreds of defeated rebels to return quietly to their homes. He was no philanthropist, but the local economy needed those men – not to mention the fact hunting them all down would be a major burden on his own military resources.

Now, though, one of his men had hurried to see him with news from one of Nottingham's gatehouses. King Edward II was at the gate, making his way to see the sheriff. It wasn't an entirely unexpected visit, but de Faucumberg had hoped for a little more notice than this.

He absent-mindedly smoothed imagined creases from his expensive robe, ran his hands over his short greying hair and breathed on his gold chain of office, working it to a nice shine with his sleeve. He looked up irritably as the newest addition to his staff strode confidently up to stand before him.

Sir Guy of Gisbourne had been sent by the king a few months earlier, to hunt the outlaws hiding in Barnsdale. Robin Hood in particular.

De Faucumberg had failed to catch Hood and his gang as they robbed a number of powerful nobles and clergymen during the last year. King Edward had grown impatient and, eventually, sent his own man to help. Gisbourne was an experienced bounty-hunter – ruthless, intelligent, and an expert forester to boot. The king expected him to soon take care of the notorious Hood and his gang, who were fast becoming folk heroes to the poor, downtrodden people of northern England.

Sir Henry de Faucumberg couldn't stand the sight of the tall, self assured Gisbourne. He had no choice but to work with him though, and, if the king's man managed to kill Hood and his men – well, good! One less wolf's head to worry about. Then the overly confident lanky big bastard could bugger off back to the king.

"Oh, get up here and sit beside me, Gisbourne," the sheriff groused. "The king will expect to see his bounty-hunter." De Faucumberg indicated the empty seat to his right, and Sir Guy stepped onto the raised dais before settling into the vacant chair with a grin at the sheriff.

De Faucumberg, nervous at the thought of meeting the king under these circumstances, suddenly leaned forward to glare into Gisbourne's surprised face.

"You watch what you say to the king," he whispered with a snarl. "Don't forget, he'll be gone in a day and you'll be left behind again…with me and my men."

There was a commotion near the doors as the steward hurried back into the great hall and lifted his powerful voice.

"His royal Highness, King Edward!"

"I'll be left behind with you?" Gisbourne quietly asked the sheriff, as the king and his retinue filed into the hall. "You're assuming you'll still be sheriff after I give my report to the king…"

De Faucumberg glared at Gisbourne, but the king's man grinned back, clearly enjoying the sheriff's discomfort.

King Edward cut an imposing figure as he strode to the front of the hall. Handsome and tall, even taller than Sir Guy, and much broader across the shoulders with long wavy fair hair that curled around his neck.

15

Gisbourne dropped to one knee, his head bowed respectfully as England's ruler approached them and De Faucumberg quickly followed suit.

"Highness, be welcome!" the sheriff intoned, eyes on the impeccably polished wooden floorboards.

"Yes, yes, very good, Sir Henry." King Edward swept past his kneeling subjects and took his seat, in the middle of the table, between the sheriff's and Guy of Gisbourne's chairs.

"Get up. I don't have time for this," the king shouted to the gathered people. He lifted the silver goblet of wine before him and drained it with a loud gasp of pleasure. A wide-eyed serving boy rushed over, jug in hand, to refill the cup, but the king waved him away irritably.

"Let me guess, de Faucumberg," Edward growled, as the sheriff took his seat and looked at the king. "These people are here hoping their men who took up arms against me will be pardoned."

De Faucumberg nodded. "Yes, my liege. It seems many local villagers joined the ill-fated rebellion. Without those men the economy will struggle."

The king nodded grimly. "I understand that. It's hard enough for these people to survive, yes?"

The sheriff nodded again, thankful that the king understood the issue so well.

"Then they should have thought of that before they rebelled against my rule!" King Edward suddenly slammed his hand on the table, his face red with anger. "You people!" He roared, glaring at the men and women gathered in the hall. "Get back to your villages, and make sure you pay your rents! When your children are starving, and your bellies are swollen with hunger again maybe your men will think twice about rebelling against their rightful king. Get out!"

De Faucumberg, his earlier thoughts of leniency to the villagers forgotten in the face of the king's rage, shouted at his guards. "You heard him! Get those people out of here, now!"

As the frightened men and women streamed out of the hall Edward leaned back and, brandishing his empty goblet, shouted for a refill.

"I understand your dilemma, de Faucumberg," the king told the sheriff, gazing up at the vaulted ceiling. "But I want these traitors hunted down and destroyed. Every last one of them." He held up a hand as the sheriff opened his mouth to protest. "You need soldiers, I know. I have them for you: another thirty men."

De Faucumberg let a small smile creep over his face at the thought of such an increase in his personal militia, and he glanced over at Sir Guy with a triumphant smirk.

"They will be under Sir Guy of Gisbourne's command."

The sheriff's face fell in disbelief as Edward continued. "You're tied up with your administrative duties in Nottingham and Yorkshire, Henry. Sir Guy will hunt down the rebels. I don't know why you look like someone's pissed in your wine – you've got it easy."

"Sir Henry is one of the best administrators I've ever worked with, Sire," Gisbourne told the king solemnly, as the sheriff listened in surprise. "I'm sure that, between us, we can hunt down these rebels while making sure the rents are paid on time." He glanced at de Faucumberg, eyebrows raised. "Eh, Sir Henry?"

The sheriff, a man who had known great power over a period of many years, felt lost under the steely eyes of the king and the smirking bounty-hunter. He nodded.

"Yes, my liege. We'll look after things for you. But..."

The king looked irritably at the sheriff. "But what?"

"Well, without their men...some of the local villages won't survive the winter."

The king shrugged his shoulders and emptied his goblet, wine running down the side of his mouth. "Fine," he said, wiping his chin neatly with a napkin. "Pardon

17

the ones you see fit. Not the ringleaders though – not the knights and noblemen. Those you will kill or imprison until I can decide their fate, yes? And what about that outlaw I sent Gisbourne here for in the first place? Have you managed to catch him?"

De Faucumberg shook his head, not wanting to admit Robin Hood and his men had been spotted within the ranks of the Earl of Lancaster's army. "Not yet" –

"Fear not, sire," Sir Guy broke in, his earlier smile replaced with a determined scowl that chilled the sheriff to the bone. "The commoners see him as some legendary swordsman – a great hero like Arthur or Lancelot. I'll show them he's nothing more than a dirty peasant with ideas above his station. Count on it, my liege: I'll bring the wolf's head to justice, one way or another..."

"Good, that's all settled then," King Edward nodded contentedly, gesturing to the serving boy for another refill. "I'll leave you two to sort it out – I'm off to deal with my cousin the Earl of Lancaster in the morning. Now...where's your entertainment, de Faucumberg? I'm looking forward to a fine evening. The sheriff of Manchester has a minstrel who can fart a tune you know."

* * *

"That stinks, you dirty bastard!"

Will Scarlet grinned, as Little John covered his bearded face theatrically with his sleeve.

"Sorry," Will laughed. "I must've eaten too much of that cabbage yesterday. It's good for the digestion they say."

"In the name of God," John grunted with a scowl. "I thought it was hell on Earth fighting the king's men but your arse is deadlier than a blade in the guts."

Winter was retreating, so, as they settled back into their old camp near Notton the outlaws were able to sleep in the open again, under sturdy shelters, rather than crushed together in a cramped cave as they had been before joining the earl's army.

They clustered around the camp-fire, enjoying its warmth and light as glowing embers crackled into the night sky, drinking ale, playing dice, and singing songs.

So far they'd managed to avoid the king's soldiers, although they'd heard tales from the locals roundabout of other rebels being caught in the forest and hanged or worse. It was only a matter of time until they'd be forced to fight for their lives, Robin mused, as he sat, staring into the camp-fire and nursing a mug of ale.

He had sent a message to Wakefield, to let his family, and Will's daughter Beth, who also lived there, know they were all alive and well, although still outlaws.

"Any idea what we're going to do?" Friar Tuck sat down with a grunt next to the young leader, an ale in one hand and a leg of roast duck in the other.

Robin smiled at his portly friend, shrugging his shoulders in reply. "Not really. I can't see anything for us to do, other than what we've been doing all along: living here in the greenwood, robbing rich folk, counting on the good will of the villagers' hereabouts...and killing anyone who comes hunting for us." He shrugged again, despondently. "If you've got any advice, Tuck, I'd like to hear it."

The friar nodded, understanding Robin's frustration. "I don't have much to offer by way of advice," he replied. "But you should take heart from the fact these men followed you after the Battle of Boroughbridge, and still trust you to lead them."

Robin stayed silent, brooding as he gazed at the black silhouettes of the tall trees, like giant sentinels all around them.

"Men like John Little and Will Scaflock are no fools," the friar had a pleasant, persuasive voice and he carried on, fixing his young captain with a knowing look. "Either of them could lead their own gang of men, but they choose to follow *you*. Look, the rebellion wasn't

19

meant to be – the earl burned Burton and he treated with the Scots." He waved away Robin's half-hearted protest. "The rumours were true, Lancaster could have crushed the Scots over the years but he always let them escape. Aye, he promised a lot and he probably would have been a better king for the likes of us than Edward ever will be but...maybe it'll turn out to be a blessing that we failed at Boroughbridge. I know it's hard to believe, with your wife carrying your child and you stuck out here with all of us, but... God will look after you. Never give up hope!"

Robin was taken aback by the vehemence in Tuck's voice.

"Trust me, lad: our Lord has a purpose for you. That much was clear to me from the day I met you. You have to believe in yourself the way these men believe in you." He spread his arms wide, encompassing the whole outlaw camp. "And they're going to need you now – that bastard Gisbourne will come for us soon..."

Robin shivered. When they'd been part of the earl's army he'd heard rumours about Sir Guy and the things he'd done. He looked across at Tuck and pushed the king's man from his mind, grinning back at the rosy-cheeked friar who drained the last of the ale in his cup and nodded towards the rest of the gang.

Despite their defeat in the battle against King Edward's forces, and their continuing status as outlaws, the men were enjoying themselves tonight. They laughed and sang around the camp-fire, seemingly without a care in the world. Every so often one of them would wave over to him, grinning and raising their mugs in salute.

Robin felt humbled by their friendship, and their faith in him as their leader.

His eyes grew moist and he looked away from Tuck, wiping the tears with his fingertips. *Never give up hope...*

The big friar stood up, and clapped his young leader on the back. "Come on, it's time you joined in."

With a smile of gratitude, Robin followed Tuck back to the fire, and found himself singing and dancing with the rest of the men, his cares, for a while, forgotten.

At the edge of the fire's orange glow, Matt Groves stood alone, watching the others enjoying themselves, his expression blacker than the starless sky overhead.

CHAPTER THREE

After Robin and the other outlaws had fled the battlefield at Boroughbridge, things had not gone well for the Earl of Lancaster's forces, or his Marcher allies. They had suffered horrendous casualties from the sustained assault of Andrew Harclay's longbow men and, in desperation, had managed to obtain an overnight truce but the majority of their remaining soldiers had deserted during the night.

The rebellion was over.

In the morning, the earl, along with his other captains, had surrendered to Harclay, who had them manacled and taken by boat to the earl's own castle in Pontefract.

Thomas had been locked in a cell with his ally, Roger Clifford, 2nd Lord of Skipton.

"What do you think Edward will do with us?" Clifford asked, gasping in pain from the terrible cut in the side he had suffered at Boroughbridge. Before imprisoning him, the king's men had poured wine on it to clean it, and roughly tied a strip of linen around his torso to stop the bleeding, but the deep wound was beginning to fester and become ever more painful.

Thomas shrugged, too weak from hunger and dehydration to offer a reply.

For three days they had languished in the freezing jail underneath the castle. The guards occasionally threw some mouldy bread in to them, and skins filled with cheap, vile tasting wine, but mostly they were left alone in the near total darkness. The cell stank, as they were forced to relieve themselves in the corners, but the mess inevitably spread. There weren't even any rushes to soak up the filth.

The earl sat contemplating the irony of being held captive in his own castle. If he'd known this was going to happen he'd have at least had the floors stocked with rushes! He almost smiled at the idea.

"Do you think he'll pardon us?" Clifford breathed, gazing at the ceiling which was filthy with years of damp and mould. "We're too powerful to be held prisoner for long, don't you think?"

Lancaster never even offered a shrug this time, his eyes glassy, as if lost in a daydream.

Both men stirred as the sound of heavy footsteps approached them. Would it be another guard to toss more scraps of food for them to scavenge off the shit-stained floor, like dogs again?

The massive door, close to four inches thick was flung open, the light from the torches their jailers carried momentarily blinding the captives.

"You. Up." It was one of the king's soldiers, a huge bear of a man with a small but distinctive scar on his upper lip which made him look even more daunting. He was flanked by two other men, not as tall as their captain, but with the enormous arms and shoulders of longbow men. All three wore the king's heraldic badge of three yellow lions on a red background, and they glared at the earl, watching as the disgraced nobleman weakly tried to stand.

"Help him."

The two shorter men moved into the cell, swearing at the stench, and grasped the wretched earl by the arms, dragging him to his feet effortlessly.

"Take him."

Thomas was half-dragged from the cell, his head spinning so badly he feared he might puke on his two 'helpers'.

"Where are you taking him?" Clifford whimpered, but the huge soldier simply slammed the door shut with a thump, throwing the miserable cell into darkness again and leaving the Lord of Skipton to his fate.

"What about me?" he shouted, his voice cracking as the burning pain in his side almost made him pass out.

As he was pulled along the draughty corridor the Earl of Lancaster felt sorry for Clifford. His wound was mortal, that much was obvious – the man would be dead in a couple of days even if the king did pardon him.

Thomas, on the other hand, would be fine once he had something to eat and drink. His mouth watered at the thought of a nice cut of roast pork and a mug of ale.

Obviously, the king – his cousin – would have to punish him somehow.

An exorbitant fine perhaps. Christ, maybe even exile. That would be terrible.

But the earl was of royal blood himself – the Steward of England and the second wealthiest man in the country after Edward himself. He had survived the king's wrath before, most notably when he had beheaded Edward's lover Piers Gaveston.

Yes, he felt pity for his ally Clifford, left to die in a piss-soaked, freezing jail cell, but at least Thomas would be all right.

He felt sure of it.

As he was taken into the great hall – his great hall! – Thomas's confidence faltered. The king sat at the table, with those loyal earls and other magnates that had supported him against the rebels. At Edward's right hand sat Hugh, the younger Despenser, with a look of malevolent triumph on his face. The Elder Despenser, along with other earls who had remained loyal to the king were also seated at the long table.

The two soldiers let their charge go at a nod from the scarred giant, and Thomas slumped embarrassingly, and painfully, onto the floorboards, too weak to lift his arms protectively as his face hit the ground.

He was offered no food or drink, and his manacles remained locked in place on his wrists and ankles, as the king himself stood to list the charges against him.

In his weakened state he could only crouch on the floor as Edward railed at him.

"You raised an army against me!"

After a while, Thomas couldn't concentrate on what was being said. His head was spinning and he longed to sleep, which seemed such a ridiculous idea that he burst out laughing.

His laughter stopped a moment later as the king sat down and Sir Henry Despenser stood to proclaim judgement. It took a few seconds, but even in his fragile state of mind the words shocked the earl.

"Thomas Plantaganet, Earl of Lancaster, Leicester and Derby, you have been found guilty of treason. You are hereby sentenced to death by being hanged, drawn and beheaded."

Exhausted and half mad, he looked up at his cousin, King Edward II with a wild stare.

Then, with tears streaking his filthy cheeks, he burst out laughing again.

* * *

"Robin!" The girl's eyes lit up as she saw her husband standing at the door, but, as she looked at him, they welled up with tears and the outlaw took her gently in his massive arms.

"I know, I know," he muttered. "The rebellion failed. I'm still a wolf's head. I'm so sorry."

They moved inside, locking the door behind them. It was before dawn and the village was mostly silent in the early spring gloom, but Robin didn't want anyone seeing him. He remembered only too well the trouble that had come to Wakefield last year as the law hunted for him and Matilda had been arrested herself as a result.

"Ah, it's you lad! We thought it was a cat scratching at the door so quietly before sunrise." The village fletcher, Henry, Matilda's father, smiled warmly at his son-in-law and moved across the small room to grasp him by the hand.

"It's good to see you," Mary, Matilda's mother added, reaching up to kiss Robin gently on the cheek. "We were worried...well, when we heard the king's men had beaten the earl's forces and were hunting you all down."

Robin nodded sadly. "We had no chance in the end. I ordered the lads to run before Harclay's men got close enough to catch us. It felt like a betrayal, running like that, but we were done for."

"You did the right thing," the fletcher said. "The Earl of Lancaster should have made more of a fight of it instead of throwing away so many lives needlessly. The villages hereabouts have lost a lot of fathers and sons. The good Lord knows what'll happen when the harvest's to be planted."

Robin waved a hand dismissing Henry's fears. "The king might be a fool, but I don't think he'll let the people starve just to teach a few peasants and yeomen a lesson. He's not that vindictive. He'll probably hang a few of the rebel leaders to make an example of them, but the earl is too wealthy for the king to do much."

"You think this will all just die down?" Matilda led Robin by the hand to the small table the family kept by the wall and bade him sit and eat some of the porridge she'd just ladled out for him.

"Will seems to think so," he replied, tucking into the warm food gratefully. "And Will understands these things a lot better than I ever will. We're going to be in even more danger than we were before for a while, though, until the king's men flush out the rest of the rebels. We'll be all right though," he smiled reassuringly at the worried look on Matilda's face. "We know how to hide in the forest, you know that. It's those other lads I feel sorry for."

"Hopefully you're right," Henry said, "and this dies down quickly, so things get back to normality, although it's been said this Guy of Gisbourne has been ordered to hunt you down" –

"Forget him," Robin broke in, not wanting Matilda to be alarmed by talk of the king's bounty hunter. "Me and the lads know how to look after ourselves in the forest."

The fletcher threw his tunic around his shoulders and nodded at Robin. "I hope so. Now, I have to get to work. It was good to see you, son."

"You too," the outlaw agreed warmly. "I won't come back around like this again, not for a while. I don't want to place you in any danger."

Mary gave the seated man another kiss on the cheek. "I have to nip out to get some things from the baker. You look after yourself, Robin."

Matilda's parents waved goodbye and left the young couple by themselves. Matilda looked almost shyly at her husband, who she hadn't seen for weeks, and he gazed back fondly, noting how she absent-mindedly stroked her swollen belly.

"How is...it?" he asked awkwardly, flushing slightly at the girl's laughter.

"'It' is fine. I can feel kicking now, especially at night. We've got a little fighter in here." She stood up and came over to stand beside her young husband, holding out her hand. "Come on, we should make the most of the time. I've missed you."

They made love, passionately but hurriedly, for fear of Matilda's mother returning, then Robin kissed the girl softly in farewell, rubbing his hand affectionately across her tummy.

"Do you have any names yet?"

Matilda smiled down at the bump. "I like Mary, if it's a wee girl."

Robin nodded. "That's perfect. Mary. I'll go with that." He eyed her belly and returned her grin, placing an arm affectionately around her shoulders. "What if it's a boy?"

The girl shrugged. "I'm not sure. I like Arthur. Or maybe Edward."

"Arthur, that sounds good," the outlaw replied. "But I'm not so keen on naming our child after a man that's sent a bounty-hunter to kill me."

"What about Adam then?" Matilda smiled impishly at him.

"That's even worse!"

They held each other in close again, smiling and imagining a future where they could both live freely, watching the life that was growing inside Matilda become a child and then an adult.

"I will visit again when I can," Robin told her, pulling away reluctantly, "but this new bounty-hunter of the king's might turn out to be another bastard like Adam Gurdon so I won't place you or the baby in any danger."

She smiled up at him and squeezed his buttocks playfully. "Don't make it too long," she warned. "Pregnant women have needs too, and I've been told they get even stronger urges as the baby grows."

"I'll think of you at night when I'm in the greenwood," he told her, his blue eyes drinking in the sight of her and committing it to memory.

"Get going, then," she giggled. "I love you."

"I love you too, both of you. And I still intend to keep the promise I made you last year: I *will* earn a pardon, somehow, and be a proper husband and father."

He hurried out into the street and, with a last, longing wave, disappeared into the shadows cast by the early morning sun.

Matilda sighed as she watched him go, missing him already. *At least I'm not alone*, she thought, holding her belly and giving thanks to God.

* * *

A week passed after what was being called the Battle of Boroughbridge, and the outlaws had settled comfortably back into their old routine. The soldiers hunting them had failed to find them. Although Sir Guy of Gisbourne was a hugely experienced bounty-hunter, he simply didn't know the forests of Yorkshire well enough yet. He had hired local guides, and was creating a detailed mental map of the area in his head, but Robin and his men were able to stay a step ahead of their pursuers easily enough.

Of course, Gisbourne wasn't just hunting Robin's gang now; he also had to find the dozens of defeated rebels who had taken refuge in the greenwood after Boroughbridge. Although those other rebels were diverting attention away from his own men, Robin had grave fears about the presence of so many lawless men roaming the region. While his gang tended to steal from the rich nobles and clergymen who passed their way, these other rebels were apparently happy enough to rob from anyone they could – peasants, yeomen and villeins, as well as those much better off. When Robin's men visited the outlying villages for supplies, they heard worse tales: rebels accused of carrying off livestock from poor families who might only own, and depend on, one or two sheep or hens; drunken men wandering through villages stealing from traders, and viciously assaulting any who complained; even accusations of rape and murder.

As a result, Robin and his friends found it difficult to get the supplies they relied on from the surrounding villages, as the locals became more defensive and began to arm themselves.

Unless the locals knew the outlaw well, they would be chased off with the promise of violence.

Of course, everyone in Yorkshire knew of Little John, thanks to his great height – near seven feet tall, and built like a bear with a shaggy brown beard to match – so he ended up having to collect the outlaws' supplies whenever they needed anything they couldn't catch or make themselves: butter, salted beef and pork, fruit, bread and eggs although those were scarce in winter.

"I'm fed up with this," John grumbled as he returned from Bichill one afternoon, dropping a pile of supplies on the ground by the camp-fire. "I feel like a woman, doing everyone's shopping for them. The sooner the rest of the rebels are caught, the better!"

Will Scarlet gave a loud laugh and came over to stand in front of John, grinning. "Hark at her! I thought you enjoyed shopping." He tugged at the sleeve of the giant's worn old brown cloak. "You always put on your fanciest dress for it."

Little John lunged at Scarlet, but Will danced back out of reach, gesturing the big man to come ahead, while Robin and the rest of the men watched the entertainment with broad smiles.

"I'm glad you all find it so funny," Friar Tuck grunted, dropping a sack of loaves on the ground beside John's supplies. Tuck had gone to Bichill with John, but he was dismayed at the stories they'd heard there.

"These other outlaws have no respect for anyone. Someone should stop them."

"It's nothing to do with us," Robin replied, glancing up from his log by the fire, where he sat stirring a big cauldron of pottage.

The men muttered in agreement, but Tuck fixed his young leader with a glare. "Will you still be saying that when they rape someone in Wakefield?"

Robin shook his head, looking away from the clergyman. "What would you have us do, Tuck? We're outlaws ourselves. We can't go around Barnsdale hunting down other rebels. All we can do is hope we meet these men and they join up with us."

The men shouted agreement at that, but Tuck shook his head. "These men aren't like us. They're desperate – starving."

Matt Groves snorted. "Desperate? I've been an outlaw for years, friar! Men don't get much more desperate than me."

"What's that in your hand then, Matt?" the portly friar demanded, gesturing towards the gently steaming bowl of pottage in Groves' right hand. "All of us here have food, money, warm clothing and a loyal friend at our side to defend us if the foresters find us."

Matt waved a dismissive hand and turned his back on Tuck with a scowl.

"You might think you're desperate," Tuck stated, looking around at the other men, his eyes finally meeting Robin's. "But I fear we're going to find out all too soon what truly desperate men will do when they're trapped in these woods with nowhere to run."

* * *

Guy of Gisbourne had been tired and irritable before he and his men had, purely by chance, stumbled upon the group of rebels hiding in the forest.

They had been searching an area of Barnsdale where reports suggested some of the insurgents were camping. They were on foot, since horses were no use for moving between the dense undergrowth and, after much of the day walking and stumbling over fallen logs and trailing plants Gisbourne was about ready to call a halt to the search for the day.

Then his second-in-command, and friend of many years, Nicholas Barnwell, a bald man with a disconcerting gaze, had caught the sweet scent of wood smoke. He held up a hand, motioning for silence and sniffed the air again, as the unmistakable smell of roasting meat came to them. The soldiers remained silent, senses straining as they tried to glean whatever information they could about the unseen cook.

A faint laugh carried to them through the trees and Gisbourne nodded to his sergeant, motioning his men – twenty five of them – to make their way towards the source of the sounds and smells.

As they carefully moved forward the gentle murmur of a number of men in relaxed conversation could be heard and, when the soldiers came to a small clearing they could make out the tell-tale grey smoke from the camp-fire a little way ahead of them.

Sir Guy gestured to his men to encircle the camp and, with the efficiency and discipline of professional soldiers they moved to obey his silent order.

Although there was a good possibility these men cooking meat and laughing together were innocent travellers – merchants perhaps, or even wandering friars – Gisbourne was too experienced a bounty-hunter to take any chances.

He carried a small, neatly made crossbow, painted black, rather than a longbow. Generally, the crossbow was an inefficient, unwieldy weapon, mainly used by peasants or untrained soldiers. But Gisbourne's smaller weapon, which he'd had specially made by an Italian craftsman, with its stock made from hazel, a steel bow and a hemp string, was deadly at closer ranges.

He carried it on a leather strap slung over his right shoulder, but now he slipped it down into his hand, placed a bolt in it and cocked it by pulling the lever down.

He waited a few moments to let his men get into position, then as Nicholas nodded, judging enough time had passed to have the camp-site encircled, Gisbourne raised his arm.

"Move in," he growled, gesturing towards the rebels.

This close to the men by the fire it was impossible to remain undetected for long as twenty five lightly armoured men rushed forward between the trees, bursting through the undergrowth to stand, weapons drawn in a loose but impressive perimeter around the small clearing where the remains of an old sheep was slowly roasting over the little fire.

The surprised rebels, in a panic, scrambled to defend themselves. It was obvious they were no merchants or churchmen from their threadbare clothing and array of pitiful weaponry which they brandished threateningly at the silent soldiers surrounding them.

Gisbourne, his mouth watering at the sight and smell of the mutton skewered above the fire, held his crossbow by his side as his eyes took in the frightened faces of the men before him.

He was a tall man, although he wasn't powerfully built, being more wiry than massively muscled, but his clothing and bearing clearly marked him as the leader of the soldiers facing the rebels. With his short black hair and stubble, dark eyes and confident, relaxed stance, every one of the rebels felt their gaze drawn to him like iron filings to a dark magnet. Clad all in black, from head to toe, with a boiled leather cuirass moulded to show the shape of his chest, he knew he was an imposing figure and revelled in the sinister power he exuded.

"What do you want?" One of the rebels asked, his voice wavering. He was a broad shouldered young man, obviously an archer, although his bow was nowhere to be seen, probably discarded when he and his comrades fled from Boroughbridge. He hefted a cheap looking sword and tried his best to look menacing. "We've done nothing wrong."

Gisbourne wandered forward and, drawing his dagger with his left hand, cut a small piece of meat from the bottom of the skewered mutton. He lifted it to his lips and blew on the crisp meat gently to cool it, his eyes taking in the men before him, resting eventually on the man who had spoken. The leader, obviously.

"You've done nothing wrong, eh?" Gisbourne took the small slice of meat in his mouth and chewed slowly, a smile of pleasure lighting his dark features. "Where did you get this meat then?"

The rebel was ready for the question, stammering his reply almost before the question was asked. "We bought it from the butcher in Wooley, you can ask him."

Sir Guy finished the mouthful of mutton and placed his dagger back in its sheath in his boot. "You men are rebels. Outlaws," he stated, ignoring the cries of denial from the men before him as he continued. "And you have stolen this sheep from some local farmer."

The men again shouted their innocence, the fear plain on their faces. These were no hardy soldiers – they were armed mostly with pitchforks, blunt hatchets and hammers. Not one of them wore even light armour.

Every one of them looked terrified and desperate.

"Please, my lord," their young leader begged. "We're just peasants. We were forced to join the Earl of Lancaster's army!"

"Peasants you may be," Gisbourne replied disdainfully, "but your king seeks justice for your treason." He raised his crossbow. "Kill them," he ordered, as he squeezed the trigger and watched the wicked steel bolt hammer into the young rebel's chest, throwing the man stumbling backwards onto the grass where he lay, gasping and crying pitifully.

The soldiers moved in and engaged the panicked rebels who offered little resistance, the pitchforks proving no match for the sharpened steel Gisbourne's men wielded so mercilessly.

One of the outlaws flew straight for the black-clad bounty-hunter, screaming with rage as he pulled his axe – more suited to chopping wood than cleaving skulls – behind him, ready to bring it down on Gisbourne's head. "You shot my brother you bastard!"

Sir Guy dropped his crossbow on the ground and sidestepped the rebel's wild downward swing, pulling his sword smoothly from its scabbard as the youngster barrelled past. The polished silver steel stood out in stark contrast against Gisbourne's all black attire as, spinning nearly full circle, arm outstretched, he hammered the razor sharp blade into the axe-man's neck.

The young man, only just into his teens from the look of his beardless face, was thrown sideways to the ground, the great wound erupting in blood as he fell.

The fight was over within seconds, as Gisbourne's soldiers cut down the frightened peasants. The victorious soldiers searched the dead men for valuables but found nothing, as their dark leader took out his dagger and cheerfully helped himself to more slices of roast mutton.

"Dig in, lads," he grinned, gesturing at the dead rebels. "These boys have lost their appetite."

* * *

Late that afternoon, as Robin and his men sat around the fire talking quietly and eating their pottage the sounds of fighting could be heard, carried by the light westerly wind that ruffled the new green leaves in the trees.

"How close do you think that is?" Much wondered, hand dropping instinctively to his waist, although his sword lay on the ground beside him. He picked it up and fastened the belt reassuringly around himself. "Doesn't sound that far off."

Will shook his head. "It sounds closer because of the wind – we're in no danger, whatever it is that's happening."

The sounds of metal on metal and men shouting, or occasionally screaming, faded soon enough; the silence that replaced it feeling oppressive and eerie under the canopy of beech trees the outlaws were using as a camp.

"You think that was the sheriff's men and some of the other rebels?" Tuck asked no one in particular, lifting his thick blanket and wrapping it around his thick torso.

"Aye, no doubt," Little John nodded, his great voice jarring in the stillness. "Those rebels don't know how to use the forest like we do," he went on, quieter this time. "They've got no chance – the soldiers will eventually get them all."

"The soldiers will leave then," Will nodded, stretching out on the grass, watching the sky as the sun set. "We'll have less to worry about when that happens. Just the foresters and this bounty-hunter the king's sent after us."

"Guy of Gisbourne," Tuck agreed. "He's tied up chasing the rebels for now, but we'll have to be on our guard for him. They say he's like a shadow, just appears beside you when you least expect it."

"The Raven," Allan-a-Dale muttered. "Black as night and merciless too."

"Trust the minstrel to have something romantic to say!" Will snorted, drawing laughs from the others.

"Shut it, Scarlet," Allan grinned back good-naturedly. "I never came up with it; the people in Nottingham are calling him the Raven."

"They can call him whatever they like," Robin stood up, carrying his empty bowl over to the nearby stream to rinse it out. "We've been hunted by Adam Bell remember – a Knight Templar, who knew this forest inside out. And even he couldn't stop us," he shouted over his shoulder, kneeling to dip the wooden vessel in the clear waters.

The men began to relax again as night drew in, knowing the four lookouts they always had posted around their camp would alert them in plenty of time to any danger. The sounds of men fighting, and dying, so close by had unsettled most of them though.

Robin decided to move their camp again in the morning.

* * *

The young outlaw had chosen a spot near the village of Hathersage for their new base. Little John and Will told him of a good place they had used once before a couple of years earlier, when Adam Bell had led them. On their way, they carefully scouted the area they had heard the sounds of battle coming from the previous afternoon.

Twelve men lay dead in and around a small clearing they had obviously been using as a camp-site. From the looks of it, they were all poor men – peasants. Their cheap clothes were threadbare, and their hands showed the tell-tale signs of years of hard labour. Only a couple carried swords, which were of inferior quality and as good as worthless or their killers would have taken them rather than leaving them discarded on the grass. The rest of the dead men had only the tools of their trade: pitchforks, hammers or axes.

"They never stood a chance," Tuck noted, moving among the corpses, closing their sightless eyes and muttering blessings. "A dozen poorly armed peasants against a force of well-drilled soldiers." He shook his head sorrowfully, gazing down at a boy no more than thirteen summers who had been almost decapitated. "May you find peace in heaven, my child."

As the outlaws travelled to their new camp-site, they brooded silently, the sight of the dead rebels dampening any thoughts of banter or good cheer.

They reached their new base not long after midday, and set about making the place secure. Most of the men had stayed here before and knew the lie of the land. Robin smiled with satisfaction as the outlaws erected their animal-skin shelters and renewed the lookout posts they had used during ther previous stay.

Will caught his smile and nodded with a grin of his own. "They hardly need a leader this lot. They know how to look after themselves."

"Let's leave them to it then," Robin agreed. "I'm going into Hathersage for some supplies – you coming? It'll take the rest of the day to get there, so we'll stay the night in the inn. Have a few beers..."

Will's grin widened – not so long ago he would have never set foot in Hathersage for all the money in the world. He had lived there once, and – he believed – his whole family had been butchered there by the former lord of the manor. But Robin had returned his beloved little daughter, Beth – alive! – to him, and as a result Will's old scars were beginning to heal over. A trip into the village would suit him well enough and he'd be glad to share an ale with his friend Wilfred, the baker.

"Come on, then," Robin said, slapping him on the shoulder, "we'll take Tuck with us too."

* * *

As they neared Hathersage the sun was setting, casting long shadows along the path, and the three outlaws glanced at each other, wondering if they were imagining things. The sounds of men engaged in combat from the night before seemed to echo through the trees again, and they halted in their tracks, listening intently, hands tightening around their sword hilts.

It was unmistakable: there was fighting in Hathersage.

"Move!" Robin cried, racing towards the village.

His two older companions followed at a slightly slower pace, Will charging wildly after his leader, sword held high, and the overweight friar bringing up the rear breathlessly, gripping his stout quarterstaff grimly, muttering to himself. "I warned you about those rebels."

As Robin raced into the village's main street, he could see they were just in time. A small group of armed men, no more than a dozen at Robin's count, stood grinning wickedly, brandishing their weapons confidently. At their feet lay a hefty white clad figure, the crimson stain forming around his midriff suggesting he wouldn't be getting up again any time soon.

A crowd of frightened villagers faced off against the men, but only one of them – the blacksmith – was armed. He hefted his great hammer menacingly, thick blue veins bulging almost obscenely on his heavily muscled arms. The other village men looked bewildered, although more appeared, with one or two finally having the presence of mind to collect their longbows from their dwellings. Robin could see more of the locals darting off into the forest – mothers carrying children, older women trying their best to move quickly but glancing fearfully over their shoulders in case their doom should find them. Even some of the village men, unused to violence of this nature, were deserting the place until things calmed down.

Of those remaining, their faces were angry, but they lacked the confidence to tackle the gloating rebels, especially when one of their own lay dead on the street in front of them.

Robin slowed, dropping his cumbersome longbow on the ground, trying to catch his breath as he walked up to stand in front of the rebels, a little way apart from the villagers. "What's happening here?" he demanded, glaring at the men before him. They were a motley lot, most of them looking somewhat malnourished after their time hiding out in Barnsdale. One of them, an ugly looking bastard with a great scar on his cheek and only a couple of blackened teeth left, stared back arrogantly at the young outlaw.

"We just came here looking to buy supplies," the rebel smirked, spreading his hands wide innocently. "Then this fat old prick tries to stab one of my friends here."

The other rebels chorused agreement, but the village blacksmith roared indignantly. "Liar! You were stealing from the traders, and when you lifted Wilfred's loaves he tried to stop you. You murdered him!"

Robin's stomach lurched and his eyes dropped to the white figure on the ground. Blood had formed a thick pool around him, and now the young man recognised the murdered villager. It was his friend, Wilfred the baker, who had done so much in helping him and Allan-a-Dale rescue Will Scarlet's daughter from her enforced slavery just a few months before.

A low growl rose in his throat as he met the scarred leader's eyes, and without thinking, began to move towards the gang, who looked surprised but not particularly worried at the sight of a single swordsman coming at them.

"Fan out!" the rebel captain ordered with a toothless grin, bringing his dull-looking sword up before him defensively. "Looks like we'll have to do a bit more killing, before we can enjoy what this town has to offer."

CHAPTER FOUR

"How long can we hold out?"

The Hospitaller knight, Sir Richard-at-Lee, glanced over at his sergeant, Stephen, and shrugged his broad shoulders, although, clad in chain mail as he was, with the black mantle of his Order over it, the gesture was hardly noticeable. "A couple of weeks I'd say, if they don't break the door down."

"Not bloody likely," Stephen growled with a confident smile. He had good reason to feel secure inside Sir Richard's castle in Kirklees. A small moat surrounded the site and, although it was almost empty, once the drawbridge was up, it meant the main entrance was impossible to reach without some sort of platform.

Although they only had a dozen men with them, it was enough to hold off any attempts by the king's men gathered outside to erect such a platform before having to batter the main gate down with a ram.

The two men – hardened veterans from countless battles in their Order's service – looked down from the battlements at the men besieging them. Twenty part-time soldiers, at most, led by some minor royalist noble Sir Richard didn't recognise. They had turned up a day after the Hospitaller had led what remained of his followers from the defeat at the battle of Boroughbridge back home.

Such a small force had no chance of either penetrating the great front door, or scaling the walls, unless the Hospitaller and his men relaxed their guard. Which would not happen. Stephen would make damn sure of that.

It was a stand-off and, with enough food and drink stored within the castle to last them a fortnight at least, Sir Richard felt reasonably secure.

"The only way they're getting in here is if the king sends more men with siege engines," Stephen mused. "Otherwise, they'll have to starve us out."

"I can't see them hanging around out there for a couple of weeks," Sir Richard grunted, stroking his bushy grey beard thoughtfully. "Those men will have to return to their own villages. Besides, there must be easier targets for them to hunt scattered throughout Barnsdale forest."

"Like Robin Hood and his mates, assuming any of them survived the battle," his sergeant-at-arms replied. "They're going to have a hard time of it for a while with all these bastards chasing around the forest after rebels."

"Robin and his men know how to hide. They'll be fine. Christ knows what'll happen to us though." The Hospitaller sighed, feeling lower than he'd ever felt in his life. Not only was he a wanted man – a rebel – but his son had been murdered by someone acting for Sir Hugh Despenser not that long ago.

As Sir Richard stared out disconsolately over the spring countryside, the nobleman leading the king's men rode boldly forward, halting as he came close enough to converse with the big knight on the battlements without shouting at the top of his voice.

"Oh-ho!" Stephen nodded. "The king's lackey wants a word."

One of their men stationed on the battlements beside them fitted the string to his longbow and pulled an arrow from his belt. "You want me to take him down, my lord?"

"What?" Sir Richard, startled from his reverie, waved a hand. "No, Peter. Let the man say his piece."

The horseman gazed up at them. "My name is Sir Philip of Portsmouth. I assume you are Sir Richard-at-Lee, former Lord of Kirklees."

"I'm the preceptor of this commandery, yes," the Hospitaller replied.

"Former preceptor," the nobleman replied. "The king has declared your lands forfeit to the crown as a result of your recent treasonous actions against him."

He waited for a reaction, but Sir Richard remained silent. This news was no surprise after all.

"No doubt you feel very secure locked up in your little fortress," Sir Philip cried, waving a hand in disdain at the walls which had frustrated his attempts to arrest the Hospitaller and his men. "Well, your castle has bought you some time: I must take my men onwards, so you can relax for a while."

Stephen let out a tiny gasp of relief as the knight continued.

"Do not think this is the end of it though, Sir Richard! Your men might slink off back to their homes in the village as if none of this ever happened, but the king has vowed to make an example of those so-called noblemen – like yourself – who planned this rebellion. Eventually, more of his men will be back for you. Better armed, better prepared to take this pitiful castle down about your treacherous ears! Make the most of your freedom while it lasts, Hospitaller!"

With that, the horseman turned his mount and kicked his heels into its sides, spurring it into a canter back to his own men and out of range of the archers on the walls behind him.

"Wanker," Stephen muttered, drawing a smile from Sir Richard.

"We'll give them time to leave, just in case they change their minds," Sir Richard said. "Then you and the rest of the men," – he looked over at the archer, Peter, beside him – "can 'slink off' back to your homes."

The look of relief on Peter's face was plain, as he dared to hope he might see his family again, and go back to his normal life.

Sir Richard slapped the man on the back with a smile, told him to remain on watch and alert for now, and then led his loyal sergeant-at-arms down the stairs and into the great hall.

43

"That…wanker," he threw Stephen a sardonic smile as he filled a wooden goblet with wine, "thinks I'm going to sit here waiting for death, or else I'm going to try and make a run for it."

Stephen filled a mug of his own from a large jug of ale on the table beside the wine and raised an eyebrow. "So did I," he admitted. "What are we going to do then?"

Sir Richard took a sip of wine and wiped his mouth with the back of his hand, eyes blazing.

"I'm not done just yet," he vowed, "no matter what Sir Philip of Portsmouth might think! I may only be a minor noble, but I'm also a Hospitaller Knight…"

* * *

"Wilfred!" As Will came into the street behind Robin and recognised the baker lying dead on the ground, he screamed in rage and, at his young leader's side, tore into the rebels who shrank back from the berserk gleam in his eyes.

"Get them!" Scarface shouted, his voice wavering as he saw Friar Tuck barrelling into the street, brandishing his quarterstaff expertly. Suddenly it seemed this might not be such an easy fight after all, especially as the young man with the piercing gaze and the enormous archer's shoulders was coming straight for him.

Robin never slowed as the rebel swung his sword in a vicious arc; he parried the blow and swept the man's feet from under him with his foot. As the man went down, Robin rammed the point of his long sword into his throat, pulled it free and carried on, swinging the bloody weapon upwards into the armpit of another rebel, almost taking the screaming man's arm off.

In contrast to Robin's unnerving silence, Will was roaring the baker's name like a madman as he battered into the shocked rebels. When his blows were parried, he rammed his forehead into the defender's face, or kneed them in the groin, before finishing them with a sword thrust.

Realising they were done for, as the villagers, led by the blacksmith, finally found their courage and ran forward to join the fray, the remaining rebels, seven of them, simply turned and began running for the forest.

"You!" Robin roared at one of the local youngsters. "Throw me your bow!"

The outlaw caught the weapon and, whipping an arrow from his belt, sighted on one of the fleeing rebels, taking a fraction of a second to steady himself and visualise where he wanted the missile to strike.

With a feral scream the rebel dropped to the grass as the outlaw leader's arrow tore into his calf.

"Let the rest go!" Robin shouted. "They've had enough."

The villagers were happy to give up the chase, as the adrenaline began to leave their bloodstream. They had chased off the invaders – that was enough for them.

Friar Tuck finally managed to halt the enraged Scarlet, who walked back to the fallen baker, sobbing with rage as he turned the man onto his back and closed his eyes.

Robin looked away from his weeping comrade, not wanting to intrude on the naked show of emotion. And yet, Robin felt a great sorrow too. Wilfred was a good man – he had helped the outlaws. He had, in fact, given Will his life back.

"He didn't deserve to die like this," the blacksmith muttered sadly, wandering over to stand beside them. Meeting Robin's eye, he carried on. "That little adventure he had with you and your mate last year made him feel like a youngster again – gave him a real zest for life. When those bastards came here acting like they owned the place, Wilfred thought he could take them all on."

"You should be proud of him," Robert nodded. "And learn a lesson from this too. Next time your village comes under attack from a gang of wolf's heads, you all

45

need to stand up to them!" He glared at the village men who dropped their eyes sheepishly. The big blacksmith simply hefted his hammer thoughtfully and muttered agreement.

"Chances are, those men will come back here looking for revenge – you better be prepared. So arm yourselves – properly."

Fifty paces away the rebel Robin had shot in the leg was groaning as he tried to drag himself away into the trees, before finally giving up and lying panting on the damp spring grass.

"Come on," Robin growled to Tuck and Scarlet. "Let's go and see what that bastard has to say for himself."

* * *

In humiliation akin to that of Christ, Thomas, the Earl of Lancaster, was forced to wear a torn old wreath made of cheap cloth and ride an old mule, with no bridle to steady himself properly, and led to the place of execution.

He had made his peace with God in the few short hours since his sentence was handed down but still, he was frightened as the worthless old mount carried him to his doom, the locals jeering loudly and pelting him with snowballs so that he almost fell onto the ground once or twice.

As they neared the platform he raised his voice, which seemed weak and thin after his days of ill-treatment, and cried out in anguish. "King of Heaven, have mercy on me, for the worthless king of England has shown me none!"

The men and women of York roared in outrage at that, thoroughly enjoying the whole spectacle, and rained more hard-packed snowballs on the defeated earl, who was dragged from the mule by two footmen, angrily trying to stop the missiles hitting them too, and thrown on his knees onto the wooden platform.

Silence descended on the place, except for the occasional sound of someone stamping their feet or rubbing their hands to try and warm themselves, breath steaming from everyone's mouths, noses running unchecked as every eye was fixed in fascination on the great earl's pitiful downfall.

The executioner, a lean man with a black hood over his head, strode forward and, raising his voice so it would carry to the furthest reaches of the crowd, grabbed Lancaster and dragged him around to face northwards.

"Turn to face your allies, the Scots. Traitor!" The executioner roared, to howls of hatred from the mass of spectators, "and receive your foul death!"

Although he had been sentenced to be hanged, drawn and quartered, the king had shown leniency and decided a simple beheading – as Thomas had done to Edward's friend, Piers Gaveston ten years earlier – would be enough.

It took three strokes of the great axe to completely sever the earl's head, and the thump as it dropped to the frost-bitten wooden platform was drowned out by the laughter and near-hysterical cheering as people who had previously supported Lancaster became lost in the spectacle and enjoyed the day's entertainment.

CHAPTER FIVE

The man screamed as Will stood on his calf beside the protruding arrow and pressed down with a snarl.

"You sack of shit. That was a good man you and your lot killed!"

Friar Tuck gently pulled the enraged Scarlet backwards and the grounded man gasped, squeezing both hands around his wound to try and dull some of the pain.

"I didn't kill the baker," he grimaced. "I didn't kill anyone."

Robin leaned down and opened the leather pouch on the man's belt. The rebel tried to slap the big outlaw's hands away but Robin cuffed him, hard, on the ear and emptied the contents of the man's purse onto the road.

"That's my money!" A heavy, red-faced older lady pushed her way to the front of the gathered villagers and spat at the thief as she knelt and scooped up the small silver coins. "I was selling ale – just made a fresh batch this morning – when that arsehole came into the house with his friends. Helped themselves to my ale and this one" – she glared down at the sullen man – "helped himself to my takings."

"Your ale tasted like piss," the man muttered, before crying out as Will booted him in the face.

"Shut your mouth or I'll rip that arrow right out of your leg!"

"Where are the rest of your friends camping?" Robin asked, crouching down on his haunches to look at the man, who opened his mouth to make a smart reply, then glanced at Will Scarlet and changed his mind, replying with a question of his own.

"Why should I tell you anything? You don't have the look of lawmen." His eyes took in the light armour

48

and weaponry of the three outlaws and he gave a small humourless laugh. "You're probably rebels just like me and my mates."

A child's voice piped up from somewhere in the crowd of villagers. "He's Robin Hood, he brought us food at Christmas!"

The injured rebel spat on the ground in disgust as the other villagers shouted agreement. "You're a real hero," he smirked at Robin. "Good for you."

"Right, fuck this," Will leaned down and began to slowly pull Robin's arrow from the rebel's calf. Tuck crossed himself sadly as the man thrashed his shoulders and screamed in agony. "Where's your camp-site?" Scarlet roared, twisting the shaft of the arrow slightly to cause the man even more pain.

"A clearing!" The rebel's voice dropped to a tortured whimper as Will released the pressure on the arrow. "About half an hour's walk from here, to the north-east."

The three outlaws looked at each other, but none of them recognised the place the man had described. "We need more information than that," Will snarled, placing his hand back on the arrow, as blood oozed thickly from the wound. "Is it near the river? A waterfall? Any trees that look unusual?"

"A waterfall!" the man shouted, eyes wide at the sight of Scarlet's hand on the arrow. "Aye, there's a waterfall! Not a very big one, but we thought it would mask any sounds from our camp-site." He fell back with a sob.

Robin looked to Will again, who stood up, nodding. "I know where he's talking about. He's right – the sounds of the waterfall will hide the sound of them laughing about the people they've murdered. It'll also hide the sound of men approaching to wipe the lot of them out."

"How many of you are hiding out there?" Robin asked the man who was now beyond the point where he cared about resisting.

49

"Twenty-two."

"Who leads you?"

"Sir Richard Willysdon." His eyes flared again, momentarily, and he stared at Will. "You think you're a hard man, but old Dick'll show you. He's a wicked bastard. He'll eat you three alive." The rebel grinned through gritted teeth, but shrank back with a whimper as Scarlet jerked his leg as if about to kick him again.

"All right, let's get the supplies we came for as quickly as possible," Robin replied. "Then we'll head back to camp and decide what to do about these rebels."

"What about this one?" Tuck gestured to the man on the ground, who had by now almost passed out from the pain in his leg.

"Not our problem," Robin shrugged, turning to the villagers. "He robbed your ale-seller and was part of a gang that murdered your baker. It's your place to dispense justice, not ours."

As the three outlaws moved away to buy their provisions and find a room for the night, the angry mob closed in behind them around the terrified rebel, who shouted for mercy.

By the time they left the inn to head back to their camp-site just before dawn the next day, the man was swinging gently by a rope hanging from a big oak tree at the roadside. His breeches were heavily stained at the front and back and crows were already gathering, watching from the branches of nearby trees until it was safe for them to move in and feast on the hanged man's soft flesh and eyeballs. Robin's arrow was still embedded in his bloody calf.

Tuck crossed himself again. "Christ, what a sight. The people of Hathersage don't waste any time, do they?"

Will shook his head. "Serves the bastard right," he growled. "And once we find his mates, they'll be wishing they'd died as quickly."

* * *

50

Wilfred the baker had been a good friend to the outlaws. Not only had he helped Robin and Allan-a-Dale rescue Will's daughter, Beth, from a life of slavery in Lord John de Bray's manor house, he had also helped them rob the same lord. They had piled his wagon high with cash, jewellery, tapestries, silk bed-clothes, silver cups and plates and a huge amount of hoarded food.

His murder at the hands of a gang of rebels had outraged Robin's men when they heard about it.

Robin, Tuck and Will had returned from Hathersage with their tale of the previous day's events, but by then the sun was beginning to set in the spring sky again so the outlaws spent a quiet night, their anger building at what these rebels were doing in the forest. Their forest.

As dawn broke the next morning, Allan-a-Dale and Will Scarlet woke the men, impatient to hunt down the rebels that had killed Wilfred.

"What about breakfast?" Little John wondered, his hair and beard comically tangled as he dragged his enormous frame from his straw pallet on the forest floor.

"Eat it on the way," Scarlet shouted, tossing the giant half a black loaf. "Get ready to move!"

A short time later Robin was leading the outlaws north-east, towards the waterfall the injured rebel had described. He called John and Will, his two most trusted advisers, to him as they made their way through the early spring undergrowth.

Although Much, his childhood friend from Wakefield, was the outlaw Robin had the closest bond with, he lacked the military skills and tactical knowledge of the terrain around Barnsdale that John and Will had. Robin sometimes felt a little guilty leaving his friend out, but he knew including Much in the planning of missions would be seen as favouritism and, being honest, the young outlaw leader knew his lifelong friend was best employed as a simple foot-soldier.

"What's the plan then?" Little John wondered. "Do we have one?"

"If they're camped where I think they are," Will replied, "they're hemmed in on two sides. The waterfall is a short way to their back, with another tributary feeding in behind their clearing, both feeding into the main course of the river which continues to the east."

"It shouldn't be hard to pin them down then," Robin nodded, trying to visualize the terrain Will was describing, although he didn't think he'd ever been there before.

"That's it then?" John rumbled. "We just come at them from two sides, knowing they've nowhere to escape? Doesn't seem like it leaves us much room for manoeuvre."

"Doesn't leave them much room for manoeuvre either," Will grinned. "That's the idea!"

John shook his great head, his long brown hair flailing. "There's sixteen of us, and there's about twenty of them, according to that lad you left hanging in Hathersage. Even if we surprise them, we're still outnumbered. We don't know anything about these men."

Robin and Will exchanged glances, realising their giant friend was right. In their rage and desire to avenge Wilfred's death they hadn't given much thought to this.

"We know their leader's called Sir Richard Willysdon – Old Dick," Will noted with a shrug. "And he's a right dodgy bastard. Apparently."

"What about the rest of them?" John asked, spreading his hands wide. "They could all be landless knights. We might be walking into the hardest fight we've ever had. I think we need a better plan."

The outlaw gang moved through the forest almost silently, their experienced eyes spotting dried twigs that might crack and give away their position, and using the available cover to remain hidden from anyone travelling on the main road.

Robin pondered the dilemma, knowing John spoke the truth. Although the dozen men they had found butchered near their camp had been poorly armed peasants, many of the defeated insurgents hiding in Barnsdale were knights or at least well armed mercenaries.

"All right then," he smiled. "How about this…"

* * *

Stephen had set off from Kirklees, early in the morning. It was raining hard, and thunder rumbled some distance off. Thankfully, the wind was behind him, so the driving rain stayed out of his face, but it wasn't long before his black surcoat was soaked through.

He wore his gambeson underneath his chain-mail, so he was warm enough, but as he became more sodden and uncomfortable he cursed the circumstances that had brought him to this point.

"Where would I go?" Sir Richard had asked Stephen the previous night as they sat by a brazier on the battlements, mugs of warmed wine in hand, gazing out at the lush countryside around them. "Aye, there's no one besieging us just now, and I could escape. But where would I go? Take passage back to the Order's base in Rhodes, to live a life of austerity as a lowly brother knight? I've had my time doing that – being given the commandery of the manor of Kirklees was my reward for many years of loyal service."

He would fight to hold onto it, rather than running with his tail between his legs.

"This is my mess," he clasped his faithful sergeant by the arm, fixing him with his steady gaze. "If you want to go, I'll release you from my service" –

"That's enough of that shit," Stephen had growled, cutting off his master with an angry gesture. "I've stuck by you for years. I've no more intention of buggering off back to Rhodes than you have. What do you want me to do?"

Sir Richard had written a letter and, dripping wax from a ruby-red candle onto the envelope, pressed his ring into it to mark it with his own personal Hospitaller seal, showing a man kneeling before a cross. He handed it to Stephen with instructions to take it straight to Clerkenwell, in London.

The Prior of the Hospitallers in England, Thomas L'Archer, had his headquarters in Clerkenwell. Although Sir Richard thought the prior had become an incompetent fool in his old age, he was still the most powerful Hospitaller in the country, with direct access to the king.

With the dissolution of the Templars just a few years earlier, the Hospitallers had grown greatly in power and influence. If anyone could help Sir Richard, it was Thomas L'Archer.

So, as dawn broke, Stephen had taken his master's letter, filled his horse's saddlebags with food and drink and the two old companions embraced one another as brothers rather than a master and his servant.

"It'll take me six, maybe seven days to reach Clerkenwell," Stephen had cautioned. "A round-trip of" –

"I know, I know," Sir Richard had nodded with a small smile. "Two weeks without you to look after me. It'll be hard, but I'll manage somehow."

"Aye, you can bloody laugh," Stephen retorted dourly. "Just watch yourself. There's probably a bounty for you. We're lucky the villagers like you, or they'd have handed you over to the law already, but that won't stop outsiders."

Richard waved a hand dismissively. "Don't worry about me – no one's coming over these walls uninvited. And, as you say, the villagers like me. I've always tried to do right by them. Travel as swiftly as you can though," he gazed at his sergeant earnestly. "Eventually someone will come and try to force their way in. And I can't sit here, cooped up like a falcon in its cage for ever."

The drawbridge was lowered, groaning loudly as the chains rotated on their axles, and, with a last grim nod, Stephen had kicked his mount forward and headed for the capital.

The Hospitaller sergeant was a hard soldier, who had spent much of his life fighting in wars. Not much frightened him: he had seen men, some of them his friends, butchered and mutilated beside him. He had decapitated, disembowelled and dismembered countless men in the name of Christ.

And yet, the thought of addressing the superiors of his order made him sick with nerves. It was so ridiculous he almost laughed.

He crouched down low against his palfrey as the rain hammered against his back and kicked the beast into a canter, hoping to cover as much distance as possible before the light failed and he had to make camp for the night.

His actions over the next few weeks would decide his fate and the fate of Sir Richard-at-Lee.

A sudden, massive rumble of thunder boomed overhead, making his horse skitter sideways nervously, its eyes bulging and he patted the beast reassuringly.

Two weeks for a gruff, uncouth sergeant-at-arms to travel to Clerkenwell and persuade a senile old prior to intervene with the king on his master's behalf.

Thunder cracked the sky overhead again and Stephen shook his head dismally at the impossible mission.

"We're fucking doomed."

* * *

"Logs? You want us to ride fucking logs down the river?" Will Scarlet burst out laughing at his young leader's suggestion.

"Aye!" Robin grinned at the rest of the outlaws as they walked through the forest. "We find a few logs, lash them together with this" – he patted a coiled length

55

of rope he and some of the other men carried on their packs – "then split up. Some of us take these rebels from the west and some from the logs. You say there's a second tributary behind them. They won't expect anyone to attack them from there."

"So they're all going to stand watching us in front of them when we turn up through the trees shouting a challenge," Little John shook his head with a smile. "While some of us sail down the river at their backs and shoot them."

Scarlet laughed again, the type of laugh that was so genuine and uninhibited it was infectious, and many of the other men joined in with him.

"I don't see why it wouldn't work, though," Friar Tuck shrugged, wiping his shaved crown, sweating despite the chill air. "I'm not sailing on any half-arsed raft though, I'll stick to dry land."

"I'll go on the raft," Much volunteered. "My da used to take me fishing in a little boat on the Calder when I was younger." His face dropped at the thought of his father, murdered in front of him, in their own mill, less than a year ago. "I like the water," he finished quietly.

"I'll go on it an' all," an older outlaw, Peter Ordevill agreed. "I used to be a sailor and it sounds like the safest place to be in this mad plan."

Another older outlaw, James Baxter offered to take a place on the raft too as Robin nodded.

"All right, you three it is: we're going to need skilled archers on the water, to take out as many of the bastards as possible. The river's not flowing that fast just now, but even so, you won't have much time to get your shots off before you'll be past."

"And then we're three men down," Matt Groves grunted. "By the time those three get off this raft of yours, the fight'll be over, one way or the other, and we're outnumbered as it is, if they've really got twenty-odd men at this camp."

"Aye, but if Much and the others manage to take out even four or five of these rebels," Robin replied patiently, "it'll throw them into chaos. They won't know which way to turn."

"What if they don't take out four or five of them?" Gareth, the thin teenager from Wrangbrook wondered. "It'll be hard to aim from the water won't it?"

"Nah," Much shook his head. "The river will be calm. It shouldn't be much different from firing the longbow at a moving target on land, as long as we have something to brace ourselves against."

They were nearing the rebel base now, as the sound of roaring water came to them, so they made sure to go well around the spot where Will expected the camp to be, and started to make their way upriver to find suitable logs for the raft.

"Will," Robin waved his friend over. "You go and scout out these rebels. Make sure they're really there. Try and see how many of them there are, weapons, armour and kill any lookouts" –

"I know what I'm looking for," Will broke in, raising an eyebrow indignantly. "I've been doing this for a lot longer than you, lad."

"Sorry," Robin smiled sheepishly. "We'll find the wood we need for the rafts while you're gone."

As Will disappeared into the undergrowth, surprisingly nimble for such a sturdy man, the rest of the outlaws walked on for a while then began to hunt for thick branches. They found plenty, torn from the trees in the previous winter's storms, and chose ones as flat as possible to make a smooth platform which Much, Peter and James could shoot from. A couple of men carried axes as their close-combat weapon of choice, rather than swords or maces, and they quickly cut the wood to similar lengths.

"Won't the rebels come and see what all the thumping is?" Much asked Robin as the fallen branches swiftly turned into somewhat similarly sized logs.

"Why would they?" his boyhood friend replied. "For a start they've made their camp beside a noisy waterfall, so they'll hardly hear this noise so far upriver. And even if they do hear it, so what? Why should they think it's a threat to them?"

Peter, the former sailor, proved to be an expert with ropes and knots and managed to lash the branches together, forming an odd-looking craft that would, hopefully, work.

"That abomination is never going to float," Matt Groves sniggered. "If one of you farts it'll sink. This is fucking madness."

"No it won't," Peter retorted, confident the hastily- built raft would float just fine on a calm and relatively sluggish river. He had directed the axe-men as they quickly cut the wood to form a flat base, a rudder and a tiller which he would be able to tie off, holding the "boat" on a relatively straight course for long enough to shoot their bows at the rebels. "It's big enough to stay steady while the three of us get off a few shots. That's all we need."

"Aye, well, you're welcome to it lads," Groves smirked. "I'd rather have my feet on something sturdier."

Will Scarlet reappeared, blowing slightly, but smiling wickedly.

"They're there all right," he reported, sitting down on a boulder to catch his breath. He gave the raft an approving grin and took a couple of sips from the ale skin at his waist before continuing. "I counted seventeen of them – some of them must be off at some village looking for supplies. Probably because we" – he nodded towards Tuck and Robin – "disturbed them yesterday, before they could take what they needed from Hathersage."

"Shit," Robin murmured, hoping the five missing rebels hadn't decided to head for Wakefield to find what they needed.

Little John could see his young captain was worried, and he clapped him gently on the back with a grin. "Don't worry – this won't take long. The numbers are almost even now."

"Terrain?" Robin wondered.

"As I described it to you before," Will replied. "They're camped right beside the river, which is to their east. To their north is a rock wall, which the waterfall comes down. It's not that all that high, but none of the rebels will be climbing up it once we attack; it's too steep for that. The lads here can get the raft around to the tributary if they head north-west for a short way and double back. West and south of the rebels it's all trees and bushes. It's a good hiding place to be honest – if that son of a whore in Hathersage hadn't told us where they were we'd never have found them."

"Sounds simple enough, then," Allan-a-Dale grunted, making sure his string was in its pouch ready to fit to his longbow.

"Aye, but take care, though," Will raised a cautionary hand as he took another swig from his ale skin, slowly catching his breath. "These aren't peasants like the ones we found butchered the other day. These men are all wearing light, and even pieces of heavy, armour. And, from what I saw, they all have good quality weapons. There's no pitchforks – it's all swords, maces and proper battle-axes."

Robin looked over at Much and the other two outlaws making ready to carry the raft round to the tributary on the other side of the rebels' camp. "You'll have to pick your targets well," he told them. "Leave the ones with the heavier armour, in case your arrows can't penetrate. Your shots might not have the same force they normally do shooting from this thing," he kicked at the hastily lashed together logs.

"Don't worry," Much nodded confidently, grasping his friend's hand with a grin. "We'll take out as many of them as possible."

"All right!" Robin shouted, looking around at his men with a determined gaze. "Let's get this thing into the water and make those bastards pay for killing Wilfred and God knows what else!"

The raft was sturdy, but light enough to be carried off to the north-west by Much, Peter and James without much trouble.

"Give us enough time to get into position back downstream," Robin told Much as the three men moved away with their burden. "Then cast off. We'll post a lookout to watch for you coming and distract the rebels just before you arrive at their backs."

"Good luck," Much smiled.

"You too. Try not to shoot any of our own lads..." Robin grinned back with a wave as he led the rest of the outlaws back through the foliage to the rebels' camp.

The waterfall grew louder the closer they came, and Robin took Will, Tuck and Little John aside.

"Me, John and Tuck will take the west side of their camp with half the men," he decided.

Tuck was no archer, so would be wasted in Will's section, while John, at almost seven feet tall, was so physically intimidating Robin always felt it was good to have him in open view.

"When we show ourselves to the rebels I'll talk to the leader and distract them," he said. "We'll set Gareth as lookout to signal us when he sees Much and the raft coming."

Gareth was a young lad from Wrangbrook, too thin to be an archer, or much of a fighter, but smart enough to be useful in other ways. Most of the outlaws looked on him as their little brother.

"You take some of the men to the south," Robin went on, looking at Will, "and when you see the signal, start shooting. Get as many of the bastards as you can before they know what's happening."

The more he thought it over, the more Scarlet liked Robin's mad plan. With his half of the remaining outlaws shooting at the scum that had killed his old friend Wilfred, and the three on the raft firing at them as well, they should be able to take out at least ten or eleven of the seventeen rebels before they even knew what had happened.

Then Robin, John, Tuck and the rest of the men would engage them from the front and the fight would be over. It was devastatingly simple. Foolproof!

"For such a young lad," Will smiled, playfully slapping Robin on the back of the head, "you've got an old soldier's brain in there."

"Aye, it's a good plan," John agreed as they came near to the rebels' camp-site.

Will picked the five best archers from the remaining outlaws, including Matt Groves, and took them off to take up position to the south, while Robin gave Gareth his orders and sent him to the top of the waterfall with a strip of white linen from Tuck's medical pouch to wave when he spotted Much and the raft nearing their position.

As they waited, the image of the rebel peasants they had found killed that morning played on Robin's mind.

"Who is this Guy of Gisbourne?" he wondered. "The sheriff must think he's got the skills to catch us."

Little John and even Tuck, who had travelled extensively over the years, had never heard of Gisbourne until a few months earlier, when he had turned up leading the Sheriff of Nottingham and Yorkshire's men on sorties into Barnsdale. Still, none of the outlaws had even seen the man the locals had dubbed 'The Raven'.

"There!" Allan-a-Dale hissed, as young Gareth suddenly appeared on the waterfall above them, waving his long strip of bandage. "The raft's coming – time to move!"

Robin gestured to his men and they drew their swords, moving forward through the foliage towards the rebel camp which was only a few yards away.

"Do you think Gisbourne really dresses all in black?" Robin asked, shoving branches out of his way and making sure he stepped quietly from force of habit, although a cracking twig would go unnoticed with the raging waterfall so close.

"I hope he does," John growled from just behind. "Black will show up easy amongst the green leaves of the forest – we'll see him coming from a mile off."

Robin nodded silent agreement, then gasped in shock as half a dozen figures appeared, like wraiths, through the undergrowth to his left.

The roaring waterfall had masked the sounds of their approach, and, as he brought his sword up instinctively before him, his eyes were drawn to the man leading them.

A tall, slim man, dressed all in black.

The outlaws recognised him straight away.

"Gisbourne!"

CHAPTER SIX

"I wondered who that fool beside the waterfall was waving at," Sir Guy of Gisbourne smiled, resting his hand on the pommel of his sword as his eyes flickered across the armed men in front of him, assessing the situation.

The outlaws stood, frozen to the spot, looking to Robin for guidance.

"You obviously know my name," the black-clad bounty-hunter noted. "How about you give me yours?"

Robin's mind whirled. Gisbourne had a lot of men with him – maybe twenty, or even more; it was hard to tell given the density of the undergrowth here. He knew he had to act fast though, or the soldiers would encircle them.

Clearly their attack on the rebel's camp would have to wait for another time, assuming they somehow escaped from this with their lives, which didn't seem at all assured.

"No matter," Sir Guy shrugged, drawing his sword. "It's clear you are wolf's heads or rebels of some sort or another and, since I'm in Yorkshire specifically to clear your sort from the forest..." he waved his left hand in the air and pointed to Robin and the outlaws, opening his mouth again to issue the command to attack.

"We're bounty-hunters!" Robin shouted. "We're here to wipe out a gang of rebels who are hiding out beside the river, there." He nodded towards the river behind Gisbourne, who had halted his order to attack, and stood looking slightly confused. "Our man up there is signalling us to attack, we have more men coming down the river on a raft – we have to move now, or we'll miss the chance to surprise the rebels!"

It was possible these men were hunting rebels, as Gisbourne was. The king had employed many such man-hunters to clear out the Earl of Lancaster's supporters from Barnsdale and its environs. As he stood gazing at the young man he heard, sure enough, men's voices, raised in laughter, loud enough to be heard over the waterfall not far from there.

"I see," Gisbourne replied smoothly, a dark eyebrow raised questioningly. "Well, let us help you then. Lead the way to this rebel camp and we'll destroy them together."

There was nothing else for it. Robin nodded and made his way past Gisbourne, expecting the man's wicked looking blade to pierce his back at any moment.

Tuck and the rest followed behind, Little John hunching over to try and appear smaller.

"How the fuck do we get out of this?" Allan whispered to Robin.

The young leader looked at the four men with him. "No idea," he admitted. "Hopefully Will realises what's happening and takes out some of Gisbourne's men. Once the shooting starts, kill anyone that isn't one of our friends, then…either make a run for it, or try and jump in the river. There's no way we can beat that lot," he gestured with his thumb to the cluster of soldiers following behind them.

"Aye," Tuck groaned. "And Christ himself knows how the rebels will react when they see us coming…"

"They're no bounty-hunters," Nicholas growled to his captain, gesturing to the outlaws conversing in hushed tones in front of them. "A young man leading a Franciscan and a giant? It's Robin Hood and his men!"

"Well done," Gisbourne replied, fitting a quarrel to his crossbow as the outlaws led them through the trees. "But there's only five of them – so we let them lead us to the rest of their gang. And, if there really are rebels hiding out here, so much the better. This will be a very productive afternoon!"

It only took a few moments for Robin and the rest to reach the outskirts of the undergrowth at the edge of the rebel's camp. He turned to Gisbourne and gestured, wondering what the bounty-hunter wanted them to do?

The man simply shrugged with a relaxed smile, so Robin turned back and, trying to find a target through the foliage, raised his sword and, as the raft carrying Much and the other two slowly came into sight, shouted, "Attack!"

* * *

The Don was calm and the raft held steady as Much, Peter and James floated steadily downriver and the rebel camp came into sight.

The men were clustered around their camp-fire, drinking from wine-skins, laughing and joking together, oblivious to the bizarre sight on the water just yards behind them.

Much let out a relieved sigh. If there had been a lookout with a bow they'd have been easy targets but Will had done his job and removed any sentries. "Ready, lads?" he wondered, standing and fitting an arrow to his bowstring, his two companions following suit.

"Don't try anything fancy," Peter warned them. "The raft might be steady now, but we could hit a branch, or an underwater current at any time, so just take the easiest shot you can."

Much couldn't help grinning, the blood beginning to really pump in his veins, as Robin suddenly burst from the trees behind the rebels, sword raised, shouting something at the startled men.

Little John, Tuck, Paul Fuller and Allan-a-Dale appeared in loose formation behind their young leader, weapons ready, faces grim, as the shocked rebels leapt up from their seats by the camp-fire, scrabbling for their own weapons.

"Shoot!" Much shouted, loosing his arrow which flashed across the short distance and hammered into a rebel's back, sending the man stumbling forward onto the grass. Peter and James also let fly, their missiles finding targets too, and the three archers quickly nocked another arrow to their bowstrings.

The rebels were in chaos, as three of them were taken down by an attack from behind, then, from the side, more arrows battered them when Will Scarlet and his men joined in.

Sir Guy sauntered into view, his men slowly fanning out behind him, and the rebels, already panicked, completely lost any semblance of disciplined resistance, looking around for an escape rather than working together to hold off their attackers.

"Make for the raft!" Robin shouted at the outlaws beside him. "Fight your way through these idiots, and jump onto the raft before it's too far downstream!"

Tuck crossed himself, his eyes heavenward, and with John and Allan at his side, they tore into the rebels, not stopping to finish their targets off, just barrelling past to try and catch the raft before it sailed away.

Robin raced towards the trees where Will and the rest of their men were still concealed, gesturing towards Gisbourne and his soldiers, screaming as loud as he could. "Run for it! Run!" One of the rebels had been taking a piss in the bushes, and, seeing Robin coming towards him, lunged at the young man with his dagger.

Without even slowing, Robin swatted the short blade aside and battered the hilt of his sword into the man's face, feeling teeth crunch and warm blood on his knuckles as the rebel fell back and Robin continued his mad dash.

By now, Sir Guy realised Robin Hood's men might well escape. "Finish those men off, quickly!" he ordered his men, pointing his crossbow at the remaining rebels, none of whom were offering any real resistance as their original attackers seemed to be fleeing. "Then get after Hood and his gang!"

"What the hell's going on?" the rebel leader, Sir Richard Willysdon shouted, as the remainder of his dazed men stared about themselves, wide-eyed. "Get a grip of yourselves, damn you! Form a circle around me!"

Will Scarlet had seen Robin coming towards him, and the man wearing the exquisite black armour could only be Sir Guy of Gisbourne, so it didn't take him long to figure out things had gone drastically wrong. "Retreat!" he shouted, turning and waving his men back towards the south. "Lose yourselves in the trees; meet back at camp later on if we get separated!"

Robin pelted into the trees at their backs, with a glance over his shoulder.

Thankfully, Sir Guy's men were engaging the remaining rebels. By the time anyone came after him and the rest of his friends, they would hopefully be long gone, disappeared into the forest they knew so well.

Little John had managed to jump onto the raft, almost capsizing it with his enormous weight, while Allan-a-Dale had landed in the water just short of it. Much and Peter helped him climb on board, as John and James moved to the opposite side of the wavering craft, trying to displace the weight so it wouldn't flip over.

Although the river wasn't moving all that fast, Friar Tuck wasn't as fit as the other outlaws. His face was scarlet as he puffed along, trying to catch up with the raft, but it was slowly pulling away from him.

Robin halted his flight, crouching down amongst the bushes, praying that Tuck would make it, but his heart sank as the craft pulled away.

"Jump in!" the outlaw leader whispered to himself. "Jump in, Tuck! Let the current carry you to safety!"

To his shock, Tuck slowed to a stop, breathing heavily, watching in anguish as the raft with his friends on it sailed inexorably downstream.

"What's he doing?" John shouted, as the mismatched fight between the rebels and Gisbourne's men came to a conclusion and Gisbourne walked towards the breathless friar who dropped his sword on the riverbank and raised a hand in defeat. "Why won't he jump in?"

"He can't swim," Robin groaned as the realization dawned on him. "Ah shit. Now we'll have to rescue Tuck!"

Gisbourne's men killed the last of the rebels, but Nicholas ordered their leader, Sir Richard Willysdon, to be spared and tied up. From his expensive-looking armour and arrogant bearing the man was clearly a noble. The king would reward them well for bringing the man to him for a public trial.

The outlaws on the raft collapsed in frustration and exhaustion as the battle-fever left them and reality hit them. As it sailed out of sight around a bend in the river Robin prepared to head back to their camp again, where they could regroup and make a plan to help Tuck.

He watched as Sir Guy ambled over to the overweight churchman, the pair talking although Robin couldn't hear what was said.

"There's another one of them!" One of Gisbourne's soldiers spotted Robin and, pointing towards the hiding outlaw, led his fellows into the undergrowth.

As he turned to sprint off, Robin saw Gisbourne lift his finely-carved black crossbow and heard the sharp crack as the bolt was released.

"No!" he sobbed, but there was nothing he could do as the wicked bolt hammered into the jovial friar and his friend was hurled backwards into the river.

* * *

The forest was quiet that night.

68

The outlaws had made their way back to camp in dribs and drabs, exhausted and, in Allan's case, soaked through.

Astonishingly, only two of the group were missing. Will had led his group back and the volatile Scarlet now sat dejectedly on his own apart from the group, thinking of his old drinking partner Wilfred and the absent Franciscan friar.

Much and the rest of the men on the raft had let the current carry them back to Oughtibridge then made their way warily back to camp.

When he arrived back last of all, Robin had told them of Tuck's shooting, but young Gareth hadn't returned either. It seemed certain Gisbourne's men must have killed him.

"The bastard knew who we were the minute he saw us," Robin spat. "He probably sent a couple of his soldiers after Gareth while we were heading towards the rebels' camp."

"Poor lad," John shook his big head sorrowfully. "Couldn't pull a longbow, or wield a sword very well, but he was a fine companion with that daft toothless grin of his."

When Robin had shaken his pursuers he had searched along the riverbank for signs of Tuck's body, but it was pointless and he'd eventually headed home in despair.

As the light faded the men had cracked open a barrel of ale and were gloomily downing the dark liquid, huddling close to the camp-fire for it was a bitter cold evening again.

"He might yet be alive," John said, wandering over to Robin and clapping his young leader on the shoulder reassuringly. "Tuck's a hard man. It'd take a lot to kill him."

"He was shot with a crossbow and fell in the river. Since he couldn't swim, I'd say that's a lot to survive." His shoulders slumped. "It's my fault. I should have come up with a better plan. Or better yet, should never have led everyone to tackle the group of rebels in the first place."

"Don't start with the self-pity crap," John growled, glaring at his friend. "Your plan was a good one – you think differently to everyone else, that's how you come up with ideas that are so mad they work. It was sheer bad luck Gisbourne and his men turned up when they did."

The giant wolf's head could see his words hadn't worked. "Listen, Robin, those bastard rebels killed our friend Wilfred – a good man, who only wanted to defend his livelihood and stand up for what he knew was right. The men all wanted to avenge the baker, you didn't just decide that's what we were doing. Mourn Tuck if you have to, but don't sit around here feeling sorry for yourself with a face like someone took a shit in your pottage."

Robin felt his temper rise, his cheeks flushing at John's telling off, and he locked eyes with the big man – but then glanced away in shame, knowing he deserved the rebuke.

They sat drinking in silence for a while, but Robin felt the need for companionship that night.

"Why are you an outlaw, John?"

Robin had never wanted to pry into the other outlaws' histories unless they offered up the information themselves, but he had been curious about this ever since the day he had met the big man and now seemed as good a time as any to ask.

* * *

John Little had originally lived in the village of Holderness, where he had a wife, Amber, and a small son, also called John. He was a blacksmith by trade, with his own little shop at the front of their house. His father had been the village blacksmith before him, and taught John the skills required to forge a plough or shod a horse.

His life was simple, but pleasant, and his family and friends in the village made him happy while his work was interesting and he always tried to improve on the small weapons and implements he crafted.

"Then," said John, "one night – autumn it was – blowing a gale outside and pitch black, my wife came back from visiting her sister and started going on about the baker, knocking his wife and kids about their house. Nothing unusual. The baker was a drunk with a vicious temper – everyone in the place knew it. He'd been spoken to before by people around the village, including me, telling him he shouldn't act like that, not with little children around. He'd act all ashamed, blame the drink, promise not to do it again – then he'd stumble home from the alehouse and knock them about worse. There were even stories amongst the village women that he forced his eldest girl into his bed, but...They were just rumours. I don't know how anyone could have known anything like that was happening...

"I didn't like any of it," John muttered, his voice low, "but... What could I do?

"Anyway, this night my wife said it was worse. The baker was going crazy, had locked them in his house and was shouting about burning their house down with them all in it. The young ones were screaming and crying, and there wasn't a sound from his wife, which wasn't a good sign since you could usually hear her crying or shouting at him to stop.

"Well, I knew what the baker was like with a few ales in him: I thought he might well set alight to his house, and you know what it's like in a village like Holderness, especially on a windy night: one house starts to burn and it sets off the ones next to it until half the place is burning. And our house wasn't too far away from the bakers.

"So, I go along to his house and sure enough, there's a lot of noise coming from inside. I knock on the door and tell him to calm down and come out.

71

"'Fuck off, Little, this is none of your business!'" he shouts, probably called me an oaf or something like that too, pleasant fellow he was."

John gave Robin a sardonic look, and carried on as the young outlaw smiled silently, not wanting to disturb the big man's story.

"I tried to reason with him – the kids are frightened, they haven't done anything wrong, you've just had too much drink – that kind of thing, but he wasn't having it, just kept shouting. I could hear him hitting the children too, so I was getting angrier myself and, when I heard him breaking up furniture to set fire to the place I'd had enough."

John's mood as he told his story had been relatively light so far, his natural good humour shining through. Now though, his expression turned dark, as he remembered the rest of that night.

"I couldn't just stand there shouting like an idiot while I knew he was trying to burn his house down, so I kicked the door in. Didn't take much: one good kick and it went right in."

The giant turned his face away from Robin and his voice became even more strained as he went on. "The bastard had killed his wife. She was lying on the floor with her neck broke, you could tell straight away. I'd never seen someone with a broken neck before but her head looked weird, didn't seem to be on right, you know....And his kids were there – three of them he had. Three girls. Two of them, the little ones, were crying and huddling against each other in the corner, while he was...he was on top of his eldest...on the bed... His own daughter... His own daughter Robin, she was only eleven! And the worst of it was, she wasn't even struggling...it was like she was used to it, she just looked at me as I came through the door with a blank look in her eyes, like she wasn't even there, like she couldn't even see me."

Little John shook his head, the pain in his voice turning to fury as he carried on, his fists clenched.

"Well, he didn't take any notice of me coming through the door, he just carried on, his horrible white arse pumping up and down, so I came in and dragged him off her, threw him onto the floor. He went down, but only for a few seconds, then he came up, flying at me. Like I said, he was quite a big man and strong – I wasn't much of a fighter back then and…I was frightened, and shocked, by everything that was happening. So when he came at me in a rage I just punched him in the face as hard as I could."

The sun had gone down by now and, in the darkness, a cold breeze whispered through the leaves of the trees surrounding the camp. The rest of the men were a little way off, talking and joking around the camp-fire which glowed a bright orange as Robin looked at it, although it cast little light outside its own small circle. John hid his face in the shadows as he continued, but the dim light couldn't hide the hurt in his voice.

"He fell right over backwards – must have been knocked right out when I hit him. By that time some of the other village men had come along and they grabbed me, dragged me outside. Of course, I was shouting and struggling and . . . in all the noise and with the children crying and whatever, no one thought to check on the baker straight away . . ." John turned, his face wet with tears that glistened in the light from the camp-fire. "He'd fallen right into their hearth. Face first. The children saw him burn to death."

The big man's head dropped and he hugged his knees in an almost childlike way. "Those two little girls ran out the house screaming and crying and started hitting my legs, saying I'd killed their daddy, they hated me, I was this and that." His open, honest face took on a look of bewilderment. "Even after what he'd done, they still loved him, he was still their da… And I'd killed him. I was the Devil to them, even though the bastard had killed their ma, raped their older sister and I'd stopped him from burning their house down around them!"

The bailiff had come and arrested Little John. He had, after all, broken into another man's house and killed him. He couldn't deny it and it didn't seem to matter that he'd only been trying to stop the drunken fool of a baker burning down the village. The baker's eldest daughter hadn't said a word to anyone since the night her father died – her mind had gone, the villagers said, and so she'd been sent off to live with the nuns at the local priory.

The corrupt magistrate would have been lenient if John had any money, but, although his family managed well enough, they weren't rich.

So Little John had been sentenced to hang. He had escaped from the bailiff's men on the way to the gallows though, and taken refuge in the forest before Adam Bell's men had found him and taken him into their group.

"That was seven years ago now. My brothers have helped my wife and son, thank God, but, you know as well as anyone, I hardly ever get to see them, even after all this time."

He looked up at his young friend. "I miss them, Robin. I miss them every day. All I did was try and help." His huge shoulders shook, his head slumped forward and he heaved a sigh that was full of hurt. "There's no justice…"

Robin sat for a moment, then he grasped John's shoulder and squeezed, trying to do something reassuring, to offer some comfort.

As the genial big outlaw sat, depressed and hurting, Robin thought again of the missing – probably dead – Tuck and Gareth, and the young outlaw captain wished that he'd never asked to hear John's story after all.

* * *

When Gareth had seen the raft approaching he had begun to wave the strip of white linen madly, but his

74

lofty vantage point gave him a good view of the landscape where Robin and the rest of his friends were.

He had seen the approach of the man in black and the soldiers, but couldn't think of any way to warn the outlaws. When he had seen Robin and the others apparently joining forces with the soldiers he had heaved a sigh of relief and looked at making his way back down to join them.

When the sounds of fighting reached him he realised there was no point in rushing to take part in the battle. He knew his limitations – knew he was much better as a scout or lookout than a fighter. His mother had struggled to feed him – and herself – when he was a child. The effects of malnutrition had remained with him as he had grown into early manhood. Although he had more than enough to eat nowadays, he still only ate sparingly and his frame remained slight as a result, unlike the rest of the outlaws.

Robin, John, Will and the rest were killing machines though, he thought. They could deal with things on the riverside without him and his sword.

He climbed back up to the top of the waterfall and looked down on the scene below.

"What the fuck?" he breathed in disbelief.

His friends were running from the battle.

As he watched a little longer, it became clear the black figure commanding the soldiers was no friend. The rebels were massacred, all except their leader who was struggling in the grip of a couple of soldiers, and Gareth's outlaw mates had all fled.

Apart from Tuck.

When the ominous black figure had shot the clergyman, Gareth had looked on in horror as his friend was thrown into the Don with a massive splash.

Without thinking about it, he ran as fast as he could to where the men had cut logs for the raft on the river bank earlier and hauled the thickest branch left over into the water, straddling it as the freezing water hit him and the current dragged the makeshift boat downstream.

The current was slow, so he kicked his legs to propel himself along faster, but it seemed to take an age before the rebel camp-site hove into view.

The soldiers were searching the dead rebels for weapons and other valuables. He could see the man in the fancy black leather cuirass talking to a bald man and, as he swept past, he took a great deep breath and ducked under the water so only his hands were visible grasping the log, offering a silent prayer to the Magdalene to make him invisible.

No one shot at him, and he came up for breath moments later, opening his eyes gingerly to get his bearings, hoping he was out of sight of the soldiers.

Although the river was moving slowly, the current had carried him well beyond the rebels' camp, so he pulled his torso onto the log, out of the freezing water, hoping the soft spring sun would dry him out before he became ill with the cold.

He continued to pray for help as the branch carried him along, his eyes scanning the water for anything that seemed out of place for signs of Friar Tuck. Although the clergyman had landed on his back, Gareth knew his head would sink beneath the surface before long – he had to find him, fast.

A dark mass came into view to his right and he dismissed it out of hand. The churchman was wearing grey, while the boulder he was looking at was black.

As the log swept by he realised the rock was actually Tuck in his sodden habit. The friar was face-down in the river, apparently snagged on something underwater.

With a desperate cry, Gareth kicked himself away from the safety of his log and swam against the current to reach Tuck.

His thin arms weren't suited to swimming, and, by the time he reached the friar, the youngster was almost exhausted. He knew his limbs would begin to cramp soon.

Sobbing with fatigue he threw himself at Tuck. His weight was enough to dislodge the unconscious friar from whatever was holding him in place and the pair began to move downstream with the current again.

Desperately kicking his legs, knowing he had to push them towards the riverbank or die, Gareth gritted his teeth and rolled the friar onto his back so his face was out of the water again.

Slowly, ever so slowly, he swam sideways until, at last, the water became shallow and, with a last agonized effort, the slim teenager propelled the limp friar onto dry land.

The young man simply lay on his side for a while, gasping from the exertion, and shivering uncontrollably from the cold. He knew he had to check on Tuck, but his tired body wouldn't co-operate until he rested a little.

"Move, you idiot!" he told himself, realising he was about to pass out.

Whimpering, he dragged himself on his hands and knees to Tuck and, making sure to avoid the crossbow bolt which was still in place, pressed on his chest, up and down, up and down. He had seen one of the villagers in Wrangbrook doing this when a childhood friend of his had fallen into the water when they were playing by the mill one day, years ago.

He had no idea what the purpose of the exercise was – it had done nothing for his friend, who had been blue when they took him from the water and had stayed blue – but it was the only thing he could think of doing to help the friar.

"Come on you bastard!" he sobbed, looking imploringly at the sky, past the limit of endurance. "God, help him!"

As the youngster collapsed, utterly spent, on the mud and stones of the riverbank, Tuck suddenly convulsed, water spurting from his mouth as if he was vomiting.

Gareth watched in disbelief as the friar curled up, gasping and coughing, looking at him through glassy unseeing eyes. With a final gasp, Tuck stopped moving and Gareth panicked again, but he could see his big friend's pale lips moving as he breathed heavily.

They were both alive. But they were far from help, Gisbourne's men were still in the area, they were both soaked to the skin in the cold spring air, and Tuck had been shot.

Gareth had saved them both, simply to die here on the riverbank.

* * *

Gareth woke, but the sunlight was bright, so he kept his eyes shut and pulled the blankets around him even tighter.

Then he remembered what had happened and sat up, fearful of what he might see.

He was lying on a crude bed of straw, beside the fire-pit in what looked like a peasant's house. There was a big pot of something cooking above the fire, porridge from the smell, which was making his mouth water. Beside it were his clothes, obviously hung there to dry out.

He realised he was naked under the blankets and felt his face flush in embarrassment.

No one else was in the room. Where was Tuck?

He scrambled up and threw on his clothes, happy to note his weapons – a dagger and a short sword – on the floor.

Where the hell was he? And how did he get there?

The sounds of a busy village came through the thin walls and he wondered what to do.

The door suddenly burst open and a man strode into the room, nodding as he saw the young man dressed and up.

"You're awake then, good." He pointed to the porridge. "Help yourself, lad, you must be starving."

Gareth's eyes cast about for a bowl, spotting one on a small table against the wall. There was a shallow wooden spoon with it, so he ladled some of the bubbling, creamy oats into the bowl and blew on it, so hungry he was tempted just to shovel some of it in even though he knew it would be burning hot.

"Where am I?" he asked, eyeing the man, who had sat in a chair by the fire. "How did I get here? And where's the friar I was with? Is he...is he all right?"

The man frowned. "He's alive, aye, but he's been unconscious since we brought him here to the village. He's at the barber's place. You're in Penyston." The man gestured to a stool. "Sit. Eat."

Gareth gratefully sat down and began to spoon some of the hot food into his mouth, hoping the local barber was skilled in medicine as well as trimming beards. It was rare to find a qualified physician – and certainly one wouldn't be working in a little village like this. Instead, small places like Penyston were served by surgeons or barbers who learned their trade by experience and from reading books – it wasn't at all unusual for a patient to die as a result of the barber's lack of medical knowledge, but there was usually no alternative in England's backwater villages.

"Me and a mate were fishing in the Don," the peasant said. "We saw you dragging the big Franciscan out of the water and came to help. It took us a little while to reach you, mind, since we were on the opposite bank. You were lucky, lad. You came ashore close to the village, so we were able to find a boat nearby and bring you and your friend back here before either of you got a killing chill."

"I owe you and your mate my life," Gareth nodded solemnly. "I'll reward you for it. You have my thanks."

The man raised an eyebrow at the thought of this skinny young man – probably a wolf's head – rewarding

79

him in any meaningful way, but his manners stopped him from making any remark.

Finishing off the porridge gratefully, Gareth stood up, stretching his aching muscles. "Can I go see Tuck?"

Recognition flared in the man's eyes at the name and he stood up to show the young man out. "Aye, come on then, I'll take you. Don't tell anyone else in the village who the friar is. Or yourself either for that matter. No one needs to know. That way when the law come round looking for you and your gang no one will get into any trouble for helping you." He looked at Gareth with fear plainly written on his face. "All right?"

"Of course," the outlaw agreed. "I don't want to bring you or anyone else any bother. I'll check on Tu – I'll check on the friar then head back to our camp for help. Like I said, I'll reward you, and the friar will be taken away from your village before trouble comes."

The barber's place was a nice two-storey building, with the shop on the ground floor and the house above. It was of similar construction to the peasant's dwelling, but bigger and with nicer furnishings.

Gareth was shown in by the peasant, who didn't offer his name before making his way quickly back home with a nervous wave and a blessing.

The barber looked gravely at him when he brought him to see Friar Tuck, who lay on a wooden bed, the crossbow bolt in his chest removed and the wound heavily bandaged. Blood had seeped through the dressing, and the smell of alcohol was strong from the solution the barber had used to try and clean the wound.

"He was fortunate," the man told Gareth, gesturing to Tuck's light armour which lay on the floor beside the bed. "His gambeson took much of the force out of the bolt so it didn't go in too deeply. It's mostly a flesh wound." The barber looked questioningly at the young outlaw. "Unusual for a Franciscan to be wearing such a finely constructed piece of light armour under his habit," he mused.

Gareth pretended he hadn't heard that.

"If it's just a flesh wound, when will he wake up?"

The barber puffed out his cheeks and shrugged. "I have no idea. Maybe never – or, if he does, he might be unable to care for himself."

Seeing Gareth's shocked look, the man continued. "He almost drowned. And if the filth in the river water got into his wound it will become infected." He shook his head, looking down on the sleeping churchman pityingly. "However, he looks a strong man, and his skin is a healthy colour so he may wake up soon and be absolutely fine. I've prayed for him, there's not much else to do." His gaze moved to Gareth and he eyed him appraisingly. "What about you, lad? I've heard how you pulled the friar out of the river then collapsed yourself. You should be resting. Or is someone after you?"

"You're better not knowing anything about that," the outlaw replied. "As for me – I'm all right. Tired and sore, but otherwise fine. I need to get back to my friends so we can get the friar away from here."

The barber nodded and led Gareth back to the front door. "Wait a second," he called, hurrying into another room. When he returned he carried a small bottle. "Here, take some of this, it'll help the chill in your bones."

The young man took the cork from the bottle and sniffed. "God's bollocks," he gasped, recoiling from the overpowering smell. "What is it?"

"My own recipe. A concoction I distilled from wine after hearing about it from an Italian merchant," the barber smiled, used to the reaction. "I've added some herbs and such to it. Drink some – just a little at a time. I guarantee you'll feel much fitter after a few moments."

Gareth took a swig and cursed even more colourfully this time. It tasted vile and burned the back of his throat. The barber motioned him to drink more though, so, hoping the man wasn't poisoning him, the young outlaw forced down another few gulps then, thanking the man for his help and promising to return for the friar soon, he stumbled into the street.

A short time later, he was sprinting through the forest heading for Robin and the rest of the gang with a happy smile on his face, wondering how much of the barber's medicine he could carry when they returned to the village for Tuck.

CHAPTER SEVEN

"You're alive!" Little John grinned as Gareth trotted into their camp. The lookouts the outlaws always had posted around their base had seen the youngster coming and alerted the rest. They crowded around, clapping him on the back, happy to see him safe.

"Sit down," Robin laughed at the puffing lad, handing him an ale-skin which Gareth grasped gratefully.

"So, what happened? How did you get away?" Much demanded, the others shouting questions of their own.

Gareth caught his breath and took a long drink of ale, raising a hand to silence his curious friends.

"We don't have much time for questions," he said. "Tuck's alive."

There was uproar as everyone demanded the tale from the young outlaw.

"Let him speak, for God's sake!" Robin roared, silencing the men.

"He's in Penyston." Gareth continued. "I saw that bastard in the black armour shoot him into the river, so I jumped on a log and floated downstream until I found him, then I dragged him out of the water."

"Nicely done," Robin smiled as the men made appreciative noises. "You must be stronger than you look to have dragged the old friar onto dry land."

"I don't know where I found the strength," Gareth admitted. "I pressed on his chest until he spat out the water he'd swallowed, but then I passed out. When I woke up this morning I was in a bed in Penyston. Two fishermen from there had found us, and taken us to the village."

The outlaws were quiet as they pictured all this unfolding in their minds.

"Tuck's alive, you said," Little John grunted, scratching his thick beard. "How is he?"

Gareth shrugged. "The local barber removed the crossbow bolt from his chest and cleaned the wound up, but he's unconscious. He might never wake up."

"So we have to go and bring Tuck back here before anyone – like Gisbourne – discovers him." Gareth nodded and took another swig of ale as his leader went on. "If Tuck's discovered, the people of Penyston will suffer for helping a wolf's head."

Robin stood up. "Right. Who's coming with me to get him?"

Little John nodded. "I'll fetch the stretcher."

Much and Will volunteered to go as well. "Tuck carried me on a stretcher when I was wounded," Scarlet said, "the least I can do is return the favour."

Gareth finished the last of the ale in the skin and, wiping his mouth contentedly, stood beside Robin. "I'm coming too."

Matt Groves snorted with laughter. "No offence, boy, but you're too skinny to be much help carrying that fat churchman. And Penyston's a good few miles away – you must be worn out already."

Gareth was used to Groves's snide remarks, so he just ignored the man, addressing Robin again. "I have a debt to pay to the men who saved us. Just let me collect some of my money from my things" –

"Don't be daft," the young outlaw captain shook his head. "We'll repay them with money from the common fund. Those men didn't just help you, they helped Tuck too."

"Aye," John agreed. "Besides, if the villagers around here know we appreciate their help, they're more likely to keep offering it."

Robin nodded to Gareth, handing him a small key which he kept on a leather thong around his neck. "That's a good point. Go and take two pounds of silver from the common chest. We'll split it four ways: seven shillings each for the two fishermen and the barber, and the remainder for the village headman to buy everyone in the village some meat and ale as a thank you from us." He grinned at the thought. "They can throw a feast in our honour."

"And when we get back here with Tuck," John smiled. "We'll have a feast in young Gareth's honour. You're a hero, lad."

The teenager laughed, embarrassed but pleased at the praise. "I've found just the thing we can celebrate with too," he told them as they made their way through the forest to Penyston. "The barber has this amazing drink!"

The barber was happy to sell them some of his strange brew, although he warned them not to drink too much. "It's a lot more potent than ale," he told them as they lifted the stretcher with the unconscious Tuck on it, a man to each corner, Gareth following at the rear carrying a few skins filled with the powerful drink.

They didn't want to attract too much attention, so Robin had given the barber his seven shillings payment for taking care of the friar, and asked him to pass on the other seven shillings for the feast to the village headman. He gave the barber a stern look as he handed over the silver, making it clear without saying anything that they would find out one way or another if the man kept all the money for himself.

Gareth quickly ran to the house of the peasant that had brought him to the village and handed over their share of the money – more than a month's wages – to the astonished man, asking him to give half to his fisherman friend, then the youngster rejoined Robin and the rest and they made their way as fast as they could back through the trees to their camp.

Tuck looked peaceful enough lying on the stretcher, but the barber had told them again that the portly friar might never wake up.

As they jogged back to camp, trying not to jostle the stretcher too much, they breathed prayers to God, his saints, and the Magdalene to help their injured friend.

* * *

"So that was Guy of Gisbourne." John mused when they returned safely with Tuck to their camp in the woods near Notton, helping himself to a large chunk of venison from his wooden plate. "Impressive, eh?"

Robin nodded thoughtfully but Will snorted.

"Impressive? What was so impressive about him? He's a soft, skinny noble. Good Christ, you were almost three times the size of him John! The only thing impressive about him was that armour of his."

The rest of the outlaws around the camp-fire murmured agreement at that. Gisbourne's light black armour may have been ostentatious, but it was obviously functional and made its wearer stand out in a crowd. It was the kind of armour men coveted.

"You never spoke to him, Will," Robin said, gazing into the flames. "John's right – Gisbourne had something about him. Something more than just fancy clothes. He had a kind of hypnotic gaze – almost made you forget he was an enemy when he spoke to you. I could imagine men hesitating for just a fraction of a second when they looked into his eyes – just before they felt his knife in their guts."

"Aye," John agreed. "He had charisma; reminded me a bit of you." He nodded towards Robin, no trace of humour on his big honest face.

The young outlaw leader waved a dismissive hand, his face flushing slightly at the compliment from his giant friend.

Allan-a-Dale, gittern in his lap, strummed a cheery chord. "My money would be on Robin if the two of them ever get in a fight," he stated, eyes on the fingerboard as he traced a short melody. "That black

86

armour looked nice, but it wouldn't stop one of you big lads if you were to ram the point of a sword into it."

"Who's taking bets on it?" Arthur, the stocky young man from Bichill shouted with a grin, raising his ale skin in the air, spilling much of it on the forest floor. "Anyone want to put money on it? Fight of the century!"

Allan laughed and stood up, hammering out a few repetitive, sinister-sounding notes on his instrument which he wore on a fine leather strap over his shoulder.

"The Wolf!"

He pointed theatrically at Robin, drawing loud cheers from the inebriated outlaws as he continued the ominously descending riff on his gittern.

"Versus...the Raven!"

The men played along, booing and laughing loudly as Allan mimicked a bird – cawing, and flapping his arms ridiculously around the camp.

No bets were placed on Sir Guy – the men had too much faith in their young captain's strength and skill with a sword to wager against him.

The evening wore on, the outlaws happy to have their friend Tuck back in the fold, even if he was still unconscious. At least the bastard Gisbourne and his cowardly crossbow hadn't managed to kill the merry Franciscan yet. For this night, he was still breathing, and the men celebrated their escape from the men hunting them like animals.

Robin looked over at the unconscious friar.

They had tried to make him as comfortable as possible, covering his grey robes with blankets and laying him out on a bed of straw under a shelter near the fire. Still, it was another cold night for all spring was on the way, with the threat of frost – maybe even snow – in the air. Robin resolved to have Tuck moved into the large cave before the men turned in for the night.

The outlaws – living a life where death was an ever-present threat – were right to enjoy the evening. They had escaped from the man sent to kill them, after all. And the scum that had murdered their friend Wilfred had been destroyed.

Things could have turned out much, much worse for them that day.

But, as the others danced and sang and downed their ale, and Gareth produced a bottle of the barber's 'medicine' with a wild grin, Robin sat thoughtfully on his own.

Gisbourne's men weren't like anything they'd faced before in the forest. They had clearly been well drilled by the king's bounty-hunter. The soldiers also outnumbered them, and were at least as well armed and armoured as the outlaws.

Robin took a long pull from his ale skin, tensing his huge bicep muscles as the bitter liquid warmed his belly. Aye, in a fair fight, one-on-one, he'd probably beat Sir Guy, he thought.

But he doubted Gisbourne was the type of man to fight fair, and, as he watched the rest of the men smiling and enjoying the evening, he realised he'd have to watch his back from closer to home. He wasn't the only one not joining in with the revelry: Matt Groves sat alone under a thick old beech tree, staring at him.

As their eyes met, Groves curled his lip derisively but looked away, draining his ale skin and wiping his wet mouth with a stained sleeve.

This has gone on too long, Robin realised. He hates me. Eventually he'll find the courage to slip a knife in my back...

The outlaw leader, half-drunk himself, glared at Groves, willing the man to react so he could finish it right there and then, but Matt never looked at him again.

As he glanced back down at his good friend Friar Tuck, unconscious, possibly never to wake up again, Robin decided.

These were *his* men now. They were loyal to him, despite his youth.

It was hard enough having men like Gisbourne and the sheriff, de Faucumberg, after them, without worrying about members of his own group.

He would talk to Little John and Will Scarlet in the morning. It was time they removed Matt Groves.

* * *

The loud crack of wooden practice swords clattering against each other filled the cold morning air.

Sir Guy of Gisbourne liked to be up at dawn to read from his bible then to practice his one-on-one combat skills with whoever was awake and not too hungover from the previous night's ale. Today, he sparred with a tall, but fat soldier. Gisbourne hadn't bothered to ask the man's name and, irritated by his opponent's lack of finesse, had given him quite a beating.

Since Thomas of Lancaster's failed rebellion, Sir Guy and his bounty-hunters had taken up temporary residence in the earl's former castle at Pontefract which was now in the hands of Sir Simon de Baldreston, although de Baldreston's seneschal, Sir John de Burton, looked after the day-to-day running of the place.

The majority of the escaped rebels – including Robin Hood and his men – had fled into the forests nearby so it was an ideal base; certainly it was closer than de Faucumberg's castle in Nottingham, so the sheriff had been quick to suggest Gisbourne seek Pontefract's hospitality for a while.

"Ow, fucking hell!" the fat soldier roared, dropping his practice sword from numb, scarlet fingers. "We're on the same side you know," he muttered, clasping the injured hand under his armpit with an angry glare at his black haired tormentor.

"You taking out your frustration on the peasants?" Gisbourne's sergeant Nicholas Barnwell, came into the courtyard carrying a mug of ale and half a

89

loaf. The angry soldier stormed off, muttering under his breath, much to the amusement of Sir Guy.

"I don't know how oafs like him dare to call themselves 'soldiers'," he replied, tossing his own wooden practice sword noisily back onto the pile in a corner of the practice area. "No defence and too fat to attack without giving his opponent time to react. Good for nothing but arrow-fodder."

Barnwell laughed. "Nothing to do with you being pissed off at Hood's escape then?"

"Aye, that too," Gisbourne shrugged with a small smile. "That fat bastard's lucky I didn't use a real sword to spar with him." His face became serious again as he continued. "I can't believe we were so close to the man we've been sent here to kill. And his whole gang too!"

"Now you know why the king sent us here," Nicholas mumbled, mouth filled with crusty bread. "Hood and his men seem to live a charmed life."

Gisbourne nodded agreement. The stories the sheriff had told him about Hood, and his predecessor Adam Bell's, time in the forests of Barnsdale suggested it would be very hard, if not impossible, to catch this gang. They were well trained, well armed, had the support of the common people who seemed to love them, and their leaders had great tactical skill. Not to mention much better knowledge of the local terrain.

"Perhaps we need to try something different..." he mused.

"Fuck it." Nicholas turned away. "Stop fretting. There'll be another time to catch them. Come and have some breakfast with the men."

"You know I don't eat in the morning," Gisbourne replied. "You go back in; I'm going to finish my practice session. I want to be ready for Hood and his men the next time we meet."

As his sergeant wandered off, ale mug raised to his lips and waving the hard bread at his leader, Gisbourne drew his sword from its ornate black sheath and began to practice with it, flowing from one position to another with an economy of movement that was breathtaking to watch.

As he spun and twisted, his mind worked over the problem of Robin Hood and his men and, as he finished – his body moving astonishingly fast to end gracefully back in a defensive stance – a smile spread over his face. A passage from the Gospel of Matthew had come to mind.

Yes. He would find thirty pieces of silver and then they would try something different to catch this wolf's head...

* * *

"Exaudi nos, Domine sancte, Pater omnipotens, aeterne Deus: et mittere digneris sanctum Angelum tuum de caelis, qui custodiat, foveat, protegat, visitet atque defendat omnes habitantes in hoc habitaculo. Per Christum Dominum nostrum. Amen."

Allan finished the prayer, watching Tuck hopefully, but the friar remained unconscious. Maybe the minstrel had got the Latin wrong? He'd heard the prayer once, as a child, when his father had been dying, and memorized it.

"What did all that mean?" Much asked him.

"No idea," Allan admitted, to looks of amusement from Much and Robin who sat crouched on the forest floor beside the friar. "I heard it years ago, when my father was dying, and I memorized it. It seemed appropriate to say it now." He shrugged apologetically, but the two young men from Wakefield nodded encouragingly. Anything was worth a try after all.

Most of the outlaws were away from camp that morning, either hunting, fishing or gone off to local villages on errands. Robin, Much and the minstrel had stayed behind to watch over the camp, while a few of the others sparred and practiced with longbows close-by.

When Robin had woken up, hungover, he'd decided not to tell John and Will about his thoughts on Matt Groves the previous night after all. What had seemed like a good idea under the influence of ale now, in the cold light of morning, seemed extreme and unnecessary.

Matt would need to be dealt with somehow, but murdering him in cold blood just wasn't in Robin's character.

He shrugged and put Groves out of his mind for now then motioned towards Tuck.

"He told me how he came to be a Friar, but he never got around to telling me why he joined us. Seemed insane to me, leaving his safe life, to become a wolf's head. Something to do with that bastard prior, de Monte Martini."

Prior John de Monte Martini was the reason Robin had become an outlaw in the first place. The clergyman's threats towards Matilda at the previous May Day celebrations in Wakefield had led to Robin smashing the prior's nose and the young man being declared a wolf's head as a result.

Much nodded. "Aye, that's right, Tuck told a few of us the story one night when we were sitting by the camp-fire. You must have been on watch at the time or something."

"He did?" Robin leaned forward eagerly. "Go on then, let's hear it. I've been curious about it ever since we first met him."

Much waved a hand at Allan. "You tell it, you're the minstrel," he smiled. "You'll make it a better story than I would."

"Well," Allan began, making himself more comfortable on the log he sat on, "you know Tuck was a wrestler but gave it up when he was accused of cheating? And he saved the life of the Bishop of Norwich – what was his name again…?"

"Salmon," Much offered.

"Aye, John Salmon," Allan agreed. "Well, Tuck went off with the bishop and, with his help, Tuck became a Franciscan. Learned to read, learned Latin, studied the bible and so on."

Robin nodded. He knew all this already. "What did he do after that?"

"Well, the Franciscans knew about Tuck's previous life as a wrestler. They knew he could look after himself, so they used him to escort valuables around the place – money, religious relics, that sort of thing – against the threat of outlaws like ourselves."

"That's what he was doing when we robbed him," Much offered, remembering the day they had stopped the friar and his guards taking a chest full of silver through the forest. The outlaws had beaten the guards easily, but Tuck had shocked everyone when he brutally knocked out their previous leader, Adam Bell, using a cudgel hidden in his grey robes.

They all grinned at the memory and Allan carried on. "Aye, he would often travel to places with groups of mercenaries and he ended up in Lewes Priory one day. The prior asked him to travel to France, to buy some religious relic or other." He furrowed his brow and looked over at Much. "What was it de Monte Martini wanted?"

"Some hair from Christ's beard," Much replied. "It had turned up in some French village – Eze I think Tuck called the place – and the prior thought it would look good in his collection."

Allan took up the story again. "That's right, the prior gave Tuck some crazy amount of money to go to France and buy this hair. Off he went on a ship with half a dozen guards and the silver. He didn't tell us much about the journey, other than to complain about having to walk up some huge mountain to reach the village! At least no one bothered them on the way. I suppose France isn't infested with wolf's heads and robbers like England." He smiled and continued. "Anyway, this Eze is, apparently, a small village, and the local priest was more than happy to sell the relic for such a huge sum of silver. Tuck and his men made their way back through France" –

"Sampling the best of the exotic local food and drink," Much laughed, nodding towards the unconscious friar's round belly, "at de Monte Martini's expense."

"I can imagine," Robin smiled. Tuck liked his food, there was no denying that. "I bet he enjoyed that journey."

"Until they returned to England," Allan nodded grimly. "When they got back to Lewes, Tuck paid off his guards and, taking Christ's hair, which was in a small, fancily decorated reliquary inside a plain wooden box, went to give it to the prior." He paused and met Robin's eyes. "Now, you know Tuck. You know he takes his faith very seriously."

Robin nodded. It was true. Although he was a man outside the law, the friar was still very much a man of God – more of a Christian than the likes of Prior de Monte Martini with his string of brothels would ever be, that was for sure.

"Well, as he sat outside the chapter house, waiting on the prior to see him, Tuck opened the little box for a last look at the hair. He hadn't looked at it since they'd bought it from the priest in France – Tuck thought it would be disrespectful to keep staring at it, so he'd stopped himself until then, but when he opened the wooden box, *Pater Noster* on his lips, for a final look at the relic…" Again, Allan paused dramatically.

"It was gone!" Much broke in to the minstrel's annoyance.

"Shut up!" Allan shouted with a glare. "I'm telling the story."

Robin and Much shared a laugh at their mate's indignation.

"The box was empty," Allan went on. "One of the mercenaries must have taken the reliquary when Tuck was sleeping off too much French wine one night. When the guards kept asking for a look at it, the daft bastard had told them no one would be opening the box until he handed it over to the prior."

Robin shook his head sadly, looking over at his unconscious big friend. "Always wants to see the good in people, does Tuck," he said. "Naïve old sod."

"Of course, the prior called him in then, and he had to tell him what had happened. It didn't go down too well."

"I see why Tuck wasn't too keen to go back to de Monte Martini when we robbed him," Robin muttered.

"Exactly," Allan replied. "The prior suspected Tuck might have stolen the relic himself, so he had him stripped naked and searched. Of course they didn't find it, and the local bailiff was called to hunt down the mercenaries. They found five of them, but one had left town as soon as they'd parted ways with Tuck, and the rest of them didn't know where he'd gone."

He shrugged. "No one ever found the relic, and de Monte Martini made Tuck's life miserable afterwards. When we robbed him on his way down to Lewes with the prior's silver, Tuck knew he would be blamed again and be thrown in jail or worse."

"So he joined us," Robin said, and the three men sat in thoughtful silence for a while.

It had been two days since they had brought Tuck back to camp, and he'd shown no signs of stirring, despite the prayers of the outlaws.

"There must be some religious relics in the churches around here," Robin mused.

"So what?"

"Well, I'm just thinking…if they're as powerful as the churchmen tell us…maybe one would help our prayers to wake Tuck?"

Allan and Much looked at each other. Why not? It must be worth a try.

"There's something – I don't remember what – in Brandesburton," the minstrel told them. "When Little

John returns to camp, maybe he'll be able to tell us more; he knows that area well."

"I'm not keen on the idea of stealing something like this," Robin said, but then he smiled and shrugged his massive shoulders. "Maybe we can borrow it for a while though."

CHAPTER EIGHT

"The fat friar's as good as dead now," Matt Groves growled over his shoulder as he relieved himself against a tree.

"Always so cheerful, you," Paul, the former fuller from Nottingham replied with a scowl.

"I'm just being realistic." Groves did his breeches up and turned round with a shrug. "Keeping him alive's not doing him any favours. Someone should put him out his misery."

Paul and James, one of the men who had been on the raft with Much when Tuck was injured, had accompanied Groves to Darton that morning. They had come specifically to Darton because a local merchant was able to supply them with rope, something only port towns normally specialized in, but the two men had grown tired of Matt's incessant grousing.

"When we get back to camp, you can sort the friar out then," Paul muttered. "Can we bloody hurry up though?"

"What's the rush?" Groves wondered, lifting his pack from the grass and following the others.

Matt had managed to conclude his business quickly in the village, while Paul and James had been forced to take more time inspecting, and paying for, the rope that Little John had asked the merchant to obtain for them on a previous visit.

Matt had spent the time waiting on his companions in the local ale-house. He'd also bought a skin of the dark ale which he'd been sipping from as they made their way back to camp.

"Guy of Gisbourne has spies in all the villages about here, now," James noted. "I'd rather not hang about in case 'the Raven' hears we're around and comes hunting us. If you'd stop swilling that ale, and pissing it out, we'd make better time."

"The Raven!" Groves hooted, taking another mouthful of ale from the skin. "Fuck him and his fancy armour. He's a fool. Had us in his grasp and let us escape." He waved a hand dismissively. "Gisbourne's no threat."

"All the same, can we hurry up?" Paul retorted, utterly fed up with his half-drunk companion. "The sooner we get back the better."

"Wait!" James stopped, holding a hand up for silence, his eyes wide.

"Oh, what now?"

"Shut up, you prick!" James glared at Matt, his hand on his sword hilt, listening intently.

The unmistakeable thundering sound of horses close behind came to them.

All three were hardy fighters, but none was a leader. They gazed at each other in fear, wondering what to do.

"Run for it!"

Paul shouted and spun to make his way into the undergrowth but a horseman burst through the trees beside them as they ran, swinging his longsword into the back of the fuller's skull.

James tried to head towards the thicker foliage nearby, but another mounted soldier charged into view, his horse clipping the outlaw on the shoulder and sending him sprawling on the ground.

More riders appeared as he tried to rise, while Matt Groves stood, sword drawn, but with a blank look on his face.

Matt instantly recognised the black armoured man as he rode up, crossbow in his right hand while expertly guiding his mount with his left.

James sprinted towards a massive old oak, trying to find some cover, as, with a dull thud, Gisbourne released the trigger and his iron bolt hammered into the cold bark of the tree just beside his head.

"Damn! Surround him!" The black knight roared with a grimace, tossing his weapon to one of his men to reload and wheeling his horse around to face Matt Groves. "This one's not hiding anyway!"

Groves held his blade before him defensively. The ale he'd swallowed that day coursed through him, making him feel invincible, even though he could barely walk in a straight line.

"Come on then, Raven," the outlaw spat. "Get down from your horse and I'll shove my sword up your arse!"

Sir Guy raised his eyebrows in surprise, and then laughed. It was a genuine, happy laugh, and weirdly out-of-place in the present situation.

"Very well."

Groves spread his feet wide defensively, the ale focusing his mind solely on the man directly in front of him as Gisbourne dropped from his mount and faced up to him, sword in hand.

Matt Groves was no unskilled peasant. He had been a member of well-trained outlaw gangs for years, and that experience, combined with his natural aggression, made him a dangerous swordsman.

He grinned as the black-clad Gisbourne walked towards him, waving at his men to stand down.

"You're the Raven, eh?" Matt growled, swinging his sword in a vicious, controlled arc, testing his opponent's defences.

"That's me," Gisbourne grinned, parrying the blow and stepping in close to ram his boiled-leather gauntleted fist into the outlaw's nose.

Groves fell backwards onto the ground, stunned, blood streaming down his face as the bounty-hunter smiled down at him.

"Bastard!" The furious outlaw pushed himself to his feet, remembering Robin Hood breaking his nose not so long ago, and threw himself at Gisbourne, swinging his blade from side to side brutally, as if he was trying to smash his opponent's weapon by sheer brute force.

Sir Guy parried the onslaught for a few moments, then deftly stepped to the left and, as the outlaw fell slightly forward, the bounty-hunter slammed the pommel of his sword into Matt's chin, throwing him to the ground, bloodied and stunned.

"Don't get up," Gisbourne grinned, holding the point of his blade against Matt's throat. "I want to talk to you." He looked to the right as his men brought a silent, bloodied James out from behind the oak and dragged him over, throwing the wolf's head onto the forest floor beside Groves.

"Now there's two of you, and I only need one."

The outlaws glanced at each other wondering what was going to happen next as Gisbourne carried on.

"I need one of you to do something for me. A...favour, let's call it." He looked down at the two men lying on their backs and smiled. "Who'll do me a favour?"

For a few moments there was silence, and then James gave a short, forced laugh. "Fuck off, lawman. If you think we're going to betray Robin and our friends you can think again" –

The king's man swept forward and shoved the point of his sword deep into James' neck, so hard it came out the other side and stuck in the grass underneath. Steaming hot blood spilled onto the grass below as the outlaw died, his eyes and mouth opened wide in shock and pain.

Matt Groves watched his companion expire then looked up to meet the Raven's eyes.

"I'll do you a favour."

* * *

"St Peter's thumb?"

Little John nodded. "Aye, father, we need it."

The Priest of St Mary's in Brandesburton looked bemused at the strange request, but shook his head firmly. "I can't just give you one of our relics John, these things aren't bread, or fish, to be bartered. St

Peter's thumb has been in the company of Christ himself. The people of our parish are proud to have it here – pilgrims come to pray before it."

"And pay you for the privilege," Will growled.

Father Nicholas de Nottingham, a small, completely bald man with intelligent eyes nodded defiantly at the glowering outlaw. "Aye, they give alms, what about it? Do you think our roof repairs itself when the January winds blow the slates off?"

"Doesn't God repair it for you?"

"He does, yes," the priest replied to a cynical-looking Scarlet. "God sent us the relic people pay to see didn't he?"

Robin laughed at de Nottingham's unassailable logic, and waved a hand for Will to give it a rest.

"Look, father, we need the relic. Our friend, Tuck, is badly injured. We hoped the relic might be able to heal him." He held up a hand as the priest opened his mouth to reply. "We appreciate St Peter's thumb brings your parish revenue. So, we'll buy it from you." He dropped some silver coins into the churchman's palm. "Three pounds. That should buy you a few roof slates."

Father Nicholas gasped at the money, his eyes wide.

Will had suggested they simply walk into the church and take the relic, but the other outlaws, more pious than Scarlet, had rejected the idea. Little John, who had lived in nearby Holderness, told them Father Nicholas was a good man – a local, not high-born, who had tried to do his best for the villagers while living frugally himself, unlike many of the other clergymen in England.

In John's opinion, the priest would spend the three pounds of silver wisely and fairly, for the benefit of the parish, rather than just buying himself jade rosary beads, new silk vestments and some imported French communion wine.

"You're good men," de Nottingham smiled. "Even that one," he nodded at Will, bringing laughs from

Robin and Little John. "But" – he spread his hands, meeting Robin's gaze – "it's St Peter's thumb! St Peter himself, our first pope! I can't just sell a relic like that; it's beyond price."

The three outlaws looked at each other in frustration. None of them, not even Will, wanted to take the relic by force, not after speaking to the sincere priest. But time was running out for Friar Tuck and they didn't have time to hunt for another powerful relic.

"Where did you get it?" Robin wondered.

Father Nicholas looked uncomfortable. "It was a gift from Our Lord" –

"Be honest with us," Robin sat on one of the cold wooden pews, looking up at the churchman earnestly. "How did something like St Peter's thumb end up in a tiny parish church in the arse-end of nowhere?"

Father Nicholas had genuinely warmed to this young outlaw, with his open face – not at all like most of the other cut-throats infesting the greenwood – and found himself being more truthful than he would have expected when the three rough-looking wolf's heads had wandered into his church a short while earlier.

"A man – from London judging by his barely understandable accent – sold it to me for...well, that's not important. He said he'd been given it as a gift for rendering some service or other to a bishop."

"And you believed him?" Will laughed.

"No," the priest shook his head. "It was obvious he'd stolen it."

"Why did you buy it from him then?" John wondered, sitting down beside Robin, his massive legs barely fitting into the space.

"The reliquary is quite exceptionally crafted," de Nottingham replied. "And it was clear the fellow was desperate. He wasn't asking much at all for it, despite the obvious value of the thing. I believe he must have tried selling it in many different places, but been turned away – perhaps even chased by the local lawmen." He shrugged. "As you say, this is a small parish in the middle of nowhere. We have some other relics, but they were nothing in comparison to this. I took pity on the man, gave him his price and sent him on his way."

"What does a thousand-year-old thumb look like?" Will asked.

The priest shrugged again. "No idea, I've never been able to open the reliquary. It's locked, I don't have a key, and it's simply too precious to damage by forcing it open."

The outlaws looked at him in disbelief.

"You've never even seen it?" Robin demanded. "How do you know it's not just an empty box?"

Father Nicholas looked at the three friends with a small smile on his face.

"You're missing the point. It doesn't matter what's inside the box. I was told it was St Peter's thumb – so that's what I tell the pilgrims that come to see it. I've personally seen people with terrible afflictions touch the reliquary and become cured. It really doesn't matter what's in the box." He waved a hand dismissively. "Besides, as I said, the reliquary is so ostentatious, so obviously valuable, it stands to reason it holds *something* of great value."

"It might hold nothing at all!" Will hooted derisively.

"Then I bought a hugely expensive reliquary for a tiny sum, what's the problem?" the little priest demanded, glaring at Scarlet who looked away, abashed.

Robin stood up, the wooden pew creaking loudly in the cool silence.

"Father, we need" –

"Yes, yes, your friend is dying and so on," the churchman butted in. "So you've said." He moved towards Robin and looked up, meeting his eyes imperiously. "You're an honourable man, so I hear."

The young outlaw remained silent, not quite sure whether he was 'honourable' or not.

"So, I'll tell you what I'll do," de Nottingham continued, turning his back on the trio and disappearing behind the altar.

He reappeared a moment later, carrying the reliquary which was finely-decorated and, as the priest had said, obviously very valuable.

"Here," he thrust it towards Robin. "You can borrow it. But – whether your friend lives or dies – I expect you to return it to me."

"You're a good man, father," Will grinned.

"I told you he was," Little John agreed, slapping the clergyman on the shoulder gratefully.

Robin took the small box reverentially and gingerly placed it into a pocket under his gambeson, nodding his thanks to the priest.

"What do we do with it?" he asked. "I mean, how do we get it to heal Tuck?"

"Place it on his chest and pray. But" – he raised his hand in warning – "don't expect too much. It may be your friend's time has come. He might be beyond healing."

With glad smiles and words of thanks the three outlaws made their way to the big oak doors, promising to return the valuable relic as soon as they could.

As they stepped out into the sunlight, squinting as their eyes became accustomed to the brightness after the dim church, Robin turned and tossed the bag of silver to Father Nicholas who scrambled instinctively to catch it.

"Hey!" the priest shouted, running after them as the outlaws wandered off. "Don't forget I want the relic back – what's this money for?"

"Your roof," Robin grinned over his shoulder. "It won't repair itself when the slates blow off in January, will it?"

* * *

104

Stephen made good time on his journey to Clerkenwell, pushing his horse close to its limit in his desire to find aid for his master as soon as possible.

In truth, he wasn't sure exactly what he would find when he got there. It was many years since he had visited the place, and he doubted he would recognise any of the brothers residing there now.

Not far from his destination – no more than two or three hours – dark grey clouds suddenly filled the sky, blown by a bitter wind from the east, and the Hospitaller cursed in frustration as light flakes of snow began to fall.

He had hoped to reach the capital tonight, but knew it would be dangerous to continue his journey in the face of a gathering snowstorm.

With an angry sigh he turned his horse about and headed back the way he had come. He had passed through a small village – Finchley according to the signs – just a couple of miles earlier. He'd noticed a small but, from the outside at least, cosy looking inn where he would spend the night.

As his tired palfrey made its way along the road, Stephen felt his disappointment lift and he allowed himself a small smile at the thought of a roaring fire, a cosy bed and a few ales.

Aye, he had hoped to be within the sturdy stone walls of the Hospitaller headquarters tonight, but you couldn't argue with a snowstorm. Besides, he'd ridden hard and spent the previous six nights under cold blankets in a simple tent – he and his mount had earned a proper roof over their head tonight.

Tomorrow morning he'd ride into Clerkenwell and deliver Sir Richard's letter to the Prior.

* * *

"Where's the three that went off to Darton this morning?" Much wondered, stirring the big cauldron of pottage over the fire, sniffing at the contents with a small smile of pleasure. "It'll be dark soon."

105

"That's why it's so peaceful around here," Allan-a-Dale looked up from where he sat resting against a tree, a broad grin on his face. "That sour-faced bastard Matt's not here."

"Don't speak too soon." The skinny youngster, Gareth, jogged into camp. He was acting as one of the lookouts and, from his vantage point high in a thick old beech, had spotted Matt approaching.

"Coming from the west, alone, no sign of Paul or James. And he's got blood on his face, looks like he's been in a fight."

"Everyone up!" Robin roared, running for his longbow and arrows, his stomach lurching in apprehension as the men followed his lead, hurriedly strapping on swords, bracers, helmets and whatever other weapons or armour they each favoured.

"What now?" John wondered. "Someone might be following him."

Robin nodded agreement. "Everyone find a place to hide. Those of you who can shoot a longbow, have them trained on the path to the west, where Matt'll appear. The rest of you, have your swords, axes or whatever ready. I'll wait here for him."

It was a measure of Robin's ever growing stature amongst the outlaws that no-one questioned his orders, the men melting away like wraiths into the dense green undergrowth, the sounds of insects and birds filling the air and lending the scene a serenity the young captain didn't feel inside.

It took a short while, but eventually Matt Groves walked into camp, looking at Robin warily.

"Where is everyone?"

"Where do you think?" Robin retorted, his eyes scanning the trees behind Groves uneasily. "We saw you coming."

Matt nodded in understanding, wandering over and lifting a wooden bowl from beside the fire which he ladled some of the pottage into.

"You can tell them to come out," he grunted through mouthfuls. "I haven't been followed, I managed to lose them." He met Robin's eyes, meat juice dribbling down his chin, but his look was unreadable. "The bastards got James and Paul though."

Robin cursed, his stomach lurching again at the thought of two of his friends not coming home to camp tonight.

"Who got them?" he demanded.

Matt placed the bowl of food on the ground, clutching his chest and scowled momentarily. "Gisbourne and his men," he replied. "Sly bastard rode us down. Shot James himself, while one of the riders stuck a blade in Paul. One of them tried to do the same to me – gave me a kick in the face the prick – but he knocked me down the side of the trail. Steep bit. I slid down a good fifteen feet, battered my chest off a bloody rock at the bottom." He grimaced again. "Still, I was lucky. Their horses wouldn't follow down after me, so I was able to get away before any of them bothered to dismount and chase me on foot."

He gulped down the rest of his pottage and lay back on the ground with a groan. Robin felt a pang of guilt. It was clear Groves was in genuine pain – the blood caking his face and the exhausted look on his seamed face weren't an act. The man had been hurt and made his way back to the safety of their camp, surely hoping for a better welcome than this.

"You're sure you weren't followed?"

"Nah," Groves muttered without lifting his head from the grass. "I don't think they were too interested in a chase – they'd killed the other two lads anyway. Bastards."

"You hurt anywhere else?" Robin asked, but he was met with silence and he realised Matt had fallen asleep.

Shaking his head, sick of the harsh life they were forced to lead, the young outlaw called for the men to return to camp, with the lookouts ordered to be extra vigilant throughout the night.

In the morning they would try and recover their fallen friends' bodies for a proper Christian burial.

Robin felt almost as tired as Matt. Their former leader, Adam Gurdon, had known the greenwood of Barnsdale better than anyone; he had been an ex-Templar knight, a man of considerable military skills. And yet, when Gurdon had betrayed them and tried to hunt the outlaws down he hadn't been able to kill even one of the group before Robin had rammed his sword through the turncoat's chest.

But Sir Guy of Gisbourne – a stranger to the area – had, in the space of a few days, managed to put Friar Tuck into a sleep he might never wake from and now he'd slaughtered two of their mates and promised to do the same to Robin.

No wonder the locals talked about this sinister black knight in hushed tones.

Little John, as he did so often, guessed what his young leader was thinking and walked over to slap him reassuringly on the arm.

"Have faith," the giant growled. "You'll see: things'll work out. A raven is no match for a wolf."

CHAPTER NINE

"I can't speak bloody Latin!"

"None of us can, this is a waste of time." Will nodded agreement with Allan-a-Dale, who had been tasked with holding the relic and praying for Friar Tuck's cure.

"Why do I have to do this anyway?" Allan demanded. "I'm not a priest. I only know the one Latin prayer, and it might be a prayer for crops to grow for all I know!"

"You know how to make a sermon though," John replied. "Always blabbering on about stuff. If you hadn't become a minstrel you'd have made a damn good bishop."

There was laughter at that which somewhat eased the tension in the air.

Although the men didn't visit church frequently – how could they? – they were all Christians. They all believed in the power of God and his saints. The presence of a true holy relic had them in awe, and the atmosphere as they gathered around their unconscious companion was both nervous and reverential.

Matt Groves had been typically condescending when the ornate reliquary had been produced by Robin, who told the men it couldn't be opened.

"Of course it can be opened," Matt had laughed mirthlessly. "Give it here, I'll open it."

"We can't damage it," Robin shook his head. "It's not ours. Father Nicholas was good enough to let us borrow it – we return it to him as he gave us it."

"Let's have a look," Peter, the old sailor held out his hand curiously. "I've seen lots of strange boxes. We used to carry all sorts of foreign cargo on the ships I worked on. Maybe I'll be able to see how the thing opens without breaking it."

Robin handed the reliquary over cautiously, but Peter took it as carefully as if he were handling a newborn babe.

Eyebrows lowered in concentration, the sailor turned the box this way and that hunting for some catch that might unlock the fancy little case, then he exhaled softly in defeat before giving it back to his leader with a puzzled frown.

"It doesn't need to be opened anyway," Robin said. "Father Nicholas told us he's seen people cured by the relic even inside its box and I trust him." He bent down and placed the box on Tuck's chest. It rose and fell slightly with the friar's shallow breathing and Little John ordered the men to get on their knees and pray for their friend.

"In nomine Patris," Allan had started before he had given up in frustration.

"Just repeat that prayer you said the other day. The Latin one. You don't have to pretend you're a real churchman." Robin nodded encouragingly at the embarrassed minstrel.

With a sigh, Allan bent his head again, the rest of the men following his lead and clasping their hands piously as he recited the prayer he'd memorized as a child. As he finished, the respectful looks the other men gave him encouraged him to continue.

"In the name of the Father, the Son and the Holy Ghost," he mumbled, before he glanced at Tuck and his voice grew in strength and confidence with the desire to see his friend well again. "We are gathered here to ask you, St Peter, to help our companion. He is a good man – a man of the cloth – who almost drowned and now can't be revived. By the power invested in this, your holy relic, we humbly pray you will cure our friend."

He couldn't think what else to say, so some of the outlaws muttered, "Amen," and Will whispered, "Is that it?"

"Just pray, for goodness' sake!" Little John hissed, and the men bowed their heads and closed their eyes again, silently sending their supplications to the venerable Saint.

Nothing happened. No flash of lightning, no angelic healing hands appeared to help Tuck.

"It'll work eventually," Robin told the men. "Have faith. We'll pray for him again tomorrow."

* * *

Matilda felt enormous.

Her ankles were swollen. Her back and legs ached, and her breasts were becoming so heavy she worried they'd hang like empty sacks when the baby finally arrived.

Her parents tried their best to help her through the pregnancy, but they had their work to do every day, as did she. What she needed was her husband beside her, to look after her and make her feel better about the changes her young body was going through.

What she didn't need was to be pawed at.

Robin had made his way through the forest to visit that morning, upset at the relic's failure to cure Friar Tuck, and knowing Henry and Mary would be out at the fletcher's shop so he could spend some time alone with his wife, despite her irritation the last time he'd seen her.

Matilda had let him into the house, overjoyed to see him, but she was beginning to wish he'd never turned up.

"Stop it!"

Robin flinched in surprise at the rebuke as he tried to caress Matilda's swollen breasts in the dimly lit room.

"They hurt," she glared at him.

He apologised with a bemused smile and cuddled her for a few moments, before the swelling in his trousers overcame his good sense and he tried to slip a hand between his pregnant wife's legs.

"Are you an idiot?" Matilda shouted, shoving the surprised outlaw away. "I told you: my body aches."

Robin looked at her in confusion and she almost felt sorry for him. He looked so young and innocent and was obviously too stupid to understand what was wrong.

"I'm sorry," he mumbled, his eyes downcast momentarily, before they rose and settled again on her swollen breast and she could actually see his erection swelling again underneath his trousers and knew exactly what he was thinking.

"I'm sick every morning. My feet ache. My legs ache. These" - she cupped her breasts, fury rising in her again as she saw Robin's eyes light up - "are breaking my back! And this baby is keeping me up all night, kicking and jumping around like a court jester!"

It was true. Matilda was exhausted. Her legs jerked when she tried to rest, and the baby rolled about inside her so distractingly she hadn't been able to fall into a proper sleep for days.

"I've never felt so tired in my whole life," she told him, glaring at him as if it was, somehow, his fault. "Sleeping rough in Barnsdale as a wolf's head was easy compared to this."

All she wanted was a cuddle and for Robin to spend a little time talking to her about what she was going through. But she could see from his expression he was only interested in sex.

He tried to hide it with a placating smile, but his eyes roved over her heavy breasts when he thought she wasn't looking and, when he cuddled her she could feel him pressing himself against her backside almost in desperation.

"Get off me!" she shouted, pushing him away. "Go back to your mates in the forest. Maybe one of them will let you stick it in them."

Again, the confused expression on his handsome face made her hesitate, but she was in no mood to deal with this.

"Go. Come back when you can be a proper husband."

Bemused and upset, Robin stormed out the fletcher's house without another word.

* * *

The inn at Finchley proved to be as cosy and inviting as Stephen had hoped.

By the time he reached the village the snow was falling heavily and the wind whistled about him, making him glad of his thick black surcoat, emblazoned with the white cross of his Order.

This far from the North he saw no reason to hide the fact he was a Hospitaller, so when the snow had started he'd taken the surcoat from his pack and gratefully put it on.

When he'd ridden into the village the locals had bowed their heads or smiled up at him respectfully. Everyone knew the Knights of St John. When Stephen had first joined the Order fifteen years ago he had been inordinately proud of the normal folks' respect for the military Orders. The Hospitallers and Teutonic Knights – even ex-Templars, if any were discovered – were generally held in great esteem by the common people of England.

After a decade and a half of travelling the world and fighting thankless battles, Stephen had grown apathetic to the views of strangers. The villagers saw a man wearing chain-mail and automatically assumed he was someone of power and significance; a man somehow worthy of respect for the horse he rode and the attire he wore. But Stephen had fought beside plenty of courageous, loyal, Godly men who'd been nothing more than simple yeomen, like the good men of this village.

He'd also known plenty of cruel, selfish and damn evil men who acted like the red, black or white cross emblazoned on their shield somehow absolved them from whatever immoral deeds they chose to be involved in.

Images of women raped, children brutally murdered and rows of worthy foes treated like cattle at the slaughterhouse by 'honourable' men in the name of Holy War filled his head and he cursed inwardly.

Aye, he had seen some terrible things before he came back to England as Sir Richard-at-Lee's sergeant-at-arms, but it didn't help to be maudlin.

Passing an old church dedicated to St Mary, he reached the inn – the Wheatsheaf from the crudely painted sign over the door – and, with long practised ease climbed from his mount, leading it towards the adjoining stable.

There were no stable-hands around, so Stephen found a vacant stall for the palfrey and made sure it was secure. He patted the beast on the neck fondly. "I'll send someone out to tend to you, lad," he muttered, feeling somewhat foolish. He'd never owned a pet as a boy, and always felt like an idiot talking to animals, but this horse – which he'd never even given a name – had served him well for years and, despite his reticence, there was a bond between them that the sergeant acknowledged.

With a backward glance at his mount, which seemed to be looking at him with an amused expression on its long face, he huddled into his surcoat and walked round to the front of the building.

The sound of music and song filled his ears as he pushed the sturdy door open, wandering gladly into the warmth and light cast by a well-banked fire on the far wall of the room. The rushes on the floor hadn't been changed in a while, so the stench of dung, urine and stale vomit permeated the air making the room smell worse than the stable, but it was to be expected in a place like this; Stephen knew he'd get used to it within a short while.

Locals nodded gaily to him as he made his way to the bar and waved the inn-keeper over.

"I'll have an ale – warmed if you please. And my horse needs tending to." He handed a coin to the man, who nodded pleasantly and shouted through a door at someone – the stable-boy presumably – to move his lazy arse and see to the gentleman's steed.

"There you are, my lord," the barkeep smiled, placing the mug of ale in front of Stephen. "There's a couple of pokers in the hearth – help yourself."

The sergeant lifted the mug with a nod of thanks and weaved his way through the crowded room to the fire. He lifted a poker from the flames and placed the red-hot tip into his ale, which hissed as it instantly warmed, and took a small sip, grinning in satisfaction as the mild heat filled his mouth and spread throughout his body. They brewed their ale strong in Finchley!

He made his way back to the bar, sipping his warm drink as he went. "I'm no lord," he told the inn-keeper. "I'm only a sergeant, but I do need a bed for the night."

"You're in luck," the man replied, with a broad smile. "I have a room for you: bed freshly made up, floor newly swept – you'll have the best night's sleep you've had in ages, I promise you."

The Hospitaller nodded. He'd heard it all before, in every inn in every town in Christendom and beyond.

"Aye, very good. I don't give a shit about the dust on the floor. I'll sleep like a babe as long as it's cheap."

The inn-keeper laughed good-naturedly and moved off to serve another customer. "A shilling for the night," he smiled over his shoulder. "I'll do you some pottage and a few ales too. Can't say fairer than that."

Stephen nodded and raised his mug in salute. "Good enough."

He took a long pull of the powerful warmed ale and looked around the room which was filled with dancing shadows cast by the cosy orange glow from the roaring fire in the hearth.

There were twenty or so villagers in the large room. Most of them were singing along with a man playing a battered old gittern. Stephen wondered how they could hear what the hell he was playing over the sound of their own tuneless voices, but they all seemed to be having a good time.

The sergeant's gaze roved across the people, seeing the usual types in a village of this sort: peasants; yeomen; a priest; a couple of hard-looking fellows that probably made a living guarding property somewhere nearby... and there was the loner, sitting by himself in a dark corner, nursing a mug. Stephen wondered what tragedy had befallen the man, whose eyes looked dead as he gazed at the table in front of him.

His eyes moved on and widened slightly as they came to rest on a beautiful red-headed girl, no more than twenty-five or twenty-six summers, seated at a table with an older man – her father, no doubt. She wore a tight fitting dress which did little to hide her ample bosom, even though it showed no bare skin at all.

Stephen found himself staring at her, admiring her figure and her clear, pale skin.

As if feeling his gaze, the girl suddenly looked straight at him and the Hospitaller flicked his eyes away in embarrassment.

He took another sip of his ale and looked over at the red-head again. She was staring at him, her full lips opened in a little smile, showing whiter teeth than Stephen had seen in a long time.

Christ, she was lovely!

He had fought in many battles, and killed many men. He had travelled the world, and seen sights most men would never see.

But he had only lain with one woman in his life, and even that single night's pleasure lay heavy on his soul, as it had been a betrayal of his Order's vow of chastity.

Vows meant little to some men. Priests, bishops, cardinals and, unbelievably to Stephen, some popes had lain with women – and men! – whenever they felt like it. Even the Hospitallers in England had been tainted by sexual scandals: the young preceptor at Buckland had been removed in disgrace after rumours of fornication with the nuns they shared a building with. The Prior of England, under instruction from his superiors in Rhodes, had eventually replaced the young preceptor with a much older man, hoping it would put an end to any more scandals.

Stephen took all his vows seriously. He had dedicated his life to the service of Christ and his Hospitaller master, Sir Richard. He had been terribly drunk the night he had slept with the lovely olive-skinned girl in Rhodes. In fact, he had been so drunk, he could barely remember what had happened, but he knew the alcohol had rendered him incapable of any legendary feats of lovemaking.

He felt guilty – dirty even, that he had broken his vows. But, deep down, it rankled even more because he couldn't remember much of it.

At least if he had a clear memory of an incredible night's loving with a dusky beauty the guilt and shame might be worth it!

Irritably, he turned away from the flame-haired girl and drained the last of his ale, shouting at the bar-keep to refill his mug.

Christ, that ale was strong, right enough!

His head swam slightly after just one mug and he knew he'd have to take it easy – and be in bed early – if he was to be off for Clerkenwell at dawn the following morning.

He sat watching the musician for a while, the ale and the warmth of the room seeping into his bones. He hadn't felt this relaxed in a long time and he savoured the feeling.

Another ale went down and he found himself tapping his foot in time with the music, although it would take an awful lot of alcohol to make the gruff Hospitaller join in with the raucous singing.

"May I sit with you, sir?"

Startled out of his comfortable reverie, Stephen looked around and was shocked to see the gorgeous red-head sitting down at his table.

117

There was no sign of her elderly male companion.

"Where's your father, girl?"

"He's had enough of Hobb's ale," she laughed, her brown eyes sparkling as she nodded towards the busy inn-keeper. "He makes it too strong, and my da can only handle a few before he can barely stand up. So I sent him home, but I felt like staying and listening to the music for a while." She looked at the sergeant-at-arms somewhat sheepishly. "A girl can't be seen out on her own though can she? I'd be the talk of the village, sitting in an alehouse, drinking by myself."

Stephen raised his eyebrows. "But you won't be the talk of the place for sitting with a stranger?"

The girl smiled again, pushing her long red hair away from her face. "You're a Hospitaller. A man of God. I'm safe with you – I might as well be sitting with the pope himself."

She was really quite beautiful Stephen thought to himself, his eyes lingering on her smiling face.

"Aye, lass, I suppose so. Unless you mean Benedict."

Pope Benedict IX had, almost three hundred years earlier, been notorious for his sexual depravity – being accused of everything from homosexuality to rape and even murder – but the girl looked blankly at Stephen, clearly having no idea what he was on about.

"Never mind," he grunted, signalling Hobb to bring another couple of ales over. "You're safe with me, but it's been a long time since I sat drinking with a woman. You might find my conversation boring."

She grinned and leaned against him for a second, nudging him companionably with her shoulder. "Let's just listen to the music for a bit then, eh?"

The girl seemed totally oblivious to how attractive she was, or she wouldn't be acting so familiar with strange men, Stephen thought. He looked at her as she watched the minstrel, enjoying the sight of her perfectly rounded nose, full lips and trim figure.

She suddenly turned to him, catching him watching her, and smiled, curling her tongue onto her teeth, her green eyes shining, before turning her gaze back to the minstrel. From any other woman such a look would have been openly wanton, yet this girl appeared to be simply having fun, enjoying life to the full.

Silently, the Hospitaller swore to himself as he felt his loins tingle and his trousers begin to bulge.

The ale had gone to his head and he felt confused. A man of his age and experience should know better, but the presence of the stunning red-head was playing havoc with his emotions. He didn't know whether he was falling in love or just desperately wanted to lie with her, but, without even realising it, he stared at the girl, his eyes drinking in the sight of her as she moved slightly, almost dancing in her seat to the music.

Every now and again she would look at him and grin.

Before too long Stephen had lost track of the time, his mission forgotten, and he found himself singing and dancing with the girl, whose name he still never knew, amongst the other drunken revellers in the Wheatsheaf.

Eventually though, the powerful drink was too much for the Hospitaller and he sat down, his head spinning, nursing the dregs in his mug breathlessly.

"You're worse than my da!" The girl laughed, leaning against him and shouting in his ear over the music. He grinned blearily, enjoying the fleeting touch of her mouth and the feel of her breasts pressing gently on his arm.

He looked at her and she gazed back, her wide green eyes surprisingly alert.

"Come on, I'll help you to your room. You need to go to bed."

Even though he was by now well in his cups, Stephen somehow stopped himself from replying, *Aye, and I need you to come with me.*

His body ached to be closer to her though, as she helped him along the narrow hallway to his guest room.

He never wondered how she knew where his chamber was, and he never noticed the disapproving look Hobb threw the red-head as she escorted the Hospitaller out of the common room.

Stephen was drunk, and, for now, hopelessly besotted; his vow of chastity forgotten once again.

When she closed and bolted the door to his room behind them and, with another bright smile, kissed him, her tongue forcing its way into his mouth, the Hospitaller felt closer to heaven than he ever had killing men in the name of God.

CHAPTER TEN

Robin awoke feeling like he'd barely slept. He worked his neck from side to side with a grimace, hearing the tight muscles pop as he made his way to the stream by their camp to wash his face.

Two of his men – friends – had died yesterday. Tuck was in an unnaturally deep sleep, despite the holy relic. And he desperately missed his wife, Matilda, despite their falling out the last time he'd seen her.

He sighed as he knelt on the grass by the gently bubbling water next to the outlaws' camp-site and threw handfuls of the freezing liquid over his face. He wouldn't let the gloom take him again, he vowed, forcing himself to put his troubles to one side and just enjoy the sights and sounds of the hazy spring morning.

It promised to be a warm one, once the sun climbed high enough to burn away the clouds.

"God give you good morning!" Much wandered over to his friend's side and mimicked his actions, stooping to wash the grit from his eyes with the fresh water of the stream. "Ah, that feels good!" He grinned, wiping his face with his palms, but his own expression fell as he looked at Robin.

Since his father had been murdered by Wakefield's previous bailiff Much hadn't been the joyful young man Robin had known growing up in the village. It wasn't in his nature to channel his emotions into rage and violence, the way Will Scarlet had done for so long.

Instead, Much had drawn into himself, some days barely managing a smile.

Robin felt guilty as he saw the grin on his friend's face disappear.

"What are we like?" the young outlaw leader asked, forcing a laugh. "It wasn't us that were killed by

Gisbourne yesterday – we shouldn't be so morose. Come on!"

He stood up, smiling, and dragged Much up with him by the arm.

"The men won't want to do much today after James and Paul were done in by that prick Gisbourne, but I don't want to hang around here feeling down all day. Fancy coming hunting with me? Or fishing?"

Much smiled in return. "Aye, that'd be good. Let's get our stuff and head out."

They made their way back to camp and gathered their weapons, along with food and some ale skins.

"Ho, Robin! Off hunting?"

The outlaw captain turned and, instinctively, felt his heart sink as he saw Matt Groves walking towards him. His annoyance turned to guilt though, as he remembered Matt's ordeal and fortunate escape of the day before, and knew he should have probably been nicer to the man than he'd been at the time.

"Aye, Matt!" he nodded, clapping the older man on the arm. "Me and Much don't fancy spending the day sitting about feeling sorry for ourselves so we're going to do some hunting and fishing."

Groves looked upset, which was most unlike him, and Robin knew the previous day's meeting with Gisbourne had taken its toll on the sullen outlaw.

"You want to come along with us?"

The words were those of a good leader. A man who wanted to do the best for his men. Yet, when they were out, Robin kicked himself. He couldn't fucking stand Matt Groves!

But Matt's face lit up, as if one of the girl's at Nottingham's *Maiden's Head* had offered him a freebie. "Aye, that'd be good! Give me a minute to get my longbow."

He hurried over to his bedroll, as Much rejoined Robin with a questioning frown. Robin simply shrugged and rolled his eyes.

They decided to head southwest, in the direction of Barnsley, hoping to bring down a young deer or at least a few rabbits, before spending some time by the bank of the River Dearne with their ale-skins.

Ah well, Robin mused as they made their way quietly through the undergrowth, the sun just beginning to appear through the clouds and fresh spring foliage. *Maybe me and Matt will be able to put aside our past differences and become friends today...*

Somehow it didn't seem likely, but they were on their way now.

* * *

When the bright sunlight coming through a gap in the curtains woke him Stephen cursed as he realised he'd overslept. His mouth felt dry and his head ached.

As the fog in his brain slowly started to lift and fragments of the previous evening returned to him, he desperately reached under the bed, hoping the innkeeper had place a chamber pot there.

Grasping the filthy metal vessel gratefully he dragged it out and dropped to his knees on the hard floorboards, vomiting copiously.

Spitting the last of the bitter bile from his mouth, gasping, he sat back down on the bed guiltily.

He'd been given an important mission to complete, yet here he was, dawn long since broken, wasting time, while Sir Richard fretted back in Kirklees.

There was no sign of the girl and, as he realised he was still fully clothed he sighed, both with relief and disappointment.

He hadn't broken his vow of chastity then – but she would have been worth it.

Shaking his head ruefully, he collected his belongings, intending to make his way downstairs, down another of those strong local ales and be on his way to Clerkenwell with all haste.

"Shit!" he cursed, as he finally noticed the coin-purse at his belt was gone. "She robbed me!"

He hadn't been carrying much money, but that wasn't the point. Furious and embarrassed at the realisation the girl had played him like a gittern he patted the pocket sewn inside his mantle and his blood ran cold.

She'd taken the letter.

He retched into the stinking chamber-pot again, his mind whirling. Maybe he'd put the letter somewhere last night?

Searching the small area frantically, he roared in frustration and hurried from the room.

It was a small inn, which was just as well, as Stephen couldn't remember making his way from the common-room to his chamber the previous night, but there was only the one narrow corridor leading to the main hall.

His weapons were thankfully still with him, and he placed his left hand on the pommel of his sword as he stormed into the bar, seeing the inn-keeper, Hobb, at one of the tables, eating a large breakfast of bread and cheese.

The man looked up with an obviously guilty expression, but he painted a smile on his round face as the Hospitaller stalked over to him.

"Morning, my lord! You'll be wanting some breakfast eh?" The stout man stood up and made to move towards the bar area. "An ale, perhaps?"

Stephen moved straight for him, grabbing the man by the throat and shoving him backwards until his spine was bent painfully over the bar.

"The girl. Where does she live?"

"The red-head you were with last night? I don't know where she lives!" the inn-keeper gasped in fright. "She's not a regular. I've only seen her in here a couple of times. Please, you're hurting me!"

"I've not even started yet, you lying sack of shit," the sergeant-at-arms growled. "You know who she is. She must have done this before to other guests of yours. Do you get a cut of whatever she steals, eh?" He squeezed Hobb's throat tighter and the man struggled to free himself, but Stephen was a powerful man who knew how to restrain someone.

"It's not like that!" the inn-keeper wheezed. "Please – her man's a maniac. They threatened to burn down my inn if I didn't let them rob people. The girl gets travellers drunk, steals their purse, and then pays me the room's rent for the night. I don't make anything out of it!"

The Hospitaller slowly released the pressure on the man's neck and let him sink to the ground, where he sat, desperately trying to suck in air.

Stephen walked behind the bar and lifted a mug, filling it from one of the ale casks. He downed it in seconds and refilled it, watching Hobb struggle upright onto the chair beside the table he'd been eating his bread and cheese at.

"Here," the Hospitaller placed the ale in front of the panting Hobb, who looked at him suspiciously, then gratefully sipped some of it to ease the burning in his throat.

"How long have they been doing this?"

Hobb lowered his head, clearly ashamed of his small part in the scam. "About two months. They're not from around here. Turned up out of the blue one day, but her man, Jacob, said he was a blacksmith. The village hadn't had a proper smith since old Simon died close to a year ago, so they were welcomed."

He sipped some more of the ale, flinching slightly as Stephen stood up, but the sergeant was simply going to get more ale for himself.

"What about her da?"

The inn-keeper looked puzzled for a moment, then shook his head. "The old man that was with her when you came in? That's not her da, just one of the locals. She sits with whoever she pleases and, to be honest, the old men are happy to have company like that for the evening."

Stephen swallowed his ale with a scowl, rubbing his pounding temples.

"I'm sorry," Hobb mumbled. "You didn't lose much money did you?"

"The money's not the problem. I was carrying a letter and she took it. That letter is, literally, a matter of life and death for my master. So, you can see why I need it back."

The inn-keeper's face paled as he understood what Stephen was saying.

"You can't just go demanding it back, they'll kill you! Then they'll kill me!"

Stephen glared at the cowering man. "They'll have a hard time killing me. As for you, you'd better speak to your village headman, because I *will* get that letter back. Tell me something – why haven't the locals run these bastards out of town?"

"Like I said, the village needs a smith. Besides, they only ever target travellers, not locals, and they never steal their clothes or weapons – generally the men wake up and are so ashamed of what's happened they go on their way without making a fuss."

Stephen checked his weapons and armour were all fitted securely, and drained the last of his ale, fixing Hobb with an icy stare.

"Well, this time they robbed the wrong man."

* * *

As the sun reached its zenith and the three outlaws had only managed to shoot a couple of small brown hares, Much muttered about a wasted morning.

"Ach, stop moaning," Robin laughed at his friend. "Maybe we'll have better luck fishing."

Matt snorted. "We can't go back to camp with nothing but a couple of hares and some fish to show for a day's work. The lads wouldn't let us live it down."

They walked on in gloomy silence for a while longer then Matt spoke quietly, his voice almost

126

reverent. "When I was going to Darton with James and Paul the other day we saw the biggest stag I've ever seen. His horns were the size of a house! Herne himself didn't have horns like that."

Robin shrugged, liking the idea of relaxing by the riverbank with their ale skins better than chasing about the forest, but Much jumped on Matt's comment.

"Where did you see this stag?"

Matt's forehead creased in thought, then he pointed off to the east. "Around Wheatley Wood. Not too far from Darton itself. It saw us though, and buggered off into the trees before any of us could string our bows."

"Let's see if we can find it then. Wheatley Wood must be only a couple of miles from here."

Robin groaned. Walking such a distance, on the off-chance that they might be able to find this great stag, seemed a much poorer choice to him than fishing and drinking by the Dearne. Matt comparing the animal to Herne the Hunter also seemed a bad omen: Robin had become an outlaw at the previous year's May Day games in Wakefield when their new prior had taken offence to the villagers' celebration of pagan times. The churchman's venomous face came back to the young man, glaring around at the villagers.

"Heathens! The lot of you!" the prior had shouted. "Animal sacrifice? Herne the Hunter? Green Men?"

Robin had eventually broken the man's nose when he'd laid hands on Matilda.

The young wolf's head would prefer to forget Herne and his great horns.

But Much and Groves, curse him, had altered course and were now heading for Wheatley Wood. Robin grumpily fell into step behind them.

He knew it had been a bad idea to invite Matt along.

* * *

127

It wasn't Stephen's style to come up with some elaborate plan. That was the main reason why he'd never been promoted any higher than a sergeant-at-arms within the Hospitallers.

He didn't analyse situations in great detail – he was a doer, not a thinker.

So, while Sir Richard-at-Lee would have found some way to get the smith – Jacob – and his female accomplice on their own, somewhere out of sight, to avoid any trouble, Stephen simply followed Hobb's directions – and the sounds of metal on metal – to the smithy near the outskirts of the village.

There was no sign of the girl, but the bald man with the ginger moustache working the forge was enormous. Standing almost as tall as the outlaw from Barnsdale that people called Little John, the smith's upper body was bare except for a leather apron. Sweat glistened on his hard arm and chest muscles as he worked a set of bellows, and the Hospitaller knew he had to be wary of the big ox.

"You." Stephen strode up to the front of the workshop and fixed the smith with a calm gaze. He rested his left hand on the pommel of his sword, but made no threatening moves. "I don't have the time or inclination to talk about this with you. I want the letter your slut of a wife stole from me."

Jacob's eyes glanced at the villagers working and passing nearby. He didn't look at all frightened by the imposing sergeant-at-arms clad in chain mail in front of his shop, but Stephen guessed his unconscious look around at the locals betrayed his desire to avoid a scene in public. The blacksmith had a good thing going here, and clearly didn't want to jeopardise it.

The big man calmly wiped the sweat from his brow and walked around his forge, removing his apron as he went and tossing it onto his workbench.

Some of the locals had stopped to watch what was happening, muttering to each other with interest.

They all knew, or had heard rumours, about the smith and his shameful wife, and the sight of this grizzled soldier coming to take the enormous Jacob to task was something no one wanted to miss. The couple were tolerated because the villagers needed nails made, weapons or tools mended and horses shod, but they weren't liked.

Especially the smith's red-haired wife. The local women hated her for her beauty and flirtatious manner, totally unbecoming in a Christian lady. They also hated her because they could see their husbands eyeing her lustfully every time she walked past.

As the smith walked out of his workshop, meaty hands raised placatingly towards the Hospitaller, a crowd of neighbouring women began to form, clustering in little groups to talk in low voices as they watched the scene with disapproving looks.

They were loving it, Stephen knew. Well, he'd give them something to enjoy if this big bastard didn't hand over the letter and his money.

"My lord" – the smith began as he came closer to the angry sergeant, but Stephen cut him off, pulling his sword from its leather sheath and pointing it towards Jacob's groin as the gossiping women squealed in obvious delight and children ran off to spread the word amongst the rest of the villagers.

"I'm not a lord, and I told you: I don't have time to talk about this. I want that letter back, or I'll" –

"You'll what?" Jacob laughed. "You wanted to share a bed with my wife, Helena, did you?" The crowd gasped in outrage at that, and the smith, apparently enjoying himself raised his voice over the muttering. "Aye, tried to get her drunk and took her back to his room to try and put his seed inside her, this so-called *soldier of God!*"

Stephen hadn't expected things to go like this, and he mentally kicked himself for not thinking things through before he barged in, sword drawn.

"Now he's angry because he got drunk and lost something, and he's turned up here to blame my good wife. Aye, she told me all about it this morning, Hospitaller! She fought you off and made her way home to me, while you must have passed out after all the ale you'd had. You're a disgrace to your Order!"

The men in the crowd muttered angrily, glaring at Stephen. This wasn't going well at all, he realised. The sorceress hadn't just bewitched him last night, she'd bewitched all the men of the village too, and now they were going to take the side of the lying smith!

He looked around warily, watching for signs of an attack, as the blacksmith gave him a smug look and some of the men began to move forward menacingly, no doubt to try and restrain him.

Oh fuck, the Hospitaller thought to himself as he hefted his sword defensively, glancing around to see where the first attack would come from. *This isn't going to go down too well with the Prior. Or Sir Richard.*

"You're a filthy liar, Jacob!"

Stephen's gaze flicked to the left, as an overweight woman shoved her way through the watching crowd, past the surprised men in front of her. She must have been a good-looking girl in her youth, Stephen thought, but she'd lost her figure through time and, no doubt, a few childbirths.

"Everyone in Finchley knows your wife's a whore!"

The smith's face was dark with rage, but he held his silence as more of the local women pushed past their men to stand by their portly leader.

"You tell him, Mary, it's time someone did!" one of the women bellowed, ordering her mortified husband to shut-up as she forced her way through the throng to stand by her neighbour.

"Your wife, Helena, gets travellers so drunk they can barely stand up," Mary shouted indignantly. "Flutters her long eyelashes at them, flashes her tits, and then steals their purses from them when she gets them alone."

The smith, almost foaming at the mouth, spotted Mary's husband in the crowd and shouted at him. "You better shut your wife's mouth, Alfred. I'll not hit a woman, but I've no problem breaking *your* face!"

Stephen found himself grinning as the crowd howled indignantly at the smith's loss of control. Things were definitely swinging back in his favour, he thought.

Jacob looked over at him, furiously, and tensed himself to move forward to attack the sergeant-at-arms, but Mary and her cronies, fuelled by their righteous anger, crowded in on the big smith, pointing their fingers and yelling, feeding on each other's outrage.

The Hospitaller slid his sword back into its sheath as he realised the danger to him had passed. The villagers – thanks to the petty jealousy of a few vocal women – were on his side.

He folded his arms, watching the scene unfold in front of him with satisfaction.

He was surprised a moment later to find himself face-down on the hard earth of the street, the back of his head exploding with pain.

* * *

By the time they reached Wheatley Wood Robin was sweating heavily. For some reason Matt had set a much brisker pace than seemed necessary, but, although he was their leader, Robin was still a proud young man, full of bravado, and didn't like to show any sign of discomfort so he simply matched Matt's hasty stride without complaint.

He was damned if he couldn't keep up with a man more than double his age.

"Christ, I'm sweating like a Templar on Friday the 13th," Much grunted. "Are we nearly there yet, Matt?"

Groves had been looking around constantly for the past while, his eyes looking for landmarks, and he nodded in satisfaction as they finally reached the main road through the forest. "Aye, this is the spot."

Robin wondered at the bright, almost manic stare in the older man's eyes, and then his blood ran cold as a number of armed men appeared from behind the foliage around them.

His eyes were drawn instinctively to the black-armoured, smiling man holding the crossbow. "Gisbourne..!"

"Well met, Hood." Sir Guy bowed with a flourish, never taking his eyes from England's most wanted wolf's head. "This time, I'm afraid you won't be escaping. Drop your weapons."

Much glared at Matt Groves, his face scarlet with rage. "You sold us out you arsehole!"

"Aye, I did," Matt retorted fiercely, turning from Much to fix Robin with an angry glare. "You've brought us nothing but trouble since you appeared, Hood. Lording it over the rest of us as if you were the king, or Hugh Despenser himself! Well, no more, you little prick! Sir Guy here will see you hung like the scum you are, and I get a pardon for my trouble."

"What about the rest of the men?" Much shouted. "How can you betray the men who've been like brothers to you for so long?"

Gisbourne cut in, shaking his head with a bored expression. "Matt here didn't tell us where the rest of your men are hiding. They're not important to me. The king demanded I bring him the head of Robin Hood, and now I have him." He waved his black crossbow towards Robin and Much. "Take them."

As Gisbourne's soldiers moved in Groves took a step back, smiling wickedly.

Much, totally enraged, felt the hurt and tension of the previous year exploding inside him. His right hand dropped to his belt and he whipped his sword from its simple leather sheath.

Time slowed to a crawl for Robin as his childhood friend's face twisted in a feral scowl, teeth bared and eyes bulging as he lunged forward, but Matt, still a dangerous man despite his middle-age, saw the attack coming.

Flicking his own sword out and around in time to deflect the blow, Groves rammed his forehead forward into Much's face, shattering the young man's nose.

Much stumbled backwards, reeling, and Robin heard the click as Gisbourne pulled the trigger on his crossbow. The bolt hammered into Much's chest just as Groves leaned forward, placing his body weight onto his right leg, and shoved the point of his sword into the miller's son's stomach.

Robin screamed. It wasn't a battle cry; it was a mournful sound, as he watched the young man who had been his friend throughout his whole life die in agony.

By the time Robin realised he should fight back, someone had come up behind him and battered the pommel of their sword into the base of his skull, throwing him to the ground, stunned.

The attacker dropped onto his spine, pressing him into the forest floor, as others grasped his arms and legs, holding him fast.

As the dark figure of Sir Guy of Gisbourne approached, Robin felt tears coursing down his face and he struggled to rise. To fight. To kill this bastard people called The *Raven*.

"Leave the dead one for the crows, and bind this one," Gisbourne growled, looking down at the young outlaw with a satisfied smile. "It seems we have a wolf's head to hang."

CHAPTER ELEVEN

For the second time that day, Stephen awoke with a throbbing head and a moan of pain.

His hand moved to the back of his skull and he felt, through the bandage someone had applied, a tender lump half the size of a hen's egg.

"You're lucky she never cracked your skull," someone told him, and he flicked his eyes to the dimly lit corner of the room. "If she'd found a bigger rock you wouldn't be here now. Crazy bitch."

It was the heavy woman from earlier – the loud one – Mary, was it? This must be her house, Stephen realised.

"Where are they?" he growled, swinging his legs over the side of the pallet he'd been lifted onto and getting to his feet somewhat unsteadily.

"Gone." Mary nodded in satisfaction, putting down the threadbare cloak she was mending and leaning forward so the dim light of the cooking fire illuminated her round features. "After that little slut hit you with the rock, we ran the pair of them out of town. The men weren't too happy at losing a blacksmith, but we couldn't have them here any more. They were wicked. Finchley's a God-fearing village, and they were turning the place into a den of sin!"

She filled a cup with ale and handed it to the Hospitaller but he waved it away. "I've had enough of the ale in this place," he muttered. "Do you have any water, lady?"

As she moved to fetch him a drink, he asked where Jacob and his wife had gone. "They have a hugely important letter from my lord," he told her. "I must get it back."

"You could try searching their house," Mary shrugged, pushing the mug of cool water into his hand.

"They weren't given much time to collect their belongings – the villagers were in a right fury."

Aye, stirred up by you, Stephen thought to himself, imagining the scene.

"There's a good chance your letter will still be there."

He handed her back the empty cup with a word of thanks and asked her to point him towards the blacksmith's newly-vacated home, shading his eyes from the early afternoon sun as he went. He cursed as he noticed the positions of the shadows, realising he must have been unconscious for an hour or two. He couldn't afford to lose this time – Sir Richard was depending on him, in the name of Christ!

It only took a short time to reach the house, a small, single-storey wooden building with a poorly-thatched roof, where he found a man and a young boy of about nine years old.

"Ah, the good knight," the man smiled apologetically as Stephen walked across. "I'm the headman – Baldwin. This is my son, Geoffrey. I'm truly sorry for the terrible time you've had in our village" –

"Forget it," Stephen interjected. "It was my own fault. I'm here to search for a letter those two stole from me. May I?" He pushed his way inside, eyes scanning the single low room.

"You're welcome to look," Baldwin replied, "but me and the lad have already searched the place and put anything valuable aside for the village. We never saw any letter, did we?" He glanced at the boy, who agreed with his father in a small, high-pitched voice.

The house had few items of furniture, so it only took a few moments for Stephen to be sure his letter wasn't hidden anywhere. He swore colourfully, and the little boy grinned on hearing a new word to tell his friends.

"Which direction did they go?" the sergeant-at-arms asked, his patience now wearing very thin.

"They took the road south, brother knight," the headman pointed vaguely. "I heard the girl saying something about London. A place called Clarkson, or Clarking, I didn't really catch it right."

"Clerkenwell?" Stephen demanded in astonishment, and Baldwin nodded.

"Aye, that was it, I think. You know it?"

One of them must have been able to read. They were taking Sir Richard's letter to the Prior!

Why, though? What could they gain from it?

His blood ran cold as it dawned on him. They were going to make up some story about him – probably say he raped the girl, the blacksmith knocked him out and they found the letter on him. They'd be hoping for a reward.

Stephen knew exactly how believable that red-headed girl could be. The Prior would excommunicate him! And God knows what would happen to Sir Richard.

"I have to stop them!" he roared, racing back to the Wheatsheaf for his horse, calling over his shoulder at the bewildered headman. "Were they on foot?"

"No – they had a good looking palfrey. Just the one mind."

Only one mount between them, but a head-start of at least an hour.

There was no choice though – he *had* to stop them before they reached Clerkenwell!

* * *

Sir Richard took a long pull of his watered wine and gazed out over the battlements at the land around his stronghold.

Stephen had been gone a week – he should, hopefully, be on his way back home with good news from Prior L'Archer. The letter Sir Richard had sent virtually guaranteed the old man would do something to help the commander of Kirklees.

Sir Richard hated to resort to blackmail, but what other choice did he have? He'd kept the Prior's secret for ten years, never telling anyone else about it. And he'd take it to his grave too, as long as L'Archer made himself useful and did something to help him.

He took another sip of the wine and heaved an irritated sigh.

"I'm bloody sick of sitting here in this castle by myself," he growled, standing up and striding purposefully down the stairs to the armoury.

The king's men had returned to the castle only once since Stephen had ridden out, and their last visit was four days ago. They had clearly given up on taking the Hospitaller.

Well, he'd had enough of eating tough salted meat and dried fruit. He lifted a hunting bow from its place on the wall, and stuck a few arrows into his belt. A nice young rabbit would make a fine stew with some of the pickled vegetables in his undercroft, which he made his way through now, carrying a torch to light his way.

Making his way past the barrels, sacks, bottles and jars of stored food to the far corner of the cool, dark room he placed the smoky torch in an iron holder on the wall and, rolling a heavy barrel out of the way, found the trapdoor, just big enough for one man to fit through.

A heavy bolt held it locked, so he undid it quickly and lifted the thick wooden door open. He kept the hinges greased with goose-fat so it opened silently and he lifted the torch again, using it to illuminate the pitch-black stairway underneath.

He grinned as he remembered when he first took over the commandery here in Kirklees and his bottler – a local man named Luke – had told him of the existence of this secret passageway out of the castle. At first he had planned on closing it off: filling the tunnel with rubble and sealing the entrances, but he had eventually decided against it. Yes, it compromised the castle's security somewhat – but it would take a battering ram to break

137

through the doors and he knew from past experience an extra escape route might be useful one day.

 He had never used it before – he'd never had to. But it was coming in handy now.

He couldn't have simply raised the great iron portcullis and walked out the huge oak front doors. With no way to seal the entrance behind him, and no retainers to guard the place, the king's men – or anyone else passing by – could have simply walked in and taken control of the castle without a fight.

He made his way along the damp, narrow corridor stooping as he went since the ceiling was only as high as his shoulders, until, after a short time, he reached an iron door – again, bolted from the inside.

He undid the crude, but sturdy, locks and pushed the door to, squinting as the bright sunlight flooded the little passageway and the sounds of birds and insects came to him on a gust of fresh air, which he sucked in greedily.

The doorway was well hidden behind a thick clump of gorse and juniper bushes and he shoved his way through the foliage, swatting branches out of the way with his hand and revelling in the sense of freedom.

The thought gave him pause, as he reflected on the fate that awaited him should the king's men capture him. Days, weeks, months in a tiny cell, with only rats and his own shit and piss to keep him company…

"Let them try!" he smiled grimly, touching a hand to the hilt of his sword instinctively, then, looking around and, spotting a pair of little brown hares lounging on the grass he pulled an arrow silently from his quiver and slid his bow into his left hand.

An hour or two, hunting in the sunshine, then he'd return to the castle, cook up a nice, fresh stew and finish the wine he'd started earlier. Only this time he'd not water it down. He might even have a go on the old citole he'd been trying to learn for the past six years.

Praise be to God, he thought. *This would be a good day!*

* * *

As he kicked his heels into his mount, forcing it into a near-gallop, Stephen was thankful he at least knew which direction his quarry must have taken.

South. Towards London and the Grand Prior.

He cursed himself repeatedly as the spring countryside passed, wondering how he could have been stupid enough to allow this to happen.

In truth, he was being too hard on himself. Although not an ugly man – quite the opposite in fact, with his battle-hardened physique and square jaw – he wasn't exactly the magnetic type. Women didn't usually show an interest in him and, despite his vow of celibacy it hurt him when his master, Sir Richard, with his easy smile and outgoing nature drew admiring glances and giggles from girls young enough to be his grand-daughter.

When Helena had shown an interest in him, Stephen had been flattered. And, given her simple beauty, love of life and apparent sincerity, the Hospitaller sergeant had been utterly smitten.

The strong ale hadn't helped matters either.

Still, he derided himself for a fool. She had played him expertly, like that Allan-a-Dale character in Barnsdale played his gittern.

He dug his heels into his mount with an angry cry, pushing it close to its limit, knowing he only had a very short time to catch up with his quarry.

As the afternoon wore on the sun moved slowly around in the sky until it was directly above and before him. The trees that lined the road cast dark shadows directly behind themselves as the outskirts of the capital city slowly came into sight and Stephen, squinting, growled in frustration.

He was almost there yet had seen nothing of the blacksmith and his wife.

The Hospitaller felt his stomach lurch in despair as he realised he had failed his master, and probably ruined his own status within the Order he'd served faithfully for the past fifteen years.

His horse was blowing hard and sweating after being pushed hard for so long, and, with a sob of rage and defeat, Stephen allowed the beast to slow to a walk.

What now?

He wondered if he should turn back. Without Sir Richard's letter, the prior had no reason to send aid to Kirklees. Carrying on to Clerkenwell was pointless.

His head had ached for the past couple of hours, and a feeling of nausea made him want to retch as he squinted at the road ahead, contemplating his failed mission, the sunlight almost blinding him even though it offered little warmth.

"Wait!"

His horse paid him no attention as it trotted along the slightly muddy road, its sides still heaving from the day's run.

Stephen's raised his right hand, shading his eyes from the sunlight as he tried to see ahead.

His sight wasn't what it had been as a younger man, and he blinked as his eyes watered from staring along the road into the harsh sun. Still, there was no mistake.

At the side of the road stood a horse and, as the Hospitaller urged his mount into a canter, the abandoned horse looked at them with a bored expression.

Could it be the blacksmith's own horse had gone lame?

Daring not to hope, Stephen pushed his own mount forward, until, finally, his heart soared in jubilation.

There, casting great shadows along the road in their wake jogged two figures: a huge man and a willowy woman.

The pair must have noticed his approach since they tried to move faster, but the city was still a distance away and the Hospitaller bore down on them like the tide at a full-moon.

He drew his sword and roared as he charged along the road after the fleeing couple, the relief at finally catching up with his prey making him smile in triumph.

The jubilant grin dropped from his face as Helena suddenly turned, her beautiful features cloaked in shadow but her mane of hair flaming from the sunlight directly behind her. She held a bow – not a longbow, but a smaller hunting bow – and, as the sergeant-at-arms bore down on them the girl loosed her arrow.

"No!" Stephen cried in outrage, not just because he saw his plans ruined, again, but for the sake of his faithful horse, which slowed to a halt, Helena's missile stuck deep in its steaming chest.

As its front legs gave way the Hospitaller could see the red-haired girl about to loose again, this time at him, and he hastily unhooked the shield he had strapped to his mount, bringing it up just in time as the next arrow lodged itself in the wood covering his face.

"You fucking bitch!" he screamed, hurling himself from his expiring horse before Helena could shoot again.

The girl shrank away from his fury but Stephen slammed the pommel of his sword into her face, feeling her teeth smash as she was thrown backwards onto the ground.

His eyes flicked to his right, expecting an attack from the blacksmith. Although the battle-fury was upon him, the Hospitaller was an experienced soldier. He knew how to fight multiple enemies – had done so on countless occasions at the side of Sir Richard in England and the with others of his Order in Rhodes.

Jacob, although be was built like a warhorse, had none of Stephen's skill or experience. As he saw his wife battered to the ground the blacksmith roared and swung his big hammer at Stephen as if he was forging a horseshoe.

It was an incredibly powerful blow. If it had connected it would have smashed right through the sergeant's light armour into his ribcage but the Hospitaller saw it coming even before Jacob had fully begun his swing and he stepped lightly to the side, bringing his sword round as the man stumbled past, and hammered the blade viciously into the blacksmith's spine.

There was surprisingly little blood for such a devastating blow, and Jacob only gave a quiet, high-pitched gasp of agony as he collapsed, face-first, onto the road, his great torso jerking spasmodically.

Helena struggled to her feet, her eyes wide with disbelief at the sight of her crippled husband but, as her bloodied face contorted with rage, ready to launch herself at the Hospitaller, Stephen stepped towards her and grasped her around the throat with a gauntleted hand, squeezing hard to choke off her shouts.

"Shut up!" he growled, grasping her right hand as it flailed among her skirts for a weapon. "You brought this on yourself, and I've no more time to fuck about with the pair of you."

She tried to spit in his face but Stephen squeezed tighter and the spittle ran down her own chin as her eyes bulged defiantly at him.

"The letter you took from me," he said. "I want it. Your man's already as good as dead so I can search him for it. But you're still alive," he pressed his face against hers, feeling a surge of shame as he did so, remembering how he had felt so drawn to this sweet-looking girl just a few hours before.

He dropped her to the ground where she lay on her back, panting and staring up at him murderously, but he'd learned his lesson not to underestimate her, and he placed the point of his sword against her breast.

"You won't fool me again. Now where's the letter, Helena?"

"Fuck off, monk."

She stretched flat on the grass and gazed at him, her legs slightly parted, panting with exhaustion and somehow still exuding an air of innocence despite her smashed teeth. But Stephen had taken enough of this.

He leaned down and battered his sword hilt against her temple, watching as her head slumped to the side and she slipped into unconsciousness.

The smith was dead, Stephen could see, as he glanced over at the man face-down in the dirt. He sighed in resignation and methodically began to search the girl's clothes for his missing letter. He felt the beginnings of panic again when he couldn't find it, before he hurried over to Jacob, turned the huge man onto his back and, with nervous fingers, almost tore the giant's clothes apart in his search for the precious parchment.

"God be praised!"

The sergeant-at-arms smiled and exhaled in relief as he pulled the document – now unsealed but otherwise intact – from a pocket in the blacksmith's leather apron.

His mission was saved. All he had to do now was deliver the letter to the Prior in Clerkenwell.

"Ah shit," he growled, looking over at his dead horse. "I'll have to walk the rest of the way."

* * *

Sir Richard had managed to bring down three decent-sized hares before deciding that was enough. When he'd picked the little carcasses clean he could come back through the secret tunnel and catch some more, so it seemed wasteful to shoot anything else.

At first he'd been wary; jumping at the slightest noise, fearful the king's men might sneak up on him, but, after an hour, with the spring sunshine filtering gently through the fresh green foliage and birds and insects going about their business peacefully after the

143

short-lived snowfall yesterday, he started to relax and enjoy the freedom of being outside again.

How did Stephen fare? he wondered. Had his man made it to Clerkenwell safely? Richard knew his sergeant was a hardy fighter, so he was sure Stephen would have made it there safely.

Would the Prior send help though? This was the question that worried the veteran Hospitaller, but he shook the fears from his mind as he contemplated the letter he'd sent to his Order's headquarters.

Years ago – more than two decades ago in fact – before he became Grand Prior of England, Sir Thomas L'Archer had been Turcopolier in Cyprus, while Sir Richard had newly come to the Order, already a husband and father to two boys.

Richard knew, from entertaining travelling Hospitallers at his commandery in Kirklees recently, that L'Archer had become quite senile over the past few years. Indeed, the old man's administrative powers – once the stuff of legend – seemed to have utterly deserted him, and, as a result of the Prior's mismanagement the Order was practically bankrupt in England, despite their growth in the wake of the Templar's demise.

The Thomas L'Archer Sir Richard had known back in Rhodes had been a rather different character though. Far from being senile, he was as sharp as an arrowhead, with an easy smile and an outgoing, friendly way with the locals on the little island.

The sight of a young hart startled the knight from his idle reverie, but it spotted him before he could even think about nocking an arrow to his bow and disappeared silently back into the bushes.

Richard grinned at the sight of the beautiful animal, then he remembered the day he'd found Thomas L'Archer in a...compromising... position back in Cyprus, almost twenty years ago in 1304.

He'd felt like that frightened hart when he blundered into the room and seen the newly promoted

144

Turcopolier, prostrate on the floor, apparrently worshipping a stone head. The face was carved with a thick red beard and long hair and it bore a terrible expression which had chilled the new Hospitaller to the bone. He'd mumbled a stunned apology to his superior before closing the door and hurrying from the castle to try and make some sense of what he'd seen, and what he should do about it.

Richard had heard rumours of the rival Order, the Templars, worshipping idols and performing strange rituals, but he'd never expected to find one of his own brethren involved in anything so blasphemous. In the end, Sir Richard had done nothing. He'd never mentioned it to anyone, not even L'Archer, and the Turcopolier had never brought the subject up either.

He liked L'Archer and he was fearful the Order would be irreparably damaged, possibly even destroyed, if something like this became public. Besides, he wasn't even sure exactly what he'd witnessed, he told himself. So, Richard had held his silence on Cyprus, and later while stationed in Rhodes, and been glad of it a few years later when the Templars had been ruined as a result of similar accusations.

Thomas L'Archer was soon promoted even higher in the Order and Sir Richard had found his own fortunes improving as time went on, no doubt thanks to the influence of L'Archer who must have been quietly helping the younger knight in gratitude for his silence.

When L'Archer's close friend, William de Tothale, had been given the position of Grand Prior in England, Sir Richard had been offered the commandery at Kirklees, a place the new prior knew Richard had ties with, his family owning much of the surrounding lands.

Richard had never even considered blackmailing his superior for his own gain – it simply wasn't in his nature, he was far too honourable a man. And he had been rewarded for his silence.

But desperate times called for desperate measures. Without the help of the prior Sir Richard and his faithful sergeant-at-arms would be destitute, jailed, hanged even, while the king would seize the manor and all its lands from the Hospitallers.

That was why Sir Richard had, with a heavy heart, put in writing a threat to Thomas L'Archer: intervene with King Edward or I'll tell everyone your secret.

When Stephen delivered the letter to him, the prior would have no choice but to help. If the story got out the scandal would ruin him and irreparably damage the entire Order.

Sir Richard moved quietly through the trees, heading for the hidden entrance back into the castle, lost in thought. Yes, the prior would help, he was absolutely sure of it.

Or the Hospitallers might suffer the same fate as the Templars before them.

* * *

When Sir Philip of Portsmouth had ordered Edmond and Walter Tanner to remain close to Kirklees in case Sir Richard should try to escape the king's justice they had gladly agreed. Sir Philip was paying well enough, and all they had to do was sit around hiding in the trees close by the castle entrance where they could see who might go in or out. If Sir Richard set foot across the castle door, they were to ride to the village of Kirklees for help in capturing the Hospitaller. King Edward wanted to make a show of the noblemen who had rebelled against him.

Edmond and Walter were brothers and it was obvious to anyone who looked at them. Sons of the tanner in Kirklees and learning the trade themselves, Edmond was older and rather taller, but they shared the same thickset bodies, stumpy limbs and thin brown hair and beards. Walter wasn't the sharpest arrow in the quiver though, and, as children, Edmond had often been forced to defend his sibling from village bullies. Even now, when they went to the local alehouse Walter's dull wit seemed to antagonise drunk people. Fortunately they

146

were both able to handle themselves when it came to it, which was why Sir Philip, when he'd heard of their fighting skills, had left only the pair of them to make sure Sir Richard didn't escape justice.

"Christ, who's that? Is that Sir Richard?"

Walter barely glanced up at his brother's surprised whisper.

"It is! Fuck me, how did he get out here? We've been watching the front door of that castle for days and it hasn't moved!"

"It moved when his sergeant came out," Walter replied innocently.

"Shutup!" Edmond hissed irritably. "You should have woken me up; it's not my fault he escaped!"

In truth, Edmond had slept late the morning Sir Richard's sergeant-at-arms had disappeared along the road to the south. Walter had seen the horseman leaving, but, since he'd been told to watch for Sir Richard, hadn't bothered to waken his hungover brother.

"Never mind him anyway; Sir Philip doesn't have to know about that. We've got more to worry about – look!"

Walter finally turned to follow his older brother's pointing finger and smiled as he saw the figure some way off, moving between the undergrowth, oblivious to their presence.

"Look, it's Sir Richard!"

Edmond grinned and slapped his slower brother on the back. "Aye, it is. And he's alone, with no idea we're here or he wouldn't be out. Hunting, from the look of the game he's carrying."

"We'd better hurry then," Walter muttered, standing up and moving in the direction of the village.

"Wait!" Edmond replied, waving his sibling back.

"We need to hurry," Walter whined. "Or he'll get away, and Sir Philip will be angry with us."

"Sir Philip will be bloody overjoyed when he sees us coming," Edmond grinned, fingering the hilt of his sword. His smile disappeared as he realised his brother didn't understand what he meant. "We'll catch the knight by ourselves! Come on, move quietly, and have your weapon ready."

He moved stealthily into the foliage and headed towards the unwary Hospitaller.

"Edmond, we can't!" Walter hurried behind fretfully, drawing his own poor quality sword silently from its worn old hide sheath. "He's a knight! He knows how to fight. We should go to the village and tell the men to catch him."

"We know how to fight too!" Edmond retorted. "He's alone, and hasn't seen us. We ambush him, take his weapons and lead him to Sir Philip. He'll reward us! Those arseholes in the village won't laugh at us then."

The pair flitted through the trees, making their way to a place Edmond knew would make a fine spot for their ambuscade.

Walter didn't like to argue with his sibling. He knew he wasn't as smart as Edmond, and he knew his big brother always tried to do what was best for them.

He set his jaw and gripped the hilt of his sword firmly. If Edmond said they could take the knight, that's what they were going to do.

They came to a large patch of juniper and Edmond motioned for Walter to hide at the back of it, where the little overgrown path came past. "Wait here. When you see Sir Richard coming, step out with your sword and order him to stop. I'll be over there." He pointed to the thick trunk of an old beech tree. "When you stop him, I'll come up behind and stick the point of my sword into his spine."

Walter grimaced. "Don't kill him, Ed, he's been a good lord to us."

Edmond shook his head and waved his brother behind the bush. "I won't, I'll just let him know he better surrender to us. Now, go!"

The knight was in no hurry, it seemed, and Edmond started to think he'd changed course or even returned to his castle by whichever means he'd exited it.

Eventually, though, the sounds of heavy footfalls reached him and he tensed, looking over to make sure Walter couldn't be seen behind the thick branches.

As if he hadn't a care in the world, Sir Richard appeared, whistling gently to himself, and Edmond smiled, the blood coursing through his veins in nervous anticipation.

"Stop!" Walter, small and short of limb as he was, had an imposing glare at times, as if he might go completely, and violently, crazy. He brandished his sword at the stunned knight, who, for a moment wasn't sure how to react.

"Aye!" Edmond slipped out from behind the beech and pressed his sword against Sir Richard's back. "Stop."

The Hospitaller vaguely recognized the small man in front of him from the village. The tanner's son: a nice lad, if a little touched. "What do you men want?" he demanded. "You realize I could cut you both down in seconds if I choose?"

Walter looked nervously over his shoulder, as if he wanted to run away, but Edmond confidently pressed the point of his blade harder into the gambeson Sir Richard wore.

"Shut up. One move and I gut you like were planning on doing to those rabbits at your belt."

As he finished speaking, Edmond was surprised to find himself on the grass, his nose bloody and the point of a sword at his throat.

The Hospitaller had moved with incredible speed, drawing his blade as he spun through one hundred and eighty degrees and hammering the pommel into Edmond's face before the young villager could react. Edmond had under-estimated the knight, and yet, the knight had under-estimated Walter.

The little man had reacted instantly as he saw the attack on his beloved big brother, rushing forward and swinging his blade with terrible force at the veteran Crusader.

Sir Richard saw the attack just in time. He brought his own sword up, pushing Walter's weapon to the side and, instinctively, reversed his swing and dragged the blade across the inside of the man's thigh.

A killing cut.

It severed the artery, and as blood bubbled from the wound Walter collapsed on the grass in shock, staring at his brother, too surprised to even try to hold the wound shut.

Sir Richard watched the lad fall, horrified, as, unbidden, the memory of his own son's killing less than a year earlier flashed through his mind.

Then there was a scream – a scream of anguish like he'd never heard before, and the world went black.

CHAPTER TWELVE

"Wake up, you bastard!"

Sir Richard felt as if he was drowning, somehow trapped underwater, and his mind tried desperately to reach the surface again.

"Get up!"

He heard the voice again, clearer now, and he felt his arm being kicked roughly but he was too dazed to react.

As his eyes opened, he saw Edmond glaring down at him, his grubby face tracked with white streaks where tears had wiped away some of the grime.

The young man bent down and tried to haul the Hospitaller to his feet, but Sir Richard was too heavy, and, with an anguished sob, Edmond let him drop, aiming a half-hearted kick at his arm again, before sitting on the grass himself.

"You killed Walter."

The young man was staring straight ahead, seeing nothing, and Sir Richard knew he should strike the boy down while he had the chance, but he was too weak. The back of his head ached, and he realised Edmond must have given him a lump the size of an egg with the pommel of that cheap sword. He was lucky if his skull wasn't cracked.

Groaning, Sir Richard rolled onto all-fours and tried to sit up, retching as his fingers gently probed the back of his aching head. "You and your brother were taking me to my death – can you blame me for defending myself?"

Edmond didn't reply as his eyes turned to look at his brother's corpse which lay in patch of crimson grass and shook his head mournfully.

Sir Richard's fingers flexed tentatively as he noticed Edmond hadn't disarmed him – his sword lay beside him, within easy reach.

The younger man noticed the Hospitaller's body language and jumped back to his feet with a snarl, pointing his blade at Sir Richard's face. "Get up you old bastard, get up! You won't get away with murdering my little brother – I'm taking you to Sir Philip. I'm going to watch you hang!"

As Sir Richard shakily rose to his feet Edmond moved in and lifted the finely crafted Hospitaller sword, tossing his own inferior weapon into the bushes. He hefted the expensive weapon appreciatively, and placed it against the knight's cheek.

"I know you have a dagger about you somewhere – give me it."

Knowing it was pointless to deny the presence of his second blade, Sir Richard slowly removed the short dagger from the leather sheath on his belt and handed it to the volatile bounty-hunter who tucked it into the frayed old rope he wore as a belt himself.

"Right. Move."

Edmond gestured with his sword, east, in the direction of Pontefract, and Sir Richard groggily moved forward.

The younger man's eyes fixed again on the body of his brother and it was clear he didn't really know what to do. Should he leave Walter lying here, where foxes and crows would come to tear the eyeballs and flesh to pieces? What about the last rites?

With another tortured sob, Edmond punched Sir Richard in the small of the back, shouting at him to move as the old knight staggered forward in pain. There was nothing else to do – they couldn't bury Walter and there was no way to carry him.

"Get on with you, Hospitaller! I'll see you to Pontefract, then come back to take care of Walter." His voice broke as he finished and he kicked Sir Richard in the backside angrily.

They moved along the overgrown trail in silence, the knight slowly coming back to full consciousness, knowing his grieving captor would, eventually, let his guard down.

And then Sir Richard would get away. Because Edmond didn't know about the other little dagger concealed in his boot.

* * *

"He's awake!"

When he saw Friar Tuck's eyes flutter open, the grin on Little John's face was so wide it threatened to swallow his beard.

"Tuck's awake!" he shouted again as the rest of the men ran over to join him.

The friar groaned weakly as he tried to focus on the figures around him. "Gisbourne shot me," he muttered. "Then I drowned. I must have died twice…If this is heaven, there's a hell of a lot of ugly men up here."

The outlaws bellowed with laughter at the joke, not because it was very funny, but because they were all relieved and overjoyed to see the cheery clergyman back in the land of the living.

"What happened?" Tuck asked, as John knelt beside him.

"You're right, Gisbourne shot you and you fell in the River Don. But Gareth here jumped in and hauled you out. He's a hero!" John grabbed the young man by the arm and pulled him down beside them.

"Really? A skinny lad like you managed to pull a fat friar like me out of that?"

Gareth nodded, embarrassed again by the attention. "Not so fat now though, Tuck," he replied, eyeing the clergyman's shrunken waistline. "You've been unconscious for a few days."

Tuck nodded slightly. "I feel as weak as a newborn babe."

"Here." Allan-a-Dale hurried over carrying a bowl of venison stew, as John and Gareth helped Tuck sit up. Allan lifted the bowl to the friar's lips, feeding him small sips while John finished the story of his rescue and miraculous recovery.

"Praise be to St Peter," he whispered, closing his eyes with exhaustion as Allan wiped spilled stew from his face like a wet-nurse. "May I see this relic of his?"

"It's right here," John nodded, lifting the ornate little reliquary from the ground where he'd placed it as Tuck sat up to eat. "Been sitting on your chest for a while now. Looks like it works, just as Father Nicholas said it would."

As the giant outlaw lifted the box for Tuck to see, the friar's eyes narrowed for a moment as he studied the meticulous carvings and obviously superior workmanship.

"Christ our Lord," he breathed, and the men grunted agreement.

"Give it to me," Tuck gasped, opening his palm, his eyes fixed on the reliquary.

"Fancy eh?" Will grinned as Little John placed the box onto Tuck's hand. "Shame none of us could figure out how it opens" –

Scarlet stopped, open-mouthed, as the friar moved his fingers and the reliquary sprung open.

"Here, that's not St Peter's finger!" Will exclaimed.

"No, it's not," Tuck agreed, still staring at the relic. "It's hairs from Our Lord Christ's beard. I don't know how it ended up in Brandesburton, but this little box is the reason I'm an outlaw!"

* * *

"We're going to hang you, wolf's head."

Robin glared at Gisbourne's sergeant, Nicholas Barnwell, as the man threw him a malevolent gap-toothed grin. "Ever seen someone hang? I bet you have –

154

you know what it does to you. You'll shit yourself like a babe, while everyone watches."

Robin held his peace. They had bound his hands behind his back and he was still in shock at the death of his childhood friend. That wasn't the only thing that kept him silent though.

He felt ashamed to admit it, but he *was* frightened. Barnwell was right – he had seen men and women hanged before. It was a humiliating and often slow death, if the hangman didn't lean on the person to ease their suffering.

Besides that, the face of Matilda haunted him. She carried his child. His life had come to nothing, and now Gisbourne would end it like he ended Much.

Yes, he was frightened. But he straightened his back and pushed out his chest, towering over the men leading him to the jail in Nottingham.

Barnwell noticed and threw him another spiteful grin.

"You won't feel so big when we get you to the castle, boy. Sir Guy will probably use you as a sparring partner before your trial. He'll tear you to shreds."

"Why don't I spar with you right now, you ugly old bastard?" Robin finally found his voice but his captor just laughed and rode ahead to join his captain at the front of the group, leaving Robin to be dragged along by a couple of footmen.

They didn't reach Nottingham until the next day and, when they arrived at the Cow Bar gatehouse a crowd was there to welcome them. Gisbourne had sent one of his men ahead to spread the word – the Raven had captured Robin Hood!

The news spread like wildfire. Robin and his men were heroes to the common people who hoped this rumour proved to be false. Hundreds of them had gathered at the gates, held back by the guardsmen who threw angry glances at Gisbourne as he rode into the city like a conquering hero, oblivious to the trouble that might arise from this.

Sir Henry de Faucumberg appeared, with a couple of dozen guards to the relief of the gatemen, although, if things really turned ugly they were still badly outnumbered. The sheriff nodded to Gisbourne as his party made their way into the city, but de Faucumberg walked past and entered the gatehouse, appearing moments later on the battlements, looking down on the gathered throng.

"People of Nottingham," he cried. "Hear me!"

His voice was mostly lost in the clamour, but some folk noticed the sheriff and pointed him out to those around them, until, eventually, an uneasy silence descended and the people waited to hear what he had to say.

"For months now, the forests around our city have been plagued by outlaws. By wolf's heads who rob, rape and murder innocent travellers – even men of God!" He hurried on before anyone could shout a smart reply. "Now, my men have captured the leader of those vicious felons – Robin Hood! Not only an outlaw, but a rebel as well: the King himself demanded I bring him to justice. And now...I have!"

He raised his hands in triumph, and the city guardsmen cheered half-heartedly. Gisbourne was furious at the sheriff taking the credit for capturing Hood, and he vowed to have words with de Faucumberg later on. For now though, as the crowd stood watching their sheriff to see if he would say anything else, Gisbourne waved his men on, towards the castle, moving to drag Robin along in their wake.

"Sir Guy!" the sheriff shouted down, beckoning the furious king's man to climb the stairs. "Bring the wolf's head up here, so the people can see him!"

The sight of the walls made Robin want to retch, and he felt panic welling up inside him as he was shoved inside the gatehouse and made to climb the stairs. He was used to the freedom of the greenwood – the thought of being encased in a gloomy stone prison, surrounded by walls like these – was almost too much for him to bear.

As they came up onto the battlements Barnwell saw Robin's hunted expression and read his thoughts. He caught the young man's eye and, with another malicious smile nodded a little way to the north, on the road to York.

Robin tried to spit at Gisbourne's grinning lackey, but his throat was dry and what little spittle he could produce dribbled embarrassingly down his own chin as he followed the man's gaze.

His stomach lurched and his tired legs almost gave way when he saw what Barnwell was looking at.

On a hill, dominating the skyline, stood an enormous wooden frame almost four metres tall. Two corpses could just be seen, hanging suspended from the sinister construction while tiny black specks – crows no doubt – wheeled in the sky overhead, taking turns to fly down and peck at the eyes and soft flesh of the dead felons. The sight of the structure was all the more ominous surrounded as it was by gently rolling fields and a couple of picturesque windmills.

The gallows.

"Take a good look, wolf's head," Barnwell grinned. "There lies your doom."

* * *

He was half-dragged, half-led down to the dungeon by a couple of the sheriff's men. Robin felt claustrophobic cooped up within the cold stone walls which grew even colder as they moved underground.

Criminals stared out at them through thick iron gates. Some shrank back as the guard's torch lit the gloom; others proclaimed their innocence, begging to be released. Robin's felt his heart wrench as one pitiful man sobbed unashamedly, asking to see his family again before he was hanged the next day.

The guards ignored the cries, leading the tired outlaw to his own cell which lay at the far end of the corridor. As he was shoved in, one of them battered the back of his head with his pole-arm. "That's for the good soldiers you and your mates have killed in Barnsdale, you piece of filth. Some of them were my friends."

Robin dropped to his knees, clutching his skull in agony as the gate was pulled shut and locked with a loud, final click. The guards left, taking the torch with them, and bolting the massive oak door at the end of the corridor at their backs, and complete darkness filled the freezing dungeon.

Stumbling into a corner, Robin sat with his back against the wall, his eyes trying unsuccessfully to adjust to the inky blackness, as the other prisoners cried out in anger, fear or madness.

His eyes welled up, but he angrily wiped them, not giving in to the self-pity that threatened to overwhelm him and he remembered Tuck's words from not so long ago: *"Never give up hope!"*

He clenched his fists and forced a smile into the darkness. It would take more than this to break Robin Hood.

It might have been minutes later, it might have been hours, Robin couldn't tell, but the door at the far end of the corridor creaked open and the dim orange glow from a smoky torch made its way along until it was outside his cell.

The outlaw stared at Gisbourne's sergeant, who had his usual wicked smile on his scarred face.

"Get up, Hood. Sir Guy feels like a little sparring practice before he has his supper."

Slowly, knowing he had no choice, Robin stood up and walked to the cell gate which was unlocked by the same guard who had battered his head earlier. "Supper eh? What are we having?"

Barnwell roared with laughter at that. "Good lad! Let's go then."

They made their way back up to the courtyard of the castle, where the captor drank in the fresh air and the early evening sunshine. He'd only been in his cell for a short time; he wondered how he would feel seeing the sky again if he was locked up for even longer next time.

"Ah, the famous wolf's head himself!"

Gisbourne stood, stripped to the waist despite the cold, his slim, yet wiry body heaving from exertion. He had been practising his combat moves, watched from a large open window by some of the giggling women of the castle.

"I've heard all sorts of stories about you, boy," Gisbourne said, lifting a pair of wooden swords and throwing one to Robin which he failed to catch. His face burned as the girls above laughed mockingly and he stooped to retrieve the weapon.

"They say you can fight three men at the same time and kill them all without breaking a sweat. They say you defeated a Templar and cut off his manhood. They say" – he fixed Robin with a piercing gaze and took up a defensive posture – "that you can't be beaten."

Robin smiled, spreading his hands wide. "The people exaggerate. How about a wager though – if I beat you, I go free?"

Gisbourne spat on the hard ground, angry at the outlaw's apparent self-confidence. "You won't beat me. Now...let's see for ourselves how well you fight."

Barnwell and the guardsman moved away, and Robin flexed his muscles which were stiff from his incarceration. The back of his head still ached – there was a lump the size of half a pigeon's egg there now – and he felt exhausted. Drained by Much's murder and his capture.

Gisbourne could see all this reflected in his young opponent's blue eyes now, and he darted forward aiming a blow at Robin's shoulder.

Instinctively, the outlaw brought up his own wooden sword and, with a crack that echoed around the stone walls surrounding the courtyard, the two blades met.

Gisbourne grinned and hooked his foot behind Robin's, dragging the younger man's leg out from under him.

The women screamed in delight as he crashed to the floor, the breath knocked out of him, and Gisbourne danced back gracefully.

"Get up, scum!" One of the women was louder than the rest, and her eyes flashed in delight at the promise of more violence.

Robin got to his feet and warded off another of Gisbourne's blows, this time using his own greater bulk to lean into the lawman's attack and force him stumbling backwards.

Wanting to finish this as soon as possible, the outlaw moved after his foe, raining blow after blow on him. Gisbourne somehow parried them all, and as Robin moved to take another swing the Raven unexpectedly jumped forward, smashing his forehead into Robin's face.

Again, the women cheered and hollered, almost in a frenzy as the outlaw collapsed on the ground, blood dripping from his broken nose. Gisbourne laughed and kicked Robin in the ribs.

"Take him away. It seems the tales of Robin Hood's fighting prowess have been wildly exaggerated."

As he was dragged by the arms back down to the dungeon, the mocking laughter and catcalls of the noblewomen ringing in his ears, Robin felt despair again, this time like an evil black wave that washed over him, filling his soul. Drowning him.

When he was thrown into his freezing cell again he curled into a ball and wept.

* * *

"Where's Robin anyway?"

It had taken a couple of days, but Tuck was just about able to sit up now and, as Will handed him another steaming bowl of spring vegetable soup, he asked the question all the outlaws had been asking.

"We don't know," Will admitted. "Him, Much and Matt went off a couple of days ago, hunting. We haven't seen any of them since."

Tuck's eyes grew wide. "You've looked for them surely?"

"Of course we have! The problem is, Robin said they weren't going far, then planned on finishing the day fishing and drinking. We've searched all around but can't find any trace and – well, Barnsdale's a big place. They could be anywhere."

Tuck tipped the rest of his soup into his mouth and sighed. "Funny they took Matt with them."

Will shrugged and explained how Matt had escaped from Sir Guy of Gisbourne while Paul and James hadn't been so lucky.

Tuck shook his head and tried to stand up, but his legs were still shaky and he slumped backwards onto the pallet, head spinning so badly he almost threw up.

"Where? Where did Gisbourne kill Paul and James?"

Will spread his hands wide, his eyebrows drawn in consternation. "I don't know – somewhere close to Darton. That's where they'd been visiting that day, trying to buy rope."

"You must send some of the lads to look close to Darton then!" Tuck gasped, exhausted even after his moment of exercise.

"John! Arthur! Come here!"

The two men hurried over at Will's shout, worried something was wrong with Tuck, but the friar explained his fears to them.

"Matt conveniently escapes from Gisbourne and his men," he breathed, resting his arm on his forehead, "then the next day he goes on a hunting trip with Robin? We all know they can't stand the sight of each other."

161

John and Will exchanged glances, understanding better than anyone that Robin had come close on a couple of occasions to casting Groves out of their group, or even killing the obnoxious older man. Arthur just looked baffled.

"None of you thought that odd?" Tuck demanded, incredulous.

"Well, no, not really." Little John looked at the ground, like a little boy being scolded by his father. "Matt seemed upset by what had happened to James and especially Paul – they were close in age. I thought Robin and Much just took him along with them because they felt sorry for him."

"Aye," Will agreed. "You know what Robin's like. Always tries to be the good leader – the better man. If Matt had asked me to go hunting with him I'd have told him to fuck off, but Robin's not like the rest of us."

Tuck recognised the truth of what they were saying, and he lay his head back down on the pallet, somewhat mollified.

"Well," he went on, his eyes closed as he fought the damnable exhaustion that had plagued his few waking moments for the past two days, "it seems to me, Matt was hired by Gisbourne to lead Robin into an ambush. It wouldn't have taken a lot for the bastard to betray Robin, would it? And the simplest place for them to take him would be wherever they'd met the previous day. So..."

He opened one eye and glared at the three outlaws. "What are you waiting for? Go and find Robin and Much!"

* * *

Will felt they were wasting valuable time travelling to Darton to hunt for their missing friends, but Little John knew there was no choice.

"We don't know if Tuck's idea is right," the giant outlaw grunted as they raced through the greenwood.

162

"For all we know they were injured by a stag or something and are lying waiting for us to find them."

"A stag?" Will laughed in disbelief.

"Now you mention it, I heard Matt saying something about seeing a big stag on his way back from Darton, before Gisbourne caught them." Arthur nodded agreement as he pushed past a small clump of gorse, pollen from the bright yellow flowers staining his brown breeches.

"There you are," John nodded at Will. "We can't just go chasing off to Nottingham expecting to find Robin and Much have been captured and taken there. Not until we check out Tuck's guess about what happened."

"What will we do if they *have* been taken to the sheriff?" Arthur wondered.

Neither Little John or Will Scarlet could offer a reply. If Robin and Much had been taken to Nottingham they were as good as dead. It was as simple as that.

A few outlaws weren't enough to storm the castle, which sat on a hill inside the city walls, and mount a successful rescue.

Little John lengthened his already enormous stride, praying his friends were safe somewhere, while Will and Arthur fell silent, conserving their breath for running behind their big friend.

"Trust in Robin," John growled, his eyes fixed straight ahead as he ran. "A Raven is no match for a Wolf."

* * *

"It hurts!"

Matilda's mother, Mary, grasped her daughter's hand, and nodded sympathetically. "I know, but it'll all be worth it, I promise you."

Matilda's baby was going to be a handful, Mary could see. The child kicked her daughter relentlessly

163

through the nights, so hard you could see the little feet pushing against Matilda's belly.

Mary didn't think the pain could be that bad, but she knew the constant movement inside you made it impossible to sleep properly and Matilda was exhausted now.

First had been the morning sickness, which had lasted for weeks, and now this. Matilda often told her parents she wished she'd never let Robin get her into this state, but they knew those feelings would pass once the babe was born.

Didn't all women feel the same during pregnancy, Mary wondered?

Still, for all her wisdom, Mary – and her husband, Henry – didn't know how to react when their daughter cursed Robin Hood. On hearing her anguished cries during the night they instinctively, inwardly, agreed with Matilda in wishing the wolf's head had picked another young girl from Wakefield to fall in love with. And yet, both Mary and Henry knew Robin was a good man who would like nothing better than to be here to comfort his pregnant wife.

"I'd have been better letting that bastard Woolemonger lie with me," Matilda grunted, doubling over on the bed. "At least he wasn't an outlaw!"

Mary glared at her husband, warning him not to respond to that. Simon Woolemonger had been killed by John Little the previous year after he'd tried to assault Matilda then informed on her to the old bailiff which had led to her being arrested. Woolemonger was scum, and Mary knew Matilda didn't mean what she was saying.

"Hush, child," she whispered to her daughter, gripping her hand tightly as Henry looked on, bewildered, as men always did when it came to situations like this. "Robin will be pardoned one day, and the three of you can be a family."

Matilda grimaced as the baby kicked again, hard, and Mary shook her head, wishing she could do more to ease her girl's pain. She knew Robin and Matilda were meant to be with each other and yet...sometimes, as a parent, she did wish her daughter hadn't fallen in love with a wolf's head.

He was probably having a great time hiding away in Barnsdale just now, she thought, looking down at Matilda's tired, pale features. He'd be drinking ale and singing songs with his friends while her daughter – his wife – tried to deal with the child growing inside her.

Men. They thought they knew about pain, but they had no idea!

CHAPTER THIRTEEN

"Even if they were ambushed and are lying injured or…" Arthur couldn't finish the sentence. "Well, they could be anywhere! We can't search the whole forest."

They'd almost reached Darton and had still seen no sign of Robin, Much or Matt.

John knew his young companion was right, but they had to keep looking.

"Why don't we go to the village and find someone with a good dog?" Will suggested, and the other two nodded agreement.

"Aye, good idea," John replied as they barrelled through a cluster of bracken that had grown right over the path. "A dog will" –

The three outlaws stopped in their tracks, staring in shock at the ground just a short distance ahead, then they broke into a run.

"It's Much!"

It was instantly obvious their friend was dead. If the terrible wound in his stomach wasn't enough, the crossbow bolt embedded deep in his chest and the blank stare in his eyes confirmed it.

"No!" Little John's anguished cry was swallowed by the trees as he knelt by the body, placing a big hand almost tenderly on the unmoving chest. "Not Much…he was a good lad – not like the rest of us!"

"That bastard, Gisbourne!" Will shouted, his eyes transfixed by the black crossbow bolt protruding from Much, voice cracking with anger and despair. "He's destroying us, one by one!"

Arthur stood at the side quietly, numb with shock, but his eyes scanned the thick trees and bushes around them.

"Where's Robin and Matt?" he mumbled.

Scarlet was lost in a world of his own, consumed by rage and grief, but John realised they could be in danger and he stood up, grabbing Will by the shoulders.

"They've taken Robin – probably to hang him. We have to take Much back to Wakefield and give him a proper burial."

"He's dead!" Will roared. "We can't do anything for him – we need to find that bastard Gisbourne and help Robin!"

John could feel Scarlet's anger as he held him by the shoulders, but he stared down, deep into Will's eyes in determination.

"They've taken Robin, probably to Nottingham for a show trial. We can't just chase after them – three of us! On foot! We take Much home, and then we talk to the rest of the lads and decide what to do."

Will glared up at the big bearded giant, but the sense of it finally penetrated his fury and he nodded, leaning down and lifting Much's arms. "Fine – one of you grab his legs then and let's move. Quickly now!"

They were all tired after their journey here, but their anger spurred them on as they made their way back towards their camp with their dead friend, taking turns to relieve one another – especially the much slighter Arthur.

"Don't despair lads," John growled, gazing at his two companions. "Robin is still alive, maybe in a dungeon somewhere, but still alive until they can make a show of him."

Arthur didn't reply, his whole body aching from carrying Much's corpse, but Will spat on the thick undergrowth beside them.

"I owe Robin for what he did, saving Beth," he muttered, to himself as much as anyone else, remembering the previous year when Robin and Allan-a-Dale had posed as minstrels to sneak into the manor house where his little daughter was being held as a servant and rescued her. "If he's in a dungeon, I'll kill myself trying to get him out. 'The Raven'," he spat the epithet in disgust, "better watch his fucking back! As soon as we've taken Much home, I'm going to Nottingham."

* * *

"How's your father?"

"Eh?" Edmond had been staring at the road ahead, but now he turned, casting a venomous look on his noble captive.

"Your father – the tanner?" Sir Richard asked again.

"None of your fucking business," Edmond spat. "You don't know him, so what do you care?"

"On the contrary," the Hospitaller replied. "Your father has been making harnesses for my horses for years. I remember you and your brother running around outside his shop as children…"

Edmond's eyes became damp again, but his throat tightened and, when he tried, he couldn't tell the knight to shut up.

"I am truly sorry for Walter." Sir Richard's voice was calm, and the sincerity in his words was obvious from his resigned tone and the look of sadness on his face. "My own boy was taken from me not long ago…I'm getting too old…seen too much death. I'm sick of it."

The tears spilled from Edmond's eyes at the thought of his beloved brother – who'd never had a real chance in life from the day he was born – lying dead and unburied miles back along the path as he shepherded their old lord to his death.

Edmond knew, deep down, his brother's blood was on *his* hands. He had been the one who wanted to capture Sir Richard, even though the Hospitaller had been a good lord to the people of Kirklees.

Edmond had been the one who'd wanted to make a name for himself by capturing a rebel.

As he thought of his brother's body lying cold and dead in the undergrowth he wondered if Sir Richard had been worth it, especially since their father had died not too long ago and Edmond was now all alone in the world.

"Shut up you bastard!" he screamed, kicking the knight in the back through his tears, almost sending the big man falling to the ground.

"You're going to hang!"

* * *

"What are we going to do?" Will Scarlet furiously repeated Allan-a-Dale's question. "I don't know what anyone else is doing, but I'm going to Nottingham to find Robin!"

"Peace, Will." Friar Tuck raised his hand, shaking his head in resignation. "This is no time to be haring off in a blind rage. We'll have to think about it."

"What is there to think about?" Will demanded. "We know Gisbourne's taken him to the castle and plans on hanging him. Sitting here planning isn't going to do anything – no plan in the world's going to make this easy."

Tuck made to reply, but Little John clapped a meaty hand on Scarlet's shoulder. "I agree with Will," he rumbled, bringing a look of surprise from the weak friar. "We don't have time to mess about, trying to think up a clever plan. Besides, Robin's the one for that, and he's not here."

Tuck closed his mouth and nodded for John to continue as the rest of the outlaws gathered round, wondering where this would lead.

"All we can do is be direct," the massive outlaw asserted. "We have to get into the castle, kill or otherwise incapacitate the guards, and somehow get out of the city with Robin."

"Is that all?" Allan snorted sarcastically. "Piece of piss."

"We can't all go," Gareth said. "They'd spot us straight away, especially you," he nodded at Little John. "Not many people in Nottingham are as big as you. Probably no one!"

"Maybe we could disguise him as a dancing bear," Allan grunted, nodding at John. "Wouldn't take much disguising."

No one laughed and Allan fell silent, embarrassed to have made the silly joke at such a stressful time.

"I'll go in myself," Will stood up, patting his weapons instinctively to make sure they were all in place. "One man has a better chance than all of us together. I'll find a way to get inside and free him."

"Wait." All eyes turned to Tuck again as he swung his legs off his pallet and shakily got to his feet. "I'm coming with you."

"Don't be bloody stupid," John shook his head in disbelief. "You're too weak. How will you be any use?"

"I'm not that weak," the friar retorted. "The journey south will build my muscles back up and I'll be able to help Will get into the city if nothing else. Remember, everyone – including the sheriff's men and Gisbourne – think I'm dead. And thanks to this" – he rubbed the short bushy beard that had grown on his face while he was unconscious – "they'll never recognise me anyway."

Will agreed. "He has a point, John."

"This is insane," the giant grumbled. "The only exercise you've had in the past few days is the odd wander around the camp. How are you going to walk to Nottingham? You might have lost some weight, but you're still too fat for Will to carry all the way there!"

"I'll go on ahead to Royston," Gareth volunteered. "I'll buy a horse and bring it back. You," he nodded at Tuck and Will, "can meet me on the way."

"Perfect," the friar smiled at the young lad appreciatively. "I can alternate between walking and riding. I've got my appetite back, so by the time we reach the city I'll be my old self again."

170

"All right then," Will began packing some food and drink for himself and Tuck. "Take five pounds from the common fund to pay for the horse and head off to Royston. We'll meet you on the road."

Gareth nodded and headed over to the big wooden chest where the outlaws stored their money as Tuck got himself ready for the journey.

"Here," Little John tossed his great quarterstaff to the friar. "You can use that to steady yourself until you get stronger."

"Thank you," Tuck replied with a grateful smile. "But it's much too big for me – it'd make me stand out and that's exactly what we have to avoid. I'll take my own staff."

Gareth gave a wave and raced off into the trees, his spindly limbs allowing him to move much faster than any of the other outlaws. Will and Tuck clasped arms with the rest of the men who wished them luck and promised to pray for the success of their mission.

John wished desperately he could go along with them, and he unashamedly grabbed Scarlet in a great bear-hug as they said their farewells.

"Be careful, Will. The most important thing is that you, Tuck and Robin make it back here alive. Don't go looking for revenge for Much. We can deal with that another day."

Will nodded at his big friend. "Don't worry, I'm not an idiot... If I get the chance though – I'll run that bastard Gisbourne through."

John smiled as Friar Tuck, swigging from his ale skin and cramming bread into his mouth in a ridiculous attempt to regain his former strength, shouted for Will to get moving.

"Just make sure you come back to us in one piece, Scarlet, you moaning faced bastard."

* * *

Gareth was true to his word, meeting Will and Tuck on the road to Nottingham with a tired-looking horse.

"Christ, we've got enough money – you could have got us something a bit stronger looking," Will grumbled, but Tuck laughed and patted the young man on the shoulder.

"You did well, lad. If we turned up at the city gates riding a great charger we'd stick out a mile." The smiling friar stood by the horse, stroking its mane gently. "This fellow will do us just fine, I'm sure."

Scarlet gave a grunt and they waved Gareth off as he hurried back through the trees to the camp-site.

"Help me up." Tuck laid a hand on the saddle and gestured for his companion to give him a shove.

Once mounted, they set off at a faster pace than they'd been able to manage with the weakened Tuck on foot. All being well, they would reach Nottingham within a couple of days.

"Maybe I should have thought this through a bit better," Will muttered, a rueful smile on his round face. "The guards might recognise me at the gates, or in the city."

"My body might have lost some of its vigour while I was out of it," Tuck replied, reaching for the pack he carried and pulling something from it. "My mind, thankfully, still works fine. Here."

He threw the object at Will, who caught it and opened it out with a grin. It was a grey robe, the same as the one Tuck was wearing. "My spare clothes," the Franciscan nodded. "Try not to lose it or get too much blood on it."

"You're a genius, Tuck!" Will threw the robe on over his head and pulled the hood up, his face instantly becoming lost in shadow. It was an ideal disguise.

"True," the friar agreed with a nod. "I deserve something as a reward." Reaching into his pack again he pulled out some strips of salted beef and grunted in satisfaction as he began chewing.

172

"Aye," Will agreed grimly. "Reward yourself as much as you can – you're going to need your strength back when we try to get Robin out of the city..."

They made good time and reached Nottingham just before nightfall the next day, when the sun was low in the sky. The air was cold with a light rain and a gentle wind making it feel even cooler, while the fading light cast long shadows on the road behind the two travellers as they approached the city's northern gatehouse.

They had made good use of their time on the road, thinking of a back-story for Will. The former mercenary had fought in the Holy Land with French armies as well as English, and picked up a little of the foreign tongue there.

"You can pretend to be a visiting French friar," Tuck told him. "The guards won't be able to understand what you're saying anyway. And if you throw in the odd Latin phrase it'll fool them long enough for us to get past and into the city."

Will nodded. "We'll find an inn near the castle and see if the local gossips know anything about Robin."

"You two – halt!" A loud voice boomed at them from above and Tuck looked up to see the guard, while Will kept his head down and under his hood in case the setting sun showed his face too clearly.

"It's late. What do you want?"

"We're travelling friars, my son," Tuck shouted back in a voice almost as powerful as the guardsman's, and Scarlet smiled. It seemed his weak companion was indeed growing stronger after his recent ordeal. "We seek to spend the night in your city, before we set off on the morrow to Canterbury."

The sound of talking, muffled by the massive stone walls, filtered down to the travellers, before the city gate was slowly opened and another guard gestured them impatiently inside. He gave them a cursory look, and waved them through as Tuck grinned and Will made the sign of the cross while mumbling, "Gratias tibi ago," at the bored looking man.

It was as simple as that. The guard gave them a wave and ran up the stairs to where his fellows huddled around a brazier at the top of the gatehouse, and the two outlaws entered Nottingham.

Although it was getting late, people still bustled about the place, while children ran between them, screaming playfully, and mangy-looking dogs sniffed at the travellers hoping for a scrap or two.

Tuck asked a local man if there were any taverns near the castle and the pair set off in the direction the man pointed to obtain a room for the night before the weather got any worse.

"I hope they have some good thick beef stew," the friar smiled, rubbing his shrunken belly. "Can't beat some good red meat for building up your strength."

When they reached the inn – so close to the castle you could actually see its great bulk dominating the skyline from the front door – they made sure their palfrey was comfortable in the rickety old stable that was attached to the building and hurried inside gratefully.

Scarlet's stomach rumbled loudly at the thought of food and he pictured in his mind's eye a cosy inn with a roaring fire, beautiful serving-girls and barrels full of freshly brewed ale.

It wasn't to be.

"Ah, bollocks!" Will cursed quietly as the stench hit him and his eyes took in the sight of the *King and Castle* common room. Smoke from the fire filled the place, while the rushes on the floor hadn't been changed in days. He carefully avoided a stinking, dried up patch of vomit and followed Tuck to the bar, noting the toothless old barmaid – breasts hanging almost to her knees – with a rueful shake of his head.

Fuck it. At least the place had a roof.

CHAPTER FOURTEEN

"Ah, Gisbourne!" Sir Henry de Faucumberg grinned and slapped the king's bounty-hunter on the arm. The sheriff's eyes were slightly glassy and it was obvious he'd had a glass or three of wine. "Good job capturing the wolf's head – I'm certain the king will reward you handsomely. I'm hosting a feast tonight to celebrate Hood's incarceration and imminent doom. I trust you will be joining us?"

Gisbourne glowered at the sheriff, still unhappy at the man for stealing his thunder at the city gates. De Faucumberg had a point though – King Edward would reward him well for his work here, and he, along with his sergeant, Nicholas, could leave this place. It wasn't that Gisbourne particularly disliked Yorkshire or Nottingham, but now that the notorious outlaw was safely locked up, there was no challenge left here. The Raven was a man who liked to pit his wits, and his sword arm, against the best – against those criminals no one else could stop.

"Aye," he agreed, forcing himself to smile back at the sheriff. "We have much to celebrate. The outlaw will hang, the king will look upon us both with favour, and I can move on. I'm sure that will please you as much as it pleases me."

De Faucumberg looked confused. "Move on?"

"Indeed," Gisbourne nodded. "Robin Hood is no longer a threat to anyone. I was sent here to kill or capture him, and my job is done. As fine as your hospitality has been," he smirked as the sheriff frowned at the sarcastic tone, "the north of England is a boring place and I'll be glad to get back to London. Who knows where I'll end up next? Hopefully somewhere warm, with a little more culture, like the Languedoc maybe."

The sheriff shook his head, a smile of his own playing on his lips. "My good man, I don't think you understand the situation. The king sent you here to take care of Hood – but his gang are still out there. You will be going nowhere until the rest of them are hanging from the gallows outside the city."

Gisbourne snorted. "I caught the ringleader, de Faucumberg. I also killed the fat friar and at least two more of them. Surely you can capture the rest of the scum? I'm a bounty-hunter, not a damned forester."

The sheriff shrugged, enjoying the moment as Gisbourne grew increasingly angry. "I have the king's orders, Sir Guy – you are to remain here until the forests heareabouts are cleared of outlaws and rebels. It seems King Edward sees you as a forester, eh?"

The smug look on de Faucumberg's face enraged Gisbourne and he burned to smash his fist into the man's throat. With an effort he controlled himself and stalked stiffly away, the sheriff's snigger ringing in his ears.

Damn the man, and damn the king!

The sounds of revelry echoed along the stone corridors, blackening his mood even further, and before he even knew where he was going he found himself at the iron door to the dungeon.

"Bring the prisoner," he growled to one of the two guardsmen.

"Which one, my lord?"

"Which one d'you fucking think, you oaf? Hood!"

The man nodded, well used to his betters talking down to him, and hurried along the gloomy hallway to fetch the wolf's head.

Sir Guy of Gisbourne hadn't always been the ruthless, brooding bounty hunter he was now. As a young man he had been quite pleasant and well-liked around his home town. He had a stable family life as an only-child, his father being one of King Edward I's keepers of the peace while his doting mother looked after the household affairs. Young Guy had loved and respected both of his parents a great deal, particularly his mother who would tell him bedtime stories about King Arthur and the quest for the Holy Grail.

An able student, he'd done well in his schooling, while lacking the required interest in the subjects to ever truly excel. Still, with the help of his influential father, he had begun working as a hayward and was on his way to becoming a well-respected local official.

Life had suited him like that. He wasn't particularly ambitious back then and he had no destructive vices. He had a natural aptitude for fighting, but it had never interested him beyond childhood games with friends, pretending to be Sir Lancelot. Even the military training his father had paid an old mercenary to give him hadn't made him want to become a soldier.

Things had changed when he met Emma.

A stunning, fair-haired girl, she had come with her father – a well-off merchant – and her younger sister, to live in Gisbourne when Guy was seventeen and she a year younger.

The innocent teenage hayward had been smitten by her easy smile, playful nature and her infectious lust for life and the pair had been married just months after meeting for the first time at one of Guy's father's parties.

Unfortunately, Emma's playfulness wasn't confined to her relationship with her new husband, and her lust extended to more than just life.

Within six months, Guy and his wife's adultery were the talk of the village and the young man was crushed by it. The sneers, the mocking laughter when he walked past, the loss of respect of the workers he was in charge of...it had all been hard to bear, but not as hard to bear as the knowledge Emma didn't care for him the way he did for her.

He'd begged her to be faithful, to stop seeing other men behind his back, but still it continued.

His father and other men of the village had told him to beat some obedience into her – she was his woman and should be made to obey him, yet here she was making him a laughing stock!

But, to this day, Guy was never the type of man to physically assault a woman even when she was ruining his life as Emma was doing.

The situation had continued for almost two years, his wife becoming ever more brazen and unrepentant over her affairs while the villagers' view of Guy had moved from mockery to pity.

Then one night Emma had gone a step further than before and brought a man back to their house. Guy had walked in after his day's work and found her astride the man, a middle-aged local shopkeeper with a pot-belly.

That was the day Guy of Gisbourne finally snapped and his aptitude for violence became brutally apparent.

The case had never come to the bailiff's attention, thanks to his father's influence, although murdering a man who was fucking your wife in your own house was hardly a crime anyway.

From that day on though, Guy had become a different person.

It had felt good to deal out justice with his own hands. The respect he'd lost over the past two years had been won back in the space of a few short, bloody minutes. The village children no longer hooted at him when he walked past, and the men who had formerly looked at him with contempt now averted their eyes fearfully when he glared at them.

He'd thrown Emma out of their home although even now he was still legally wed to her, then he had sold the house and, with a letter of recommendation from his father, gone to London to find employment.

Starting as an assistant to one of the city bailiff's Guy had performed his duties with relish and eventually come to the attention of the king's own chamberlain who hired the brooding young man to work on behalf of Edward II himself.

Gisbourne shook his head ruefully as he thought back on it all now. Things could have been so different if Emma had just been a loving wife. They would have had children – lots of them – and, once he had saved enough money, lived in a big house by the River Ribble which was something he'd dreamt of since childhood. He'd always loved being close to water, particularly the Ribble where he'd spent many hours with friends as a child, fishing and sailing little wooden boats.

He would have been content.

As the notorious young wolf's head was led along the hallway towards him, Sir Guy's fingers tightened around his sword hilt and he pushed the old dreams from his mind. His life had turned out differently to how he would have chosen, but he was exceptionally good at his job. Good at bringing justice to those who flouted the law, like this boy Hood.

Well, Gisbourne was going to bring his own form of justice to the big bastard now.

Robin walked like a dead man as he was led along the dimly-lit stone corridor towards the bounty-hunter standing in the shadows.

"I'll take him from here," the king's man told the guard, who tried to object – his orders from the sheriff were to make sure Hood stayed locked safely away – but the furious, slightly insane, stare Gisbourne threw him turned the man's blood cold and he backed away, hands raised placatingly.

"Right, wolf's head. Move it. You know the way to the practice area. You're going to show me what you're made of, or in the name of Christ, you won't make it to the gallows alive."

The practice area was empty; the guards were all either at their posts or joining in with the feast which was now under way. The entire courtyard seemed eerily silent as Gisbourne and his captive walked out onto the grass and the bounty-hunter lifted a pair of wooden swords.

"I noticed the spark of hatred in your eyes when you saw me there, wolf's head. There's no one else here – if you're man enough, you can kill me and probably walk right out of the castle before anyone notices." He tossed a sword to Robin, who caught it and gazed at his tormentor.

Robin knew there was no chance of escape – the guards wouldn't allow him to walk past them when they saw him approaching the gatehouse, but there was a possibility of killing this black-clad bastard and the thought made the blood pound in his veins.

Gisbourne smiled as he saw the colour rise in the outlaw's face, and moved in to try a thrust, but Robin sidestepped and moved backwards, trying to work some strength into his muscles. He hadn't slept properly for days, and the cold, damp cell floor had made his whole body ache, not to mention the psychological torment he'd suffered recently.

Gisbourne aimed another blow at his opponent's side, which was again parried, but Robin was slow and before he knew it Gisbourne had reversed his strike and hammered the heavy wooden sword into Robin's ribcage.

Crying out in agony as he felt bones crack, the outlaw transferred the practice weapon to his left hand so he could clutch his injured side.

Gibourne was in no mood for mercy though, and attacked with a flurry of strokes which Robin desperately managed to parry until, inevitably, Gisbourne landed another blow, this time on Robin's thigh, deadening the limb.

Roaring in pain again, the young outlaw tried to move back, away from Sir Guy, in an attempt to buy some time for the pain from his injuries to hopefully lessen.

"You were supposed to be a test for me, peasant," Gisbourne spat in disgust. "But you're nothing. You fight like any other farmer. Will you be more of a challenge for me if you're angry? What if I tell you the king won't let me leave here until I've hanged every one of your band of friends?"

Robin, hoping to stall for as much time as possible, tried to laugh but the pain from his damaged ribs made him grimace. "Good luck with that. If Will doesn't kill you, Little John'll do it."

"The angry man and the giant," Gisbourne feinted left as he spoke and Robin, in his exhausted and injured state found it impossible to defend himself as the edge of the lawman's wooden sword cracked off his face and he fell to the ground, dazed and almost passing out from the blow. "I'll kill them both, just like I'm going to kill you. Fuck de Faucumberg and his show trial, I'm going to finish this now!"

By now, the celebration inside the castle was in full swing, and the joyful sounds of drunken revelry filled the courtyard. The young women who had cheered Gisbourne in his previous fight here had again come to the balcony and squealed delightedly at the sight of the outlaw being beaten so viciously.

As Robin unsteadily rose to his feet, the sheriff appeared on the balcony, shoving his way past the women to see what they were all watching. When he saw the state of his prisoner, and Gisbourne's body language, he ran back into the castle, roaring for the guards.

"Fight me!" Sir Guy shouted, punching the hilt of his sword into Robin's nose. Blood spurted onto his hand as the outlaw fell on his backside, grimacing up in pain and hatred at his persecutor.

"Fight back!" Oblivious to the fact Robin was almost unconscious and in no state to defend himself never mind retaliate, Gisbourne came in again, swinging his wooden blade down into his opponent's sword hand.

The pain was too much now and, mercifully, Robin's body began to shut down, a wave of blackness swamping him as his crazed attacker bore down on him, kicking and battering his unmoving body with the practice sword.

Even the drunk girls on the balcony above had stopped cheering now, as they realised they were witnessing a young man being brutally beaten to death.

181

The courtyard filled with the sound of stamping feet as Sheriff de Faucumberg and four guardsmen appeared, running towards Gisbourne. The bounty-hunter had to be wrestled to the ground and held down by the guards as the sheriff screamed in rage at him and shouted for a surgeon.

Eventually, Sir Guy came to his senses and the men let him up.

"What the hell are you doing, you fool?" de Faucumberg demanded. "This is my castle, and that is my prisoner! Have you lost your damn mind?"

Gisbourne took a deep breath and puffed out his cheeks, before closing his eyes and exhaling. As he looked into the sheriff's eyes it was clear the madness had left him, but he glanced at the ruined outlaw and shrugged.

"Whether you hang him or not makes no difference to me – King Edward wants him dead however it's done. Looks like your public hanging is off, sheriff."

The king's man calmly walked from the practice area, placed his wooden sword back in its basket along with the others, and strode into the castle out of sight.

"The man's a lunatic," de Faucumberg muttered, shaking his head in disbelief, before shouting over to the surgeon who had finally arrived. "If he's not dead already, do what you can for the wolf's head – he must survive until the weekend, so we can hang him."

* * *

Tuck and Will paid the landlord – a small, skinny man with a terrible red rash on his face – for a room. They weren't entirely sure yet if they'd need it: Will, as usual, wanted them to make their move as soon as possible.

"Don't be impatient," Tuck scolded him like a naughty child. "We should sit in here for a while and see if we can hear anything about Robin. He's a hero to most of the people in Nottingham; surely someone will be talking about him. We can't just wander around the castle walls at this time of the evening without attracting attention!"

Will knew the friar spoke sense, so they sat nursing two surprisingly fresh ales, pretending to chat but straining to hear other people's conversations.

Thankfully, Tuck was right – the sheriff's capture of Robin Hood was the talk of the place. The outlaws turned their attention to one particular pair of men seated at a table by the window, one of whom appeared to have a brother in the sheriff's guard.

"What's the word on Hood?" a dark-skinned fellow asked the man seated across from him.

"James says he was just coming off duty for the night when that scary bastard Sir Guy of Gisbourne came down to the dungeon looking for Hood. James thought he was looking for another sparring match."

"I thought he'd already beaten him the other day?"

The guard's brother put down his mug and messily wiped his mouth with the back of his hand. "Aye, so he did, Godfrey. He had a mad look in his eyes though, or so James said."

"What happened then?"

"Dunno – James left the castle. I'll tell you tomorrow when he comes back home!"

The men sat silently for a moment, then Godfrey muttered. "I hope Hood gave him a fucking hiding."

Tuck led Will over to the table the two men were sitting at and addressed them apologetically. "I'm sorry to disturb you, gentlemen," he began. "Would you mind if me and my brother friar share your table?" He gestured around at the busy inn. "All the tables are occupied."

The men moved along the bench with respectful nods of their heads, too inebriated to care much who sat with them. "Of course, father. Please, sit."

Tuck dropped onto the seat beside the guard's brother with a grin of thanks, while Will, hood still up lest anyone recognize him, grunted and gave a small wave of his hand.

"So, Robin Hood eh?" Tuck shook his head sorrowfully. "They say he's a wicked murderer. A blasphemer. A thief. And yet the people seem to love him."

The dark-skinned man called Godfrey leaned towards the friar earnestly. "The common people love him because he's one of us," he said. "Aye, Hood's a thief, but he steals from the rich lords and the likes of your bishops. He's done a lot of good for the villages around Yorkshire from what we hear. That's why the sheriff wanted him captured."

"What about his men though?" Tuck wondered, sipping from his ale. "Won't they try and rescue him?"

"No chance!" The guard's brother shook his head vigorously. "He's locked away in the dungeon. Those outlaws might be good at fighting in the forest, but there's no way into the castle; it's too heavily defended, even if they could get inside the city and through the castle gates. Mind you, tonight would be the time to try – the sheriff's throwing a banquet to celebrate Hood's capture at last."

Tuck shared a glance with Will, but let the men's talk move onto other things, while he paid the bar-keep to bring them more ale. It didn't take long for the locals to become quite drunk and the friar neatly steered the conversation back to the sheriff's prisoner.

"When do they plan on hanging the wolf's head?" he wondered.

"Two days," Godfrey replied sadly. "The sheriff wants as many people as possible to see it or he'd have done it by now. Bastard."

"Ach, to be fair," the second man shook his head. "Sir Henry's just doing his job. He's not the worst sheriff we've had in this city – not by a long shot. The outlaws undermined his authority, especially when they killed his man Gurdon last year."

Tuck saw Will's fingers clench convulsively around his mug – the outlaw had thought Adam Gurdon was his friend and it had hurt him deeply when the man had betrayed them. Thankfully, though, Scarlet remained silent and Simon growled at his friend.

"You're just saying that, Roger, because your brother's one of his guards and hoping to win a promotion. I bet you wouldn't think so highly of de Faucumberg if he found out about James sneaking out of the castle that time. The sheriff would have *him* hanged alongside the wicked wolf's head and you know it!"

"Shut up, you idiot," Roger retorted, glaring furiously at his companion. Although he was well in his cups, he didn't want gossip about his brother getting around the city.

Tuck roared with laughter, and patted Roger on the arm reassuringly. "Never fear, lad. We hear much worse things at confession every day – a friar knows how to keep a secret." He winked and drained the last of his ale, shouting to the landlord to bring another four mugs.

"It's true," Godfrey grinned at Tuck. "His brother's lady-friend was leaving to live in Scotland, but James was desperate for one last night of..." he remembered he was talking to clergymen and trailed off sheepishly. "Anyway, he couldn't get the night off, and he couldn't let anyone see him leaving or he'd be in trouble. So he climbed out the latrine on the east wall, then, before anyone noticed he was missing, he climbed back in the same way!"

Tuck's eyes were wide with disbelief as he listened to the tale, and Roger laughed, as the bar-keep placed the fresh ale on the table. "The worst of it is," Roger leaned over conspiratorially, making sure no one else was listening, "he was covered in shit and filth, so his girl wouldn't touch him!" The laughter left his eyes though and he became thoughtful. "He's a bloody fool. Just as well he made it back inside unseen or they'd have hanged him for leaving his post."

185

"Didn't his captain have anything to say about the smell?" Tuck asked.

Roger shrugged. "I think he managed to wash most of the crap off once he got back into the castle, or at least mask the worst of the smell."

Tuck grinned and, again, turned the conversation onto other things. It was late now, and, once they drained the last of their drinks, the friar and Scarlet bade their new friends goodnight and made their way up to the room the landlord had provided for them.

It had been a productive evening.

"I hope you don't mind me getting shit and filth all over your spare robe," Will grinned.

"Not as long as you wash it afterwards!"

CHAPTER FIFTEEN

"Do we really have to do this tonight?"

"You heard them," Will growled, making sure his weapons were all in place and ready under the grey Franciscan robe. "Half the castle will be roaring drunk tonight, while the minstrels and singing will drown out any unusual sounds. There'll also be more strangers than usual about the place; de Faucumberg will have invited all sorts of people for this. So, yes: we have to do this tonight."

Tuck shook his head. It made sense, but he'd hoped for at least one night in a real bed. "I'm too weak to go climbing up some latrine though; what will I do?"

Will laughed and poked the friar in the belly good-naturedly. "Even at your fittest you wouldn't have been able to climb a latrine, big man." He shrugged. "I don't know – come with me to find the place in case we run into anyone. You can do your clergyman thing until I deal with them. I'm going to need some light to find handholds too – you can help with that. Then, I suppose it'll be down to me. At least we know Robin's in the dungeon."

It was an insane plan; they would need God and all his saints on their side if it was to have any chance of success. "Just as well we have this," Tuck muttered, clenching the holy reliquary in his hand and offering a silent prayer to St Nicholas, patron saint of thieves, which seemed most appropriate.

"Let's move."

Their room was on the ground floor, so it was a simple matter to open the wooden shutters and climb out onto the street, even for the weakened Tuck. The city was shrouded in darkness, although a gibbous moon cast just enough light for them to move between the buildings. The castle was easy to spot, its great black bulk huge in the darkness, and many small points of yellow light shone from the windows and murder holes. It was an eerie sight and the outlaws felt the hairs on their necks stand up as a chill breeze blew along the slumbering street.

They headed for the east wall, moving silently up the hill that led to it, although Tuck struggled to keep up and was breathing heavily as they drew close to the castle. They had heard others out and about, but found it easy enough to remain unseen in the gloom and, before too long, stood by the massive wall of Nottingham Castle.

The latrine was simple enough to find – the stench was overpowering. Will had no doubt the mountain of shit that must accrue here every day would be used by some tradesman for something or other. They probably paid the sheriff for it too.

"Unbelievable," Tuck whispered. "A fortress, with walls almost as thick as I am tall, massive iron gates, defended by a garrison of hard men...and anyone that knows about it can climb in through the latrine!"

"I haven't done it yet," Will cautioned. "Besides, it's not that much of a security risk is it? You have to be inside the city walls to get here – so it's not that much use to an invading army. And who in their right mind wants to break into a castle, using a fucking *latrine* to do it? It's madness."

Tuck grinned, the moonlight reflecting off his yellow teeth. "Aye, you're not wrong there. Good luck with that."

There was a locked door barring the way into the building, but it was wooden and, thanks to the dampness of what it guarded, it was badly rotten. "The lock probably won't give, but the wood might," Will guessed, leaning down and aiming a kick at the bottom of the barrier, which splintered with a wet thud. Another blow took the bottom half of the door off and, after waiting a while to make sure no one came to investigate the noise, the companions crawled into the stinking toilet.

It was pitch black inside, so Tuck produced the torch he'd taken from their room in the *King and Castle* and rummaged in his pack for his flint and steel.

"Wait," Will hissed fearfully, guessing what the friar was doing. "I've heard stories about farts catching fire! You might blow the whole castle up if you light that torch in here!"

Tuck burst out laughing. He couldn't stop himself. The high-pitched sound rang out, bouncing off the steep stone walls, and he bent over, covering his mouth with his hand in an attempt to muffle the sound.

"What's so fucking funny?" Will demanded, trying to keep his voice low. He would have grabbed the friar if he could see him, but the darkness was total inside the fetid room, and he had to wait until the friar came to his senses.

Eventually Tuck wiped the tears from his face and lit the torch. As it flared into life he grinned at his furious companion. "The farts in here have long gone: out the door you kicked in. We're quite safe."

"Arsehole," Will growled, prompting another snigger from Tuck.

Thankfully, there was more than one opening in the wall to the latrine. Will only had to climb up one storey before he could make his way inside the castle proper.

The problem was the wall was covered in green slime and white mildew so thick and hairy it looked like it might get up and climb into the castle itself. Will threw a hand up to his mouth and gagged.

"Here." Tuck handed the ornate reliquary that held Christ's facial hair to his friend. "You're going to need this."

* * *

Matilda awoke in a sweat, tears streaking her cheeks in the darkness. The house was silent and she

189

absent-mindedly stroked her swollen belly, the nightmare fresh and raw in her mind.

Robin had been in terrible danger, although she had woken up as the great black faceless figure had swept its sword down into his body. She shuddered and pulled the blanket tighter around her, telling herself it was just a dream.

She thought it must be her mind's way of reproaching her for the way she spoke to Robin the last time he'd visited, chasing him off as if she hated him. Which was, of course, nonsense – she loved him! – but the pained look on his face as he'd walked out the door had stayed with her and she wished she could see him to make friends again.

Sighing, she sent a silent message to him to let him know how she felt, hoping, somehow he would hear, or feel it, and closed her eyes to sleep again.

* * *

Climbing the wall of the latrine proved to be every bit as disgusting as Will had feared. Once he had looked at the hand holds, and fixed a mental image of the place in his mind, he told Tuck to extinguish the torch in case someone from the castle came in to relieve themselves and found the outlaws.

They had went back outside and found some old branches with as much foliage still attached as possible which Will used to scrape off whatever filth he could before attempting the climb. The mortar between the stones was old and loose and it was fairly easy for him to find good hand and footholds, but, by the time he was halfway to the opening he was drenched in sweat, not to mention the sticky grime that coated his hands.

He was almost at the top when he heard the creak of a door opening somewhere and he froze, pressing his body instinctively into the filth-encrusted wall, praying he'd be able to hold onto the wall.

The sounds of distant laughter and revelry filtered down through the latrine, and there was a dim glow which cast shadows on the walls, clearly from a torch in the room above.

The loud voices of two drunk men boomed off the stone walls, sharing inanities and laughing at nothing. Suddenly, for just a moment, there was silence, then Will almost screamed with fury as a stream of warm piss hit the top of his head and ran down the back of his neck.

Somehow, the outlaw closed his eyes and clung to his position in outraged silence, as the men above resumed their inebriated conversation and, at last, the stream of urine stopped.

The dim light, and the sound of their voices faded as the door closed behind them, and Scarlet cursed them and their children to the tenth generation. It took him a moment to clear his mind and begin his ascent again.

From the darkness below, Tuck's voice carried cheerfully up to him.

"At least they didn't need a shit."

* * *

"Do you know how far it is to Pontefract?"

Edmond glanced over at his captive and growled at him nastily. "No, but I know how to get there. We just have to follow the road to Wakefield then continue along and it'll lead us straight there. Then I'll see justice done."

Sir Richard plodded on for a while, then turned to look back at Edmond. "Pontefract is twenty miles from here. On foot, like this, it'll take us forever to get there."

The younger man's face fell, then he laughed nervously. "You're lying. Sir Philip wouldn't ask me to take you all that way."

"Sir Philip was probably expecting you to have a small group of men with you. Or horses. What happens at night, when you have to sleep? Or when you have to do the toilet?"

Edmond didn't reply as they walked along the little path, heading for the main road that would take them east, in the direction of Pontefract.

"I tell you truly, I wish your brother hadn't died. I was just defending myself, as is a man's right. You would have done the same thing in my position."

Still, Edmond remained silent, tears rolling down his cheeks as he pictured Walter's face in his mind. Poor Walter. His life had been hard, and his death even harder.

"Come, lad," Richard went on, looking up at the trees as if he was talking to God himself. "You'd be as well killing me now – there's no way you can hold me hostage for the length of this journey. Tell me what Sir Philip is paying you to capture me."

"It's not just about money, Hospitaller! I wanted to do something brave, and noble, and noteworthy. Something that would show those arseholes in Kirklees that Walter wasn't the useless idiot they made him out to be. The money is just a bonus."

The knight looked round at Edmond, taking in the stumpy body, large fish-like lips and short limbs. He guessed it wasn't just Walter that had been the butt of the villager's jokes.

A memory suddenly flared in Sir Richard's head. "Aren't you married? I'm sure I remember your father telling me his son was betrothed. He was very proud – as a father should be." His voice trailed off as he thought of his own son, killed before he could find a woman to share his life with.

"She died," Edmond snarled, his thick lips spraying saliva before him. "Same as my da!"

No wonder the man's so angry, Sir Richard thought, holding his peace for now. *He and his brother bullied for years, his wife dead, his parents dead, and now I've killed his only surviving kin...Christ above,* he prayed, *help me!*

As he mouthed his silent supplication, the weight of everything that had befallen him in recent months came down on his old shoulders and the Hospitaller knew what he had to do.

He stopped in his tracks and Edmond stopped too, leaning back into a defensive stance, the knight's sword held before him.

"Why are you stopping? Move on! Sir Philip never said I had to take you to him in one piece."

Richard raised a hand. "Calm down, lad. You can relax." He clasped his hands and gazed at his captor. "I'll travel with you to Pontefract Castle. I give you my word as a Knight of St. John, I won't try to escape. Whatever happens, I will allow you to take me, as your prisoner, to Sir Philip."

Edmond's eyes flickered from side to side warily, half-expecting men to burst from the trees to aid the Hospitaller. Surely this was some trick.

"Why?"

Sir Richard sighed, his bearded face falling, and suddenly Edmond noticed just how old the man was.

"My wife and my youngest son are dead. The king himself wants me hanged. I'm a disgraced rebel who's spent the last few weeks hiding like a frightened woman in a lonely castle." He smiled ruefully at his captor. "I have my eldest son – Edward – but he has his own life, far away in Rhodes...God has allowed me to fall into your hands, so...I will go to Pontefract with you, freely. You may sleep – or relieve yourself – when you must, without fearing I'll kill you or sneak off."

From the wary, and somewhat frightened expression on Edmond's face, it was obvious the young man had no idea what to make of this.

In truth, Sir Richard felt desperately sorry for the man. And guilty for taking his one sibling and friend from him. If he'd analyzed his own motives more honestly, the knight might not have made his promise to the tanner's son. But it seemed to him like this was a thing he could do to make Edmond's life better. He knew he couldn't hide out forever in Kirklees Castle – it would drive him mad before much longer, which was why he'd even been out in the open in the first place.

"I have your oath on this, Hospitaller? You're almost a priest right? Your oath, before Christ, has to be binding!"

Sir Richard nodded. "You have my oath."

"Thank God," Edmond grunted, dropping the sword onto the grass and pulling his breeches down about his thick thighs. "I've been desperate for a piss for ages."

The young villager continued to eye him suspiciously, warm urine splattering and steaming on the grass, and Sir Richard turned away, looking thoughtfully into the dense trees.

It felt like a weight had been lifted from his shoulders. He *would* go to Pontefract with Edmond. The young man would be well rewarded by Sir Philip, and be able to go back to Kirklees with a tale that would finally earn him the respect from the villagers that he so desperately craved.

Would the king hang him? Yes, Sir Richard knew he would. It would give Edward the perfect excuse to seize Kirklees – Hospitaller lands – permanently.

As Edmond pulled his trousers back up with a satisfied grunt, and stooped to retrieve the dropped sword, Sir Richard moved off along the overgrown trail again, casting another prayer skyward.

Lord, I place myself at your mercy. But it would be nice if my sergeant-at-arms turned up in time to save me from a humiliating death on the gallows!

* * *

When he finally made it to London Stephen was exhausted. He had pushed his body to the limit trying to make up for lost time and the fact he was now on foot. As he passed through Enfield he was able to buy a tired old palfrey, but by then he was close to collapse from the physical and mental pressure he had placed himself under.

When the Moorgate of London came into view he could have cried out in relief if he had the strength, but his elation soon left him as his eyes took in the sight of hundreds of people queueing to get into the city.

Making sure his shield was easily visible and the cross prominently displayed on his black surcoat, he led the palfrey off the road onto the verge and kicked it into a canter, racing past the patiently waiting queue. Most people, quickly spotting the Hospitaller livery and his arms and armour, kept their mouths shut, although one or two braver than the rest cursed him for skipping the line.

Stephen never even heard them, tired and focused as he was on entering the city at last. The crowd was a blur until he came closer to the gates and reined in his mount, roaring at the top of his voice for people to move and let him through.

Not everyone was quick to obey, and Stephen knew he was courting disaster as he rode the old horse directly into the queue of people, scattering them.

"Stand aside!" he shouted, trying to summon his most powerful parade-ground voice from protesting lungs. "Hospitaller on official business!"

Three men, wealthy merchants judging from their clothes and haughty manner, stood their ground, glaring at the sergeant-at-arms bearing down on them, but Stephen was in no mood to slow his progress now.

"Get out of the way you arseholes or I'll ride you into the ground!" To emphasise the point he pulled his sword free from its sheath and held it above his head.

The merchants, realising the crazed soldier wasn't slowing, scattered to the side of the road shouting curses at his back as he rode past them up to the gate.

The guards, used to seeing things like this all the time, stopped the Hospitaller to ask his business but quickly waved him on his way. Sometimes they would be rewarded with a coin or two when they fast-tracked someone in a hurry, but Stephen offered nothing. Despite that, the guards were glad to send the wild-eyed sergeant on his way before he caused any trouble.

He had a vague idea of where the Hospitaller headquarters were situated but it was a few years since he had last visited and his memory wasn't very clear. Stopping for a moment, he asked for directions and walked his horse through the streets in the direction indicated by the eager locals hoping – fruitlessly – for a small reward from the soldier.

It felt like an age before he finally reached the grand stone building that housed the Grand Prior of England's chapter of The Order of St John, and when he saw it, he felt his stomach lurch anxiously.

He shook his head with a rueful grin. He'd almost been killed numerous times in pitched battles with the Saracen, where it felt like hell had come to Earth and yet the thought of facing Prior L'Archer and possibly failing his master Sir Richard frightened him more than any fight he'd had since he was a raw young recruit.

Almost oblivious to the sights, smells and sounds around him, Stephen slowly dismounted, the muscles in his legs screaming in pain, and led his horse through the imposing archway that led into Clerkenwell Priory.

He was finally here, and, praise be to God, he still had Sir Richard's letter to the Grand Prior.

Let me be in time to help my master, Lord!

CHAPTER SIXTEEN

At last, panting and stinking, Will reached the top of the wall. The wooden bench that people sat on to relieve themselves pushed out of the way easily enough and the filthy outlaw scrambled into the room as quickly as possible.

Divesting himself of Tuck's sodden robe and feeling much cleaner for it, he hid the wet garment under the bench which he shoved back into position, then moved to the door, opening it a crack to make sure no one was around.

The corridor appeared to be empty, and as his eyes adjusted to the flickering light he took in the layout of the place. Closed doors led to what he supposed must be bedrooms, and a flight of stairs led up and down just outside of where he stood.

He crept down the stairway, hand on his sword hilt and shook his head. This was madness! He had no idea how to get to the dungeon, and chances were he'd be found if he just wandered about the place, but he didn't see what else he could do.

He reached another landing, on the ground floor he guessed, where the sound of the party was louder, but the steps stopped here so he slowly made his way along the corridor, praying no one was about. Again, closed doors led off to God-knew where and, thinking it wise to have a hiding place should someone appear, he listened at the first one he came to. It was impossible to know if anyone was inside over the noise of the feast which was obviously close-by.

Drawing his sword, he gritted his teeth and tried the handle. The heavy door opened easily and he moved inside, eyes flickering from side to side seeking any threats.

The place was empty and appeared to be a storeroom for bed clothes, curtains and other soft furnishings which were folded neatly or hung on rails. The fresh smell of lavender filled the air and the outlaw wished he could sleep on sheets like these every night. Exhaling softly, he decided to wait for a short time, to see if anyone would come past that might be able to lead him to the dungeon.

Leaving the door open a crack, he watched the corridor. Revellers passed every so often, obviously making their way to the latrine, or, in some cases, couples were looking for somewhere private to get to know each other better. Thankfully they all continued along the corridor and up the stairwell – Will had no desire to kill innocent civilians should they stumble on his hiding place.

As another drunk middle-aged man stumbled past humming to himself, Will cursed and decided he'd wasted enough time; the feast wasn't going to last forever, and he hadn't even found Robin yet, never mind freed him.

He began to pull the door to the storeroom open, then quickly closed it again as two stocky men wearing the sheriff's livery appeared in the hall, making their way towards him. They carried pole-arms, but appeared lightly armoured, and Scarlet's mind whirled as he wondered what to do.

Hurriedly, he pushed the door shut and hid behind one of the great curtain rails close to the door then, trying to judge when the guards would be passing the room, he made a high-pitched squeal. Not a threatening sound, or too loud to be overly obvious he hoped.

Suddenly the door was pushed open, and Will heard the men wandering into the room.

"What was it?" one of them asked. "I never heard anything."

"Dunno," his companion replied. "Christ above, where's that smell of shit coming from?"

The voices moved in front of Will, going further into the room, and, steeling himself as they came near, he silently pushed through the curtains and plunged the tip of his sword into the side of the guard nearest him.

The man cried out as the outlaw pulled his bloody sword free, and, as he collapsed onto the floor his companion spun round, eyes wide with shock, before Will punched him in the guts with all his strength.

The door to the room was lying open, so he ran over and pushed it shut, then made his way back to the downed guards. The one he'd stabbed was no threat – he was already dead and Will nodded, knowing his thrust had been a good one. The second man had pushed himself back to his feet despite Scarlet's heavy blow, and now aimed a wild swing at the outlaw's head with his pole-arm.

Ducking just in time, Will launched himself at the guard and the pair fell back onto a pile of bed-sheets, struggling for their lives. The man was strong and obviously well-trained in hand-to-hand combat, but Scarlet's massive upper-body strength was too much and, forcing the guard's hands down onto the sheets, the outlaw slammed his forehead into the man's nose, then, when he went limp, Scarlet leaned back and hammered another punch into the guard's stomach.

Vomit and bile filled the unfortunate man's mouth and his face turned red as he began to asphyxiate before Will pulled him onto his side, retching and spluttering as the foul liquid spilled out and his airway cleared.

Panting himself, Will sheathed his sword and drew his dagger, pressing it against the sobbing guard's neck.

"I already killed your pal," he growled, tossing the pole-arm away into the corner. "The only reason I didn't let you choke on your own puke is that I need information."

"Who are you?" the guard gasped. "What do you want?"

"I'm a friend of Robin Hood," Will replied. "I'm here to take him home. And you," he pressed the dagger against the man's neck, drawing blood, "are going to tell me how I find him."

"Fine! I'll tell you, just take that away."

Will released the pressure on the dagger, hopeful the man would be true to his word. He had no stomach for torture, but this guard *would* give him the information he wanted, one way or another.

The man lay still for a moment, trying to catch his breath, then, wiping the wet sick from his mouth and cheek, he leaned his head up from the dirty sheet and glared at Scarlet.

"I've no love for your leader – him and the rest of your gang have killed more than a few of my fellows. But I also have no love for that bastard Sir Guy of Gisbourne. He's made me spar with him twice now, and battered me black and blue both times. Sadistic, arrogant wanker he is. If you manage to free Hood, Gisbourne won't be quite the hero any more, and if you die trying, it'll fucking serve you right."

"How do I get into the dungeon then?" Will asked impatiently.

"Here, take my surcoat," the guard said, pulling the light blue garment with the sheriff's coat-of-arms emblazoned on the front over his head and tossing it weakly to the outlaw. "Hopefully it'll stop any of my mates challenging you. The stairs to the dungeon are at the far end of the corridor. There's a door, but Charlie on the floor there has the key. You'll have to get the key to Hood's cell from the jailer down in the dungeon though – Adam's the only person that carries the keys for the cells. Don't kill him like you did Charlie, will you?"

Will found the key on the dead man's belt and placed it in his pouch before turning back to face the guard.

"What are you going to do with me?"

Will shrugged. "I can't leave you to raise the alarm" –

"Don't kill me," the young man mumbled. "Please. I have two little boys, Matthew and Andrew,

I...please..." His voice trailed off as he pictured his children and he held his head in his hands.

"Matthew and Andrew?" Will repeated, thinking back to the man in the inn. "Are you James?"

The guard looked up in surprise. "Aye, how did you know that?"

"I had a few ales with your brother earlier on. He told us about you climbing in and out of here through the latrine – that's why I stink of shit and piss. Never mind the rest," Will grunted, raising his hand to silence any more questions. "I don't have time. I also have no wish to kill you."

With his dagger he tore one of the sheets into strips and used it to bind the guard's hands and feet, then used another strip to gag him.

"I expect someone will come looking for you and your mate eventually. I just hope me and Robin are gone by then." He opened his pouch and took out some silver coins – probably six month's wages to the guardsman – and stuffed them into the small pocket sewn into the man's gambeson. "Look after your little boys."

With a wink, Scarlet stood and left the room, closing the door behind him.

* * *

"Don't think I trust you, or we're friends or anything like that, Hospitaller. Your warped sense of honour may be telling you to come to Pontefract with me, but you still murdered Walter and I'll watch you hang for it."

Sir Richard nodded at the young man's rant. They had been travelling for hours and he was tired and bored. Any attempt at conversation had been met with stony silence or threats of violence; sometimes Edmond would lash out physically as he just had, almost as if reminding himself of their roles.

"I didn't murder your brother: you two attacked *me*, remember. I saw two young men coming at me with naked blades – how would you have reacted?"

201

Edmond growled but didn't reply.

"You look a hardy fighter to me," Sir Richard went on, turning to eye his captor's powerful, if short, arms and a nose flattened from many brawls over the years. "I'm sure you'd have done the same as I did."

The tanner's son knew the knight had the right of it, and it gnawed at him to realise Walter had died because of him and his stupid plan. Two village boys overpowering a Hospitaller Knight, a man who had fought, and won, countless battles in the Holy Land! The idea seemed ridiculous now, and Edmond shook his head sorrowfully at his own hubris.

"Your mother died when you were young, didn't she?"

Edmond glared at Sir Richard, but the knight's face was open and sincere, with no trace of malice in it, and he muttered a reply. "She died giving birth to Walter."

"And your father?"

"He died two months ago. I took over his shop."

They walked on in silence for a while, the road wide and open at this point as the ancient Romans had paved it and the trees hadn't managed to reclaim the ground yet. Dark clouds filled the air and Sir Richard huddled into his cloak which wasn't a thick one since he hadn't been expecting this long journey when he'd left his castle.

"Did the villagers make things hard for Walter?"

Again, Edmond looked at his captive's face, trying to read the man's expression, but all he saw was apparently genuine interest. What harm would it do to talk to the knight? It might help ease his own guilt, if even a little.

"Walter was a nice person. The children his own age used to hit him because he was different to them – slower. But he never hit them back, he didn't really have it in his nature. He would come home and sit by the hearth crying. Da would tell him he had to stand up for himself, but he wouldn't, and that just made it worse."

202

The images came to his mind and he clenched his fists in anger at the cruelty of the boys. "Then one day he came in and his shoulder was out of place. The barber said it was..."

"Dislocated?" Sir Richard offered.

"Aye, that," Edmond agreed. "His face was pale and he screamed in agony when the barber put it back into place. Four of the children had..." his voice cracked in disgust, but he carried on through gritted teeth. "They had tied a noose around his neck and pulled him up onto a branch! The rope snapped and he'd landed on his shoulder – the boys had run off when Walter got his breath back and started screaming."

They walked on, the clouds growing ever more threatening, and Sir Richard let Edmond gather his thoughts for a while.

"How could children do something like that? So...evil? Walter was only eight! A little boy!"

The Hospitaller stared along the road, his own memory replaying images of cruelty and hatred perpetrated by men supposedly fighting for the glory of God.

"Did you" –

"Aye, I did!" Edmond replied. "I found out who had done it and I did the same thing to one of them, but his da told the headman and I was warned not to go after any more of the little bastards. To this day, whenever Walter and I would go to the inn for an ale after work, those boys – grown men by now – would snigger at him and make choking motions." The rage left him and he gazed at Sir Richard with wide, damp eyes. "All because Walter was born a little bit slow-witted."

The rain began to fall on them then, gently. "So you wanted to show the men of Kirklees that Walter was as much of a man as any of them by capturing one of the rebel leaders."

Edmond nodded, bringing the sword up threateningly as if just remembering where they were going. "Aye, but you ruined it; you, and this." He looked in disgust at the blade in his own hand.

Sir Richard held his peace and they plodded on, the rain becoming a torrent, ending any possibility of further conversation, but the old knight understood Edmond much better now. It was clear from his body language that he hadn't just wanted to prove Walter's worth to his peers – he had wanted to prove *himself.* With his stumpy little body and odd-looking facial features, Sir Richard knew the village bullies would have made Edmond's life a misery, almost as much as they had Walter's.

The rain coursed down his face and dripped from his grey beard but the Hospitaller felt too tired to wipe it away. So much hatred and pain in the world. At his age, after everything he'd seen and done in his long years, he would have hoped to be able to make sense of life. But he had no better understanding of the ways of men now than he did when he was Edmond's age.

He sighed and bowed his head to let the rain drip off onto the old Roman road. *These stones have been here for centuries, and nothing's changed: men still can't stop hurting and killing one another...*

* * *

Will forced himself to keep moving along the corridor as the door to the great hall opened and a figure came through. If it was another guard, Will would surely be recognised and that would be the end of his rescue attempt.

"You – where's the latrine?"

The man fixed Scarlet with a drunken glare and the outlaw let out a sigh of relief. Just another reveller, thank Christ.

"Up the stairs, and straight ahead, my lord," he replied deferentially, as the man staggered off without another word.

"Noble twat." Will hurried to the opposite end of the corridor, to the great door that stood closed, and fitted the key he'd taken from the dead guard into the lock. It turned easily and he moved through onto another stairwell, which led down into the dimly lit, and damp-smelling dungeon.

He left the door unlocked: no one would come down here by accident, even if they were drunk: it was obvious the stairwell led to the dungeon, and leaving it unlocked would speed their escape once he had Robin.

Voices came to him as he reached the bottom of the steps. Men shouted for water, or food, or freedom. One seemed to be singing a children's song and Will shook his head, knowing the prisoners would have been physically and mentally abused horribly down here where no-one could hear their tortured cries.

Well, that wasn't his problem – some of them probably deserved it anyway.

Setting his shoulders confidently, he strode up to the two guardsmen who sat at a table playing dice. They looked up curiously, but the sight of the light blue surcoat Will had put on stopped them from reacting immediately with alarm.

"What's up?" one of them asked, squinting up at him. Will had stood directly in front of a guttering torch, so the guards couldn't make out his face in the brightness behind him, and he made the most of the few extra seconds it bought him.

"Adam?" he asked.

"Aye, what is it?" the man demanded impatiently. "Why are you down" –

Scarlet hammered the point of the pole-arm he'd taken from the dead guard in the linen room into Adam's chest, hurling the man backwards into the wall, where he stood for a moment, before sinking slowly to his knees, a look of disbelief on his face.

Before the second guard could react, Will withdrew the pole-arm and brought the blunt end round in a ferocious sweep that sent the shocked man

205

sprawling onto the floor. Reversing the weapon the outlaw plunged the bloody point through the groaning man's windpipe.

"Shit!" He cursed as he searched Adam's body for the keys to the cells. He hadn't wanted to kill the guards – if there had been just the one he would have overpowered him and locked him in his own cells. But it was too risky to try and beat two trained soldiers so there had been no other choice if he was to get Robin out of here alive. The guards had to die.

When he had exploded into violence, the sounds from the cells had stopped completely, and the eerie atmosphere closed in on him as he hastily made his way to the cell at the end of the stinking stone hallway.

The other prisoners pressed their faces against the iron gates, watching the man who had just murdered two of their hated jailers.

"Let us out of here," one of them shouted. "You have the keys, let us out!"

Will ignored them all as he reached the final cell and peered inside at the figure lying on the cold floor. "Robin!" he hissed, but the figure never moved.

The jailer's ring held a number of keys, all of similar shape and size, and he had to try half a dozen before the gate finally popped open with a harsh creak.

Warily, he made his way over to the prisoner lying on the ground, in case the man attacked him. "Robin," he muttered again, and this time was rewarded with a small groan from the prone figure.

By now, Will knew he'd found his friend – he recognised the clothes and the closely-cropped brown hair. Kneeling beside him, he laid a hand gently on Robin's arm and gave a gentle squeeze. "I've come to get you out of here," he told his young captain. "They're throwing a party upstairs to celebrate your capture, so I was able to climb inside. We have to move quickly though. Get up and let's go before we're discovered!"

The outlaw leader never moved, so Will carefully pushed him onto his back and gasped. Robin's eyes flickered open and his face split in an agonised grimace.

"I won't be climbing anywhere, Will."

"Holy Mother, what have they done to you?" The sight of Robin's blood-caked and terribly bruised face made Scarlet's blood run cold, and he guessed the rest of his friend's body was just as badly injured underneath his clothes.

"Gisbourne," Robin replied softly, obviously with great effort. His eyes filled with tears as he forced himself to continue. "The bastard killed Much!"

Will slumped onto the filthy stone floor and cradled Robin's head in his lap, feeling no shame as tears filled his own eyes at the sight of his broken friend.

"I know," he whispered. "We found him. I thought I'd be able to get inside here, we'd escape, and then we could hunt Gisbourne in the forest." He shook his head in frustrated rage. "I can't carry you out of here! I had to climb up the fucking latrine to get in, and it's the only way we'll be able to get back out!"

Robin shuddered as a wave of pain tore through his body and he gasped an apology to his would-be rescuer.

"Thank you for coming for me, Will. You're a true friend. But I can't even climb to my feet never mind climb down a wall. Leave me. You and John can lead the men. Take them away from Barnsdale – Gisbourne won't stop until he's killed every last one of us."

Scarlet hugged his friend's head as the tears of rage and sorrow rolled down his grime-encrusted face. He knew Robin was right: they couldn't just walk out of the castle past the guards at the gatehouse. It was over.

"Go!" Robin urged. "Before someone finds you!"

There was a sound from the end of the doorway above and Will growled like a rabid dog as he realised someone was coming down the stairs.

"Too late." He stood up and grasped his sword, gazing along the corridor. "Looks like we die here together, my friend."

CHAPTER SEVENTEEN

The rain had let up and thankfully the sun had broken through the patchy clouds, but it offered little heat and Sir Richard shivered in his sodden clothing.

Edmond was better off in his thick hooded cloak but he was huddled into it, clearly feeling the cold.

"We should stop and build a fire to dry ourselves and our clothes," Sir Richard said. "Unless you want us both to come down with a chill and be too sick to make it to Pontefract."

Edmond was lost in his thoughts and his head snapped up in surprise at the suggestion. "Aye," he agreed. "Fair enough. Night will be on us soon anyway. Let's hope we can find enough dry kindling to get a blaze going."

They moved off the road, Edmond watching his captive warily the whole time, sword still held ready even though his arm must have been very uncomfortable under the weight by now.

"Don't think about running" –

The Hospitaller waved him to silence and began hunting for firewood. A couple of old oaks grew near the roadside and they managed to find a few dry twigs and branches to build a small fire. "You get it going," Sir Richard suggested, as Edmond placed the little bundle in a pile. "I'll find more – we don't have enough there to dry us."

The thought of a warm blaze cheered Edmond as he set about constructing a small camp-fire and the big knight disappeared into the trees fringing the road. *Should I bring him back and keep him in sight?* He wondered. No, he had to trust the man's oath would hold – there was no way Edmond could watch him every moment of the day after all.

There was precious little dry kindling anywhere close to their makeshift camp, Sir Richard realised, widening his search irritably. He'd hoped to get a roaring fire going as soon as possible: the chill was seeping into his joints, making them ache, and he detested such pain for he knew it meant he was growing old. Christ, his own body-heat would have dried his soaking clothes twenty years ago! Now, he worried about catching his death if he didn't build a fire soon.

He shook his head ruefully, picking up what sticks he could find, discarding all but the driest.

Strangely, given his situation, he felt relaxed and somehow at peace. A captive on his way to what would very possibly turn out to be his death at the end of a rope, yet a comforting calm seemed to come over him as he searched for firewood and, as he looked around at the beauty of a spring forest coming into life again, he felt the joy of life for a while again and he smiled in appreciation.

The desperate scream of agony broke his train of thought, and he raced back towards the roadside, hand grasping for his missing sword.

* * *

"Can you stand?"

Will held the pole-arm he'd taken from the castle guard towards his injured friend, but Robin shook his head, clenching his teeth in pain. "I don't think so." He took the proffered weapon and with a super-human effort, managed to haul himself upright, but his vision blurred and he almost threw up as a wave of nausea swept over him.

"You'll do," Scarlet grunted appreciatively at Robin's display of willpower.

In truth, the young man had all but given up on life – he was physically and mentally utterly beaten. But the knowledge that Will had risked his own life to climb into this stronghold just to rescue him had given him back a little of his spirit.

Enough at least to face death like a warrior.

A man appeared, stopping momentarily to check on the two guards Will had dispatched, then, finding them dead, he stood and moved towards Robin's cell.

Will held his sword behind his back so it wouldn't gleam in the light of the torch that was being carried along the corridor towards them, while Robin clung to the thick wooden shaft of the pole-arm and prayed to the Magdalene to grant him the strength to wield it.

The torch-bearer moved straight along the passageway towards them, holding the light in his left hand and a quarterstaff in his right.

A cold sweat broke out on Will's back and neck; it was clear the man was coming straight for them, and felt confident enough in his own ability to take on whoever had killed two of the castle guards. It had to be Gisbourne himself.

Will could fight. He'd done so with distinction alongside the military Orders in the Holy Land after all. But he would be the first to admit his style was one of brute force, power and more often than not, sheer recklessness.

He knew he couldn't best Gisbourne. The only outlaw that could ever have beaten him was propped up on the stolen pole-arm next to him, gasping with the effort of holding himself upright.

Tensing himself, pulse thundering in his ears, Scarlet waited for Gisbourne to reach the cell door, determined to land the first blow; maybe he could take the bastard's hand off before he knew what was happening!

The king's man reached the cell and, with a roar, Scarlet threw himself at the cell gate, battering it open, but his target moved, stepping to one side and allowing the furious outlaw to barrel past.

"What the hell are you doing?"

Will faced his opponent in confusion as the torch was raised and he realised his mistake. It wasn't Sir Guy of Gisbourne that came hunting them after all.

"Tuck! How the hell did you get in here?"

The friar threw him a grin as he moved into the cell to check on Robin who still stood, swaying, as he clung onto his makeshift walking stick. "Walked in the front door. Much cleaner than climbing in through that latrine."

His eyes took in Robin's terrible injuries, but he too had served in the Holy Land, so he didn't allow his emotions to take control of him. They had no time to waste on questions or even rudimentary first-aid.

"We have to get out of here. Now," he said. "Where's that spare robe of mine you were wearing?"

"I left it in the latrine, under the bench," Will replied. "It stank, remember. Why?"

Tuck whispered a very un-Christian oath. "We might have been able to disguise Robin with it and leave the same way I came in. The guards weren't interested in looking at me too closely – I told them the sheriff had summoned me to preside over a wedding and I'd been late. They let me in without a fuss, despite the hour. They'd probably been drinking. But even so, there's no way they'll let me back out with Robin beside me."

"How high's that latrine?"

Will and the friar turned in surprise at Robin's question.

"Too high for you to climb in your state," Will replied sadly.

"How high?"

"The height of three or four men. Like I say, too high" –

"We need a rope then," their young leader mumbled through cracked lips. "You two should be able to lower me down, eh?"

Will thought about it for a second then nodded. "Aye, that'd work. We can make a rope out of the sheets in the room beside the latrine. I don't know how we'll get you along the hallway back there though. Anyone that sees you will know what's happening and raise the alarm. We can't fight our way out of here – Tuck's not much fitter than you, he's just woke up remember."

Tuck placed his torch into a sconce on the wall and shrugged out of his grey robe and pulled it over Robin's head, arranging the hood so it hid the young man's battered face. "Come on, let's get the hell out of here."

"Wait. Hold him," Will said to the friar, taking the pole arm from Robin's thick purple fingers and leaning it against the cell wall. He drew his sword again and carefully, but powerfully, hacked down on the shaft of the long wooden weapon, taking the steel blade off the end. He handed it back to Robin with shrug. "Looks a bit more like a clergyman's staff now."

The friar recovered his torch and then they walked as fast as possible back along the corridor, ignoring the pleas for help from the other prisoners, only stopping so Tuck could remove one of the dead guards' surcoats and put it on.

Two of the sheriff's men and a feeble old Franciscan friar... Maybe they'd get out of here alive after all...

They had to move slowly, with Tuck and Scarlet supporting Robin as they climbed the stairs back to the ground floor. If any of the other guardsmen had appeared it would have been the end for the outlaws, but somehow the friar's eyes retained their mischievous sparkle and Will's indomitable spirit saw him carry most of the weight of his injured leader.

"You'll have to walk from here," he said to Robin as they reached the top of the stairs and the door that led out onto the main corridor. "If we support you it'll look suspicious."

Robin sucked air in through his teeth and nodded in silent determination.

Will pulled the heavy door open and, all three of them praying silently, they moved into the hallway.

The sounds from the feast had grown louder as more wine and ale had been consumed – even through the doorway men's voices could be heard raised in jest or argument, while women laughed shrilly and the minstrels tried to be heard over the whole cacophony.

"Move!" The hallway was empty, so Will strode forward, grasping Robin by the upper arm, his eyes fixed on the final door on the right where he'd left the guard, James, bound and gagged, and where they'd find the sheets to make a rope for Robin to climb out of this place.

Tuck did his best to keep up and between them, he and Will practically carried their hooded friend for what seemed like an eternity, until they came to the door they were heading for and Will turned the handle to let them inside.

It refused to move.

"What's wrong?" Tuck demanded as Scarlet wiggled the latch and cursed.

"It's locked from inside," the infuriated outlaw replied, eyes flicking nervously along the hallway as he continued to try the handle. "The latch must have fallen when I left the room earlier!"

The sound of footsteps came to them then, and a man's voice, singing softly to himself, apparently drunk.

"Come on, Will!" Tuck hissed, but the door was locked and no amount of shaking was going to free it.

The singer – an obviously wealthy man from his expensive clothing – appeared from the stairwell to the latrine and cast an inebriated eye over them, an idiotic half-smile on his face. He nodded inanely at them as he moved past, and the outlaws felt a moment of relief.

The man stopped a few paces along the corridor and spun round unsteadily. "I know you!" he shouted, staring at Scarlet. "You're that" –

"Open the door, Will!" Tuck roared, and launched himself at the drunkard.

Robin was left to steady himself on his staff, as Will stood back and hammered kick after kick into the sturdy door while the friar landed a flurry of punches into the unfortunate nobleman who collapsed in a heap on the stone floor.

"Open it, now!" Friar Tuck glared at the red-faced, panting Scarlet and leaned down to drag the unconscious nobleman over to the doorway which, finally, burst open with a massive crash.

Robin limped into the room, as Will grabbed the right bicep of the unconscious party-goer and he and Tuck dragged the man inside.

They pushed the door shut behind them, just as a clamour of voices came to them from the feast. From the sound of it, at least half a dozen men had decided to go for a piss at the same time, and the outlaws shook their heads in relief.

"Just as well you got that door open," Tuck said to Will, who threw him a sour look as he finished with, "it took you long enough."

"Hurry," Robin muttered, slipping to the floor, his eyelids fluttering weakly.

"Right." Will nodded, taking in the sight of the guard, James, still safely bound on the floor, watching them intently. "We can use these." He grabbed a pile of neatly folded white sheets and hurriedly tied them together. "Four or five will be enough...are you going to have the strength to hold onto this as we lower you down?"

Robin watched his friend as if in a daze, and Will shook his head in frustration as he looked over at Friar Tuck. "I'll make it six so we can tie one around his waist. He's not going to be much help like that."

"What about him?" Tuck asked, nodding at the guardsman lying tied up on the floor. "He'll give us away. I'm pleased, but surprised, that you left him alive in the first place."

Will shrugged as he tied the sheets together. "We shared a few ales with his brother earlier tonight. He's the guard that climbed out the latrine to see his girl, remember?"

Tuck locked eyes with the bound guard whose expression was unreadable. He walked over to him as Will finished tying the last of the sheets together and leaned down, their eyes still fixed on each other's.

"Your brother seems a good man, and, from what he told us, so are you," the friar said. "So are we." He gazed earnestly at the man. "Look at what your Sir Guy of Gisbourne did to our friend. Robin Hood: a man who helped the poor to eat in winter! A man who steals from those who are obscenely wealthy to give to the likes of your brother. Gisbourne almost killed him, and Sir Henry de Faucumberg *will* hang him if he can."

Scarlet tied off the last of the sheets and bundled the lot together in his arms. "Don't give us away James, eh?"

The guard looked at Will, then at Tuck, and finally, nodded his head. Will smiled, praying the man would keep his promise.

"Let's get out of here."

* * *

Edmond, trusting the Hospitaller would return, had crafted a small fire and, exhausted by their long journey, sunk into a kind of a trance state once he'd managed to get a blaze going with his flint and steel. The camp-fire filled his vision and the heat drove the ache from his muscles as he gazed into the hypnotic dancing flame and pondered his life.

His brother was dead, but he still had the knight. Sir Philip would reward Edmond with silver once he turned over the Hospitaller – enough to expand his father's old tannery on the edge of town so he could continue to support himself.

The thought both comforted and sickened him. He would be able to make a comfortable living until he was elderly, which was all a man could ask for. But at the same time, he knew those bastards in Kirklees would continue to look down on him as if he was beneath them.

He felt old. Much older than he should have at his twenty-four years. He shook his head angrily. Once he built a bigger tannery he would be able to earn more money and he could find a new wife. The village men didn't care about looks when it came to marrying off their daughters, only status and, more importantly, money mattered.

He would have enough money to marry whoever he liked!

Then...then the men would respect him.

He slammed his fist onto the ground in frustration. He was as bad as them, trying to impress them, to be accepted for his wealth, as if their fucking opinion mattered.

For his entire life, Edmond had been confused, wanting to be accepted and respected, and resenting his brother for holding him back socially. The warm tears filled his eyes as he thought of Walter, innocent Walter, who simply wanted to be everyone's friend.

A cold rage filled him then, as the injustice of his whole life filled his head, and it was just as well, as a figure flew from the trees towards him, sword held high ready for a killing blow.

Edmond somehow managed to lift the sword he'd taken from Sir Richard and parried the attacker's blow awkwardly as he jumped to his feet. He felt his wrist twisting as the steel blades met with a deafening noise and pain lanced along the length of his arm, making him cry out.

He held the Hospitaller's sword before him, eyes flickering wildly, as two other men appeared either side of his attacker.

"What do you want?" Edmond demanded, his voice stronger than he'd expected, given the fear coursing through his veins at the odds stacked against him.

"Your fire," his original attacker grunted with a confident grin. "And any food you have – we're starving, see?" He patted his round belly which looked as if it had been filled with both food and ale often enough over the years, then his face became deadly serious. "And we'll have that fine blade."

Edmond's eyes moved between the three robbers and the anger built inside him again. People always treated him like a piece of shit! Even the dregs of society, like these toothless outlaws, would order him around as if he was nothing.

It didn't matter to Edmond then that the three men were well-armed and decently armoured, the rage was in him now and he didn't care if he lived or died.

All he wanted to do was kill these dirty, smug bastards.

Sweeping Sir Richard's sword up into the air, Edmond gave a hoarse war-cry and launched himself at the three robbers.

He would die here, but rather that than have anyone else treat him like filth.

* * *

When the hallway was quiet the three outlaws made their way out of the linen store and headed up the stairs to the latrine. Will went first, to deal with anyone that might get in their way, but there was no one there and they made it safely into the room.

Tuck had been forced to support his terribly beaten young leader up the steps, even though he himself was badly weakened from his own recent ordeal. By the time the pair reached Will, they were both breathing heavily and obviously struggling.

Will had shoved the wooden bench aside and retrieved the Franciscan robe, which he handed to Tuck as he hobbled into the room. "Stick it on. Aye, it stinks, but it'll keep the shit on the walls off you when you climb down."

"We can't all go down at once," the friar said, pulling the stained robe over his tonsured head. "Me and you will have to lower him down." He nodded at Robin who lay with his back against the wall, bruised face screwed up as the constant pain from his numerous injuries racked his body. "What if someone walks in? A guard?"

Will began tying the sheet around Robin's waist. "I'm dressed like one of them," he replied, patting the blue surcoat. "If anyone comes up the stairs we'll hear them and I'll tell 'em the latrine's busy. If it's a guard..." He shrugged. They'd deal with that if it happened.

"Come on, Robin," he knelt down and used his great arm and shoulder muscles to help the young man up. "You'll have to wake up a bit," he said, staring into his leader's eyes. "Otherwise you're going to end up lying in a pile of shit when you reach the bottom."

Robin gave a weak nod and glanced towards the opening as Will dropped the hacked-off pole-arm into the void.

"Right, let's do it."

Tuck and Will helped Robin over the edge of the wall, making sure they held the tied-together sheets firmly, and then they started to slowly lower him down to the ground.

They played the fabric out, hand over hand, their young friend doing just enough to keep himself from battering painfully off the grimy wall, then Will froze, his heart sinking as someone came into the room behind them. Turning, he heard the sound of a surprised breath being drawn before the man challenged them in a commanding voice.

"What the hell are you men doing in here?"

CHAPTER EIGHTEEN

Tuck didn't seem to hear the question, but Will's head spun round and he looked at the nobleman watching them in bemusement.

Concentrating as they were on lowering Robin down the stinking shaft, the friar and the ex-mercenary hadn't heard the tall man coming up the stairs. Will cursed inwardly as he took in the man's height – bigger than he and Tuck – and his apparently alert expression; this party-goer didn't seem to be anything like as drunk as the rest of the fools that had been stumbling around the castle for the past few hours.

Thankfully, the newcomer had taken in the guard's surcoat Will wore and, despite his curiosity, didn't seem too alarmed at what was going on.

"I dropped something down the latrine," Tuck smiled ruefully at the man. "My rosary beads. Archbishop Melton gave them to me," he added sadly. "This guard was kind enough to help me try and recover them without climbing in amongst all the...filth...down there."

As the man walked forward to look down the shaft where Tuck was gesturing, the two outlaws continued to play out the sheet until, thankfully, they felt the material go slack and knew Robin must have reached the bottom.

The big man peered down into the inky darkness just as Will released the sheet and brought his right fist up to hammer into the man's jaw, but, before he could collapse backwards onto the floor, Tuck grasped the back of his head and pushed him forwards, down the latrine shaft.

There was a wet thump as the stunned man landed face-first in the pile of shit below and Tuck couldn't suppress a shudder.

"He's unconscious," the friar said, looking over the edge, the light from the torches guttering in the room they stood in casting just enough orange light below.

"Or dead," Will growled in reply. "Get down there, in case he wakes up. Or drowns." He gestured to the sheet that still lay hanging down the shaft, tying it around the bench which he shoved against the wall as Tuck disappeared below.

Will stood, hand ready on the pommel of his sword, but no one else came into the latrine until the friar reached the bottom of the latrine wall.

He untied the white sheet and tossed it down the shaft so no one would see it and wonder at its purpose, then he carefully made his way over the ledge, his feet and hands finding the gaps in the mortar that he'd used to make his original ascent. He stretched up and pulled the mildew-encrusted bench over the opening behind him, casting the shaft into almost total darkness.

A man came in to the latrine to take a piss as the outlaw climbed slowly down into the void, but Will smiled thankfully as the warm liquid passed him some way to the side, splattering noisily onto the mound of waste beneath.

Below, Tuck's grasping fingers finally managed to find the torch they had left there earlier that night, and, as Will reached the bottom, the pitch flared into life and the outlaws shielded their eyes against the brightness Tuck's spark had ignited.

Robin sat near the door, his eyes closed as if in sleep, but Will could see the young man's chest rise and fall and he thanked Christ for it. That they had managed to get this far was a miracle, he thought.

The nobleman Tuck had shoved over the ledge hadn't fared so well, Will saw, taking in the sickening angle the man's right arm lay at in relation to his body. Clearly the bone was broken. They pushed him onto his side, hoping the faecal matter wouldn't infect the open wound where the snapped bone had torn through the skin.

"He'll live," Will growled, shaking his head contritely. "Unlike us if we're found. What do we do now, Tuck?"

Tuck looked at his friend in surprise. "I don't have a clue. I never expected us to get this far!"

Will shrugged his big shoulders. "We can't stay here; they'll rip the whole castle apart once they discover Robin missing and this one starts screaming," he nodded down at the unconscious noble. "We'll head back to the *King and Castle*. It's not far and our disguises should see us past any nosy guards. We can hide Robin in our room and pay to stay a couple more nights until we think about what to do next."

Tuck nodded uncertainly, his face pallid and sickly-looking in the torch's flickering glow. "What about that guard James? If he tells his brother what's happened tonight, word will spread and the sheriff will know where to come looking for us."

It was a gamble they had to take. There was no other choice. Even if Robin and Tuck had been fully fit, they couldn't have just climbed over the walls out of Nottingham, in the dead of night, without being spotted.

"Come on," Will replied, taking the torch from the friar and extinguishing it in the mound of human waste with a noisome stench that caught in their throats. "Let's head back to the inn. All we can do is pray God brings us luck. We're going to need it..."

* * *

Sir Richard was gasping for breath by the time he made it back to the camp-site, but he didn't have time to rest as his eyes took in the scene before him.

Edmond, blood covering his sword-arm, had been forced back against the thick trunk of an old beech, and desperately parried the attacks from two enraged men. A third man knelt on the ground behind them clutching his side which was also drenched in blood.

222

Awkwardly freeing the concealed dagger that was strapped to his calf, the big knight burst from the trees, surprising the attackers, and hammered the small blade into the nearest man's guts, forcing it up with all his strength and ripping it out with a wet sucking sound.

The man collapsed onto the grass, his eyes wide in shock and fear as his hands tried to cover the obviously mortal wound. Sir Richard kicked him in the face and grabbed the sword which fell from his limp fingers.

The remaining outlaw, terrified now, looked at the old knight, saw the feared Hospitaller cross on his black surcoat and decided to make a run for it. Before he could move though, Edmond swung his stolen sword in a high, wide arc and felt it bite into the side of the outlaw's skull, sending the man face-first onto the grass already dead.

Knowing the fight was over, Sir Richard placed his hands on his thighs and sucked in lungfuls of air.

Edmond, rage still burning in his veins, stalked towards his original attacker, who knelt, pale-faced, on the ground, blood seeping from the gash in his side that Edmond had inflicted on him.

"You win," the man growled, his face twisted bitterly. "Just let me" –

Sir Richard winced as Edmond hacked his sword down into the outlaw's shoulder, slicing halfway into the man's torso.

"Here," the tanner's son whispered, turning and throwing the sword onto the grass in front of the Hospitaller. "Have your sword back." Then he walked over to sit by the fire, staring into it in a daze as Sir Richard stooped to retrieve his weapon.

As the knight wiped the blade clean using one of the dead outlaws' cloaks, silent tears streamed down Edmond's face. It had been a hard couple of days.

Sir Richard searched the corpses, finding little of value other than some food and an ale-skin, then he dragged the bodies out of sight and hurried back to where he'd dropped the firewood he'd collected before the fight.

When he returned with arms full of kindling the sun had almost crested the horizon and it was rapidly growing dark. Edmond hadn't moved, so Sir Richard built up the fire and finally sat down beside the grieving young man.

Silently, he handed Edmond the ale-skin he'd found. "Drink. It will help settle your nerves."

Sir Richard leaned back on the grass, more tired than he'd felt in his life, but then he remembered Edmond had been hurt and, muscles protesting, pushed himself to his feet and moved over to the wounded man.

It was a long cut, which explained why there was so much blood on his arm, but it wasn't deep, thankfully. The Hospitaller moved into the trees where he'd dumped the bodies of the would-be robbers and returned with a blouson which he tore into strips and used to bind Edmond's arm.

The young man grunted his thanks, an odd look in his eyes, and Sir Richard shrugged. "Finish the last of that ale and eat a little of this." He handed over some of the food – cheese and bread – that he'd taken from the dead men. "Then get some sleep. I'll keep the fire banked and take first watch."

"Watch?"

The knight smiled. "Aye, lad, watch. Those three arseholes might have friends about here that'll come looking for them. You want to die in your sleep with a sword through your stomach?"

Edmond nodded, his expression now almost childlike. "I never thought of that."

Without another word, he ate the proffered food and finished the ale, then curled into a ball close to the fire and shut his eyes. Either he'd forgotten Sir Richard was supposed to be his captive, or he simply didn't care any more.

Or perhaps he trusts me now, the old man mused, and the thought made him smile.

He'd fought well, the lad. He had a natural talent for it. If Sir Richard hadn't been a wanted rebel he might have helped Edmond find a place as a sergeant-at-arms in the Hospitallers.

At that, his thoughts drifted and he wondered again where his own faithful sergeant was. Had Stephen even made it to London and the Order's headquarters, or had some evil befallen him on the road?

Sir Richard shook his head sadly. The way things were going for them recently, it wouldn't be that much of a shock if his friend had met his doom on the road to Clerkenwell.

Or if the Grand Prior has killed him to save a scandal...

* * *

"More ale, here, inn-keep!"

Will smiled and shook his head at the friar, who had finished two bowls of mutton stew with half a loaf of black bread and now sat patting his stomach in satisfaction.

After they had escaped from the castle they'd made their way, unhindered, back to the *King and Castle.* Although it was only a short distance, by the time they reached the inn, Robin had almost passed out from pain and exhaustion, and Tuck couldn't have walked any further.

Will had helped Tuck in through the window, then, between them, they hauled Robin in, before locking the wooden shutters behind them with relieved sighs.

The room had two beds, which were little more than flimsy wooden frames with dirty old straw mattresses placed on top, but it was just what Robin needed after lying on a cold stone floor for days. He fell into a deep, healing sleep as soon as his two friends helped him onto the bed, and Will had quietly but firmly told Tuck to take the other pallet while he collapsed into a rickety old chair, the only other piece of furniture in the room.

The next day, Will had woken feeling good, but dirty. The filth that had caked him as he climbed up and down the latrine had dried into his skin and the room stank worse than it had when they'd first arrived at the inn. Still, he grinned as he looked at his two sleeping companions. They'd done it! Rescued Robin from a heavily defended castle, right under the nose of the sheriff!

His grin faded as he realised they weren't in the clear yet, far from it. The guards would have discovered their prisoner was missing by now; the castle would be in uproar. Sir Henry de Faucumberg would be livid and Christ knew what Sir Guy of Gisbourne would do.

The sun had already risen and was streaming through the gaps in the window shutters, so Will got up and shook Tuck gently awake.

"Give me your robe, and whatever else is covered in shit," he ordered. "I'll get it all washed somewhere. You'll have to help me get Robin's stuff off him too – he won't be able to do it himself."

In the light of day, Robin's injuries made Will and Friar Tuck wince as they undressed him. The young outlaw's entire body seemed to be covered in red, purple, green and yellow bruises. His fingers were terribly swollen, as was one side of his face. Dried blood caked his nose and mouth.

Scarlet felt rage building inside him as he took in the sight of his friend so horribly beaten. That bastard Gisbourne would pay for this.

Eventually, Will had the dirtiest of their clothes clutched in his hands and he pulled Tuck's spare robe, stinking as it was, over his head. He would need it to make his way through the city without being recognised.

"I'll be back soon," he promised. "Keep the door locked."

With that, he'd opened the shutter on the window and waited until the street outside was empty, before jumping out. After obtaining directions from a local man, he hurried off towards the eastern part of the city, and the local wash-house, where he knew he would find women to wash his pile of clothes for a coin or two.

It was easy enough to have the garments, and himself, washed and he made his way into a deserted alley to take off the still-dirty grey robe he was wearing and pull on the wet, but freshly cleaned spare robe. Thankfully, the sun was high in the sky so he hoped that and his own body heat would soon dry the material before he caught a chill.

He took the final dirty robe to a different washer-woman and paid her to clean off the waste caked into it, slipping her an extra silver coin to silence her questions, then he made one last stop before heading back to the inn.

As he climbed in the window, freshly scrubbed and grinning in satisfaction at Tuck and Robin, there was a hammering on the room door.

"Open up, in the name of the sheriff!"

CHAPTER NINETEEN

He had been left to wait on an audience with the Grand Prior, and, although he had been made comfortable with meat and ale, Stephen sat picking at the dry skin on his fingertips wishing the prior would call on him.

"When's the last time you were here, brother?" one of the sergeants based in Clerkenwell asked him. He was a younger man called Henry, barely in his twenties, yet he had an impressive black moustache and a ready smile which even the grumpy older Hospitaller appreciated.

"Years." Stephen shrugged, sipping a little from the cup Henry had just refilled for him.

They sat in the impressive great hall, at one of the long benches pushed in against the cold grey wall. Occasionally, people would pass through the room, some of the knights or other brothers offering a greeting, while those here merely on business – cleaners or delivery boys – kept their eyes respectfully on the ground as their footsteps echoed softly off the stone walls.

"A word of warning," the young sergeant muttered, moving closer and glancing around conspiratorially. "The prior is not quite the man you remember..."

Stephen dipped his head in acknowledgement. The men stationed here in Clerkenwell knew who he was – sergeant-at-arms to the outlawed preceptor of Kirklees – and they'd guessed his mission here.

Stephen appreciated the gentle warning, and he prepared himself mentally for the sight of Prior L'Archer, a man who had run the English Order of St John into the ground so badly that they were almost penniless.

"His moods are changeable," Henry went on in a low voice, stroking one side of his moustache thoughtfully. "If you find him in a cranky state of mind, your mission, whatever it may be, has little chance of success. If, however, he is in one of his benign stupors, there is a good chance he will acquiesce to whatever you ask of him."

Stephen grimaced as he pulled a little piece of skin on his thumb too hard, drawing a spot of blood and he sucked the stinging wound as Henry continued.

"Unfortunately, he's not often in a benign mood, and it's almost impossible to make him see sense, which is why we're living here in near-poverty."

The older man smiled sardonically at the suggestion Henry and his fellows in Clerkenwell were living in anything like poverty and he guessed the young sergeant came from a wealthy family and was yet to see action, or any other kind of service to the order, anywhere other than here in London.

They sat in silence for a while as Stephen fretted at his fingers and tried not to finish his ale too fast. He wanted to have a clear head when the prior finally deigned to see him.

Eventually the door at the far end of the hall creaked open and a stocky, bald man waved a hand at Stephen. "The Grand Prior will see you now."

He shared a nod with Henry and followed the steward along an oppressively narrow corridor, fingering his master's letter nervously, his heart thudding in his chest as if he were about to go into battle.

I suppose I am, he thought. *The result of this meeting will mean life or death for Sir Richard. I'll have to be on my guard here as much as I have in any fight I've ever been in.*

The steward showed him into a surprisingly small, cosy room. A fire burned in the hearth and a large glazed window allowed the early-spring sunshine to light the room and the ancient-looking man seated in a high-backed chair behind the huge oak desk that dominated the room.

The Grand Prior was staring at something on his desk: financial records Stephen guessed. Finally he looked up and gazed at the sergeant-at-arms through watery eyes.

"You are Sir Richard-at-Lee's sergeant, are you not?"

"Yes, Father."

"How is your master? I hear he has been disgraced. His – *our* – castle in Kirklees is under siege by the king's forces; and he has brought our Order into disrepute with his selfish actions. Frankly," his rheumy eyes, which had been wandering around the room, flicked back to bore into Stephen's. "I'm surprised to see you here. It would be better for everyone if you and Richard had been killed in the rebellion. As if we didn't have enough to worry about. Yet...here you are. Why?"

The grizzled sergeant wanted to tell the Grand Prior his financial mismanagement had done more damage to their Order than anything Sir Richard might have done, but he swallowed his retort and framed his reply more carefully.

"Father, I believe you know my master from many years ago: you served and fought together in the conquest of Rhodes. You should know, then, that he would not have acted as he did for any selfish reasons. What he did, he did for the good of his tenants, and for England."

L'Archer leaned forward in his seat, his brows lowered angrily. "His tenants, and England, are not his priority! His loyalty is, or at least should have been, first and foremost, to the Hospitallers. We can ill afford to lose the rent monies Kirklees provided, meagre as they may have been. Who knows what the king will do with the lands now? I hear he has already seized control of them and, although they are still legally ours, Edward will be in no rush to return their control – or rents – to us."

He sat back again, his thin arms resting on the big chair which seemed to dwarf him, then went on.

"You're right. I served with Richard for a time in Rhodes, and before that in Cyprus." He paused as his thoughts drifted back through the years and he remembered being a younger man, rising rapidly through the ranks.

Stephen thought the prior had fallen asleep, he remained silent for so long, but, after a while the old man sighed and gently shook his head. "Richard always wanted to do the honourable thing. I remember one of the battles we were involved in not long after he joined the Order. We were fighting in Armenian Cilicia, helping the Mongols defend some little town I forget the name of, but we were well beaten by the Mamluks. They'd been in the desert for weeks, low on food and water, and when the town fell we pulled back and left the Mongols to it. The inhabitants of the town were slaughtered: men, women, children. Raped. Tortured for sport." His damp eyes met Stephen's. "You know what I mean: you've been in sieges yourself. When the town falls, the place becomes hell-on-earth."

The sergeant nodded with a grimace, knowing it was true.

"Sir Richard personally tried to save every one of those townspeople: running here and there, dragging men off women, protecting children, stamping out fires... Eventually a couple of our brothers managed to pull him away and we made our retreat...Maybe he did some good there, who knows? I doubt it. Such is the way of war."

He shrugged. "Richard, as you say, must have been acting in the interests of the people of Kirklees. But, as in that town in Cilicia, his efforts were misguided and pointless. If you're here to ask me to speak up on his behalf with King Edward, you've wasted your time, I'm afraid. Richard is a good man; a man whose sword I was glad to have by my side in the East. Indeed, your master is the perfect knight in many respects. But his idealistic sense of honour always held him back – he would have been promoted far higher than preceptor in some little English backwater had he not been so damn...chivalrous.

231

I'm afraid Sir Richard must fight this battle by himself – he has overstepped the mark this time. The Hospitallers will not intervene on his behalf."

Stephen felt his heart sink as the prior went on, his hands raised placatingly.

"The king will, I am sure, not be seeking any sort of vengeance against you, though. You may remain here in Clerkenwell, until I can find a suitable posting for you. They are always looking for experienced sergeants in Rhodes, for example, and it would get you out of the country."

"I thank you for your offer," Stephen replied through gritted teeth. "But if the Order will not aid us, I shall take the Great North Road back to Kirklees and stand by Sir Richard's side."

The Grand Prior tutted in annoyance. "I am your superior, sergeant. I could have you stripped of your rank and court-martialled for insubordination." He waved his hand dismissively towards the door. "I must admit, though, I admire your loyalty. You and Richard must have made a formidable team. Be off then. Refresh yourself and your horse and ride back north to your doom."

Taking a breath, Stephen pulled Sir Richard's letter from his pocket and stepped up to the desk. "Before I leave, Father, I ask that you read this."

L'Archer eyed the envelope suspiciously, then, with a speed belying his withered appearance, snatched it from Stephen's hand.

"The seal's been broken."

Stephen felt his cheeks flush. "The letter was stolen on my way here by... thieves. By the time I found them, they had opened it, no doubt hoping it contained something they could use for financial gain."

With a grunt, L'Archer pulled the parchment from the tattered envelope and began to read, his wrinkled mouth forming the words quietly as he did so.

Stephen watched as the old man's face turned first scarlet, then chalk white, and the burly steward moved forward from the doorway, concerned, as was Stephen, that the prior might faint and fall off his chair.

"Leave us," L'Archer growled at the steward, halting the man in his tracks.

"Leave us!" he ordered again when the worried man failed to move back.

The steward threw Stephen a murderous glance but he moved past him and let himself out the door, and the sergeant-at-arms realised with some surprise that the old prior was, despite his recent disastrous incompetence, still held in great respect – affection even – by some of the Hospitallers in Clerkenwell.

As the door slammed shut, the prior glared at Stephen. "Have you read this?"

"No. I was ordered not to, and I did not."

"The two...thieves, you say stole the letter from you. Did they read it?"

"I believe so, Your Grace," he replied, then raised a hand to halt the furious prior's next question. "Have no fear, neither of them will be a problem. One of them is dead, the other..." He stopped himself from admitting one of the robbers was a woman. "The other I left with smashed teeth on the Great North Road, miles back, just south of Finchley. Even if they were to tell anyone what they read, no one would believe them" –

"When you leave here, and before you return to Kirklees, you will find this other person and make absolutely certain they will never talk about this letter. Do you understand me?"

Stephen hesitated. He was no assassin, to hunt someone down like a wild animal.

"Do you understand me?" the Grand Prior demanded, his eyes suddenly clear and hard as iron. "You do want me to help your master, don't you?"

The sergeant nodded. Assassin or no, he was a soldier, and he followed orders. "I understand."

"Good." L'Archer replaced the letter back in its envelope, his hands shaking, whether from age or fury Stephen couldn't tell. "Once you have taken care of the thief, you may return to your master and inform him I will move with all haste to secure for him a pardon from our king, Edward."

Stephen felt the corners of his mouth twitch, but he knew it would be a mistake to grin. "Thank you, Your Grace."

"Get out, sergeant. I hope never to see you or Sir Richard again. Go!"

Hastily, Stephen let himself out of the room, the anxious steward pushing past him to check on the frail prior who sat, ashen-faced, staring into the merry flames in the hearth.

He had told L'Archer the truth: he had not read the letter. He had no idea what Sir Richard might have written in it. Whatever it was, though, it had worked.

Now, all he had to do was make sure Helena didn't talk, and make it back to Kirklees in time to make sure his master wasn't captured by the king's men.

* * *

"Get under the bed!" Will hissed at Robin as the pounding on the door intensified, gesturing to Friar Tuck to help move the injured young man beneath the wooden frame.

"Here!" He tossed Tuck a robe before removing his own and pulling on a dry one that matched the one he'd given to the friar.

"Open up, Franciscan, before I break the door down!"

Tuck looked dazed, but Will nodded reassuringly and, with a last glance to make sure Robin was well out of sight, gestured at the friar to take the lead and pulled the door open.

Two soldiers wearing the light blue of the sheriff's castle guard stood at the door, swords drawn. They looked confused as they took in the men before them.

"Forgive me, my son," Tuck smiled, rubbing his eyes theatrically. "My brother and I had a long night. We

234

were still asleep when you came knocking. How can we help you?"

"We're looking for two friars," the foremost guard replied, glaring into the room suspiciously.

"Then you have found us!" Tuck grinned, raising a hand towards Scarlet who kept his face hidden in the folds of his robe.

The guards looked at each other. "We're looking for Franciscans," the leader replied. "Franciscans wearing grey robes that are probably covered in sh – I mean excrement, brother."

Tuck's face dropped. "Ah, well then, you've come to the wrong place. We are of the Order of St Augustine. And our robes are, I hope, quite clean." He cocked his head and placed a hand on the guard's arm. "May we be of service? Or must it be Franciscans?"

"Come on, it's not them," the guard at the back sheathed his sword, and his companion followed suit, eyes roving around the little room in confusion.

"No, thank you, brother. The landlord told us he had a couple of Franciscans staying here. I'm sorry we bothered you."

Tuck smiled beatifically at the retreating guard. "God's blessing on you, my son. May you find what you are looking for one day."

He closed the door behind him and threw the small bolt into place again, then sat down shakily on his bed. The outlaws remained silent, praying the soldiers wouldn't talk to the landlord and return, but moments later they could hear the guards passing in the street outside, discussing where they should try next in their search for two grey-robed Franciscan monks.

"You're a genius, Will." Tuck blew out his cheeks in shocked relief. "Buying these black robes was the best idea you've ever had!"

Will smiled sheepishly. "I didn't do it on purpose. When I washed all our gear it was soaking wet – there was no way it'd be dry for ages, but I knew the landlord would be expecting to see us in his common room at some point today. We couldn't go along for dinner wearing wet robes when it's not rained all day. So I looked for some new ones to buy. It was sheer luck that the old woman selling these," he tugged at the fabric of his garment, "only had them in black."

Tuck laughed loudly and looked piously upwards. "You work in mysterious ways, Lord!"

"Get me off this fucking floor."

Will and the friar hastily dragged their friend out from the floorboards under the rickety bed, and helped him on top of the straw mattress."Thanks lads," Robin mumbled. "I was getting claustrophobic there. Did one of you mention dinner?"

Between them, they decided Tuck and Will should head along to the common room and have a couple of ales, just to let everyone – especially the landlord – know they were still there.

"You rest for now," Tuck said to Robin, before he realised the young man was already asleep. Shaking his head with worry, the friar led the way out of the room and Will followed behind, pulling the door shut and praying no one would go into their room and find Robin.

"Two ales, please, my child." Tuck grinned at the serving girl as they walked into the common room. It was getting late and most people had eaten their evening meal, but they found an empty table with two chairs and sank into them contentedly.

"What's the food today?" Will grunted as the barmaid set the mugs of ale on the little table.

"Beef broth," the woman replied. "We have plenty of fresh bread to go with it too."

Will's mouth watered at the thought and he and Tuck ordered a serving each.

They sat drinking their ale, quite relaxed, as the food was being prepared for them.

"Ah, brothers!" They looked up and saw the landlord carrying their wooden bowls of steaming broth along with a full loaf of bread, all of which he set down on the table before them.

The man eyed them suspiciously. "I could have sworn you were in grey robes yesterday night when you came in," he said.

Tuck shook his tonsured head indignantly. "You should really be more observant, inn-keep," he growled, glaring at the man. "We are Austins, we wear black. The soldiers you sent after us today, thankfully had better eyesight than you." He tore off a piece of bread and dipped it into his bowl of broth. "Franciscans indeed!"

Will felt like he should say something too. "Franciscans? Us?" he muttered, stuffing broth-soaked bread into his mouth. "Bloody grey-robed wandering arseholes."

The landlord didn't know whether to laugh or be shocked, so Tuck laid a comforting hand on the man's wrist. "Don't mind brother William," he whispered. "He had a bad experience with some Franciscans a long time ago."

"Right. My apologies, brothers..." the man backed away, a bemused look on his face, as Tuck shovelled more bread into his mouth and smiled at him from gravy soaked lips. "If you need anything else, just give me a shout."

Tuck waved merrily as the landlord disappeared into the back. "Wandering arseholes, eh?"

Scarlet smirked, watery brown soup dripping down his chin, eyes sparkling. "No offence."

The pair finished their meal, which was delicious after their previous night's exertions, then they sat chatting for a while over another mug of ale. To anyone watching they would have looked like any other innocent travellers enjoying the hospitality of a cheap inn.

They called the landlord over again and paid to stay in their room for another two nights, which he was clearly pleased about.

"My friend here is very tired, and we must retire for the evening, though." The friar gestured at Will who nodded in his cowl as Tuck handed over the coins for the accommodation. "But I'm still ravenous – your broth was delicious!"

The inn-keeper smiled proudly. "My own recipe, brother friar," he replied. "I'll make you up another bowl, you can eat it in your room if you prefer. Just remember to bring back the bowl in the morning."

Tuck smiled. "You have my word on it. I'll take some more of that lovely warm bread too, if I may? And could you fill our ale-skins too?"

"Aye, no problem," the man laughed, the rash on his face flaring scarlet. "I'll bring it all over to you, good friar, and welcome."

A short time later they made their way back to the ground-floor room, laden with food and drink.

Robin managed some ale and most of the broth, but it hurt him too much to chew, so Tuck finished off the bread before the three of them settled down for the night.

It was still quite early, and the sounds of merry-making drifted along from the common room, but the outlaws had full bellies, plenty of ale, and were happy to simply relax and try to recover their strength.

They were safe for now. But they would have to escape from the city eventually.

* * *

The next day Will and Tuck spent some time wandering around the city, trying to pick up bits and pieces of gossip about the search for the escaped wolf's head.

Robin was unable to move from the bed, and seemed content to simply lie there anyway, his eyes vacant and listless. Tuck in particular worried about the young man's frame of mind, but the most important thing was for his battered and bruised body to regain some of its strength so they could try and escape into the forest again.

They left their injured companion at the inn, praying the landlord wouldn't get nosy and discover Robin hiding in the room.

It was a fine spring day and the pair made their way here and there along the bustling streets and busy little marketplaces, sampling the local food and eavesdropping on conversations about Robin's miraculous escape, while Tuck doled out blessings happily.

The feeling amongst the populace seemed to be overwhelmingly one of repressed excitement, even joy. The people loved to see authority's nose out of joint, even if they appreciated the fact Sir Henry de Faucumberg wasn't the worst sheriff they'd ever had. More than that though, the citizens were drawn to Robin – he really was a folk-hero to them. Will and Tuck already knew this, to some extent, but it was humbling, and inspiring, to hear people supporting them in hushed voices.

Not just the lower classes either: well-to-do merchants and tradesmen grinned at each other in the streets, wondering if each other had heard about the outlaw being spirited out of the castle while the sheriff and his guests partied.

When they returned to the *King and Castle* in the middle of the afternoon, they carried a loaf of bread, a wheel of cheese and skins full of beer which Will hid under his cassock while Tuck engaged the inn-keeper in conversation.

"It's lamb for dinner tonight," the friar smiled as Will let him into the room and threw the bolt on the door so no one else could wander in. "I'll soon be back to full strength at this rate."

Will grunted sarcastically. "Full strength? Fat bastard more like."

"How dare you?" Tuck replied in mock indignation. "Fat bastard or not, I'll still kick your arse, Scarlet."

Will rolled his eyes and sat on the bed beside Robin who was watching the exchange with a hint of a smile on his cracked lips.

"The sheriff's got all his men out looking for you," Will said, tearing off a chunk of the loaf and soaking it in beer before feeding it to Robin who gingerly rolled the food around with his tongue until it was soft enough to swallow without chewing. Then Will crumbled some of the cheese in his hand and held some of that to his friend's mouth as well.

It wasn't the nicest meal Robin had ever eaten, but it would build him up again. They couldn't afford to keep asking the landlord for extra helpings of dinner to take back to the room every night – the man would become suspicious. Assuming he wasn't already, after their change from Franciscans to Austins.

After he finished eating Robin fell asleep so Will and Tuck sat for a while talking, wondering how they would be able to get out of the city before someone found them.

It seemed an impossible task.

"Something will turn up," Tuck promised, standing up. "The Lord will provide, you wait and see. For now, the landlord will provide. Come on, let's go and have some of that lamb while Robin gets some sleep."

The common room was quiet as it was still quite early in the day, so the pair sat at the same table they'd occupied the night before and ordered two helpings of dinner along with mugs of ale.

The food, when the serving-girl brought it steaming from the kitchen was hearty if bland. There wasn't much lamb in it, but both of the outlaws finished their bowls and shouted for second helpings.

They were happily filling their bellies when two men joined them.

"God give you good day, brothers," one of the newcomers said, staring into Tuck's eyes.

It was Roger and his friend from the night before. Tuck cursed himself for not expecting the men to return to the inn – it was their local after all, of course they would turn up!

And if Roger had spoken to his brother, James, the guard at the castle, he would know exactly who they were.

The friar's hand instinctively curled around the dagger concealed under his cassock and his mind whirled. Even if he and Will escaped into the city, Robin lay, unable to move, in their room. This was the end of them!

"Relax, friar. We won't give you away."

Will had been so utterly absorbed in his lamb that he hadn't taken any notice of the two men sitting down at their table, but he looked up now, gravy streaming down his chin and his eyes widened.

"I swear it!" Roger whispered, knowing exactly how dangerous these two seemingly incongruous "friars" could be if provoked. "James told me you were kind to him. Well, as kind as you could be in the circumstances," he smiled lopsidedly at Scarlet. "We're on your side."

His friend, Godfrey, nodded earnestly. "You can trust us, lads. We wouldn't be here otherwise, would we? We'd have sent the law and claimed the reward the sheriff's offered."

It was a good point, and Will nodded before scooping another mouthful of meat into his mouth. "Is your brother all right?"

Roger nodded as the serving-girl brought two mugs of ale over for them with a near-toothless grin. "Aye, he's fine," he replied as the girl hurried off into the kitchen to fetch some food for the newcomers. "Bit sore, since you beat the shit out of him. But those coins you slipped him will help his injured pride heal nicely." He placed his mug on the table and wiped his lip with his sleeve. "He sends his thanks. That was a lot of money you gave him, when you could have just slit his throat."

"Why didn't you anyway?" Godfrey asked seriously. "Kill him I mean. Seems a bit risky leaving witnesses alive."

Tuck broke in before his friend could reply. "We're not murderers. We're good men, like you and Roger and James, just doing what we must to survive. It's as simple as that. We don't kill for pleasure, we do it only when there's no other option."

Will grunted agreement. "I took a chance, aye, maybe a stupid chance. But after what you told us about your brother I didn't want to leave those nephews of yours without a father." He gazed at the two men disconcertingly. "Make no mistake though: if someone is a threat to us, I'll not lose any sleep if I have to tear their windpipe open."

Roger and Godfrey looked away, feeling the force of Will's glare before he wiped the gravy from his chin and began spooning the last of his meal into his mouth.

"So?" Tuck sipped his ale. "Why *are* you here if not to give us away?"

The serving-girl burst through the door from the kitchen carrying a small loaf and two bowls of food for Roger and his companion and the table fell silent as she dropped off the meals and moved away to serve other customers.

"To help you." Roger tore off a chunk of bread and dipped it into his gravy before taking a bite and moaning gently in satisfaction.

"How can you help us?" Will wondered, shoving his own empty bowl into the centre of the table and leaning back against the wall. "The city's heaving with the sheriff's men. Your brother's just a regular guard, not a sergeant or captain."

Roger shrugged sheepishly. "It's true, James can't get involved. He wants you and Robin to escape, but he won't help. If he's found out..."

"We expected you would have a plan," Godfrey growled, with a somewhat accusatory stare. "You're the experts at this. We can help create a diversion or something while you two sneak Robin out of the city?"

Will thought for a moment then turned to look at Tuck. They nodded. It was as good a plan as any and, since they hadn't come up with any plan at all, there didn't seem to be much choice.

"All right, let's think about this then," the friar nodded, clasping his mug in his hands and staring at the table, trying to work things out in his head. "Robin can barely walk. He needs someone to support him, or even a stretcher to carry him out of the city."

Will muttered agreement. "That's the easy part. The hard part will be getting past the soldiers patrolling the streets and then making it through one of the gatehouses without the sheriff's guards recognizing us. And they're going to be ten times more vigilant than normal too, to make sure Robin Hood doesn't slip past them."

"We can carry Robin on a stretcher," Godfrey suggested, looking at his friend earnestly.

"Nah," Will scowled. "We can do that ourselves. It's a diversion we need."

"But what?" Tuck muttered, clasping his mug in his hands and staring thoughtfully into it's frothy depths as the rest of the inn's patrons bustled about the room, casting dark shadows on the walls against the flickering orange light from the hearth.

"No matter what diversion we come up with," Roger told them, "the gatehouse guards will never leave their posts. So you'll still have to fight your way past them one way or another."

Will drained his mug, a thoughtful look on his face. "They don't have to *leave* their post...they just have to be distracted long enough for us to get out..."

"Blowjobs."

Roger and Godfrey stared at Friar Tuck in shock and Will couldn't help roaring with laughter. He caught himself, not wanting to draw attention to their table, but no one in the place took any notice of another man in his cups enjoying himself.

"Blowjobs?"

"Aye, Roger." Tuck agreed, looking at the man as if he was simple. "There's no better way to distract a guard than a blowjob."

"You distracted many guards, Tuck?" Will asked innocently before the friar rammed an elbow into his friend's ribs, drawing a gasp of pain and a grin.

"Do you know any prostitutes?"

Roger nodded. "Aye, friar, a few."

"Good. Find some that still have most of their teeth and with tits that aren't dragging along the ground. We'll pay them handsomely to...distract the guards at the Cow Lane gatehouse while you two," he nodded at the men, "create a diversion that will take out the rest of the sheriff's men."

"Before we make our move though," Will broke in. "We need someone to take a message to Little John and the rest of the men."

* * *

"Will you look at that?" The young guard gazed down at the well-endowed middle-aged woman in the street below. "I wouldn't mind getting a grip of that."

"She's old enough to be your mother, Jupp, you dirty little bastard," his sergeant laughed as the lady looked up and smiled coyly before disappearing into the crowd. "Now get your eyes off the ladies, and watch who's going out the gate. The sheriff's offered a big reward to whoever catches Robin Hood or his conspirators trying to leave the city."

The pair were stationed on the north, or Cow Lane, gatehouse that afternoon and had a good view of the countryside around the city from their lofty vantage point. It was a fine spring day, and the sun shone brightly, casting a golden glow on the world around them.

Jupp's eyes roved across the city hopefully. "Hood's probably already gone."

"Not a chance," the sergeant, Gerbert, replied. "The city's been locked up tight since he escaped the castle. Everyone that's went out has been searched. He's still in here somewhere."

"I couldn't care less if he gets away," Jupp said. "He seems a good sort, from what I hear."

"Aye, well, you better keep that opinion to yourself, or the sheriff will throw you off of here himself. Now: watch the people!"

The sergeant pointed into the city, which heaved with morning business as merchants and travellers made their way in through their gatehouse and met the bustle of humanity that spent their day making money – or trying to – in Nottingham. As he turned away from Jupp, though, his eye caught a flicker of movement in the trees outside the city.

He placed his hands on the battlements and stared out, but he saw nothing moving now.

"Jupp! Here! You see anything over there?"

The young guard followed his superior's pointing finger, his forehead wrinkled in concentration.

Suddenly, a figure darted out from the foliage and ran parallel to the castle walls. Two more men followed, clad in brown clothing and crouching low to the ground.

"I see them," Gerbert growled as Jupp opened his mouth to speak. "They're making for the west gatehouse." He turned to look at his subordinate. "It's Hood's men, it has to be: they're here for him."

"What do we do?"

The sergeant stared out over the battlements, looking for more signs of movement, hoping to gauge the strength of the force coming for them.

"Raise the alarm," he replied. "Tell the sergeant to fortify the western wall. There's no way Hood's men can break in here now we know they're coming. Move it, lad!"

"How do you know it's Hood's gang?" Jupp gasped, fingering the pommel of his sword in excitement.

"Who else could it be? Besides, my eyesight isn't *that* bad; I could tell the man leading them was a giant. It has to be John Little. What the fuck are you waiting for? Go!"

CHAPTER TWENTY

Robin and Will were back at the inn, while Friar Tuck, in his Austin disguise, had ventured out into the city to watch for the guards' movements. When he saw a force of a dozen men making their way hastily to the city's western wall he knew it was time and hurried back to the *King and Castle*. They would get out of Nottingham now, or they wouldn't get out at all.

"Come on," he urged, as Will opened the door to their room and he bustled inside. "John and the rest must be here: the sheriff's men have reinforced the western gate."

They had asked Roger to take word to their friends in Barnsdale, outlining their plan to Little John.

Now, they would find out if it would work.

The three outlaws, all dressed now in black robes, climbed out the window into the street, bringing curious stares from passers-by, but it was too late to worry about that now. They headed for the north gate, Tuck and Will supporting Robin as he limped along between them.

The sound of distant shouting reached them and they guessed John and the rest of the men had started their "siege" on the castle walls. Of course, the outlaws wouldn't be so stupid as to seriously attempt to force their way into the city, but it would, hopefully, provide enough of a diversion for the three trapped men to escape while the guardsmen were otherwise occupied. Hopefully Roger and Godfrey had arranged the prostitutes to make things a little easier.

Robin was so badly injured he became almost a dead-weight as they made their ponderous way towards the northern gatehouse and Tuck was sweating before they'd covered even half the distance.

The guards would realise soon enough that the outlaws outside the castle didn't have the numbers, or equipment to pose a real threat. Then the soldiers would drift back to their usual posts and the opportunity to make it out would be gone for the friar and his two friends.

"Come on, Tuck," Scarlet growled, raising Robin higher on his side to ease the friar's burden a little. "We have to move quicker."

They reached the stables where Tuck had, two days earlier, paid for two horses to be ready to leave that day and, offering smiling blessings to the stable-master – and another silver coin – they lifted Robin onto one, as Tuck climbed on behind him to make sure the wounded outlaw didn't slip off into the road.

Will vaulted onto his own palfrey, and, with a cheery wave from the happy stable-master, who pretended not to notice the swords sticking out from under the black cassocks, they made their way at a trot towards the gatehouse.

"We're moving too slow!" Will growled.

Tuck knew the ex-mercenary was right, but they couldn't whip their horses into a gallop through the crowded Nottingham streets without attracting attention from the guards who still patrolled the area.

They approached the north gate and Tuck's heart sank as half a dozen soldiers jogged past them. The one at the front, a younger man, shouted up at the sergeant gazing down from atop the battlements. "It was just a diversion – only a dozen or so of them! Gisbourne says Hood must have been hoping to sneak out while most of us were defending the western gate."

"Oh shit," Will muttered, looking over at his companions. "Now what do we do? Head back to the inn? How the hell are we ever going to make it out of here now?"

The sergeant on the wall grinned down at his subordinates as they reached the gatehouse and began making their way back inside. "A diversion eh? They'll have to do better than that then!"

Even if Robin wasn't almost crippled the three outlaws couldn't have fought their way through the garrison on the wall in front of them. "Come on, let's turn back, before they see us." Tuck jerked his head in the direction of the *King and Castle*, the blood pumping nervously through his veins as he realised they were probably going to die in this city now.

Suddenly, from the south, there was a huge roar and the distant sound of people screaming filled the air. Everyone around the northern gate froze in shock, wondering what had made such a noise.

Then, into the silence there came another, even louder, thundering crack and the outlaws' mounts skittered nervously, eyes bulging in fear as the breeze carried the unmistakable smell of burning to them.

The soldiers on the wall looked to their sergeant for guidance, but he was unsure himself.

Then, from the direction of the noise and smell, voices could be heard, raised in panic, and the fear spread like wildfire through the thronged citizens, who began to make their way to their homes, where they could lock their doors and hide from whatever was happening. Soon, words could be distinguished through the babble.

"Robin Hood's men! Robin Hood's men are attacking!"

Tuck and Will Scarlet looked at each other warily, wondering what the hell was going on.

Suddenly, one of the sheriff's personal guard appeared, shoving his way through the throng, his face black with soot, eyes startlingly white in contrast.

"You men!" he roared up at the soldiers on the gatehouse. "Hood's men are attacking the Chapel Bar gate! They've used fire to destroy some of the buildings. We're in danger of being overrun, come with me, now!"

The soldiers, finally offered some leadership, rushed to obey, running down the stairs in the gatehouse to follow the sheriff's man who had disappeared off to the west.

"That was Roger, he must have borrowed his brother's uniform!"

Tuck grinned as the guards raced past, swords drawn. "Aye! Come on, I don't know what's happening, but he's emptied the gatehouse for us!"

They spurred their horses forward, and Will jumped to the ground, heading for the great wooden beam that held the two massive gates locked shut. He put his hands underneath it and heaved.

"You, friar, get the fuck away from there!"

The area was almost empty, the bewildered locals having made themselves scarce, so the sound of descending footsteps carried clearly to Will as he gave an almighty grunt and forced the heavy wooden lock from its fixings.

The guard sergeant, Gerberd, burst out of the tower with his sword drawn and headed straight for Will.

To him, it looked like a party of three clergymen – one of them seriously ill – had decided to try and escape the apparent carnage inside the city. But, as he closed on the Austin that had unlocked the gate, something made Gerberd hesitate.

Perhaps it was the way the friar held himself, or maybe it was the steely eyes that gazed out at him from under the cowl. Whatever it was, Gerberd pulled up before he reached the gate and raised his sword before him.

He was just in time, as Scarlet threw aside his cassock and pulled his own sword silently from its leather and wood sheath.

The two blades met with a sharp metallic ring, and both men instinctively spread their feet wide defensively.

"How come you didn't go with the rest of your men?" Will asked, bringing his sword round in a blur. "Too scared?"

The guard halted the outlaw's attack, batting Scarlet's sword to the side and aiming a blow of his own which was also parried.

"No – too smart!" Gerberd gasped as the weapons met again with bone-crunching force. "There was no way anyone would have had time to get up here from Chapel Bar so soon after those noises. It was a setup. It's just a shame the rest of my men were too stupid to realise it."

The man was good with a sword, and Will, hampered by the ill-fitting black cassock was forced onto the back foot as Gerberd aimed blow after blow at him.

Suddenly the outlaw stepped on the hem of the ridiculous robe and stumbled into his opponent who reacted with glee, showing Scarlet backwards, sprawling onto the ground with the breath knocked out of him.

He raised his sword triumphantly and collapsed sideways as Tuck's quarterstaff hammered against the back of his skull with a horrendous crack.

"Get it open!" the friar shouted at Will, gesturing towards the gate.

Scarlet scrambled to his feet, shoving his sword back into its sheath and threw his weight against one of the sturdy gates which opened readily enough.

Tuck and Robin rode out as Will hauled himself onto his own horse and followed behind them.

Somehow they'd escaped from Nottingham, but, as he spurred his horse to catch up with his friends Will looked at Robin's limp form and wondered if their young leader would ever be the same again.

* * *

"What will they do to you? Hang you?"

Sir Richard nodded as they walked on towards Pontefract, his expression thoughtful. "No doubt. The king wanted bloody revenge against those who rebelled, and Sir Hugh Despenser – Edward's closest friend – is no friend of mine. There's little chance I will get out of this alive, but we'll see what fate God chooses for me."

Edmond looked at the big Hospitaller, admiring the man's stoicism and apparent courage in the face of a near-certain death sentence.

Truth was, Sir Richard, rather like his friend Robin Hood not that far away in Nottingham, had felt his spirit break. His love of life had gone and the desire to fight no longer drove him. It wasn't courage that led him to Pontefract; it was simple apathy.

Yet Edmond took in the knight's proud bearing and felt himself warming to the prisoner he was about to deliver up for judgement to the king's men.

They hadn't spoke much since the robbers had attacked, but a mutual respect had developed between them. Sir Richard, for his part, felt pity for Edmond and the lamentable fate life had dealt the man, but he didn't allow it to show in his eyes, knowing it would crush Edmond even more.

The young tanner's son from Kirklees, given time to replay the botched ambush that led to his little brother's death, had come to grudgingly accept that Sir Richard wasn't to blame for it. And the Hospitaller had saved Edmond's life when the outlaws had struck after all.

Sir Richard's noble grace and bearing, and savagery in battle, impressed Edmond greatly and he found himself wishing he didn't have to hand him over to the law. Still, the knight apparently felt they were following God's will, so...he might as well make the most of the situation: take the money and the respect he would gain from capturing such a high-profile rebel.

If it was God's will, who was Edmond to question it?

Sir Richard looked over and gave him a sad, yet somehow encouraging smile, and the young man sighed.

An hour later, Edmond saw the top of Pontefract Castle towering over the treetops in the near-distance, and pointed it out in a subdued voice.

"Where?" the Hospitaller replied, screwing up his eyes and cursing, but all he could see so far off was an indistinct blur. "My eyes aren't what they used to be, lad. I'll take your word for it. Just in time eh? My feet are aching."

"Will Sir Philip be there, do you think?"

Sir Richard had no idea. "I hope so," he replied. "The sooner we get this over with the better for everyone."

Take care of Stephen for me, Lord, he prayed, wondering again where his faithful sergeant-at-arms was and hoping that, since he obviously hadn't succeeded in procuring aid for Sir Richard from the Grand Prior in time to help him, he might at least find some other place for himself within their Order.

Traffic on the road became a little heavier as they neared the castle.

Merchants and waggoners delivering food and drink eyed them curiously, wondering at the proud Hospitaller being shadowed by the nervous-looking commoner.

"Here." Sir Richard handed his sword to Edmond as they neared their destination. "You'll want to make it look more like I'm your captive. Stand up straight. Try to look like a man that bested a Hospitaller knight not some scared peasant that can't wipe his own arse."

The crisp commands were uttered in a friendly tone yet Edmond found himself almost involuntarily obeying the older man, his shoulders pushing back and a grim expression coming over his face as he brandished the knight's sword menacingly.

Sir Richard nodded and smiled encouragingly. "Let's go get your reward, and see what the king has in store for me."

They walked up to the castle gates, the two guards eyeing them suspiciously, but the Hospitaller had allowed his proud shoulders to slump and his face looked old and haggard as he gazed balefully at the soldiers, who visibly grew in confidence as they took in the strange pair coming towards them.

"State your business," the eldest of the two demanded, grasping his halberd threateningly, although he didn't seem sure who to address: the defeated looking yet expensively armoured knight, or the unattractive sword-wielding commoner who seemed to be in charge.

Edmond spoke up, his nerves making his voice hoarse. "I am here to see Sir Philip of Portsmouth. He tasked me with capturing one of the rebel lords. As you can see, I have the man." The young tanner pointed the sword at the knight's back. "Sir Richard-at-Lee."

The guards looked at each other, although they seemed unimpressed and Edmond found himself feeling irritated at that.

"Move on then," the guard waved the pair through the gates as a heavily laden wagon rattled up behind them. "The steward will show you where to take your prisoner until Sir Philip sees you."

They walked through the imposing entrance, into the courtyard, and Edmond felt his stomach lurch. This was it. They were inside. No going back: Sir Richard would be hung, and it was his fault, just like it was his fault Walter was dead.

What have I done?

The steward, a tall yet strangely effeminate man appeared, hurrying over to them. He was flanked by two stocky guardsmen who moved quickly to search Sir Richard, none too gently, for concealed weapons. They removed the dagger strapped to his calf then took up positions either side of him, satisfied that he posed no immediate threat but alert nonetheless.

"Come. Sir Philip has been informed of your presence."

Edmond didn't have time to think about what was happening now, as the steward, who recognised the captured Hospitaller from numerous previous visits there over the years, led them through a thick door and along a short corridor that fed out onto the castle's great hall.

The large room was deserted, as Edmond and his prisoner were made to stand before the massive main table which was laden with jugs of wine and ale.

A short time later the eastern door of the hall was thrown open and six men strode into the room.

Sir John de Burton, newly appointed seneschal of the castle, led the way, followed by Sir Philip of Portsmouth and four more soldiers, one of whom wore a different livery to the rest of the guards they'd seen so far. Sir Richard assumed the man was Sir Philip's own captain.

The two noblemen took seats behind the big table and, staring almost gleefully at the defeated Hospitaller, filled their cups from the jugs before them.

"So..." Sir Philip turned his gaze to Edmond, who bowed comically, having no idea how to behave in this situation. "You managed to capture him! I have to be honest, I never expected this. A knight of St John, captured by a common villager!"

"Not just me, my lord," Edmond told him. "My brother Walter too, although the Hospitaller killed him..."

"Yes, well, congratulations, young man. You and your brother have my thanks, and the king's too. You will be well rewarded, have no fear."

The nobleman nodded and one of the castle guards moved forward, gently taking Edmond by the arm and leading the surprised young tanner from the room.

The door was pulled shut by the soldier and Edmond was led back out to the gatehouse where the castle steward stood talking to a merchant.

"Ah, the hero of the day," the steward smiled. "You have performed a great service to England, and Sir Philip has given me this for you, with his thanks." He pressed a small bag into the young tanner's hand and gestured to the gatehouse. "You may return to your village and tell them all you single-handedly captured a Hospitaller knight."

"It wasn't single-handedly, my brother Walter" –

The steward nodded, still smiling condescendingly, and looked at the guard behind Edmond, who again took him by the arm and steered him off towards the castle exit.

255

Too dazed to protest, the young man found himself back outside the castle, looking at the heavy grey clouds that threatened to burst upon the land at any minute.

Clearly Sir Philip and Sir John's gratitude didn't extend to offering him a meal, a room, or even a pallet in the servant's quarters for the night. He pulled his cloak tighter around him, trying to cover the top of his neck where a draught always seemed to get in, and resigned himself to making the long journey back to Kirklees.

"Fucking arseholes," he muttered to himself. Still, he had his reward, and he found his spirits rising again as he moved along the road back home and grasped the little coin-purse. He emptied the money into his hand, imagining what he'd do with his new-found wealth.

The sky above him split asunder and torrential rain hammered down on him as he gazed at his reward for capturing Sir Richard-at-Lee.

He wasn't great at counting, but Edmond knew the silver he held added up to fifteen shillings. To a peasant this was a great sum of money. But he wasn't a peasant, he was a tradesman who owned his own shop now – a tanner. This was no more than he could earn himself in a few weeks!

The rain poured down his face, mingling with tears of rage and he collapsed onto his knees on the soaking road. His brother had died for this? He was hardly better off than he was yesterday! His dream of expanding his father's shop was crushed, his family was gone, and, he knew, the people of Kirklees would hold him in the same contempt they had for his entire life.

He raised his face to the sky and screamed in fury until his breath gave out and he held his head in his hands in despair.

CHAPTER TWENTY-ONE

Stephen had left Clerkenwell at dawn the morning after his meeting with the Grand Prior. L'Archer would have liked to have thrown him back onto the streets directly after their meeting, but a lifetime of offering hospitality had forced him to allow the sergeant-at-arms to spend a few hours in bed and be furnished with some provisions to see him back along the Great North Road.

Pushing his mount, although not too hard now since he'd carried out his mission, he had found the spot where he'd ridden down the blacksmith and his wife, but there was no sign of either. There may have been a shallow grave somewhere in the undergrowth beside the road, but Stephen didn't have the time, or need, to hunt for it. He had to find Helena before she showed Sir Richard's letter to the Grand Prior. Judging by L'Archer's reaction, the information could have disastrous consequences for both himself and possibly the Order as a whole.

With no clues to her whereabouts, Stephen decided the most likely place to find her was in the nearest village, Highgate. Chances were that some locals had stumbled upon the injured girl with her dead husband, and would take her back to their village for medical treatment. What man could resist that innocent face?

He removed his black surcoat with its distinctive white cross that marked him as a Hospitaller, in case Helena had told anyone about him and tried to stop him from finding her.

It proved a wise move, as, on approaching Highgate, a pair of young men passed him on their way to their labouring job at a nearby farm. Greeting them cheerily, and asking after news in their village, he feigned shock when they blurted out that a beautiful girl had been terribly wounded and her husband murdered by a rogue Hospitaller knight.

Little of interest ever happened in Highgate, which was a tiny little place, so the two young men were glad to tell Stephen everything that they'd heard, shaking their heads and asking what the world was coming to as if they really cared.

The sergeant let them speak, nodding and gasping in apparent outrage as the men talked and, eventually, they told him she'd been taken to the local inn, which also doubled as a barber's shop.

Waving goodbye to them, Stephen kicked his palfrey, its big blanket bearing the Hospitaller cross also removed earlier that morning, and rode straight into the village, eyes scanning the surroundings for any sign of the girl. The labourers had said she was terribly wounded and had been confined to bed by the surgeon, but Stephen knew Helena was more than capable of having him beaten to death by a mob of angry men if she turned on her considerable charm.

The village was small, and the inn stood out like a cow in a chicken coop, but Stephen knew it was foolhardy to just walk in the front door and ask to see the injured girl. Night was approaching anyway, so he left his horse hobbled to a tree in the thick woods outside the village and, when darkness descended, made his may back through the gloomy streets to the alehouse, which beckoned through the chill spring air to weary travellers seeking some meagre comfort and warmth.

It seemed unlikely that whoever had brought the injured girl here would have carried her, or made her walk, up the stairs to the upper storey, but, having no idea which room she might be in, Stephen had no choice but to find a way inside and try each one until he found her.

If anyone tried to stop him, he would have to remove them as silently as possible. He was a natural, and highly skilled, fighter but he couldn't take on an entire village at once.

Stealthily making his way to the rear of the building, where passers-by wouldn't be likely to discover him, he chose the first unlit window he came to and stood outside, straining his ears for signs of life inside. Hearing nothing, he pried open the crude lock with his dagger and hauled himself into the room, praying to St John that the girl would be here, in a deep sleep, so he could get the hell out of there quick, and back to his beleaguered master.

The two low beds were unoccupied though, so he moved quickly to the door and, satisfied the hallway outside was silent, he moved out and along to the room on the left. If he had to check every room, he would. There could only be half-a-dozen guest bedrooms in a small village inn at the most anyway, and, even if he startled someone, any shouts of alarm would hopefully be drowned out by the racket coming from the common room which sounded like it was heaving with merry locals tonight.

Helena wasn't in the next room, or the one after, and the Hospitaller began to feel tense and angry, beads of sweat running down his back and making his armpits uncomfortably sticky.

He moved onto the fourth room, on the opposite side of the corridor, now working his way back to the room he'd started in. He felt like the Angel of Death, knowing his heightened state would probably lead to him killing anyone should they stumble from the common room into this quiet hallway. He stopped for a moment, slowing his breathing and forcing himself to relax.

"Give me a simple fucking battle any day," he muttered to himself, knowing the knot in his stomach was down to the fact he was here to assassinate a woman, and a beautiful woman at that.

Had it been a big, hairy-arsed outlaw, or one of the countless Saracen soldiers he'd faced before he'd followed Sir Richard back home to England, he would have been as focused and calm as a cat stalking a blackbird.

Exhaling a huge breath, visualising his nervousness leaving his body along with the spent air, he pushed open the next bedroom door and slipped inside, trying to get his bearings in the unfamiliar surroundings. The previous three bedrooms, on the other side of the corridor, had all shared the same layout, with the bed in the far right corner from the door, but he couldn't be sure these rooms would be the same, so he stood peering into the gloom, senses straining for anything that would allow him to get his bearings.

"Who's there?"

The voice that came from the left was unmistakable, although quite different to how Stephen remembered it, no doubt because most of Helena's front teeth had been smashed out by him the last time they'd met.

Knowing the girl would likewise recognise him should he speak, he remained silent but moved quickly towards the direction the voice had come from, cursing inwardly at the almost total darkness which would make this even harder than it already was.

The shape of the bed came into view and he stretched out to where he hoped her throat would be, grasping his dagger grimly in his other hand, his legs weak at what he knew he must do.

Understanding her nocturnal visitor meant her no good, Helena suddenly screamed, the sound filling the little room, but giving away her position almost as well as if daylight had flooded the place.

The Hospitaller reached out and closed his hand around her neck, squeezing hard enough to strangle the desperate cry and, despite the suffocating darkness, their eyes met and recognition flared in Helena's horrified stare.

"Please..." she gasped. "Please...!"

The sounds of revelry from the common room carried on in the background, as they looked at each

260

other, but Stephen hesitated, his sense of honour rebelling at what he was doing, and he released the pressure on the girl's throat, his dagger remaining by his side.

For what seemed like an age they gazed at each other, both breathing heavily. Then, Helena's lip curled in disgust and, with a smile of satisfaction she whispered. "You! Even in the dark you're revolting." She laughed gently at his weakness, despite his hand still being on her throat. "The last time we were alone in a room like this you thought I was going to let you fuck me." Her voice rose again, almost shouting, yet still Stephen couldn't move. "You ugly old bastard – no woman would let you touch them!"

His right hand rose and fell and his dagger hammered into her chest, four, five, six times, and he felt warm blood spurting from her mouth onto the hand that squeezed her smooth neck.

As he stood there, numb, not quite understanding what was happening, the door at the end of the hall opened. The sound of at least a dozen men laughing and drinking seemed to deafen him and he came back to his senses with a start.

"You all right in there, lass?"

The voice was a woman's, and the Hospitaller knew he didn't want to kill anyone else this night. Without thinking, he launched himself shoulder-first at the shutters on the window, feeling them burst open with a loud crack. He fell through the opening and landed on the muddy road outside, breathless.

Inside the room, the woman, whoever she was, had come in, a candle lighting her way, and a scream filled the night.

Stephen, panting like a dog, ran instinctively through the village towards the trees where he'd left his horse, the meagre light cast by the crescent moon aiding his desperate passage as men's voices added to the woman's scream, filling the gloom behind him.

Stumbling, the air seeming to burn in his lungs, he crashed through the undergrowth, eyes flashing left and right, searching for the old palfrey that was his only chance of escape.

Sobbing at what he'd done, he cried out in relief as a soft, frightened nicker came to him from close-by and he hastily untied the horse before dragging himself into the saddle and, heedless of the dangers of low branches or trailing roots, kicked the animal savagely into a canter through the trees and onto the main road, clinging to the reins in fright.

Christ! Forgive me!

* * *

Little John was pissed off, and confused too. Since they'd brought Robin back to their camp in Barnsdale their young leader hadn't been himself. It was perfectly understandable, given the beating he'd suffered at the hands of Sir Guy of Gisbourne, but John had expected his friend to come out of his depression after a couple of days at the most, when some of the physical pain had started to ease.

But he hadn't; he was as lethargic and disinterested as he'd been when they met him at Nottingham's gates and brought him home. John didn't know how to deal with it.

He'd seen men change before, of course. When bad things happened, a person's character was bound to change, especially if they weren't that mentally tough to begin with. John had seen Robin as an immensely strong young man though – inside and out.

It worried the giant outlaw greatly. Not only was his friend a shadow of his former self, but without Robin they lacked leadership. He and Will Scarlet were more than capable second-in-commands, but neither of them had the vision or charisma to see them safely through a summer which promised to be tougher than ever before, with Gisbourne and the rest of the king's bounty-hunters searching for them.

The mood in the camp had been affected too. They had lost a few men recently, and been betrayed by one of their own, but for all that, the audacious rescue of their popular leader from right under the nose of Gisbourne and the sheriff had cheered the outlaws greatly. The first night back in Barnsdale after their trip to Nottingham they had celebrated with meat and ale, singing and ghost-stories. The sense of camaraderie had never been stronger John thought.

It didn't last long though, as the days passed and Robin sat, melancholy and morose, ignoring the men even when some of them tried to snap him out of it. Allan-a-Dale had made jokes, Tuck had spoke of God and the Magdalene, while John himself had got angry with the young wolf's head. All to no avail.

John shook his head, embarrassed at his treatment of Robin, but he couldn't just stand around and watch while his friend sickened himself into an early grave.

Finally, this morning, tired of sitting about the camp, constantly on watch for Gisbourne and the sheriff's men coming looking for their stolen prize, John had decided to take the fight to them.

Most of the outlaws knew this part of the forest well, having camped here for weeks at a time on different occasions over the past few years.

If Gisbourne and his men came looking for them, rather than moving on, today the outlaws would strike back.

John and Allan-a-Dale had led some of the men – twelve of them in total – into the trees, armed and ready to let out their anger at the past few months' events.

"D'you think we'll get a fight?" Allan asked as they pushed their way through the trees on one of the almost invisible little pathways the outlaws knew so well.

John shrugged. "I don't know. I hope so, but...to be honest, I just wanted to get out of the camp and feel like I'm doing something worthwhile. The king's men have been coming into Barnsdale in small groups for weeks now and, with Robin escaping the city, there's a chance even more of them will come hunting us." He hefted his great quarterstaff and grinned wickedly at the minstrel. "The bastards think they have us on the run, beaten down and terrified. Most of the rebels that are hiding out around here probably are. We'll give the soldiers a fright though, if they turn up anywhere near here today."

It was mid-afternoon, the men fed-up and grumbling, before, at last, they saw the signs of a body of men passing through the trees around them. Freshly snapped branches, grass still bent against the forest floor, and damp patches of urine where a couple of men had relieved themselves against one of the mighty oaks that stood like giant sentinels all told John that someone was close.

Friend or foe, they would soon find out.

"They're heading west," the massive outlaw noted as the rest of the men gathered around him. "They've stuck to the obvious path, which suggests they don't know the area as well as we do. They might be bounty-hunters looking for us, or they might be other rebels who're trying to stay ahead of the law." He fixed half-a-dozen of the outlaws with a steely gaze and ordered them into the trees following the path to the left. Allan-a-Dale was tasked with commanding the group.

"The rest come with me, we'll take the right. Move fast, but do it silently and try to keep in sight of each other, all right Allan?"

The minstrel nodded self-assuredly.

"If I attack with my men," John went on, watching Allan earnestly, "wait until the bastards have engaged us, then hit them silently from behind."

The forces split and, like dark wraiths, disappeared into the undergrowth either side of the beaten path, making their way west towards their quarry.

It didn't take long before John heard the men in front of them. They were moving at a leisurely pace, making a fair bit of noise, and he cursed. Obviously Gisbourne wasn't leading these men, or they'd be acting in a much more professional manner.

They could still be dangerous though, so John waited until they caught up with the travellers before making any uninformed judgements on their competency or deadliness.

Reaching a point a small way ahead of the men blustering through the trees as if they hadn't a care in the world, John brought the outlaws to a halt and they peered through the early-summer foliage, watching the party of hard-looking men that came towards them.

It was the sheriff's men. They wore the light blue livery of the Nottingham Castle guardsmen, and the outlaws realised Sir Henry de Faucumberg had weakened his own garrison in order to send out as many men as possible to hunt the escaped Robin Hood.

As tough as they looked, the soldiers were clearly no woodsmen. They blustered through the foliage, cursing as branches slapped and swatted them, stumbling over concealed roots, obviously confident in their numbers and official status.

On the opposite side of the path, John's trained eye could see the stealthy movement of the rest of the outlaws as they moved into position and, with a shake of his head at the incompetence of their would-be captors, looked along the line at his own half-dozen men and, hefting his quarterstaff, gave a nod.

There were fifteen soldiers, and, to their credit, they fell into a tight defensive formation when the first of them to notice the attacking outlaws gave a shout of alarm. John's men made no war-cry as they hit the blue-liveried guardsmen. The didn't use their longbows, in case they hit their fellows on the other side of the path – instead they fell on the soldiers with their swords, while John parried their leader's own thrust and rammed the butt of his staff into the man's face.

The sheriff's men, panic in their eyes, fought back savagely, and were, for a while, able to hold their own. They might not have been skilled at moving through the forest quietly, but they knew how to wield their weapons, and their light armour was of a good quality. Despite John's enormous quarterstaff, and the skill of his six men, the soldiers began to win ground, pushing the outlaws back.

Then, just as it seemed things would go badly wrong, Allan-a-Dale led his party of outlaws into the fight, appearing from the thick trees like wood-spirits and hacking at the backs of the soldiers.

Panic spread quickly through the embattled men as half of them fell in the space of a few moments, and the remainder tried desperately to fight on two fronts.

The outlaws had trained for, and used in combat, this sort of manoeuvre countless times though. When one of the sheriff's men turned his head to counter an attack from behind, one of Little John's men plunged his sword into the soldier's back or side.

It didn't take long before the battle was almost finished, but one of the soldiers shouted, "Robin Hood! We're here to talk to Robin Hood!"

John heard the shouts and roared at the outlaws to stand down and move back. The battle had been so quick that none of the outlaws had become lost in a frenzy of bloodlust, as so often happened in war and the giant wolf's head was pleased as the men lowered their weapons and moved back breathlessly to let the sheriff's man speak.

Three guardsmen remained alive, all breathing heavily, but no fear showed in their eyes, just determination and anger, and John found himself respecting their courage.

There was a short period of quiet, as everyone regained their breath, then John pointed his staff at the guard who had been shouting.

"You. What is it you have to say to Robin Hood?"

The guardsman, a short, stocky fellow with a great dark beard, glared at John and spat into the grass.

"You'll be "little" John."

"How did you guess?"

"We're here with a message, from Sir Henry de Faucumberg, Sheriff of Nottingham and Yorkshire."

John waved a meaty hand at the man. "Go on then, I know who he is and we don't have all day. We've got more of your mates to hunt down and butcher."

The guard ignored the taunt, although his two fellows fidgeted and eyed the outlaws nervously.

"Sir Guy of Gisbourne will fight Robin Hood in a duel. To the death. If your mate wins, he will be pardoned."

"Fuck off," John growled. "We've heard a story like that before from de Faucumberg last winter, and he double-crossed us. We're not going down that road again."

The previous year, not long before Christmas, the sheriff had promised a pardon for Robin's wife, Matilda, but had set a trap to kill the entire outlaw gang when they turned up to make the deal. John knew their leader wasn't stupid enough to make the same mistake twice, even if he'd been fit enough to fight "the Raven".

"This won't be like that," the guard retorted. "Hood can name the time and place of the duel, and your men can escort Sir Guy to it if you like."

The rest of the outlaws laughed and shook their heads. "Do you think we were born yesterday?" Allan-a-Dale demanded. "What's to stop us just slipping a blade between your damn Raven's ribs once we have him?"

The guard shrugged. "If you do that, Hood doesn't get his pardon."

"And if Gisbourne wins?" John shouted. "Why would we let him go? What's to stop us from killing him then?"

The soldier cursed. "I'm just delivering the message I was told to deliver."

"Let's kill these pricks and get back to camp," Peter, one of the men who had been on the raft with Much not so long ago, growled. The others muttered their agreement. The sun would set soon and they all wanted to get back for some warm food and a few ales. They'd had their victory for today and it felt good – now they wanted to celebrate, not bandy words with de Faucumberg's flunkies.

"Sir Guy's captain, Nicholas Barnwell, will meet you to discuss the terms if you agree." The guard, understanding his time was rapidly running out, shouted at Little John, desperation beginning to creep into his voice which had, until then, been somewhat arrogant.

John waved his laughing men to silence. "Fine. I can't speak for Robin: he does that for himself. But I won't refuse any chance of a pardon for one of us, even if it hinges on some ridiculous "duel" like this. You can go. Get back to the sheriff and Gisbourne and tell them we'll talk to Robin about this."

The three surviving guardsmen heaved an audible sigh of relief and began to inch their way along the path.

"You're going the wrong way," Allan grinned, shaking his head in disbelief. "Nottingham's that way."

The men halted their progress and silently moved back in the direction the fighting-minstrel had indicated, eyes warily fixed on the outlaws.

"Tell them to send you back with the terms," John said to their leader.

"How will I find you?"

"Don't worry about that: we'll find you, boy. Now get moving."

The three, sensing the danger pass, turned and began to make their way at a trot along the path back to the city.

As they went, Allan-a-Dale took his longbow from his back, pulled the hemp bowstring from the little pouch where he stored it and nodded at Peter to do the same. Sliding an arrow from his belt he fitted it and, waiting on Peter to match him, took aim and shot into the soldier on the left's back, directly between the shoulder blades. Peter's shot took the rightmost guardsman in the lower back.

As the last surviving soldier turned, eyes wide with shock and fear at the sight of his fallen companions, Allan aimed another arrow at him and shouted, "Run you bastard!"

"Let's get back to camp," Little John grunted as the man sprinted into the trees in terror, shaking his head ruefully at the killings. "Maybe this'll be exactly what Robin needs."

CHAPTER TWENTY-TWO

He should have known better.

When he returned to Kirklees, sick at heart over his brother's death and his part in the capture of Sir Richard-at-Lee, Edmond had hoped to at least continue with his life as before.

The small reward Sir Philip had given him had been enough to provide a burial for his brother – whose corpse he'd carried back to the village from outside Sir Richard's castle by himself – and at least repair or upgrade some of his father's old tanning equipment.

He'd repainted the sign that hung above the shop-front to try and make things look a little nicer and had the local carpenter mend the vats they used to treat the animal skins.

But the loss of his brother played on his mind constantly. His life had been fairly unhappy so far, but he had never, until now, felt lonely, not even when his young wife had died. He'd never loved her, it had been a marriage of convenience for both bride and groom and he'd shed few tears when she'd succumbed to fever a few months into their marriage.

He had loved Walter though, and had felt he was needed in the world while his brother was around looking for someone to take care of him.

But now...he felt unloved and useless.

Working every day, enduring the same old stares from the other villagers – pity, distaste, amusement – only to go home to an empty house with nothing but local ale to brighten the gloom. For a little while at least, until the brew took effect and left him feeling even worse.

Anyone else would have been a hero! He'd captured one of the rebel leaders – a knight! – and been rewarded by the king's man. He had expected the people of Kirklees to look at him with respect in their eyes when he returned from Pontefract and began telling his customers what had happened.

Instead, the villagers had shunned him even worse than before. Sir Richard had been a good lord to them, and the people didn't like the fact the unpleasant-looking young tanner from the God-accursed family had somehow beaten the Hospitaller in combat then betrayed him to some faceless agent of the unpopular King Edward II.

The fact that most of the Kirklees men had been out with the bounty-hunters trying to capture their erstwhile lord didn't seem to make any difference.

He paused, threw a hide into the big vat of urine he used to strip his animal-skins of hair, and took a swallow from the ale-skin at his side. He hadn't been much of a drinker before, but had gradually started to rely on it to get him through the days. "Shit." He cursed as the last few drops spilled into his mouth, and a passer-by, already wrinkling his nose in disgust at the smell from Edmond's workshop, situated on the very outskirts of town because of the hellish stench, threw him an angry look.

"Damn you to hell," he shouted at the man who, knowing the tanner could use his fists as well as anyone in the village, ducked his head and hurried on his way, muttering under his breath.

Edmond pulled the cover over the vat of urine, wiped his hands on his apron, and locked his shop behind him.

If he didn't have any ale left, he'd have to go to the inn for some.

Kirklees had a proper inn, rather than just a house one of the villagers brewed ale in as in many other villages around the country.

Edmond shook his head angrily, as he realised it had been Sir Richard who had funded the building of the inn, after the people had petitioned him to build one for them.

271

He walked along the road, ignoring the hooted laughter and catcalls of children too young to work, but old enough to have learned their parents' prejudices.

The inn was, thankfully, quiet at this time of day. The people of Kirklees were all out working, so only the innkeeper, Fulk, and his sour-faced, skinny wife, Agnes, were in the building when he went inside.

Fulk nodded to him. The inn-keeper neither liked nor disliked Edmond who had become a good customer recently, with a little extra coin from his reward and the black mood of a man that wants to spend that coin trying to find solace at the bottom of a mug.

"God give you good day, tanner. You'll be lookin' for some ale, eh?"

Agnes snorted and muttered something to herself, but Edmond ignored her and dropped a silver penny onto the bar.

"Aye. Refill this for me." He handed the empty skin to Fulk who took it with a nod and moved to the barrels behind him.

Fulk's wife, who was moving around placing fresh rushes on the floor to replace the ones that had become sodden with ale and puke and god-knew what else over the recent days, continued to mutter to herself, shaking her head and tutting in his direction every so often.

Clearly, she wanted Edmond to hear her, as, when the young man didn't respond she moved closer and raised her voice slightly.

Although he still couldn't make out full sentences, certain words were hissed with extra venom and the tanner found himself growing even angrier.

As Fulk returned his ale-skin to him, Edmond removed the stopper and swallowed almost half of it. "Shut your whining mouth, woman," he growled, glaring at Agnes whose eyes went wide, surprised at being challenged.

Her mouth turned up at one corner in a half-smile though and she threw a small clump of reeds at his feet. "You drunk already, boy? Again?"

Like most drinkers, Edmond hated to be reminded of the fact he was in thrall to the stuff, and he felt his temper rising as he turned to Fulk. "You better shut your woman's mouth, before I shut it for her."

The inn-keeper, a man used to dealing with violence from drink-sodden customers, pointed a long finger at the tanner. "Don't you threaten my wife, you ugly bastard."

He moved around the counter to stand protectively beside his wife who smirked, enjoying the drama. She'd tell everyone all about this later on when the workers returned from the fields!

It was too much for Edmond. The grief, rage and guilt bubbled inside him and, like a poorly constructed tanning vat, his temper exploded.

He found himself with his hands around Fulk's throat, trying to squeeze the breath from him, but the inn-keeper had seen the attack coming and managed to ram his knee between Edmond's legs.

The pain was intense and the tanner responded with similar violence, kneeing, kicking, punching and trying to throttle the man who fought back desperately, knowing the crazed young tanner had lost control of himself.

Agnes tried to drag Edmond off her husband and the three of them, snarling and spitting, battered off the wall and the bar.

It started as a furious, loud fight, with the men grunting as they traded blows and the inn-keeper's wife screaming at Edmond, but after a while the room became almost silent as exhaustion overtook them and the sounds of fear and desperation became almost obscene as the two men lost themselves in the struggle.

Eventually, Edmond managed to get a hand on the back of Fulk's hair and, forcing the older man's head sideways, battered it against the wooden wall with a thump.

There was a high-pitched whimper from Agnes as Edmond smashed her husband's head against the wall again. And again, but this time there was a cracking sound and the fight left the three of them.

Edmond let go of the inn-keeper who had become, literally, a dead-weight, and the body slumped to the ground, followed by Agnes who stared in shock at her man's unmoving body.

In a daze, the young tanner walked to the front door and, without a backward glance, walked out into the village.

His hands and clothes were blood-stained and, as Agnes appeared at the inn door screaming murder, none of the villagers nearby wanted anything to do with him.

He passed unmolested along the street; even Godfrey, his brother's childhood tormentor, moved quietly back into the shadows at the sight of the bloody tanner.

Vaguely, the sound of the inn-keeper's wife screaming came to him as he walked out of the village and was swallowed up by the looming forest of Barnsdale.

* * *

Stephen knew something was wrong.

The Hospitaller had stopped at Cossebi for provisions as he made his way back to Kirklees. Cossebi was a small town, so the two men following him were easy to spot. In their chain-mail and carrying swords they stood out from the locals.

Idiots.

The problem was, Stephen had no idea who they were or who might have sent them. They couldn't have come from Highgate, to bring him to justice for killing the girl, surely? No, he doubted that: the girl wasn't important enough. The villagers would have banded together and hunted for him with their pitchforks and wood-axes, but they'd not have sent these two mercenaries after him, even if they could have afforded the price.

The king's men? Stephen was still a rebel after all.

He shook his head. The king had more important people to worry about than a lowly Hospitaller sergeant-at-arms.

The small marketplace only boasted a few stalls, and those were poorly stocked, but he wasn't a man of opulent tastes so there was enough here to keep him going until he made it home again.

"When did you bake this, lad?"

The youngster at the bakers stall shrugged his thin shoulders. "My da baked it this morning, my lord. All our stuff is newly made today, see?" He picked up the loaf nearest him, squeezing it to show how soft it was.

"Good. Give me that one then."

The boy handed over the fresh loaf with a sullen look. It was obvious most of the wares on show were at least a day old, more in some cases, and Stephen had taken the nicest, and freshest, loaf on the stall now.

The Hospitaller smiled and tossed a small coin to the boy who scrambled to catch it.

"That's for this too." Stephen lifted a small meat pie along with the loaf and walked away, biting into the savoury as if he hadn't a care in the world. As he swung his head from side to side, checking out the rest of the goods and produce for sale at the stalls, he saw the two burly men following him at a short distance.

He was in no mood to be hunted all the way back home, though, so he nonchalantly made his way towards the far outskirts of the market and the centre of town, to a deserted street with gutters so choked with shit and piss even the local dogs seemed to shun the place.

He slipped into an alley, placed his prized fresh loaf on the ground and waited for his pursuers to come past. He drew his sword and breathed deeply to try and offset the effects of the blood coursing nervously through him as the sound of fast-moving footsteps approached him.

As the men passed his hiding place, the sergeant dived out and battered the pommel of his sword against the temple of the man nearest him, who went flying sideways, unconscious, into the filth of the street.

The second man was fast though, and as he saw the attack coming in his peripheral vision, had whipped his own blade free from its sheath and brought it up defensively in front of him. His eyes took in his fallen companion and their quarry, standing before him with a murderous look on his face.

"Who are you?"

The man moved closer, his sword held expertly before him. "We come from Sir Hugh Despenser."

Stephen's blood ran cold at that, and he felt the hairs on his neck rise. Despenser? The man had murdered Sir Richard's youngest son, Stephen, and obviously held a grudge against the Lord of Kirklees.

The Hospitaller flicked his sword down and placed it against the Adam's apple of the man lying on the ground. "How did you know where I was?" he demanded.

Despenser's man smiled, confident that his size and skill would be enough to kill the Hospitaller once the talking was over. "Your own Order gave you up, fool. I don't know what you did to piss them off, but they sent word that you were heading north and were to be stopped."

Stephen's mind whirled and he guessed it had been the Prior's bald steward who had betrayed him.

"Stopped?"

The man grinned again, rolling his shoulders and head to work out any kinks in his muscles. "Stopped, aye. Meaning killed."

The man on the ground groaned and rolled to his side, retching from the effects of the blow to the temple.

Stephen booted the prone figure as hard as he could in the face, then swept his sword round in an arc to block the attack from the big man in front of him.

"Is that your best, you ugly sack of shit?"

276

Despenser's man was more than competent with a sword and held his temper despite the Hospitaller's annoying smile.

They traded blows for a while, neither giving ground, content to play it out until an opening presented itself. Stephen's mind was working though, and the realisation that his own Order were actively seeking to make an end to him was a sickening thought.

"What about my master?" he asked, parrying another raking blow from the left.

His opponent laughed and pressed the attack again. "No idea, but my lord Despenser's probably got something good in store for him too."

Stephen slipped as he parried yet another crushing blow and felt as if the earth was swallowing him as he fell face-down on the hard road. Despenser's man saw his chance and stepped forward, kicking at the fallen Hospitaller's head.

Desperately, Stephen threw both his feet round in an arc, grunting as the move paid off and his attacker stumbled over his legs, falling onto the ground beside him.

Baring his teeth in rage, the Hospitaller straddled the man and slammed the pommel of his sword into his attacker's face. He was rewarded with the sound of bone and cartilage cracking as the man's nose broke and he fell backwards with a roar of agony.

Almost insane with rage now, Stephen threw himself like one of the old berserkers on top of Despenser's mercenary, hammering his fist repeatedly into the man's left cheek until it was a bloody mess.

He lay there, sucking air into his burning lungs for a while, before getting shakily to his feet. The second of his pursuers whimpered and Stephen shoved the tip of his sword deep into the man's throat.

His own Order had sent men to kill him. The king's closest companion, Sir Hugh Despenser, wanted his blood. And God knew what fate had befallen his master.

Shaking his head he picked up his loaf of bread and stumbled back through the marketplace towards his horse.

God's bollocks! Today wasn't a good day.

* * *

They came for him at dawn. Bleary eyed and sullen from the previous night's drinking in Pontefract Castle's great hall.

They'd been glad to tell him who they were and where he was going when he asked them.

Nottingham. His heart had sank at the news the sheriff was going to hang him. Sir Henry de Faucumberg hated him after he'd helped Robin Hood and his gang escape the sheriff's "justice" last year.

Now de Faucumberg would have his revenge by publicly hanging the disgraced lord of Kirklees.

Sir Richard was frightened, but more than that, he was angry that his life would be ended, in front of a baying mob, on de Faucumberg's orders. Despair washed over him, but only for a moment, then his faith galvanized him and he rode, shoulders back and head held high, from the castle, out onto the road towards Nottingham surrounded by a dozen of Despenser's men, all heavily armed and riding great warhorses while he trailed along beneath them on a sway-backed old palfrey.

The journey took up the whole day and was uneventful: Despenser's men were well-disciplined and bore him no ill-will. He was fed regularly and given ale – indeed, he could have drank himself into a stupor for all his captors cared. As long as he gave them no trouble and stayed on his horse, they were content.

The men ignored him when he tried to start a conversation on the road though, and, on reaching Nottingham, they handed him over to the sheriff's men as if he were a common criminal.

God, give me the strength to get through this, he prayed. When he'd decided to give himself up to the

278

king's justice it had seemed like the noble, honourable, Christian thing to do. Yet now, imprisoned in de Faucumberg's dungeon beneath Nottingham Castle, Sir Richard wondered if he'd made a terrible mistake.

He was frightened. Scared to die. Not for his own sake, but, although Sir Hugh Despenser had murdered his youngest son, Simon, Sir Richard had another son in Rhodes and the tears streamed down his lined face at the thought he would never see his boy again.

Hadn't he been a good Christian? A good man?

Christ's words on the cross came to him and he bowed his head in despair. *Father! Why have you forsaken me?*

CHAPTER TWENTY-THREE

"I can't best Gisbourne, John. Even before he beat the shit out of me, I wasn't a match for him. And now...look at me!" Robin shook his bruised knuckles at his big friend. "The man's unbeatable, trust me. I'm not walking into a duel with him, it's madness."

Little John threw his hands in the air. "You have to get over this. You can't hide here forever."

"I'm not" –

"Three months ago you would have jumped at the chance to fight Gisbourne," John cut in, pointing at his young leader while the rest of the men looked on, unsure whose side they should be taking in this discussion. "You're the best swordsman of us all. If anyone can beat the bastard, it's you." He walked over to stand in front of Robin, towering over the younger man. "I know you lost hope when you were in jail. I know they tried to break your spirit. But this is your chance to prove to Gisbourne – and yourself – that you're" –

"What?" Robin demanded. "What am I? I'm a yeoman from Wakefield. Not even that any more: I'm a wolf's head. A nobody. What have I to prove to anyone?"

John's face turned red with anger and he grabbed his friend by the front of his gambeson and hauled him off the ground as if Robin were no more than a child.

"You're supposed to be our leader! You're a husband. You're about to be a father for Christ's sake! It's time you started acting like a man again, instead of sitting around here brooding about what the big bad Raven did to you."

Robin glared at the giant but made no effort to fight him off.

"See," John dropped him back to the floor, waving a hand dismissively. "You've no fight left in you. Maybe it's best you don't meet Gisbourne like this after all. Go sit by the fire again, with your ale, listening to Allan's songs, while the rest of us make sure the sheriff and king's men don't kill us all."

"What's going on?"

Will Scarlet strode into camp with two of the other men. They'd been visiting New Mylle on Dam that morning, buying provisions and gathering news from the locals.

"Ask our famous leader," John spat towards Robin, turning his back and storming off through the ranks of sympathetic men.

Will looked curiously at the bowed head of his young friend, but Robin moved away without explanation and sat down with a heavy sigh beside the little camp-fire.

"Robin won't take on Gisbourne," Gareth offered. "He doesn't think he can beat him, injured like he is."

Will walked over to stand on the opposite side of the fire and looked down at the brooding young man. "Well, here's some news that might get your fight back: the sheriff's captured Sir Richard-at-Lee. They're going to hang him on Saturday. Looks like they've found a nobleman to take your place on the gallows."

Robin's head snapped up and he met Will's stare in disbelief.

"Don't even think about trying to rescue him. Me and Tuck were lucky to get you out of there before. That was a miracle that won't be repeated. They'll have tripled the guard on the Hospitaller and sealed the city until he's swinging. De Faucumberg lost a fine prize when you escaped – he won't make the same mistake twice. Word is, the Despenser had a hand in his capture, so his men will probably be guarding Sir Richard too. He's as good as dead already."

Robin shut his eyes and bowed his head. How many more of his friends must die? Sir Richard had helped them when they needed it. He'd introduced them to the Earl of Lancaster and, if the rebellion had succeeded, they'd all be free men now thanks to the Hospitaller.

Things hadn't turned out like that though, and here they were. Condemned men, waiting to die. And Sir Richard-at-Lee would be next to go.

Never give up hope! Tuck's words rang in Robin's head again and he felt the rage of the past few weeks building up inside him.

Little John had returned to listen to Will's news, and Robin glanced up at him now, his eyes blazing. "What day is it?"

"June the 8th. Tuesday," the big man replied, with a confused look.

"When did Gisbourne want to meet me?"

"Next Monday."

"Two days after they're to hang the Hospitaller," Will noted.

"Fine." Robin stood up and made his way over to where the practice swords were stored, lifting the heavier one he always used. "Spar with me, John. I have a few days to get my fitness back if I'm going to beat the bastard. We might not be able to save Sir Richard, but maybe I can stop the Raven killing any more of us."

The gathered outlaws cheered as if they'd all been granted a pardon.

* * *

Stephen knew something was wrong when he rode into Kirklees on his way back to the castle and the locals paid him no heed.

As far as he knew, he was still a fugitive, wanted as a rebel by the king's men. So how come people were turning away from him as if they were embarrassed, rather than calling out the tithing to chase after him as he'd expected?

In the name of Christ, some of the villagers were even waving at him!

Whatever had happened, he clearly wasn't in any obvious danger. Which was a bad sign.

"How goes it, Justin?" The sergeant pulled his horse up and slid to the ground, addressing the local smith as he did so. "Any news?"

"News? You haven't heard?" The man looked at him in disbelief. "Where the hell have you been?"

"I've been away in London," Stephen replied.

Justin grunted in reply and eyed the Hospitaller as if he'd just returned from the moon. Like the vast majority of the villagers, the smith had never travelled anywhere outside Yorkshire. "Well," he grunted, swinging his heavy hammer down on the horseshoe he was working on, "Sir Richard's been taken. Two of the local lads – the tanner's boys – captured him. Your master managed to kill one of them but the other took him to Sir Philip of Portsmouth at Pontefract Castle."

Stephen felt numb. His fingers tingled weirdly, as if the blood had been cut off from them and he moved to sit on a huge old log the smith kept as a chair.

"The lad that captured him – Edmond – came back a while ago, but people were angry at him. He attacked big Fulk, the inn-keep, and disappeared. No one's seen him since."

"Angry at him?" Stephen looked up at the smith in confusion. "Why? I'd have thought he'd have been a hero."

Justin shrugged half-heartedly and went back to beating the horseshoe. "Because Sir Richard was a good lord to Kirklees, and Edmond handed him over to the law. People didn't like it, and they let him know it too." He smiled ingratiatingly at Stephen, as if the Hospitaller should be thankful for the villagers' loyalty.

"Bollocks," Stephen spat, getting to his feet again. "Me and my master were left alone in the castle when the king's men came looking for us. I didn't see you or any of the rest of them standing up for us then."

The smith opened his mouth to protest, his eyebrows lowered indignantly, but Stephen waved a hand to silence him and climbed back onto his horse.

"Forget it, I care nothing for the tanner's sons, or for the rest of you. Where's Sir Richard now? Still at Pontefract?"

"No. We heard he'd been moved to Nottingham. The sheriff's going to hang him after at the weekend. They'd captured Robin Hood, but he escaped, so de Faucumberg's making a big deal out of this to try and make up for it."

Despite his shock, Stephen smiled at the idea of Hood escaping the sheriff's clutches. The wolf's head led a charmed life, sure enough.

"Kirklees Castle has been taken over by the king's steward," the smith shouted as Stephen kicked his horse into a walk past the inn and back towards the main road. "Sir Simon de Baldreston. You'd best steer well clear! They might have forgotten you for now, but if you show up causing trouble anywhere they'll hang you too!"

The sergeant-at-arms waved a hand in reply and spurred the big palfrey into a trot. It had all been for nothing. He'd taken too long getting to Clerkenwell and now, even if the Prior had sent a letter to the king on Sir Richard's behalf, it was too late. His master was to be hanged for treason.

It was all Stephen's fault – he should never have allowed that girl to sidetrack him! All he could do now was ride to Nottingham to witness his master's death.

Christ and St John only knew what would become of him after that.

* * *

He had no trouble joining the crowd on Gallows Hill outside Nottingham. Why would he? A middle-aged man, of average height and build; just another visitor come to see the Hospitaller Knight swing.

Of course, he'd left his black surcoat with its give-away white cross back amongst the trees on the roadside, along with his chain-mail, his horse and even his sword. He wasn't here for a fight, and a weapon like that would only draw the guards' attention to him.

He lost himself in the surging mass of people. The atmosphere appeared to be one of celebration and a younger man might have felt sick at the glee these folk seemed to feel at the idea of watching a good knight die in such a horrible way.

Stephen had seen it too many times before to let it affect him visibly though. Of course, it surprised him, as it always did, that normal, everyday people – mothers with their excited children; whole families in some cases, from the youngest babe to the oldest doddering, cackling crone – could get so excited at another person's miserable death, before heading back to their homes to continue their lives as normal.

But he'd made a career – a life – from killing men, who was he to question humanity's baser instincts? Hadn't he just murdered a woman in her sick-bed?

The crowd washed him up like a piece of flotsam on the outskirts of the audience awaiting the hanging, so he discreetly but firmly pushed his way through the tightly-packed people, silencing anyone who tried to complain with a murderous glare, until he made it almost to the front. He positioned himself behind a small group of women so he could see over them straight to the sinister-looking wooden construction which would end his master's life before the day was out.

Small children pushed their way between the gathered people, offering meat pies and pastries; merchants hawked more exotic snacks like oranges, figs and dates; men and women discussed their favourite executions and how they imagined the Hospitaller would go to his death. Most of those around him thought Sir Richard would be stoic and proud to the end, but Stephen had to restrain himself from punching one drunken loud-mouth who claimed to know the former Lord of Kirklees was a coward.

Of course, there were more people to be hanged than just the knight. The sheriff wanted to make this a day the inhabitants of Nottingham would enjoy – a day that would make up for the loss of the wolf's head, Robin Hood. The people had been looking forward to that, which sickened Stephen – he knew the lower classes saw Hood as a freedom fighter and a hero. A man who outfought and outsmarted the bastard noblemen that bled the people dry.

And yet many of them had been disappointed to miss out on a day's entertainment when Hood's men had led him back to the safety of Barnsdale Forest and robbed them of a good hanging.

The sergeant-at-arms gazed around at the people and shook his head in a black rage. Fucking idiots. So starved of joy and excitement that the sight of a man convulsing as his last breath was stolen from him by a length of rope was a highlight of their week. So easily led, that even the ones who knew inside this was wrong would stand cheering and laughing until they were hoarse just so they could be like everyone else.

Idiots.

His eyes swept the crowd in disgust until he noticed a young man and a spark of recognition flared. He looked again, taking in the thin beard and flat nose, and his heart missed a beat. Edmond: the tanner's son. The bastard that had brought Sir Richard to his doom, standing here, waiting to see the knight die!

Fingering the dagger strapped to the outside of his thigh, Stephen began to force his way through the crowd towards the young man. A few people tried to stop him as he barged past but the sergeant had lost any sense of danger and he simply battered anyone that stood in his path out of the way, leaving a trail of confusion and pain in his wake.

The blood was hammering in his veins as he neared the tanner's son and, from the direction of the gallows he could hear a man's voice raised to address the people. Sliding the dagger free from its leather sheath, Stephen held it in his clenched fist, with the blade under his wrist, ready to slip it between Edmond's ribs.

The crowd suddenly cheered, as Sir Henry de Faucumberg, Sheriff of Nottingham and Yorkshire, raised a hand with a smile and the disgraced rebel knight, Sir Richard-at-Lee was led up the stairs onto the gallows.

Stephen knew what was going on now, and he wanted to look at his master to see how he was holding up, but, as he came within arm's reach of the tanner's son and prepared to plunge his blade into the man, he was shocked to see Edmond cry out in anguish and try to push his way towards the gallows.

Assuming he'd misheard the sheriff and it was some other man about to be hung, Stephen looked round and felt as if an arrow had pierced his heart. Sure enough, his master stood, head bowed, looking like an old, old man, rather than the proud knight his sergeant had left on the ramparts of Kirklees Castle just a few days before.

His eyes roved across the crowd again, searching for the tanner's son who was by now a couple of rows in front of him, shouting and crying, although the sergeant couldn't make out the words.

A couple of the sheriff's men were watching Edmond curiously. He was too far away to be a threat, yet, but they hefted their great pole-arms and Stephen knew they would skewer the tanner's son before he could get to the gallows and do whatever it was he was planning in his near-hysterical state.

With a curse, Stephen used his strength to force his way through the crowd towards Edmond who couldn't command the same level of respect – or fear – as the grim sergeant and, as a result, found his way to the gallows was a slow one.

"Boy!"

Edmond ignored the voice close behind him, and, with a snarl, tried to shrug off the hand that had grasped his shoulder like a vice.

"Boy!"

Turning, ready to fight whoever was trying to restrain him, Edmond stared at the man and knew instantly who he was. Images of Sir Richard walking through Kirklees past his father's shop came into his mind. The smiling knight with his thick beard – which had been turning to grey even when Edmond was just a teenager – chatting to the tradesmen and accompanied, always, by his scowling sergeant-at-arms. The same man who held him now, like a jailer, by the front of his cloak.

Edmond's face crumpled and fresh tears made tracks in the grime on his cheeks. "I'm sorry! I'm so sorry!"

The guards were still watching – more in amusement now than anything else, but Stephen knew they'd be quick to break a few heads to reach them if they felt anything was amiss so he met Edmond's eyes and grasped his shoulders firmly.

"Get a grip of yourself, boy, now. The sheriff's men are watching us. You keep this up and they're going to come for us."

The sergeant's commanding tone – so like Sir Richard's as Edmond remembered from their short journey together – surprised the tanner's son and he met the calm stare of the older man.

"I'm sorry," he repeated, this time in almost a whisper. "I never wanted this. I thought capturing Sir Richard would make everything right. It's made everything worse!"

"Forget it," Stephen growled, his eyes drawn to what was happening on the gallows behind the weeping Edmond.

While they'd been talking Sir Richard had been led to stand in front of the crowd and the sheriff now read out the charges laid against the Knight Hospitaller. The people booed and cheered, laughed and hooted, cursed and joked as the list was read out and de Faucumberg played the part of master of ceremonies to the full.

The bastard will be loving this, Stephen thought, watching the sheriff ham it up. Sir Richard and the Earl of Lancaster had made a fool of him the previous Christmas by rescuing Robin Hood and his men from the trap the sheriff had set for them. Now it was payback time for the sheriff.

"Keep your hands by your sides."

The voice came from directly behind them, startling both men.

They had been so engrossed in their conversation, and what was happening on the gallows, that they'd failed to notice the soldiers coming up through the crowd at their backs. Four of them, two armed with swords and two with pole-arms levelled directly at their midriffs.

Singly, Stephen knew he could have taken them or at least evaded them in the crowd. They didn't have the look of killers. They did have the confident look of competent guardsmen though; men used to violence and dealing with it.

There was no escape.

"Don't even think about it," he said quietly to Edmond, whose eyes were flicking between him and the guards as if uncertain what to do. "Even if you got away from this lot, you'd never get out of the city. So relax."

He made a show of patting the tanner's son on the back as if he was calming a child after a tantrum. These guardsmen had no idea who he was, and Edmond wasn't an outlaw, so Stephen hoped they'd be left in peace if the guards knew there was no threat to them.

Unfortunately, Robin Hood's recent escape had made the sheriff and his men jumpy. They weren't about to let anything similar happen again.

Stephen collapsed on the ground as the pommell of a sword cracked against the back of his head, and Edmond fell a moment later with a cry of rage.

"Stay down!" the sergeant-at-arms grunted through teeth gritted in pain, grasping the angry younger man by the arm.

The four soldiers moved in, ringing the two downed men and disarming them, while the crowd which had hemmed them in so tightly just moments earlier pulled well back in case they should suffer the same fate.

The sheriff's men, fully in control now, ordered the pair to their feet and shepherded them through the crowd, past the gallows and towards the castle.

A tall man, dressed all in exotic-looking black armour, watched as they passed and Stephen met his gaze, knowing it must be the man the people called The Raven: Sir Guy of Gisbourne. The king's hunting dog.

Gisbourne stood with a bald, hard-looking man by his side, and three of the sheriff's men behind him. As Stephen and Edmond were marched past them, one of the blue-liveried sheriff's soldiers swung his head to watch, staring at the sergeant with a bemused look on his face.

"That's the knight's man! The Hospitaller!"

Gisbourne and his bald companion turned to look at where the soldier was pointing. "Hold!" Sir Guy commanded, looking at the shouting guardsman. "Let's hear what this man has to say."

"I remember him from last year when we tried to ambush Robin Hood and his men," the man shouted as Stephen and Edmond were forced to stop moving. "He was with them, wearing the Hospitaller cross."

Stephen wished he hadn't left his sword back in the forest now, but he still had his dagger and its weight on his thigh was reassuring, although he knew it would not be enough to let him escape from this.

It was clear Gisbourne knew Stephen was a dangerous man, but his confidence was unmistakable as he moved around to stand directly in front of the sergeant.

"Is that true? "

"I'm Sir Richard's sergeant-at-arms, yes."

Gisbourne smiled, but it was a strange smile and Stephen wondered if the man was all there.

Nicholas Barnwell suddenly reached out towards the guard holding Edmond and took the tanner's confiscated sword from him. "This is a nice blade," Gisbourne's man whistled, noting the fine craftsmanship. "A Hospitaller knight's blade I'd say. I'd better hold onto this."

"Come to rescue your friend?" Sir Guy asked Stephen, who glared at Edmond, assuming the young tanner had stolen his master's old sword.

"No," Stephen shook his head sullenly. "I'm no fool. There's no way anyone could rescue my master from this. I came to pay my respects, that's all."

"And you?"

Edmond glared at the dark bounty-hunter. "I came to try and undo the evil that I've done. I should never have turned the good knight over to you lot."

Gisbourne laughed, and turned back to Stephen. "You are also a wanted man. A wolf's head. I will have you taken onto the gallows beside your master...you can die together."

Stephen looked impassively at the king's man, honestly not caring at that moment whether he lived or died. It seemed a foregone conclusion anyway.

"Where would you go if I release you?"

"To my Order's headquarters in London," Stephen shrugged, caught off-guard by the sudden change in the conversation and forgetting that the Hospitallers no longer required his services.

Gisbourne laughed. "Your Order? Why do you think your master is here? Your Prior's steward sent word to the sheriff saying Sir Richard was a traitor and should be hanged, along with you if you were caught. You see," he leered into Stephen's face, "you are an outcast. A rebel, wanted by the king, and disowned by your own Order. You are dead."

There was silence then, as the bounty-hunter smiled, fingering the black crossbow that hung from his shoulder and the two captives looked uncertainly at their supremely confident captor, wondering where this was all going.

"And yet...I need a messenger." Gisbourne spread his hands. "Another one I mean. My last one saw his friends shot in the back and that's made it hard for me to find another one. You," he nodded at Stephen, "are, according to the guard here, acquainted with Robin Hood."

"We've met."

"Good. Then his men won't shoot you before you can deliver my message. Are you listening?"

Stephen shrugged.

"I said, 'are you listening', monk?" Gisbourne's open hand slapped him a stinging crack across the face and the Hospitaller was shocked by the speed of the blow. He hadn't seen it until his head was rocking backwards from the force.

"Aye, I'm listening," he growled.

"Good. I sent word to Robin Hood a few days ago that I wanted to meet him in the forest on Monday. I've heard nothing since. He is, no doubt, hiding somewhere, like an old woman awaiting the grim reaper."

"Or maybe he's waiting until you ride through Barnsdale so he can stick an arrow in your throat."

"Maybe." Gisbourne shrugged. "I wouldn't be surprised. He couldn't beat me in a straight fight, so if he resorted to hiding in the trees and shooting me from a distance, well...like I say, I wouldn't be surprised."

Stephen said nothing to that. He didn't particularly like Hood or his men. They'd held him and Sir Richard up as they travelled through the forest last year. He'd wanted to attack them, even if there had only been the two of them against the outlaw's entire gang, but his master had ordered him to stand down. In the end they had, together, ruined one of the most corrupt noblemen in England, a man who had hoped to destroy Sir Richard and steal his lands.

So Stephen remained silent as Gisbourne insulted Hood.

"We know the general area of the forest where the outlaws are living," the Raven went on. "You will take my message to him." He spoke and Stephen listened, nodding as the enigmatic bounty-hunter finished telling him what to say to Robin.

"What about this one?" a soldier asked, shoving Edmond forward with the butt-end of his polearm.

Gisbourne waved a hand dismissively. "He's nothing. Look at him. He can go with the Hospitaller – sorry, I should say, *former* Hospitaller. Let them watch their friend hang first though."

The wicked laughter followed them as they were led back to the gallows by the soldiers.

"What now?" Edmond asked quietly.

"Now?" Stephen muttered. "Now we say a prayer as my master draws his last breath. And then we find Hood and watch him tear that bastard Gisbourne's head from his shoulders."

CHAPTER TWENTY-FOUR

"So he's changing his tactics," Robin nodded after he'd heard Stephen's message from Sir Guy of Gisbourne. The Raven's intelligence on the rough whereabouts of Hood's gang had been accurate, and the sergeant, with Edmond silently trailing him, had been spotted by Allan-a-Dale as they moved none too stealthily through the undergrowth that morning. Moments later the two men had found themselves surrounded by heavily armed outlaws who appeared, seemingly, from nowhere. Edmond had almost shit himself.

"Instead of threatening us with violence and killing our men," Robin went on, "he's trying to play on my pride in order to flush me out."

The Hospitaller nodded. It was true: many men would rather face death in a hopeless battle than be called a coward and have their reputation sullied. Gisbourne's message had simply demanded, again, that Hood meet him in a neutral location and fight one-on-one, like warriors, to the death. If Robin didn't show up, the whole country would know he wasn't the fearless legendary hero of so many folk-tales told in ale-houses all over the north of England.

"I don't really care, for myself, if people think I'm a coward," the outlaw leader said. "And, honestly, the idea of facing that bastard again does frighten me. But one of the reasons we've been able to endure life in the forest is because the people in the villages around here respect and even, to an extent, fear us. They know we'll reward them if they help us and they know we'll hunt them down if they betray us to the law. The legend that's grown up around us is an essential part of our survival – if the villagers think I'm a coward they'll begin to lose respect and life around here will become even more difficult."

He wasn't just thinking of himself, or the men. Matilda and the rest of his family in Wakefield were left in peace, partly because they were well-liked in the village, but also because the people there had seen what happened to any who betrayed Robin's friends. Little John had killed Simon Woolemonger the year before, after he'd told the former steward, Adam Gurdon, that Matilda had been helping the outlaws. The girl had been arrested and almost raped before they rescued her – and Woolemonger had paid the price, publicly, for crossing the outlaws.

News of that episode had travelled far and wide and had, so far, made anyone else with a big mouth too afraid to inform on the gang.

If Robin refused to face Gisbourne that fear and respect he commanded would be gone and, with his wife due to give birth to their first child, it was never more imperative that his family were left in peace.

"Where am I to meet him?"

"Dalton, to the south-west of here." Stephen described a small stone bridge not far from the village. "It's a short walk from Watling Street, Gisbourne says."

Robin looked at Little John who nodded. "True enough. It's a small bridge, just wide enough for a cart to cross, with a lot of trees around either bank. If you fight him there, the rest of us can hide amongst the foliage. If he brings his men and betrays you like the sheriff tried last winter, we can shoot him down and escape back into Barnsdale."

"Presumably that's why he chose the spot," Robin mused. "So we know we can trust him. He'd have picked somewhere more open if he wanted to ambush us."

"You really think he's just going to turn up and fight you, alone? Without trying to capture or kill the rest of us?"

"I do, aye. I think he's a vain man, desperate to make a name for himself. We've become famous" –

"Notorious!" Will Scaflock grinned.

"Aye, that too," Robin smiled. "Everyone's heard of us now, and the daft tales of me being a giant, with eyes of fire, that can beat ten men single-handedly...Hunting us down isn't enough for Gisbourne. He wants the whole country to know the Raven defeated me, fairly, in single combat."

Stephen agreed. "He was more interested in fighting you than anything else," he told them. "By rights he really should have had me handed over to the sheriff, to hang beside my master. Two Hospitaller's on the gallows...de Faucumberg would have loved that. Yet Gisbourne decided to let me carry his message to you instead. The man's a maniac."

The outlaws bowed their heads in silence for a moment, still upset at the news Stephen had brought of Sir Richard-at-Lee's death.

"What if Gisbourne does beat you, though?" Little John wondered. "It'll demoralize the people."

"And make many of them more likely to turn the rest of us in if they get a chance," Friar Tuck muttered. "They'll see your death as the beginning of the end for us."

"He won't beat me," Robin growled, glaring round at the men. "He won't."

"If he does," Will shrugged. "I'll stick an arrow in him before he can enjoy his victory."

"No! If he beats me, you let him and his men go. If we hope to be treated honourably we must act the same way, or no one will ever trust us again. If I lose, I'd suggest you all move camp, maybe even move out of Yorkshire altogether."

The faces around him were grim, imagining the worst.

"What are we all worrying about?" John shouted, forcing a grin onto his big bearded face. "Robin's the best of all of us with a sword. If anyone can beat that bastard Gisbourne, it's him." He looked up at the sky, noting the sun's position. "And we'd better get a move on if we're to reach Dalton by mid-afternoon."

The men moved silently, thoughtfully, to gather their weapons and strap on whatever armour they owned, while John stood in front of his young leader and grasped him by the shoulders, staring into his eyes.

"You will beat Gisbourne," the giant told him. "You must, for all our sakes, and for your family. Remember: the wings of a raven are no match for the jaws of a wolf."

Robin met his friend's stare and nodded, but, in truth, his guts were turning themselves inside out at the thought of meeting the black-clad king's man again.

"What about you?" the outlaw captain asked, turning to the former Hospitaller sergeant. "I'm sorry about Sir Richard...he was a good man. I'm proud to have met him."

Stephen bowed his head, acknowledging Robin's comment but also hiding the pain in his eyes at the thought of his master's hanging. "Fuck knows. My order betrayed me, and I can't go back to Kirklees." He looked out at the trees surrounding them. "I suppose this is my home now, the trees of Barnsdale – I'm a wolf's head, just like you."

"Then you'll join us," Robin replied, making it a statement rather than a question. "A man of your knowledge and experience will be very welcome in our ranks."

The sergeant gave a small smile, relief plain on his pock-marked face. "Thank you, lad. I'd be honoured to serve under you, until I can clear my name with my Order." No matter what, Stephen would always think of himself as a Hospitaller.

"Let's move!" Little John's massive voice split the air, and he hefted his great quarterstaff south, in the direction of Dalton. As he passed he handed a sword, one of the outlaws' spares, to the weapon-less Hospitaller who took it gratefully.

"What about him?" Stephen gestured to Edmond who had stood silently beside him since they'd been surrounded on the path by the outlaws, and now looked up sullenly at the famous young wolf's head, expecting to be turned away – or worse – once his part in Sir Richard's death became clear. It seemed his place in life was to forever be rejected.

Robin shrugged, pulling the laces tight on his gambeson and moving off after John and the rest of the men with a preoccupied look on his face.

"He can come with us, for now, if he wants," Little John shouted over his shoulder. "Once this is over we can hear his story and decide what's to be done. Get yourself a weapon from the pile of spares over there, lad. You didn't hear anything in Nottingham about the lads that helped Robin escape with Tuck and Will did you?"

Edmond and the gruff Hospitaller shook their heads and John shrugged, hoping that was good news. Roger and Godfrey had sent a messenger into the forest to let the outlaws know they'd started the fires in Nottingham and spread the word to panicked citizens which explained the unexpected diversion that had allowed Robin and his two friends to escape the city. John had sent a sizeable reward back to them with the messenger, but he worried the two men might have been found out by the authorities.

It seemed not though – Gisbourne and the sheriff would have surely made a big deal of their capture if their part in the famous wolf's head's escape had been discovered. Barnsdale would have been alive with the news if anything had befallen Roger and Godfrey.

"Come on, lads," John shouted, breaking into a jog. "Pick up the pace!"

Stephen, happy enough with the longsword Little John had given him, shoved it into the sheath at his side and, none too friendly – he was still unsure how to deal with the tanner's son – beckoned Edmond to follow.

Sir Richard's captor must be able to handle himself in a fight – he'd bested a Knight Hospitaller after all – and that might be useful in the next few hours. One way or another, Stephen thought, things would forever change for the outlaws today, and the more swords raised on Robin Hood's side the better.

They moved out, to Dalton. And Sir Guy of Gisbourne.

* * *

Andrew was a fast runner, and agile, despite his youth. He had been sent into Barnsdale once before, a year ago, to take news to Robin Hood and his men.

That time it had been bad news: Matilda, Robin's lover, had been arrested by Adam Gurdon.

This time he had better news, and he pumped his legs as fast as he could, ignoring the stitch in his side until it eased and he found the wolf's heads' camp, and Friar Tuck.

The outlaws had kept the horses the friar had used to escape from Nottingham with Robin and Will and it was just as well, as Tuck was the only person left on guard in the camp and young Andrew's news had to be carried to Robin as fast as possible.

"God's thanks to you, lad!" the friar roared, as he hauled himself onto the back of one of the palfreys. "Get back to Wakefield now. I'll take your news to Robin!"

The horse was fresh and Tuck had picked the strongest of them so he made good time. He knew exactly where the outlaws were going, having passed through Dalton with Will not so long ago on their way to rescue Robin.

"Christ, please let me be in time." he prayed, whipping the big horse furiously along the road. "Robin has to know!"

* * *

They were all there. Usually only a few of the men would go on a job, led by Robin himself or one of his two captains, Little John and Will Scaflock, but today, for this, everyone apart from Tuck had come and Robin was glad of it although he had no doubt Gisbourne would hold to his word and meet him one-on-one as promised.

When they reached the agreed meeting place Robin had stood on the bridge and looked around, taking in the surroundings, looking for anywhere he could use to his advantage during the fight. John was looking for direction in where to set-up the men in case the Raven didn't hold true to his word and the sheriff's men attacked, but the young wolf's head was off in a world of his own, visualising how the duel might pan out and Will eventually took charge, directing the outlaws to the trees on their side of the little brook that fed into the River Don, making sure they were all well hidden with a clear line of sight to the bridge.

They didn't have long to wait.

Sir Guy of Gisbourne arrived, accompanied by at least twenty soldiers, including his own bald-headed second-in-command, Nicholas Barnwell. He waved them to a halt long before he reached the stone bridge though, ordering them to take up positions along the bank, in plain view. They carried small, but sturdy, shields and Robin smiled. They were learning to fear the outlaws' arrows at last.

Barnwell tried to argue with his commander but Gisbourne sternly waved the man back to stand with his men. There was to be no interference – one of these two men would die today, and no one could stop it. Barnwell moved back, face as black as the thunderheads gathering overhead, and the Raven walked confidently forward onto the bridge, his left hand resting on the pommel of his sword.

"Your bruises are healing."

Robin gritted his teeth at the hated voice which brought back vivid memories of the terrible beating he'd suffered at this man's hands the last time they'd met in Nottingham. It wasn't his style to offer taunts though, so he remained silent, watching Gisbourne for the attack which would certainly come.

300

"I'm glad you decided to meet me. Killing you will make me famous. You're something of a hero to the peasants, you know. Although I can't see why. No offence, but you were no better a swordsman than a dozen other men I've fought and killed."

The boiled-leather cuirass, greaves and bracers Gisbourne wore shone like metal despite the clouds overhead, and, when he drew his sword and held it in a two-handed defensive stance, he looked like something from a fairy tale. Tall, grim and dark; death seemed to hover around him like a black cloak.

Robin felt it, the sense of dread this man somehow exuded, but he too knew the power of appearances, so he hid his fear and continued to stare steadily at his opponent, gently flexing the great muscles in his shoulders and rolling his head to release the tension in his neck.

"Not in the mood for talking?" Gisbourne smiled and Robin shuddered at it for it was a genuine smile of pleasure. There was no trace of fear or trepidation in this man's eyes – he obviously trusted implicitly in his ability to defeat the younger, stronger man.

In contrast, Robin felt like puking. Never before, in his entire life, had he felt such fear going into a battle. Bigger, faster and more agile than the boys in Wakefield, he'd grown up knowing he could deal with almost anyone that tried to stand against him. When he'd become an outlaw and joined up with the men he now led, he'd learned fast, and suffered many beatings on the way, until he knew he could best any of his men – even John – either unarmed or with sword in-hand.

So why did he feel like his intestines were about to worm their way out of his mouth? He stared into the hazelnut eyes of Sir Guy and breathed deeply, trying to marshall his thoughts.

Without thinking he drew his sword and brought it up across his body, parrying the thrust Gisbourne had suddenly thrown.

Christ, but the king's man was fast! Faster than anyone Robin had ever faced before.

Gisbourne threw a few more experimental blows, parried easily enough by the young man from Wakefield, but Robin knew this was just the beginning. He expected to be played with, as he had been in Nottingham, but this time he didn't intend to stand by while it happened. He'd been in shock from the death of his oldest friend when he'd been captured by this man previously and it had slowed him; made him a much easier target than he would normally have been. Now, Robin meant to exact revenge for Much, James, Paul and Sir Richard-at-Lee. And for the torture he'd suffered himself at the hands of this dark monster of a man.

Sir Guy of Gisbourne was a man who pushed himself mercilessly to be the best. He tried to eat well without being a glutton, paid a surgeon to bleed him regularly, and he drank little alcohol, knowing his body would suffer if he indulged too much. Once he'd left his life in Gisbourne and been employed by the king he had remembered the bedtime stories his mother had told and begun to see himself as Sir Lancelot – a charismatic, flawed genius that could best any man alive with a sword. Indeed, his whole persona had been moulded on those old tales of Camelot and the round table. His armour had been influenced by the mythical Black Knight, knowing the colour inspired a primal fear in even the most hardened of warriors. His mistrust of women came from his adulterous wife, Emma, and, of course, Guinevere who had betrayed her own husband, King Arthur.

Parsival's quest for the Holy Grail was, right here, embodied in Gisbourne's battle with Robin Hood, a man the stupid peasants had started comparing to the mythical Arthur!

There was no holy cup filled with some mythical figure's blood. Gisbourne knew it was a metaphor – a symbol that showed those with the wit to see it as the

302

way to enlightenment and self-improvement. The way to become a god.

He grinned in fierce pleasure as he aimed an upward swing at Hood's midriff, feeling power and self-belief coursing through his veins like righteous fire. He became utterly lost within himself as he traded blows back and forth with the wolf's head on the old stone bridge which had seen better days but had been neglected in recent years by the local lord.

His movements flowed effortlessly and he revelled in the feeling of invincibility as the young outlaw parried his blows desperately, rarely giving anything back, yet somehow managing to remain untouched himself.

It was a fine battle, Gisbourne admitted to himself as he danced into another attacking position. But the wolf's head was only doing enough to survive; he wasn't skilful enough to pierce the Raven's defences, and so it would end soon.

He bared his teeth in a joyful smile and went on the attack again.

When Robin had first joined the outlaws he hadn't been much of a swordsman. He could use a longbow better than most people, thanks to his years of practice growing up, like all the other boys in Wakefield. And he could handle himself in unarmed combat thanks to his quick reflexes and powerful build. But he'd rarely taken out the old sword his father kept stored under his bed. When he'd begun sparring with the outlaws all those months ago he'd been beaten and bruised mercilessly until, eventually, he'd learned how to fight with a blade in his hand.

As their leader, he wanted the outlaws to look up to him as a true warrior despite his age. And they did. Because he was the best of them.

He knew he couldn't beat Gisbourne though. It was becoming increasingly obvious that the king's man had almost supernatural abilities. When Robin launched an attack, Gisbourne knew it was coming and was able to either move out the way or parry it, seemingly without much effort. In contrast, the bounty-hunter's moves were so fast, so fluid and so relentless that the wolf's head was desperately tired already, both mentally and physically.

He couldn't hear his friends behind him, but he could feel their nervous stares boring into him as they watched the hated enemy, the Raven, gain the upper hand.

On the opposite side of the river, from the corner of his eye, Robin could see Gisbourne's soldiers watching, although their lack of movement or sound as their leader battered him relentlessly suggested they held little affection for their charismatic leader. Only his second-in-command, Barnwell, seemed excited by the whole affair, shouting encouragement to his master and hopping excitedly, almost like a child, from foot to foot as each blow was thrown and parried.

It couldn't last forever, though. Robin was fast becoming exhausted and his parries were beginning to come slower, with less strength behind them, and he was throwing fewer and fewer shots of his own as time went on.

The young man tried to rally, picturing Matilda's face in his mind's eye, holding their unborn baby in her arms. He so desperately wanted to be a father to that little child, and, for a few moments, another surge of determination allowed him to force Gisbourne onto the back-foot. But it didn't last before he tired again, his arms feeling like they were encased in lead, and the grim king's man took control again, his wickedly sharp blade – so finely polished it almost glowed in the setting sunlight – moving so fluidly it seemed to be made from liquid steel.

Robin knew he was going to die here today.

* * *

304

Friar Tuck literally fell off the big palfrey as he came at last to the bridge and found his friends watching the fight between their leader and Sir Guy of Gisbourne.

"What are you doing here?" Little John demanded, trying to keep an eye on the one-to-one battle before him while dragging the big clergyman off the grass as if he was no heavier than a child. "You're supposed to be resting at the camp. And watching our stuff!"

"Never mind that," Tuck retorted. "I have news! Robin has a son!"

The outlaws, nervously watching the fight between their leader and the man known as the Raven, suddenly cried out as they heard the friar's news.

"A son!"

"Robin has a son!"

"Are you sure?" John demanded, glaring into Tuck's eyes. "Robin's suffered enough in the past few weeks without hearing something that'll turn out to be nonsense."

"I'm sure," Tuck nodded, trying to catch his breath and rubbing his elbow where he'd landed as he dropped from the horse in his haste. "A boy, born on the Ides of June. Tell him!"

Little John grinned. "If you're sure, I'll let him know." He hefted his great quarterstaff over his head and gave a deafening shout. "Lads! Let's tell him."

Filling his massive lungs, the giant outlaw opened his mouth and bellowed across to the bridge and the men locked in mortal combat there.

"Robin! You're a father now. Matilda's had a son!"

The men behind him joined in and added their joyful congratulations, roaring and shouting happily.

"Matilda's had the baby!"

CHAPTER TWENTY-FIVE

He had a son!

Images of a smiling little boy racing through the forest and the streets of Wakefield filled Robin's mind as he knelt in the mud under another of the Raven's relentless attacks. A boy with fair hair, eyes shining, gazing up at him – his father – as they played together in the thick green summer foliage.

The outlaw rose unsteadily to his feet and parried the unrelenting blows from the wiry king's man, desperately trying to stay alive as attack after attack rained down on him.

And then it happened. A simple stumble was all it took, as a foot failed to find purchase on a damp patch of grass and the blade was coming down, slicing mercilessly through skin and flesh, before scraping agonizingly down through cheekbone and jaw.

It took Gisbourne a moment to realise what had happened, before he held his left hand up to his ruined face and screamed, an outpouring of fear, pain and rage.

All his years of training to be the best, and a damp patch of grass was his undoing.

Robin could hear his friends now – cheering and whooping in happy relief as he stepped back to catch his breath, sword held loosely in his hand as he watched Gisbourne struggle back to his feet, still clutching his cheek which was bleeding terribly now.

"You lucky bastard." The bounty-hunter mumbled as he moved back into a fighting stance, and Robin shivered as he saw Gisbourne's crazed eyes and the crimson stain that was leaking steadily between his fingers. "I'm not done yet, Hood. I still have enough left to beat you."

Robin threw his sword up again, stunned by the speed the injured Gisbourne hurled himself back into the fight, and again they traded blows. This time, though,

Robin knew he had the upper hand. Gisbourne's depth-perception was off as he tried to hold his face together and he was struggling terribly to keep up with the speed they were moving at.

Again, Robin's sword raked across his enemy's face, this time diagonally upwards, from left to right, taking the side of Gisbourne's nostril off, narrowly missing the eye, and the bleeding man continued to fight on, tears of fury spilling from his eyes and spreading the blood even more shockingly down his face, but refusing to accept defeat at the hands of this outlawed yeoman.

Both men were tired now, locked in their own little world of pain and blood.

Gisbourne tried a powerful overhand cut but totally misjudged his opponent's position and the bright steel whistled harmlessly down, lodging point-first into the grass.

They had been moving backwards as Robin's superiority forced Gisbourne onto the back-foot and were now standing in front of the old stone bridge. The sound of rushing water was the only thing the young outlaw could hear as his hated enemy stood, beaten and unmoving, looking at him through his insane dark eyes.

"You murdered three of my friends. One of them I'd known all my life – he was a good man, and you gutted him in front of me."

Gisbourne stared, mouth open, drooling slightly, his entire face, neck and that beautiful black boiled-leather cuirass covered grotesquely in blood. He never replied – indeed he didn't seem to know where he was any more, and Robin kicked him in the stomach, so hard that Gisbourne was thrown backwards to lie on the bridge.

Still lost in a place where only he and his foe existed, Robin moved forward with a murderous glint in his eyes and raised his sword to plunge it down into Sir Guy's heart.

He hadn't noticed Gisbourne's men being urged forward into a charge by the bounty-hunter's sergeant

Nicholas Barnwell though, or his own men running desperately to reach him before the soldiers did.

Barnwell reached the bridge before anyone else, sword in hand, and he screamed in fury as he swung it at Robin who only now noticed the bald man not five paces away from him.

An arrow sliced through the air, catching Barnwell in the left thigh and he spun to the side before another arrow hammered into his chest knocking him onto his backside. He sat on the bridge, a look of surprise on his face, gazing down at the missiles lodged in him.

Gisbourne's soldiers seemed to have little enthusiasm for a fight as they moved slowly towards the bridge, clearly not looking to engage the outlaws even though they outnumbered Robin and his men and Will Scarlet was shouting obscenities at them.

"Move!" Robin felt himself grabbed from behind by strong hands as Little John hauled him off the bridge, the rest of the outlaws holding drawn swords or longbows aimed at the soldiers on the opposite side of the river.

Moving backwards, still staring at the mutilated, bloody face of Sir Guy of Gisbourne, Robin Hood allowed himself to be led away into the trees by his enormous friend, their men forming a protective barrier behind them in case Gisbourne's soldiers decided to come after them.

Stephen suddenly ran past them onto the bridge and pried Sir Richard's sword from Barnwell's dead fingers before he moved back towards the trees with the rest of the men.

"You did it! You fucking did it!" John's bearded, open face was split by a wide grin and, despite his facial hair and great size, Robin marvelled at how childlike the man seemed at times.

"He slipped."

John dismissed that with a wave of his hand as Friar Tuck moved in beside them, helping the giant to support their tired leader as they disappeared back into the forest towards their camp.

"Whether he slipped or not – and I never saw it – you beat the bastard."

As they moved deeper into the trees the excitement and blood-lust wore off, the realisation of what happened began to sink in and Robin grinned. "I beat the bastard. I'm still alive!"

If they hadn't been so disciplined, the men would have sung for joy.

Robin had won!

"Come on!" he shouted, stumbling through the mud. "I have to visit my son!"

* * *

"Will you leave us then, Tuck?"

The outlaws had made it back to their camp safely, elated after their young leader's victory over their feared enemy, and now they sat celebrating their good fortune around the camp-fire.

It was a cold evening, but the cosily crackling flames cast a homely glow on the small clearing and generous amounts of ale and roast venison had warmed the men nicely.

Robin had ridden straight off to Wakefield to see his new son, accompanied by Will who wanted to see his own little daughter, Beth. Now, the rest of the men were enjoying themselves and Little John gazed across at the jovial friar, who sat looking at the valuable reliquary they'd borrowed from St Mary's in Brandesburton.

"What d'you mean?" Tuck asked, looking up in surprise. "Why would I leave?"

John pointed at the holy relic cradled in Tuck's palm. "If you were to take that to Prior de Monte Martini in Lewes, he'd welcome you back into the church with open arms."

Tuck sat for a moment, lost in thought. He hadn't even considered that idea, but John was right.

"I can't take it," he replied at last. "You promised to return it to Brandesburton."

John shrugged. "Aye, so we did, but it was stolen from the Prior so I don't think Father de Nottingham would mind too much if you returned it to its rightful owner."

It was probably true. Tuck turned away from his big friend and gazed thoughtfully into the fire. He loved these men – like brothers, some of them. But he wasn't as fit as the rest of the outlaws and his recent health problems had taken their toll on him, both physically and mentally. He didn't feel as comfortable sleeping rough in the forest as the others, especially when winter came.

Maybe God had sent him the relic, as a way to leave this life as a wolf's head...? If that was so, it would be sinful not to use it for the purpose the Lord had intended...

"What's to be done with him, then?" Allan-a-Dale shouted suddenly, standing up and pointing.

Edmond looked up, his cheeks flushing as the outlaws turned to look at him.

"Can you fight, lad?" someone demanded.

The tanner nodded, but his eyes remained self-consciously on the grass and soft old leaves carpeting the forest floor and Tuck instantly felt sorry for the young man who muttered a reply.

"Aye, well enough."

"That's enough for us, then, eh?"

Most of the men, half-drunk by now and in a happy mood, cheered Allan's words, but as Tuck saw the beginnings of a smile tugging at the corners of Edmond's fleshy mouth another voice spoke up.

"Hold on." It was Stephen. He had taken his fill of the ale like the rest of them, but he was mourning the death of his master, and friend, Sir Richard, and clearly didn't feel so much like celebrating that night. He walked over to stand in front of Edmond, looking down at him with an unreadable expression on his pock-marked face. "It's time you told us what happened between you and

Sir Richard, boy – you owe me an explanation. And it had better be good."

Tuck clenched his fist protectively around the priceless reliquary, refilled his wooden mug and settled back to listen as the tanner from Kirklees began to tell them his tale.

Edmond wasn't much of a story-teller but the emotion betrayed in his voice – the obvious pain and sense of loss as he told the band of outlaws his tale – made up for his lack of eloquence.

Even Stephen felt sorry for the young man by the end of it.

Little John stood up as the men quietly digested Edmond's words. "Enough of this, we're supposed to be celebrating! Allan!" He glared at the minstrel who jumped to his feet under the giant's murderous gaze. "Give us a tune."

As Allan expertly strummed his gittern and the sounds of a merry jig filled the camp the men were pleased to shake off the sorrowful atmosphere Edmond's story had weaved around the place. The glad sounds of singing and dance filled the shadowy forest and the celebratory mood was kindled again.

John made his way over to Edmond and sat down beside him with a nod. For a long time they sat together in silence, watching the others enjoying the music and ale.

"I'm truly sorry for what I did," Edmond finally said to the bearded giant, tears making clean tracks in the grime on his face. "I know Sir Richard was your friend."

Little John leaned over and grasped the tanner by the arm, staring into his eyes earnestly.

"Listen to me. Every one of us here has a sad tale to tell. We all wish our life had turned out differently. But we're here and we live this life as best we can. As wolf's heads, aye, but as friends and brothers too. Forget your past, forget all the shit that life's thrown at you – you're one of us now."

311

The giant grinned and moved away to join in with the celebrations.

Edmond sat watching the outlaws singing, dancing, drinking and laughing together, all grinning merrily at him as they passed in their revelry and he felt the tears spill from his eyes again, only this time his heart soared and he thanked God.

Finally, he knew he had found a place where he would be accepted for who he was.

* * *

"Where is he?" The door burst open and the people in the house shrank back, eyes searching instinctively for something to use as a weapon.

"Where's my son?"

"Robin, you bloody idiot! I nearly shit myself there – have you never heard of knocking before you open a door?"

The big outlaw muttered apologies to Matilda's father and the rest of the relieved people gathered in the Fletcher's house. His own parents were there, Martha and Thomas, with his little sister, Marjorie who ran over to give him a cuddle, a big smile on her thin teenage face. Will's daughter, Beth, was there too and she followed Marjorie's lead, jumping into her grinning father's open arms as he followed Robin into the modest house.

Robin's eyes settled finally on the old chair by the hearth, where his wife sat cradling a small bundle in her arms.

Matilda's eyes sparkled joyfully as she looked down at the child then up at her beloved wolf's head. "Your son has your nose," she told him.

Grinning at his parents he moved past them and stooped to look down at his child, placing a big arm around his wife and cuddling her in close as he gazed at the little person they'd created together.

"You can hold him," Matilda smiled, offering the sleeping baby to him, but he shook his head and leaned back, almost defensively. "No, no, you hold him, I might drop him."

Mary snorted from behind him and shook her head at her daughter. "Get used to that. Men are all the same – think they're so strong they'll break their own baby, or so clumsy they'll drop it on its head."

Robin never even heard his mother-in-law, transfixed as he was by the sight of his beautiful tiny son. His own mother, Martha came over and hugged him proudly.

"Congratulations, daddy," she said.

"Thanks, grandma," he replied.

"Come on," Henry's big voice boomed out in the low room, "everyone sit by the table, there should be enough space for us all to fit somewhere." He gestured at the things his wife had laid out for them: meat, bread, cheese and ale. "Eat. Drink. Robin, you're looking, well...battered, truth be told. What the hell happened?"

The outlaw had taken a seat right next to Matilda and the child, and he looked up from them now, his face twisted in a grimace.

"Sir Guy of Gisbourne."

The room seemed to grow smaller and darker at the very mention of the Raven, but Robin poured himself a mug of ale and nodded confidently. "He murdered Much...and would have killed me too if it hadn't been for the sheriff pulling him off. We needn't fear him any more though. I've just taken half his face off."

There was an awkward silence for a few moments as the celebrating families didn't know how to react to Robin's news.

"Kicked his arse for him, right enough, never seen a fight like it in all my life," Will nodded cheerfully, trying, unsuccessfully to lighten the atmosphere. "But Robin beat him good. 'The Raven' will be dead by now, after what Robin did to him."

313

"Are you all right?" Martha's maternal instincts took over and she stared at her son, who would always be her own little boy, no matter how big he was now.

He forced a smile back onto his face and stuffed a chunk of bread into his mouth, pushing the image of Much's corpse to the back of his mind. "Aye, I'm fine! I beat the bastard and my wife and son are well. A man couldn't ask for any more."

"A pardon would be nice," Mary muttered sarcastically to laughs from the rest of the group.

"What are you going to call him?" Marjorie demanded, moving around the table, followed by Beth, to touch the baby's tiny hands and nose.

Robin looked at Matilda, remembering their conversation months ago. "Arthur," she nodded, and her husband grinned approval.

"Aye, Arthur. Much better than Edward or Adam."

The rest of the evening, what remained of it, passed quickly with much laughter and joy as the ale flowed and Robin and Matilda's parents – and Will too – told stories of their own children's younger years, warning the proud new mother and father what to expect from their own mischievous little one. The women, along with Marjorie and Beth, were happy to take the babe for cuddles whenever he woke up and didn't need Matilda to nurse him.

Eventually, knowing they all had to work early the next morning, the Hoods made their goodbyes and left for home, taking Will and Beth with them. Henry and Mary retired to their own bed, leaving Robin and Matilda to bond, alone together, with their child.

"Arthur," Matilda whispered. "It suits him. He's perfect."

"He is. Just like his mother." Robin's arms pulled them in close and the little family stood together, savouring the blessing God had bestowed upon them.

"I'm tired, let's go to bed."

As they lay beside each other, listening anxiously for the gentle sounds of their baby's breathing as all new parents do, Robin thanked God and the Magdalene for his beautiful son.

As he drifted off into a fitful sleep, though, he remembered growing up in this village with his best friend, Much, and wished the miller's son could have been here tonight to share their joy.

That bastard Matt Groves thinks he's safe, somewhere, but I'll find him one day, and I'll make him pay. As God is my witness, I will find him, and I will kill him for what he's done!

* * *

Things had worked out perfectly. He had a drink in one hand and some giggling whore's soft little tit in the other, with coin to afford quite a few more nights like this before he'd have to find a way to earn more. Gisbourne had paid him well for betraying Robin Hood and that other idiot from Wakefield so Matt had made his way east to Hull, which would be far enough away that he'd never run into any of his former outlaw 'friends' by accident.

He'd been a good sailor before turning to piracy and, as a result of that, ended up on the run from the law in Barnsdale. Here in Hull he knew he'd be able to find work on one of the many wool ships that plied their trade between England and Flanders.

He spilled ale down his chin and groaned loudly as the girl's hand finished its work. He lay on the stinking old pallet for a while, grinning, before tossing her a coin and ordering her out of the room.

Aye, things had worked out perfectly for him...

* * *

"He's dead, my lord sheriff."

Sir Henry de Faucumberg fixed the soldier with an angry stare. "I can see that, you idiot. What happened?"

"Robin Hood and his men."

The sheriff hadn't known Gisbourne was taking men off to fight a private duel with the wolf's head, and he shook his head angrily at what he saw in front of him now. Today should have been a day of celebration: they'd hung the Hospitaller and the king would be pleased at the news. Now this...! Gisbourne and Barnwell were the king's own men, sent here by the monarch personally, to deal with Robin Hood originally and, latterly, to help round-up the Contrariant rebels.

The thought of telling King Edward that Robin Hood still lived after all this made the sheriff's stomach flip over and the back of his throat tightened. He coughed, trying not to puke as he looked down at the corpse in front of him.

The sound of agonised screaming suddenly came through from the room next door, so loud that even the thick walls of the castle couldn't muffle it completely, and de Faucumberg sighed.

"At least it won't all be bad news I'll have to send the king."

"My lord?" the soldier asked in confusion.

"God be praised," de Faucumberg replied sarcastically, turning to leave the room. "Unlike his dead sergeant here, the surgeon tells me Sir Guy of Gisbourne will live, despite his terrible wounds. I expect he'll want revenge for what Hood's done to his face. If Gisbourne was a lunatic before, Christ only knows what he'll be like once he's fit again..."

Author's Note

Hopefully you enjoyed *The Wolf and The Raven* and, if you read the earlier story, *Wolf's Head,* you liked how the story and characters have developed. I have to be completely honest and say I didn't actually plan things to turn out like this though!

Originally, as you may know, I had wanted this series to be a trilogy. Too many authors find success with a character or formula and string it out until it becomes a shadow of its original self and I didn't want that to happen with my first foray into the world of writing.

However, when I sat down and started to work on this book the characters of Sir Richard and Stephen seemed to take over and, being the type of writer who plans very little and lets the people in the story dictate much of it, some of the things I wanted to do got overlooked here.

Little John for example, is someone I'd like to explore in more depth yet he ended up having little to do in this tale. Similarly, Matilda plays very little part, being pregnant as she is, and it would be nice to look at the role Robin's wife and family might play in the future.

So, if I was to make the next book the last in the series I would have to shoe-horn in a lot more than I'd be comfortable with.

For that reason, I'm now planning on adding an extra volume to the trilogy, making a total of four books – a tetralogy! Of course, who knows what the characters will do in the next one once I get started..? What I *can* tell you is that Little John will play a much greater part, as will hopefully Robin himself and, along the way, there may be a few more surprises.

Please stick around, and join me to find out what the future holds for our merry men and women!

Steven A. McKay
18 March 2014

If you enjoyed *The Wolf and The Raven* please do leave a review on Amazon, Goodreads and anywhere else you browse. Word-of-mouth is *so* important to a self-published author and I really do appreciate it when readers take the time to post their thoughts.

Keep up to date with my writing and join in the discussions here:

www.Facebook.com/RobinHoodNovel

http://stevenamckay.wordpress.com